The Truth
Between

Emma Louise
JORDAN

POOLBEG

Published 2010
by Poolbeg Press Ltd.
123 Grange Hill, Baldoyle,
Dublin 13, Ireland
Email: poolbeg@poolbeg.com

A catalogue record for this book is available from the British Library.

ISBN 978-1-84223-387-0

Typeset by Patricia Hope in Sabon 10.5/14.5

Printed by
CPI Cox & Wyman, UK

www.poolbeg.com

Note on the Author

Emma Louise Jordan is a Poolbeg Crimson pen name for writer Emma Heatherington (*Playing the Field,* Poolbeg Press, 2009).

Emma lives in the village of Donaghmore in County Tyrone with her husband Dalglish and three children Jordyn, Jade and Adam. She works freelance as a writer/ arts consultant.

Learn more about her writing at:
www.emmaheatherington.com

Also by Emma Louise Jordan: *Beyond Sin* (Poolbeg 2009).

Also by Emma Louise Jordan

Beyond Sin

Published by Poolbeg Crimson

as Emma Heatherington

Playing the Field

Published by Poolbeg

Acknowledgements

Penning *The Truth Between* was more than a challenge to me as a writer.

To explore a young woman's search for answers and take her through a journey of desperation and obsession was a test of how I dealt with my own past when my mother died from a sudden illness aged just thirty-six.

Sudden death, be it through suicide, a road traffic accident or illness, leaves those behind with many questions and an emptiness that may never be filled.

I would like to thank as always my agent Ger Nichol who continues to believe in everything I do – even if I do make her head spin with my manic lifestyle!

To everyone at Poolbeg, especially Paula Campbell, thank you for giving me the opportunity to stretch my writing abilities by taking a chance on Emma Louise Jordan.

Thanks as always to my editor Gaye Shortland, whose sharp eye and encouraging comments kept me going when the going got tough – and it did get tough, believe me!

To my fellow "Northern Girls" – Claire Allan and Fiona Cassidy. It is an honour to be part of the team and we have had lots of fun on our library tours and photo shoots (I want a shadow!). Long may our friendship last and continued success to you both.

I have made many acquaintances and indeed good friends throughout the Poolbeg network – thanks to Mary

Malone and Michelle Jackson in particular for sharing ideas and thoughts along the way.

And finally, to all my friends and family – thank you for continuing to support me in everything I do.

*For all those affected by sudden death
who are searching for answers*

1

Her house is clinically silent.

It is clinically clean too because cleaning her house is all I can bring myself to do during the day right now. Clean the oven, clean the fridge, mop the floors, and mop them again. I have never been so domesticated in my life. My friends would barely recognise me now, neither physically nor in my new-found obsessive characteristics – blonde shoulder-length hair in need of a haircut, face pale and make-up free, dark circles round my eyes and a permanent outfit of pyjamas and bare feet – and a domestic goddess to boot. Not, in any way, my finest hour – no insult to domestic goddesses everywhere. It just never was my thing.

I'd much more likely be found in a room full of loose leaves of music manuscript, empty coffee mugs surrounding me and music blaring from a CD system or from the violin I play for a living.

Now, I am permanently busying myself in my mother's

pristine and picture-perfect cottage on Ireland's beautiful north coast, in hiding from the real world as I know it. Except things aren't "picture perfect" here any more in this idyllic hideaway my mother proudly called her home. They never can be again.

The sun is bursting through the clouds this morning and its glow looks promising so I take my coffee outside and sit on a patio chair, tilting my head back to let the morning sun warm my face. I try to focus on the positive but my brain refuses to shift gears. I think of the sun, its natural heat caressing my neck and shoulders and I force my mind to drift into a tick-box exercise of minor, everyday achievements which now seem like individual mountains on my mental "to do" list . . .

Yes, I have reached several little milestones lately, I suppose.

Death leaves an open wound in the soul that stings and burns so painfully that I have always doubted there was ever a cure, but today I can feel the edge of my wounds soften slightly even if it is in the most miniscule way. There are of course a lot of things I have yet to do to help me get back to some sort of real life again.

Number one, I have to go back to work. That is an obvious step forward but one which I am continually putting off. But going back to work means moving back into my apartment in Belfast that Ronan (my boss who has recently become the other half of my Aunt Caroline) has been looking after – watering the plants, collecting the mail and making sure everything is safe in my absence. And going back to Belfast will mean leaving this cottage and my mother's memory and the very thought terrifies me.

On top of all this, I have never as much as lifted my precious violin from its case since that horrible Friday morning in July.

My mother taught me to play as soon as I was old enough to hold a fiddle. She loved to listen to me on summer days like this, and she would sometimes even join in.

I remember one day, when I was in the middle of giving a class at the summer school, I looked towards the back of the classroom and saw that she had slipped in unannounced. She stood there with her eyes closed, just listening to me talk about arias and duets and tunes about flying away and she seemed totally at home with the mood and the music. We went for lunch in Belfast that day and she seemed so happy and so content. That was in February. It was cold and wet and neither of us had an umbrella so we huddled together and dodged traffic and puddles on Great Victoria Street as we raced into the warmth of the restaurant where we both laughed with the relief of being out of the torrential Irish winter weather.

And now, it is summer and she is gone.

Next on my list of things to do is to put my relationship with Ben into the past, once and for all. I need to make a clean break from him and I need to tell him not to call here any more (despite my late-night pleas) and not to phone me because the more I see him the more I want him and I know I can't always get what I want.

And God, I want him so.

And then there is the box of course. I have to open the box with the diary again. The box I assume I was never supposed to find – the box that my mother should have destroyed a long time ago. She was careless, leaving it under the bed amongst a stash of childhood photos and letters from past loves. But it is mine now and I will open it and I will take out the diary and read it and I will find the answers, no matter how much it kills me. I need to read it, I need to accept it and I need to absorb what my mother never wanted me to know.

I feel angry when I think about it. Angry that I found it, angry that she didn't get rid of it, angry that she took her own life so clumsily and spontaneously and that she didn't even bother to clean up her past so she could protect me from mine.

The very thought of what lies inside the pages of that diary inside the box makes my stomach curdle and I hug the cup of coffee with my hands as I battle with my senses. I know I should forget about it. I know what I read is going to tell me what she has protected me from forever. I know from the date on the diary that it will tell me who or what my father was or is, and where I might begin to find him. But I just have to know now. There is no way I can resist. It was her mistake. The diary, I mean, not me.

My phone bleeps a message and it makes my mind jump away from my internal list-making and I reach into my dressing-gown pocket, press "Read" and, just as I had predicted, it is my Aunt Caroline's early-morning greeting.

"Hey Hollie. Have you read the diary yet? Please don't. Please I am begging you."

I text her back straight away.

"I will read it. You know I will. Just not sure when."

The phone rings and I roll my eyes.

"You know, I wish I hadn't said anything to you about the box," I say. "Now you're going to go on and on and on and –"

"Look, Hollie, I've been thinking about this all night." Her voice is urgent.

"You are hung-over," I say.

"Yes, but in the depths of my hangover I am more adamant now than I was last night. I don't think you should read the diary. Please, please don't."

I sigh and rub my forehead. We've been through all this the night before at Caroline's house and I think I made myself very clear.

Caroline lives just ten miles from here, towards the city. My mother used to joke that it was close enough for her little sister to call in for coffee when she felt like it, but far enough to keep a healthy distance from someone who is so overprotective of everything we ever do.

"You know I am going to anyhow, Caroline. You know I have to. *You* would. Anyone would."

"Don't read it yet, then," she says. "I'm driving right now so I can't talk, but put the kettle on and I'll be with you in a few minutes. Just don't read it yet. Not until I talk to you first. That's an order."

I go back inside the house and it feels cool in contrast to the sun's early morning glow which makes me shiver. I let my eyes adjust to the dim light of the kitchen and switch on the radio, which is still tuned in to my mother's favourite station and, once again, I feel as if this is all a lengthy nightmare and that she will come in any minute and sing along as she boils eggs or cooks bacon for breakfast. Caroline's fears about what her diary entries might reveal, although I try to deny it, have heightened mine but in a sick way it makes me want to know more and more and more. I feel dread seep through me again and the sensible part of me hopes that Caroline is just simply nervous and jittery about what girly secrets Mum might have left behind. She was my mother's only sister and I know she is protecting her honour as much as my sanity. They were closer than most sisters, so she must know more than she is pretending to and that freaks me out. I am the last to know. The last to know about me.

I sit at the table and wait and the radio presenter's rants become clearer as I try to concentrate on anything other than what is ahead of me today. The presenter is talking about internet addiction and I listen in, marvelling at how I have managed to live hardly using the internet here in the cottage. There was a time when I would have automatically checked my emails, Facebook account and surfed on eBay before I even left the house for work. I listen intently and then, realising Caroline will be here soon, I fill the kettle and pop some bread into the toaster. Caroline's mood has certainly shaken me.

I take some cheese from the fridge, knowing that most likely Caroline will not have had breakfast and will be more than happy to grab a quick snack before she heads off to work in her boutique in Belfast.

Then the sound of the key in the door tells me I am soon to find out more at last.

"Something smells good. Yum, I'm starving!" she says.

She shivers when she comes into the kitchen and lifts a slice of toast and butters it before I have a chance to offer her some. She pours her own coffee with gusto too.

"Bad hangover?" I say.

"You could say that," says Caroline, biting into her toast. "Yeah. Definitely. I'm cold and jittery and have an insatiable hunger plus a lot of demons in my mind and the sun is shining outside. To me, that spells hangover with a capital 'H'. I'm getting way too old for wine."

I laugh, a surface laugh again – a courtesy laugh that acknowledges how Caroline really cannot cope with the morning after the night before. She never could.

"So are you going to tell me what these demons are or are you going to leave me hanging?" I ask her, way too lightly for the subject matter. "You have me on eggshells since you called. This had better be good because I'll be climbing the walls soon if you don't spit it out."

Caroline's eyes look sunken and glazed.

"No, it's not 'good', Hollie, but then you know that already. I didn't sleep too well last night, despite the influences of the wine and heavy pizza."

"And? Oh for Christ's sake, Caroline, tell me! What's in this goddamn diary? Maybe if you and Mum had been more careful with your secrets and lies you wouldn't have to lose sleep over what I might find out!"

Caroline stops chewing her food and swallows. She is hurt and I am sorry.

"Really, Hollie, I wouldn't have called at this time of the morning if I didn't think it was necessary."

She sits down and I mirror her movements, my eyes wide with fear and my insides racing because of what I am about to hear.

"When you told me about the diary yesterday on the beach," she says, "I pushed any fears that I had aside. I tried to convince myself that you could cope with what you might find, that you are a grown woman now and not my little pigtailed niece who must never, ever know. But then during the night, Hollie, I thought of the shock it will bring to you and the life that it may lead to. I know now that I need to at least prepare you for what you may find out."

I gulp my coffee. "Prepare me for what? Tell me, Caroline!"

Caroline breathes out, a long forced breath that comes from the pit of her stomach. Her eyes flick to the ceiling and then back to me.

"You know already that you were born just after your mum started university? She had just turned eighteen. My God, it seems like yesterday . . ."

I don't know why but I feel my defences rise. Yes, of course I know my mum was young when I was born but it was the late eighties, not the forties or fifties. It had never been an issue. Had it?

"That's no secret," I snap. "She told me that as soon as I was old enough to understand but she always said she had no regrets. Is this what this is about? Do you think she was sorry she went ahead with her pregnancy? Is that what I'm going to read in this bloody diary?"

"God, no. It's not that, baby – no, it's not." Caroline takes my hand and I can tell she truly fears she is jumping the gun but that she wants to take the risk and tell me something. "Look, I was in America at the time, as you probably know."

I shake my head. "At the time of what?"

"When Estelle found out she was pregnant. I was on an

8

exchange trip in New York with my school. I wasn't at home when she realised she'd have to drop out of uni and . . . Look, all I'm trying to share with you is what I know . . . that something bad happened to her. Just so you . . . just in case she has left her story behind."

I can feel my insides churn and last night's wine gurgles in my stomach as I sense from Caroline's face that the worst is yet to come.

"Something bad like what, Caroline?" I ask and I push her hand away. "Don't pussyfoot around me like this! I need to know."

"I shouldn't have said anything, I knew it," says Caroline and she stands up, scraping the chair against the floor. "I'm jumping to conclusions that she might have written about it, even Ronan said so. I should never have –"

"Wait a minute! *Ronan*? Your boyfriend – my fucking boss – knows about this? Ronan knows about my mother's past and I don't?"

"No, no, Hollie! None of us know anything much about it. You see, that's the thing. She told no one who – or why – or how it happened."

"Tell me now what you know!" I yell. "I don't care how bad it might be or how you think you might be jumping to conclusions with your guessing games! I have a right to know. My God, I can't believe she kept this from me. What happened?"

"I would only be guessing," says Caroline, her voice shaking as she speaks. "She kept the details from everyone. She wouldn't tell a soul, not even our parents and, believe me, our father did everything in his power to find out. He went to the university. He even knocked on doors around the student area asking questions – if anyone witnessed anything. He even went to the police but they were of no use because Estelle refused to talk. It was a horrific time and I landed back from America in the midst of it. I was thirteen years old and I had no idea what the fuss was all about. And I still don't think I want to know! And maybe it's better if you don't know either!"

A flurry of possibilities race through my mind and I feel dizzy and sick to the core. Something happened to my mum and then she announced she was pregnant. It didn't take a brain surgeon to work out what might have gone on. I feel physically wounded and my skin crawls as if it is dirty and scarred. I push the plate of toast away from me on the table, not knowing what to say to Caroline right now and thoughts of pity and revolt and then anger spin through my head and the internet conversation on the radio sounds like a fuzzed hum in the background.

"I'm just afraid that some of the answers might lie in that box. They are in the pages of that diary. I just know it," whispers Caroline and she sits back down at the table, watching as my world as I know it comes crashing down round me once again. "And I'm afraid that you won't be strong enough now to cope with it."

"Cope with what, Caroline?" I ask her, already knowing the answer.

She holds her hand over her mouth, unable to say the words without feeling repulsed.

"Hollie . . . your mother was raped."

10

2

"I . . . I'm going to be sick."

I leave the table and make it to the kitchen sink where I heave and retch but nothing will come up, just tears of shame and self-pity for being left in the dark for so long. I feel like an intruder in my own skin. I don't know myself any more. I feel alien.

Caroline looks as scared as I am.

"She told us never to mention it again and even when we heard her cry at night or sob in her sleep she wouldn't tell us a thing more. Dad even tried to have her talk to a counsellor – hell, he even called the priest but still she wouldn't talk. Hollie, I just don't want you to find out from some old diary or jotted-down notes of anger-filled memories. I never wanted you to hear of any of this. You don't need to know."

I wipe my mouth with a paper towel and look at Caroline. She looks broken and scared but I am bursting

11

with rage now and I want to shout at her for holding this back and then telling me just because she has some hunch about the diary.

"So you just assumed you'd walk in here and tell me this now? Just in case? Is that it?"

"No, Hollie. I'm just so scared that you will find out more than you should ever know. I'm just afraid of the truth, Holl."

I know Caroline is right – I know what I read will be painful, but like a drug or some magnetic force I feel the diary calling me, urging me to take the chance and see if I can find the truth between its pages.

"What if there's nothing like that in the box?" I ask her. "What if it *is* full of happy memories? Why the hell would she record all of that bad stuff and keep it for me to find now? Why hold it from me in life and leave me to come upon it now when she's gone so that I can't ask questions, can't ask why? No!"

"Hollie, please listen to me," pleads Caroline. "I know that when you found the box part of you was full of hope and excitement, as well as a little dread of finding out more about when you were born, but I just don't want you heading for a fall. And I hope to God that there's nothing at all in the diary that leads to this mysterious past, I swear I do."

Caroline gets up and puts her arm around me but I pull away like I have been burned by her touch. I feel betrayed by her, by my grandparents, by my mother. I want to scream and punch them and tell them how this is so unfair.

"She should have told me!" I sob. "I'm a grown woman. I can take it! *You* should have told me!"

I grab the nearest thing to hand, a half-empty coffee cup and I smash it onto the floor, feeling anger surge out with the shower of broken delph. "But what's the point in telling me now in some spineless box of whatever when I can't ask her those questions or even try to understand what she was going through? Was I such a burden to her that she had to get away from me? Did I repulse her so much?"

Caroline takes my hands and squeezes them tight as tears explode down my face.

"Shh, Hollie. Please don't cry like that. I know how hurt you must feel but –"

"No, you don't!"

"I do, because I am hurting too. I miss her so much!"

She leads me back to the table and waits until my tears subside and I feel my heart rate settle but my head feels like a cement block. I want to run out of here right now. I want to escape from the past and close my ears and forget about what I have just heard but I know I have to face the truth.

"Now," says Caroline, her voice more settled and soothing, "let's just take this one step at a time, can we? Either you decide to read it and deal with what it tells you, or you decide to put it away and leave the past in the past. It's up to you."

I nod and sniffle, looking at the table all the time.

"But whatever happens, you are not to blame for any of this," she says, holding my sodden hands again as she speaks, trying to make eye contact with me, but I cannot look her way. "You *know* how much your mum adored the very ground you walked on. She loved you so much, Hollie."

"Did she? Did she really?"

"You know she did! You know how proud of you she was, how she was bursting when you got the job at the university and the summer school and that you played in the orchestra and how gifted a teacher you are. She told me every time I saw her that you were her pride and joy and that she cherished every day you had together. But I often thought that the past still haunted her . . . I just didn't realise how much."

The room is cloudy but the soothing tone of Caroline's voice makes her words sink in somehow.

"I just can't understand how no one knows exactly what happened," I say. "Someone must know."

Caroline shakes her head. "We may never know," she whispers, "but perhaps reading the diary *will* give us an idea where she was deep inside and why she felt her time here was up. Or . . . "

"Or?"

"Or maybe it will make things worse for all of us," she says. "Carrying secrets can be a heavy burden that can eat you up while you wade through everyday life and feel like a ton of bricks on your heart when you're on your own. Whether you read it, or whether you don't, this is something that isn't going to go away."

I nod and look at the mess on the floor where tiny pieces of what used to be a red shiny cup are scattered through a pool of pale-brown, cold coffee. I didn't realise I had such a temper. It's amazing what adrenaline and anger can turn you into.

"She used to tell me stories about my father," I say with a faint smile and my lip trembles. "Now I realise

14

how wonderful her imagination was. What a contrast, eh? Where the hell did she come up with the fling with a wealthy American doctor out of that fucking fiasco?"

I glance up at my aunt and then look away again, trying to push the feelings of hurt and humiliation out of my mind.

"You never did believe the wealthy American doctor story, did you?" says Caroline, with a hint of a giggle in her voice. "We Lynches couldn't be so lucky if we hung around a hospital morning, noon and night, could we?"

I giggle too. "Of course I didn't believe it. Well, not after the age of five or at any rate since I was old enough to realise that if I had any medical genes in my body I wouldn't crawl the walls at the sight of blood or a needle. I do believe such a fear is inherited."

Caroline manages a light smile and wipes a stray tear from her own cheek.

"You know what she told our parents?" she says, this time with a hearty laugh. "She told them that she had a one-night stand with a rock star from Idaho! A rock star from *Idaho*? You can imagine how that went down! Like, why Idaho of all places?"

It is probably down to shock and nerves but my giggle turns into a throaty laugh now too at the thought of my stoic grandparents' reaction.

"Oh my God, I can imagine the twisted face of Grandma! It would have been a sight! Imagine, her daughter bedding a rock star!"

"It was a sight. They were so bent on Estelle giving them his name that she finally gave in and said that he was a music student who had flown back to America to be the next Billy Idol and that Dad had no hope of ever finding him! I mean, a rock star! I think that was worse in my dad's eyes than the truth could ever have been!"

I have no problem in believing so. Not that they live such a conventional life themselves. My grandparents are what my mother would have often referred to as "rich, educated gypsies," who travelled the world with their inheritance as soon as their daughters were old enough to boil a kettle and could be left behind to fend for themselves. No wonder my mother turned out so independent and proud and carried her secret truths with her to an early grave.

"Speaking of whom – any word from them?" I ask. It dawns on me that I haven't heard from my grandparents since the funeral as they were recuperating with a fortnight in Egypt, as you do.

"No, of course not," says Caroline, rolling her eyes. "Look, Hollie, I hope you don't think I've stepped out of line. I just had this vision of you finding out what we have never known and wondering why I hadn't the grace to at least tell you the tiny bit that I do know. I'm sorry to have upset you so much."

I nod and, when Caroline takes my hand again, this time I don't pull away.

"I'm going to look at the diary tonight," I announce. "And I'm sorry for going a bit mental but finding out your mother went through the wars to have you is not something you hear every day. I'm glad you told me though. Thanks, Caroline."

Caroline's smile fades from her face and she looks away in deep thought.

"It has always been one of those things that we were

16

never, ever to mention in her company. It was a huge white elephant in the room on every occasion we were all together that just gave our parents more reason to travel the world and forget we existed – but maybe that's the end of it now? Maybe what I've told you is all we'll ever know and hopefully we can move on and live the life that Estelle would have wanted us to."

I shrug and lift a dustpan and brush, and then I crouch down to clear up the mess I have left on the floor. I need to keep moving or else I'll stop and crumble and I can't afford any more scenes of emotion.

"I can't see that I will just leave it like this," I say, sweeping up the tiny chunks of blood-red ceramic, mixed with cold milky coffee. "But one thing is for sure. I will do my damnedest to find out exactly what happened to my mother and why she took a selfless vow of silence from such a young age about it. That, I promise."

It is almost 2 a.m. when I pluck up the courage to go into the bedroom to fetch my mother's box.

Ronan and Caroline had once again distracted me from the inevitable by insisting I drive the ten miles or so in to Caroline's apartment where Ronan had made a delicious stroganoff for dinner. I arrived with more wine which was left unopened on the shelf following our heavy overindulgence the night before but the stroganoff with its strong rich flavours was just what we all needed. I bade them farewell and Caroline promised she would stand by the phone should I take a late-night urge to open the box. I had wished her a good night's sleep and thanked her for her never-ending support and concern.

But now I am alone, with just Jinx my mother's beloved black Labrador, for company and the box on my knee. I have moved to the sofa in the sitting room where I can hear the clock tick from the hallway, urging me with every swing of its pendulum to open the box and see what my mother wanted to protect us all from so badly.

I lift the lid, my heart punching my chest beneath my skin and my cold hands shaking. A fresh lilac smell fills my senses and I peer inside at the notebook wrapped in white tissue paper that rustles when the box moves on my knee.

I decide I need a drink and I go to the kitchen and pour a large glass of wine before returning to the sofa, carefully placing the bottle on the floor beside it. Then I take the notebook out of the box and flick through it, seeing it is written in a more careful girlish hand than she later developed.

I glance around the room with a sudden feeling that I am being watched.

Perhaps she is here with me now, awaiting my reaction, wondering how I will respond to the brief story she has left me. I curl my feet underneath me, take a deep breath and begin to read.

3

My Story by Estelle Lynch – 20 October '81
No 1 Single – "It's My Party"
Favourite Movie – On Golden Pond
Fashion Icon – Singh Moshiro
Best Friend – Singh!
Crush – Simon Le Bon (and a few college boys!)

Dear Diary
I'm alone, but not lonely. Alone.

There's a nice, gentle silence in the house and my roommates are all away to class but it's my day off so it's just me and the house.

I'm very well used to my own company. My God, I spent most of my summers drifting from house to house as Mum and Dad holidayed together, leaving me and my sister with everyone and anyone who would have us. I think they would have left us with the neighbour's dog if they couldn't have lumbered anyone else with us.

I'm serious.

They are a strange couple, my parents. So in love with each other I think that they forget about us sometimes. Forget we even exist.

"Just a wee second honeymoon," Mum says every year as they take their third or fourth foreign break of the summer. "We'll bring you back something nice."

And they always do. I think I have a fan from every country in Europe. And dolls from Amsterdam. Well, I could sell them.

We got our turn of course every summer too, Caroline and I. Seven days in Tenerife in August made us stand out from the other kids first day back at school with our fresh tan and bleached, braided hair. We would splash in the pool, eye up the boys while our parents sat at the bar or Mum topped up her tan at the furthest point from which she could maintain the slightest eye contact with us.

Don't get me wrong, my parents were never cruel or bad to us. We didn't want for anything as children. Well, apart from affection, I suppose. Kids need affection. When I have kids I will smother them with hugs and kisses. For every kiss I give my daughters, I'll give them a second for me as a child and a third one for my sister, Caroline. They'll have lots of love. And my husband and I will include them in everything we do. They will be born out of love and into love and they'll take that with them everywhere they go.

We were born out of our parents' love, that's for sure. But being a product of our parents' love didn't mean they were sharing any of it around. No, they kept it all to themselves so Caroline and I, well, we just got on with things as children. We still do. I'm good at getting on with things.

University life is better than I expected. Way better.

I feel properly independent, like I can put my so-called home life behind me and build a proper one here in the city where there is so much to see and do.

I'm good at that too. I can easily shut a door on part of my life and never look back at it again. Gone. Done. Over.

I feel like that about my childhood. Sad, isn't it?

Still, I wonder how long it will be until my parents call me or come and visit me in my student bedsit. Part of me wants them to. All of me craves the attention they'll never give to me. It's already been a month since my mum called to say they were touring the States and might call in to see Caroline on their way through New York and that they are flying back into Dublin so they might drive home via Belfast so they can see where I'm living.

Might.

Well, if they don't call in to see their youngest daughter in New York, who they haven't seen in weeks, what's the chance they'll come and see me here in Belfast?

Slim, I say. So I'm sitting them out on this one.

I'll always have Singh, anyway. I know that for sure. Singh Moshiro. How's that for a posh name? And here was me thinking Estelle was exotic! Singh is my new best friend here. I call her "Sing Song" and she laughs and shakes her head and the flowers in her hair – Singh always wears flowers in her hair – shake too but none ever fall out.

21

It was destiny that we met, or so we both believe. There I was in the middle of Freshers' Week, absorbed in a novel at the canteen table at the Students' Union, cigarette burning in an ashtray in front of me and a can of Canada Dry at its side and she walked up to me, asked for a light.

The first thing I noticed was the big red flower she wore in her jet-black hair, then the book that was under her arm.

"Snap!" she said and she dropped it onto the table. The Powers That Be, *by David Halberstam.* *The same book that I was engrossed in with its tales of America's fast media.*

So she sat down and we got talking about the book. She was two chapters behind me and it took me all my strength not to mention parts she hadn't read and we would stop now and then, wondering how freaky it was that we had bumped into each other this way. I mean, there were at least 300 students in the canteen that morning and the book was already two years old so it's not like we lifted it from the recent bestsellers list. We reckon it was fate. Fate, destiny, whatever you want to call it.

You see, she had made no other friends either. She had come from Japan on her own to study – I thought I was brave coming all the way from the far side of the Antrim coast on my own! She lives in Student Halls but the girl in the room next door is a racist cow who calls her names and the others just ignore her.

It's their loss, I say. I tell her that all the time because it really is. Singh is a beautiful person inside and out. She makes me laugh when she makes up poems and jokes and she makes me cry when she sings me her favourite songs in Japanese. Then she cries too because she misses home a lot. She misses her friends and her dog and her brother and her bedroom and she misses her parents.

I don't miss mine. I don't think you can miss something you never had.

So, this is my home now. This will always be my home.

I must go and make dinner for me and the house. Think I'm in a Spag Bol mood. And Duran Duran. Yes, that sounds like a plan. This house needs some Duran Duran.

Estelle x

I lift out a picture that accompanies the diary entry. *Singh Moshiro.* Who the hell is Singh Moshiro? I have never heard my mum mention that name before but in the photo they certainly look like best pals, arms around each other in a photo booth, making faces at the camera like they hadn't a care in the world. The Japanese girl certainly looks exotic. She is wearing a braided band across her forehead and I am sure I can see a butterfly tattoo on her left hand. Yes, it is definitely a butterfly with Japanese text on its wings. My mother was wearing a white T-shirt with **"Frankie Says"** written on it in huge black text and her hair was layered and extra blonde with streaky highlights on the crown.

I flip over the page and continue to read, scanning through some of the notes she made in her early days at university. Most of the diary entries are everyday activities

23

of a typical student, some are long, historical happenings and some are snippets of daily activities or random rants of feelings on current affairs. Every single day she wrote, she would list her favourite movie, her favourite song and crush, but most of all she always mentioned her adventures with the mysterious Singh who she truly seemed to love and was in total awe of. I can't help but weep as I read and then I laugh as I read and I wonder at how this happy-go-lucky young girl seems like a stranger to the woman I knew as my mother. I don't feel the time passing by as I read through the notebook, peering in through the window to a life before I existed.

At seven thirty in the morning, I wake up, the diary still in my hands. Without as much as a pause I read as I walk to the kitchen, as I pour a coffee, as I open the blinds, as I walk out onto the tiny patio and embrace the early morning sun. I am engrossed in her world and I don't want her story to end. Ever.

4

Max Kelly awoke with a thumping headache and reached for the glass of water he always kept by the side of the bed. His mouth was dry and the bed in the spare room felt empty and cold as it had done ever since he got back from his little disappearing act.

Sandra had gone to work early and the boys would be on their way to school by now. His family was living in a different time zone, in a different world almost, and he didn't have the energy to keep up with them.

He threw the duvet back from his body and sat up on the edge of the bed, then rubbed his two-day stubble and vowed to shave before he had breakfast.

"Sandra?" he called down the landing, just in case it was earlier in the morning than he thought. "Sandra, are you still home? Josh? Charlie?"

He looked into the boys' bedrooms as he passed but as he predicted they were empty, but full of signs of teenage

25

life. Thirteen-year-old Josh's red bass guitar sat propped against the sofa and a PlayStation 3 lay strewn across the floor where bean-bags and CD covers fought for space. While Charlie's room was tidier, his bed was unmade and a faint smell of smoke lingered in the air – a crass habit the seventeen-year-old had developed as a latest sign of rebellion.

Max reminded himself to chastise his son once again for smoking the next time he saw him. He had been reminding himself to talk to his son about a lot of things lately, but somehow he never got round to it.

In the bathroom he turned the dial on the power shower and stripped off, then stepped into the steam and went in under the hot pumping water that pulsed from the sunflower-style showerhead. He used to sing in the shower, he remembered. He hadn't felt the urge to sing in the shower for a long, long time. He pushed his hair back and smoothed it down, then reached for the shampoo, letting its minty fragrance slowly wake him up properly but every time he closed his eyes, Estelle Lynch's haunting face filled his mind. For three days he had wandered the windy roads of Ireland thinking of her and her tragic end. She had never, ever left his mind and he knew that his unfinished business with her had led to his path of emotional destruction. Now she was gone and it would remain unfinished forever.

The shower and a close shave made him feel slightly more human and he dressed in fresh clothing, unsure if he would make it into work on time. He still hadn't checked the clock.

Downstairs, the kitchen felt cold and he reached out to switch on the heating, cursing himself for not setting the timer to stay on a bit longer in the morning and the fact that central heating was needed in July at all. There was a faint smell of burnt toast and three used cereal bowls sat by the sink. Sandra must have been in a hurry when she left. She was normally meticulous about leaving the house tidy so she would find it that way on her return.

He heard a car pull into the driveway and he looked at the clock for the first time that morning. It was just after nine thirty and he wasn't due into work until eleven. Sandra normally started at nine.

He heard her heels clipping along the driveway and her key turn in the door. She hadn't gone to work. His stomach felt sour and he flicked the switch on the kettle, sensing that the shit was about to hit the fan as far as his marriage was concerned. The shit was about to hit the fan *again*, he corrected himself.

"So, you've decided to grace us with your presence?" said Sandra, slamming bags of groceries down on the kitchen table and letting her car keys fall with a rattling thud. Her blonde hair was unkempt and she wore no make-up. Sandra always wore make-up, even for an impromptu visit to the grocery store.

"Why aren't you at work?" he asked in defence. "It's well after nine."

"At work? At *work*? Jesus Christ, Max, are you even on the same planet as the rest of us in this house? I can't work, I can't eat, I can't sleep, for crying out loud! This is killing me, seeing you like this. Look at the state of you! You don't talk, you don't come home and when you do you walk around like a zombie avoiding conversation and our very existence! What the hell is going on?"

Max chewed his bottom lip and searched his mind for answers. He couldn't explain how he was feeling. How could he tell his wife about his long-held guilt over Estelle Lynch and the recent pathetic end to her life and how he felt he had played a part in it? How was he supposed to tell his wife he had a woman's death on his conscience? A woman who she didn't even know existed?

"Sandra, just give me time and I'll be back on track, I promise. Please, honey. I need you to give me some space so I can sort my head out."

"Space?" Sandra took off her jacket and flung it over the back of a chair. She had hurt etched all over her face and Max hated to see her like this. "Jesus, Max, of all the men in the world you have more space that anyone else I know! It's like having a stranger living in the house lately. We don't know you any more!"

Max turned away and stared out of the kitchen window. They lived in a quiet cul-de-sac of self-builds with two fairly decent cars in the driveway, neatly cut lawns and admirable décor – all that was missing was the picket fence. To a visitor it would have seemed like a very happy home. Yet Max never related to it in this way at all. Not in the past few months, not in the past few years.

"I know," he said. "I know how selfish this all seems to you and the boys and if it was something I could explain, my God I would, but I don't even understand it myself. I don't know which way to turn right now."

He could hear Sandra fidget behind him and then pull out a chair at the kitchen table and sit down. Her voice quivered when she spoke and it cut his heart in two to know she was in such turmoil over his behaviour and state of mind.

"Is there . . . is there someone else, Max?" she whispered, dabbing her nose with a tissue. "By God, you better tell me if there is. At least give me the grace of being the first to know this time. Save me the humiliation of being the last to know."

Max swung round, feeling defensive now. "*This* time? Why the hell do you always have to drag that up? Why is it always your first defence when anything goes wrong in my life? No, it damn well *isn't* someone else! Why on earth do you have to automatically assume that every time I'm getting things a little tough in my life that I'm having a goddamn affair?"

"Because you've done it before! You've done it before and this is exactly how you acted back then."

"And don't you think I learned my sorry lesson all those years ago? Is that what you think of me, Sandra? Have you and Will been having little heart to hearts and putting two and two together and coming up with six behind my back?"

Sandra stood up to meet his level. He could tell she was fighting back tears of anger and frustration.

"Will is as concerned for you as I am, Max! Look at you! You are never at home, you are always at work even when you don't need to be and if not you're in the pub and then you disappear for days and don't answer your phone to me or the kids."

"I left it behind. I left my phone behind. I already told you all of this!"

"On purpose?"

"Yes, maybe I did leave it here on purpose! I needed to get my head around some things. I needed some time out, to get my head straight, but instead it's like I've taken ten steps back. I have things on my mind, Sandra."

"Well, why don't you tell me what those things are? At least let me try and understand!"

"I can't, Sandra. I can't." His voice softened and he looked into his wife's eyes. Her tear-filled, sad blue eyes that were bursting with worry seemed so far away from him. He was sorry for her and sorry for him and sorry for the mess he was creating for his family. But he couldn't fight this any longer. He was going under fast and he knew it.

"I thought you said you were going to take a break?" said Gina when she saw Max get out of his car in the rear parking lot at Blue Heaven. "You look like shit. Even worse than shit if there is such a thing."

"Cheers, Gina. Thanks for the vote of confidence. Will has called a meeting for eleven thirty. Did you get his text?"

Gina rummaged in her handbag for her phone as they walked together in through the back doors of the restaurant. It always was darker inside than it was outside in the natural glow and their eyes adjusted to the dim light.

"Looks like I did," said Gina. "My kids are always shouting at me to keep an eye on my cell phone but I'm a disaster. So what's the meeting about or is that a silly question?"

"It's actually about recruitment," said Max and he held a door open for her. "Not about errant Head Chefs or knives flying around behind backs or anything of the sort. Contrary to popular belief."

He faked a smirk and Gina playfully hugged him around the waist. She felt sorry for Max lately. Of her two bosses, he was by far her favourite. Will was a sweetheart too, but because Max worked in the kitchen she had got to know him much better down the years. When she needed time off if the kids were sick, or if she had to attend a dental appointment or if a last-minute crisis came up she knew that getting time out was never a problem with Max. He was so handsome too and she'd heard rumours down the years of his fling with a young waitress just after the restaurant opened its doors but she didn't let that cloud her judgement. He was a very attractive man with a beautiful family and he should be on top of the world as his business was ticking along nicely too, unlike a lot of its competitors. Yet he seemed troubled and restless and Gina had no idea why.

But she wouldn't push it. Not now, not again. It was none of her business.

"Gina, Max."

Will greeted both of them without looking up from his paperwork when they entered the office on the first floor of Blue Heaven. His desk was normally exceptionally tidy, more down to his wife Patsy's excellent admin skills than his own eye for detail. Between himself and Max he was the one that crunched the numbers and laid down the rules. Max, they both had learned, was the creative spark of the duo with an eye for décor, ambience and recipes to die for and together they clicked to make Blue Heaven one of Dublin's top eateries.

"Sorry for the short notice but I thought I'd grab both

of you before the lunchtime rush. I've had a look at the staffing structure over the past few weeks and something isn't working. We've had more sick days than ever before at this time of year and I'm wondering if I'm missing something on the ground. What do you think? You two are the eyes and ears of this place. I'm just the number-cruncher."

Gina was perched on a high stool near the door of the tiny office while Max sat on a chair at his own desk which was opposite Will's.

Max shrugged. "I know some of the students on the floor are knee-deep in exams at this time of year and some are itching to get into holiday mode so perhaps their mind isn't on the job as much as it should be. Would that be a factor? Gina?"

Gina twiddled the edge of her skirt and bit her lip.

"Gina?" said Will. "Come on. Spit it out."

She glanced at Max and then at Will and Max felt his stomach sink. He had a feeling this was going to fall on his head. Somehow this was going to be all his fault. Great.

"Well, all I can say is that I've never seen morale at such an all-time low," she whispered. "Look, Max, please don't feel I'm speaking out of turn but I've already touched on this with you. You guys have no idea how much your moods filtrate down throughout my staff. There's been an atmosphere lately and, to be honest with you both, it stinks. Max, I'm not going behind your back by saying this but I think you need some time out. I've already told you so but you don't seem to listen to me. Maybe you'll listen to Will."

Max looked across at Will and could see the colour of his face gradually go puce. Will's blood pressure and the fact that he was carrying so many extra pounds were well-known health-risk factors and Max knew this wouldn't do him any good at all.

"Tell me more, Gina," Will said. "Max, I want you to listen up."

"Hold on a minute," said Max and he pushed himself up from the desk. "Why do I feel I'm being treated like some naughty schoolboy here? How can everything that goes wrong around here be my fucking fault?"

Gina got up from her stool. "Max, I'm not necessarily –"

"That's enough, Gina! I think you've said enough!" he shouted. "Can you give Will and me some time out? I want to talk to him alone about this."

"No, I invited her along," said Will. "Gina, don't go anywhere!"

"Guys, I think it's better if I do go," said Gina and she gathered her things. "You should sort this out between yourselves. I'd rather stay out of it."

She slammed the door behind her and Max leaned over the desk to Will.

"What the hell are you playing at?" he said. "I thought you wanted to talk about recruitment? Like this time every other year when we re-recruit to keep up with the tourist trade?"

"Well, maybe if you'd have given me time to get round to that, I might have had a chance to bring it up, but no! Instead you go off on another of your 'poor me' rants! It was Gina who hinted any blame your way, not me."

"*Our* way, you mean. She was throwing it both our

ways. Do you think the staff don't notice when you come into the kitchen and throw your weight about with me, speaking to me like there's no one else around? Do you think they don't listen in and then talk about it afterwards? Your management skills are as much to blame as mine!"

Will stood up to meet his business partner at eye level and they glared at each other like gladiators in a ring.

"There is no way that my management skills should be questioned. You're the one they say needs a break. You're the one who has reached boiling point, Max! You're the one on everybody's lips. Not me!"

"I'm a Michelin-star chef!" he yelled. "I'm the fucking one with the stars in this place! Me!"

"Oh, how low can you go, buddy? That's grasping at straws! It takes two of us to run this show and you know it! How dare you!"

Like a defeated animal, Max slid back into his chair and leaned his face into his hands. His forehead was hot and slippery and he felt his whole body tremble. His hands shook uncontrollably like a freight train coming off the track. He felt like he was freefalling and the room spun so hard that he had to grip his head to make it stop.

"Make this all stop!" he shouted, his words muffled and clumsy. "I – I can't take this any more, Will. I swear I can't. Everything is wrong – I've ruined everything. Oh God, make this stop!"

Will moved around the side of the desk and crouched down by his colleague's side.

"Max? Max, what the hell? Max?"

Max looked up to see a blurred vision of Will beside him.

"Has something happened?" said Will urgently. "Are you in trouble? Tell me! First you disappear for days and now this? Tell me!"

Max sank his head in his hands again and rocked in his chair. "I . . . I can't cope with this guilt, Will. It's eating me up. It's haunting me day and night. Oh my God, I can't go on like this. She's dead and I never got to tell her . . . I never got to explain what happened . . . she's dead and it's on my dirty conscience now. My dirty, filthy rotten conscience. She's dead."

Will got up and leaned against the wall. "Stop talking rubbish, Max. What the hell are you saying? Who is dead?"

Max looked up at Will and his face was wet with sweat and tears and his eyes bulged with fear and anxiety.

"I didn't tell her what I should have. I didn't tell her I was sorry. And now . . . now, she's dead and it's my fault. It's all my fucking fault!"

Will walked back to Max's side. Max looked up at his friend and Will held him by his shoulders and gave him a light shake but Max dropped his head again.

"Look at me, Max. Look at me! For God's sake look at me!" Will reached under Max's chin and jutted his face upwards. "Now, I don't know what sort of craziness you've got yourself into, but if someone is dead, then this is a whole new level. You have got to tell me about this. Now!"

He let go and opened the bottom drawer of a filing cabinet where he kept a bottle of brandy and a glass for nights when he would be working late, but now it was needed for medicinal purposes. If Max didn't settle down he'd give them both a heart attack. He poured a large glass of brandy and pressed it into Max's hand.

"Here, drink this and talk to me as you do. Then I'll see what the hell we're going to do to get you out of this one."

5

I read all that day. I laugh at my mother's account of her parents' eccentricity and constant travel, I empathise with her as she struggles with lectures, as she passes remarks on the boys on her course, as she tortures herself as to who is more handsome – John Taylor or Simon Le Bon from Duran Duran.

But eventually, the entries become more sporadic, more rushed and I see a change in her tone. Even her handwriting is less orderly and she has abandoned her usual structure, jotting down random notes and worrying concerns and this makes me sit up and take more notice.

I slow my reading pace away down. I don't want it to finish. I don't want to know.

But then I *do* want to know and so I read on . . .

My Story by Estelle Lynch – 27 November '81
No 1 Single – "Every Little Thing She Does is Magic"

Favourite Movie – no time for movies
Fashion Icon – Singh!
Best Friend – Singh (when I can find her!)
Crush – It's a secret – but he knows who he is!

Dear Diary
I've met this guy and have been spending some time with him in the library at university. He is nice and he likes me too. I'm trying not to use the "L" word too soon but I think it might go that way. It's a secret for now so I won't tell you any more than that – but watch this space!

On the other hand, maybe I'm clinging to that notion because it's hard to keep up with Singh these days and I miss her terribly. I think she's struggling with money but no matter how many times I offer to help, she refuses and goes off on a rant in her native language and I don't understand. We went out the other night and when I suggested going back to her place to crash out like we often do, she clammed up and shouted at me and told me to mind my own business.

I followed her. I followed her to find out what the hell was going on and when she got to her bed-sit there were two guys waiting outside on the road. One was small and skinny and he wore his jacket zipped right up to his chin. The other was bulkier and seemed to be in charge and he was holding Singh's arm but she didn't seem annoyed. She seemed to know them. I think the bigger guy might be her boyfriend because of the way she was looking at him, and the way she kept running her fingers through her hair and the way she didn't flinch when he grabbed her arm. He gave her a parcel and at first I thought it might be a present. The smaller guy spat on the pavement and lit up a cigarette while the bigger one did the talking. I think they wanted Singh to invite them in but she was saying no. The big guy was angry and he kicked the wall, then they both stormed off and the small guy was laughing but the other one wasn't. Singh ran inside. She seemed upset and I called after her. I even went to her door but she didn't answer. It's like she's hiding something from me but maybe not. Maybe she just doesn't need me any more. Maybe she's moved on. Like she just used me for a while and now she's found a boyfriend and I'm totally forgotten about. But I don't think she would do that to me. Singh is not like that. She's kind and gentle and she doesn't shout or swear and I never ever have heard her say a bad word about anyone. Dear Diary, I think Singh is in trouble. I think she is spending money on drugs and what she can't pay for, she is making up for in other ways with the men who call at her door.

I think Singh is in trouble and I want to help her, but she won't let me. And I'm so scared.

E xx

6

Max Kelly zipped open the empty suitcase on the bed and wondered where to start. It was hard packing when you didn't know how long you'd be gone for.

"Sandra?" he called, but she didn't answer and he didn't try again.

Why should she? None of this was her fault. He didn't expect her to understand his mindset when he couldn't even bring himself to tell her the truth. No one would or could understand the mental mess he was in right now.

He stared into the empty suitcase and then sat down, defeated, on the bed. He concentrated on breathing and clutched the covers beneath him, his hands slipping on the satin finish of the deep purple bedspread. The spare bedroom was empty and unlived in most of the time, but he had been glad to sleep here recently . . . since the demons in his head and the guilt that oozed from his every pore, when he looked at Sandra sleeping soundly beside him, became too much to take. In this room he could suffer alone away from reality and the pressures of everyday life. Yes, it was selfish, and yes, he was weak but everything was different now. He realised now that he wasn't getting better. Time wasn't healing his pain and with Estelle's death the time-bomb ticking in his head had reached a whole new level.

It was when he saw his young sons that he felt at his lowest ebb. A knowing glance from his eldest boy who used to hold him in such high regard was enough to make his insides crumble. And young Josh would follow him around, making such an effort to have things back to normal that Max could physically feel his heart shattering at the sound of his pleading voice. And Sandra . . . well, even saying her name hurt like hell. He was ruining his family and he couldn't stop. Like a runaway train, his mind constantly flashed back to the past and what he did and didn't do and how he could never, ever make it better now. Her face haunted him at night and in the day he would see her in a bus queue or hear her laugh in the supermarket or see her seated in his restaurant. She just wouldn't go away. He felt useless and dirty and he hated himself from the inside out. He was no good for his family. He couldn't even pack a bloody suitcase.

The bedroom door clicked open and Josh came in, a stern look of disappointment etched on his young face.

"Mum sent you in these shirts. She pressed them using the nice water in the iron, the one you buy in the shop that makes the clothes smell fresh. She said that's how you like them."

Josh laid the shirts down on the bed and spilled a bundle of socks and underwear from his other arm.

"Thanks, mate," said Max. "Tell Mum I said thanks."

He patted the bed beside him and Josh sat down, automatically tucking himself under Max's arm.

"I don't want you to leave, Dad," said Josh. "Please don't go away again."

Max rubbed his son's soft spiky hair and stared out of the window in front of him. This was torture. Every day of his life was torture now.

"I'm sorry, buddy. I don't want to leave you either. I really don't want this at all but I can't help it."

"That's what Mum says."

"Mum knows best as always," said Max. "I just need some time out, that's all. Not time out from you. Time out from me. I really need to do this or the stress I'm feeling right now is going to make all of our lives even more miserable."

Josh nodded. "She's been crying again, you know. When she was ironing your shirts she had to stop a few times to wipe her eyes. You do know she's been crying for weeks now? Are you two going to get divorced?"

Max pushed his pride to the side and looked his son right in the eye. Josh was so like Sandra, always had been with his fair complexion and light freckles round his nose and the way he cut straight to the chase when he had something to say. He was pretty for a boy and his blond hair was styled in the latest trend and though Max could see that he was slowly turning into a young man, his eyes were full of childlike innocence.

"No, we are not going to get a divorce," Max said and gave his boy a strong squeeze. "I promise you that much, Josh. This is just a tough time for us but we're strong and we'll get through it."

Josh leaned into his dad and lay there for a moment in silence while Max thought his heart was going to explode with guilt and sorrow, and waves of emotions flooded through his insides. Josh was emotional like his mother too, whereby Charlie would clam up and keep all his emotions inside, just like his father.

"Mum says we're stronger than we think," said Josh eventually. "We're the Kellys, isn't that what you used to say? We're the Kellys!"

"We are, son," Max said. "Believe me, we are. We're the Kellys."

A horn tooted from outside and Josh jumped up from the bed and looked down at his father, his chin tilted and manly again.

"That'll be your lift," he said.

"That'll be Will," said Max. "On time as always." He put two pairs of jeans into the case, then his toiletry bag and carefully laid the shirts on top. Then he zipped up his case with a sigh.

"You will call?" said Josh. "It's not like the last time, is it, Dad?"

Max lifted his case and looked at the floor, the reality of what he was about to do just hitting him now. Never in his life could he have imagined his mental state driving him to measures like this.

"Of course I'll call. I'll call every day. Every single day." He felt heartburn in his chest and he realised he hadn't packed any remedies or medicines for his trip. Heartburn was a regular visitor these days along with all the torture and emotional baggage he carried around with him. "Come, walk me out. Please."

"Okay, Dad. Come on."

Max stopped when he reached the bottom of the stairs and inhaled the scent of home, wishing he could bottle it and take it with him. A family portrait sat on the telephone table and he stared at it, taking in the toothy grins of his two sons who were so much younger and innocent then. He was ruining their lives right now and he hated himself for it. He looked at Sandra in the photograph, a nervous smile on her face, doubtful, almost as if she was expecting their family bubble to burst at any given second. Her hand was on top of his but it wasn't rested. It looked uneasy, as if it just skimmed his skin. Then he looked at his own face, distant and vacant. Ungrateful, he thought, and again he cursed his feelings. He had always been ungrateful for all the good he had in his life. He had much more than he deserved.

"You should hurry up," said Sandra. She stood at the kitchen doorway, her arms folded and her mouth tight as if she was fighting back what she really wanted to say. "Will has been there almost ten minutes now."

"I . . . I just need to get . . ." Max made his way towards her and she handed him a pack of heartburn tablets. "Oh . . . thank you."

Sandra looked at the floor and then back up again and when her eyes met his she couldn't decide if anger or pity was her strongest emotion.

"Just be sure you know what you want when you come back," she whispered. "I really hope this works, for all our sakes."

"I promise you," said Max. "I promise that I will make everything better. Will said . . . Will said this is a good place for me to sort out my head. I hate to let you down, I really do. I love you, Sandra. Please believe me."

Sandra folded her arms again and looked away. "My family think I'm mad, you know. How many second chances can you give him, they say. And I *have* given you far too many, Max Kelly. I have fought tooth and nail to make this marriage work. Tooth and bloody nail and you just seem to mess us around all the time."

"I know I do, I know I have – but I want to make it all better. I want to be a better person. Please, Sandra . . ."

"And as for our boys . . . what this is doing to them you will never know . . ."

She stopped and let out a high-pitched breath, unable to control the fear that bounced from the pit of her stomach.

Max swallowed hard and heard a shuffle from the stairs. He looked around to see his eldest son leaning over the banister, staring at him like he had just murdered his entire family.

"Why don't you just run ahead, Dad?" he said. "Run away like you always do, but this time I don't care if you ever come back! We don't need you! Don't come back!"

Sandra walked away and closed the kitchen door behind her.

"Charlie, son, this is for the best," Max said.

"Get out! Go! Now!"

Max could hear Sandra fall against the door on the other side and her muffled sobs seep under the doorframe.

He lifted his case and, without looking back, he walked through the front door, down the pathway and into the car where Will was waiting for him.

"Are you sure this is what you want, Max?" asked Will, turning down the radio when his friend got settled in the passenger seat. "I don't want to force you into this, but I think it will help. I just want to help."

"It's not what I want, Will. It's what I have to do. It's my only chance," replied Max and he folded his hands on his lap, then leaned across and turned the radio up again.

Will put the car into gear and fixed the rear-view mirror.

"Charlie is watching through the window," he said. "Aren't you going to wave goodbye?"

"Just drive on," said Max. "I can't look at his face. Please, Will. This is killing me inside. Just drive on."

Blessington Abbey, a secluded mansion in the depths of County Louth, towered over Will's family car as they cruised along its long winding entrance drive. Max could almost smell religion seeping from the walls of the building and his fears of being judged or found out terrified him already. He had tried to hide his nerves the entire journey by talking incessantly but avoiding any conversation as to why he needed this stay.

"*Visitors, this way,*" he said, reading the sign. "I can get out here. No need to park up. Really, I can manage from here."

He felt hot and sticky after the journey from Dublin and, despite what Will already knew, he didn't want his friend to witness his checking in for therapy and counselling and cleansing of the soul, even though it was Will who had arranged it. He had sworn Will to secrecy but this was as much as he could bear.

"I'd rather be sure you had it all sorted – you know, that you haven't forgotten anything or arrived on the wrong day. I'll come inside with you and then I'll be out of your way before you know it."

Max bit his lip as the car slowed down and Will parked in an empty space across from the building's fine entrance.

"Thanks, Will. Thanks for everything."

Will shrugged. "Hell, what have I done only kick your ass a bit lately. I hope you don't think I'm pushing you into this. I just feel you need to get a few demons off your chest. Find some forgiveness in yourself for what you have or haven't done. It's a good place, Max. I wouldn't bring you here if I didn't believe it would help you."

Max unlocked his seat-belt and gathered the remnants of a shop stop-off from the car floor. An energy drink, a newspaper and a few packs of chewing gum were all he would bring in with him apart from his case. He reached into his side pocket and lifted out his mobile phone, then switched it off.

"I think it's best I cut myself off for a while," he said, handing it to his friend. "Don't worry, Will. Hopefully this stay here will help clear my head and leave the past in the past where it belongs. You never know, I might even learn a few things about myself. I'll be a whole better person, just you wait and see."

"Well, that's the least we can hope for 'cos this little sojourn is set to cost us a fortune in donations!"

Max opened the car door and hesitated.

"I'm scared, Will," he said. "I'm so scared I might be making things worse by running away like this."

Will closed his own door and held his hand up, ready to give the speech he had planned in his head all the way to Blessington.

"Max, you are not running away. You're facing up to things at last. You're a good man who has hit a bump in the road – a huge bump in the road that would finish any man, and you just need help in getting over it. You've been beating yourself up for years now, never feeling good enough, never feeling like you deserve all you've been given in life because of this horrible guilt you're carrying around. You may not look it but you're kicking the ass of fifty and do you want to spend the next twenty years, if God spares you, living in the past?"

"Of course not, but –"

"No buts! You've wasted enough of your life on 'what-ifs' and 'buts' and 'maybes'. Go and switch off for a while. Talk to strangers who can't judge you. Spill your heart out to them, scream if you want but for God's sake help yourself so that you can then get the happiness you deserve. And you do deserve it, Max. We all deserve some happiness. Even if we've made terrible mistakes. We can be forgiven."

Max swallowed hard and then pushed the car door open again.

"And then what?" he asked. "What do I do when this week is over and when I'm feeling better? What do I tell my sons and my wife? How do I explain why I've let them down so badly?"

"Do what they want you to do," whispered Will. "Go home and hold them tight and tell them you're back and you'll never, ever leave them again. That's all they want.

They want their daddy back. It's all they've ever wanted."

Max and Will were met by a man dressed in neat black trousers and a plain black shirt. He looked younger than Max had expected a monk to look yet his eyes were full of wisdom and he had a serene presence surrounding him. He introduced himself as Father Bernard.

"You must be Max?" he said in a lilting Cork accent, extending a warm handshake.

"Yeah," said Max, glancing at Will and signalling to him to go.

"You are very welcome," said the monk. "Come inside and we'll have a chat. Get you settled in."

Will took the cue to leave. Without saying anything he nodded at his friend and walked away, then stopped and went back again.

"Call me if you need anything," he said and gave Max a reassuring smile.

"I will. I'll keep you posted with all my tales of my revolutionary road to discovery," said Max and at that he lifted his case and followed Father Bernard into a tall library, already feeling the pangs of homesickness and guilt rise in his gut.

7

The beach is busy and I walk to a quiet, secluded spot, knowing that I now have only a few more pages of my mother's diary to read. I am truly becoming more and more absorbed as I read the later entries of her friendship with Singh and her worries as she watched her friend slip over into the dark side and of her desperate attempts to help her.

Yesterday I barely moved from the same spot and everywhere I went in the house, the diary came with me. Sometimes I stopped, for fear of finishing and not having any more to find out. Sometimes I started all over again and re-read entries, savouring every mood my mother experienced, every joy she felt, every fear she witnessed as she became more and more embroiled in the dark and dangerous life of Singh Moshiro.

Then, in the evening, I did stop. Close to the end. I was afraid to go on. Afraid of what I would find but also simply afraid of having no more to read, of coming to the end of this wonderful unexpected contact with my mother as a young woman. Afraid it would be like losing her all over again.

So I put the notebook away.

But today I dressed in a light sun-top and a pair of white shorts and I even sprayed some perfume on. Holding the diary close to my chest, I made my way to the beach.

Now I sit down on a sand dune and read.

Date – 3rd December 1981

Dear Diary
I can't find Singh today. I've looked everywhere but it's like she just vanished. She didn't turn up for any of her classes. I went to her place but it looks like she hasn't been there all weekend. I invited her to my parents' house for a break from it all but she didn't show. She has become so frail and gaunt and she won't talk to me like she used to and every time I mention Christmas she changes the subject and says she doesn't care much for Christmas any more.

Even when we go out for a night, she gets terribly drunk and talks about people I have never met. There are so many that I don't remember any of their names – I joke with her that she must know most of Belfast now and she seems to like that idea. But I don't. I don't like that she has lots and lots of so-called friends who seem to come and go. I passed her on a corridor just yesterday and she was with a group of boys. I don't think they were students. Two of them looked like the ones I had seen outside her bedsit that day. They looked at me so strangely, like I was so far beneath them, like I was dirt on their shoe and when I asked Singh to join me for lunch, she stared right through me and her face was so pale and I noticed she had no flowers in her hair and her make-up was horribly black and smudgy. But her clothes were new and she was showing the boys a new music cassette she had bought so at least she has money now. That's one thing I don't have to worry about when I wonder what she's up to.

I waited for her to introduce me like she used to do and proudly tell everyone that I am her best friend, but she didn't. She stared at me and her eyes were glassy and lifeless. She looked like she was drunk but she didn't smell of alcohol. I thought I was going to cry.

"Singh," I said, "why are you being like this? I'm worried about you."

She slipped the cassette into her bag and shrugged, then the boys led her away, the two I thought I recognised linking her arms. She walked with them across the lawns and out of the university campus.

I haven't found her since.

Do you think I should tell someone? But who? I don't know any of my lecturers long enough to know who to approach and I have no idea how to contact her parents. I don't even know any of the people on my course because from day one it has been just me and Singh. And when I mention her name to my housemates they just roll their eyes and say, "Oh, here we go again, Singh, Singh, Singh!' and then they laugh and change the subject. They don't *see how concerned I am for her safety. It is concern, isn't it? Or am I just jealous?*

Maybe I am. Maybe I'm fussing and paranoid and a bit jealous of Singh and her new friends. Maybe I should just forget about her and try to make new friends. We were far too close too soon. It was like she had become my family and I had become hers.

She was like my family. She was like my security net in this big strange city where I know no one else.

No, I have to stand by her and try to help. If she is in trouble like I know she is, then it's up to me to help her. I am all she has and she is all I have. I'm going to look for her again tonight.

E xx

PS I wish I could say that romance is blooming slowly in the background or even simmering at least but I haven't seen him in a while. Bummer! So I'm heartbroken into the bargain! Life sucks.

I turn the page for more, and another photo comes loose from the diary. I flick on through for more text but there is nothing, just blank, then blank, then blank and then I come to the very last page of the notebook. The handwriting is almost the same, but it is neater and more mature and it is written with a different pen. My heart races and I know that my mother's story is finally coming to a close. I want to press "pause" and brace myself for this moment and think about what I am about to discover. I want to close the book and never open it again as a new-found fear engulfs me – but I can't, so I pack up my belongings into my canvas bag and I walk back up to the cottage, go back inside – ignoring a barking Jinx in his pen – and close the door.

I get a bottle of water from the kitchen, slip off my shoes and sit down on the couch. Then, with the clock ticking in the background, I open the diary again and to my surprise I see that the last chapter is written directly to me. I hear my heart beat and pins and needles crawl over my wrists and down into my hands. I wish I could hold her and tell her I understand, but all I can do is read her words.

To my sweet daughter Hollie,

I am writing this but I never want you to find it. I plan to destroy this diary and this evidence of what happened to me and move on to make a new life with you, if I possibly can. I know that I will love you and care for you and never will I look on you with any memory of how you came into the world. Writing this is therapeutic, like closure almost, and perhaps some day I will forget everything and my life will begin again.

But one night in December 1981 my life ended. It was like I was plunged into the deepest, darkest hole and nothing or no one could ever help me out. Writing this down is like a release, but I fear the shame of it and I wonder if the fear will ever really go away. What happened that night spiralled me into a world that I never imagined – a world I have tried to forget about but the blankness in my mind and the things I was forced to do almost led me to become a very desperate, very dark person.

When I went to find Singh, her house was dark and cold, but the door was slightly ajar. I called her name in a whisper, afraid that she might be asleep and that I might wake her and scare her.

It wasn't very late – about half past nine I think and I hoped with all my heart to find her like I used to, laughing on the sofa in front of the latest American sitcom she had discovered. She really was a lively girl and to me she was like a drug. I wanted to be with her all the time and I had thrown all my energies into clawing my way back into her life.

I could hear the hum of the television from the small sitting room and I walked towards it, still calling her name, but there was no reply. I don't remember feeling scared at all. If she was with her new friends, this would be the time she would introduce me properly and then everything would be back to normal. I would push my jealousies to the side.

God, but I was so bloody naïve! So desperate to be needed by someone, so desperate to impress her that I didn't even stop to think of what was really going on. It was only when I heard a faint cry from her bedroom that I began to feel the first flutter of fear, but, even then, it wasn't for my own safety, just the safety of Singh and what was going on behind that door.

"Singh, it's me! It's Estelle!" I shouted, my heart thumping in my chest as adrenaline pumped through my body. I knocked on the door. "Singh, let me in! Are you okay?" Then her door opened and the big guy stepped out, the one I'd seen with her before. At the same time I heard the front door slam shut behind me.

"What's going on?" I asked him. "What have you done to my friend?"

He was angry looking, really angry like I'd gate-crashed his party and I knew right then that it wasn't the type of party I'd have been invited to anyway. I darted around him and made for the front door but his skinny friend was guarding it and he was laughing at me, looking me up and down and shaking his head. I begged them to let me go. I tried to scream but I could hardly breathe with fear. My first thought was for Singh but when I said her name, the big guy slapped my face hard and then they dragged me into the sitting area where another one sat – this time someone I recognised – with a needle stuck in his arm and a sickly, scary expression on his spaced-out face. What happened next is too horrendous to describe and I have tried my best to blank it from my memory, but no matter how much time has passed, no matter how much older I have become, I have never, ever recovered from what happened to me that night.

I died inside right then.

I have bottled it up inside me for years and years and years and it has eaten at me like a cancer, day in, day out. I could never tell anyone the details because it has always made me feel so dirty and used and like I am no more than a wet rag that is past its use that should be thrown away with the garbage.

I know it's not my fault. Well, maybe it is. You see, I can't decide. I just wanted to help my friend but I was so young and innocent that I would never have imagined the trouble she was in, or the dark path she had found herself too far along. But Singh was like a magnet to me. I was *like a moth to a flame. She had this beauty that I cannot describe and I still believe, even to this day, that she was a good person who let bad things happen to her. She was a good person who surrounded herself with bad people who did bad things and unfortunately, in a way, she let very bad things happen to me too.*

I know now that what happened to me that night ruined any chance of ever loving a man or finding someone who could love me back. It blurred my vision on life, it stunted my faith in humanity. You see, one of the men – well, he was more a boy – was the one I was meeting in the library. Someone I liked. Someone I trusted. Someone I thought I might even be in love with.

I pushed everyone away after that night, most of all my parents who I have to admit surprised me with their support – especially my father. Caroline was too young to know the true story and I have never been able to tell her because, despite the mess I was when she came back from America, I was still her big sister. Sometimes I think she blocks out any memories she has from those days, but if she thought back in detail she would remember the endless tears, the screams in the night, the flashbacks I had in broad daylight when I thought they were coming for me. I can still see their faces. I still know their names.

For a whole night they kept me in their drug-binging, partying, drinking circle – with lots of money exchanging hands. It was a sick and solitary experience but it was then I realised that Singh was on a merry-go-round of this lifestyle and she was in far too deep to help me. Or for me to help her.

I remember the face of the guy who tried to stop me

next morning when I made my escape. He was still drunk and I managed to get away.

I rang my parents and pleaded for help and they took me home but I was too ashamed to accept their care. I ran away to a friend's house and begged for some understanding. My friend tried but it didn't last. It couldn't.

Then, when I found out I was pregnant, I tried to end it all – I can't describe to you how alone and desperate I was back then. My parents were devastated and a doctor friend came to talk to me and offered to take me to England and fix things – with an abortion. It was then that I was aware of what I had to do. Taking my own life was one thing, taking yours was another. I decided that day that I would have my baby and focus on her care and that it would make everything all better. And it did, almost. The pregnancy flew by and no one thought I would have the strength to give birth. I was still on the edge and my mother never left my side. Everyone watched with bated breath after you were born to see if I could cope.

I think I did cope, Hollie. I think I did the best I could but every day was a battle. I have lived life like I've been wearing a mask. I can scream and scream and still wear a smile. I can cry without shedding a tear. I have climbed mountains when I barely have the energy to climb stairs.

Please don't think this is your fault. You are innocent in it all and I will love you every day of my life – that is the one thing that will always be real to me. I know that you will give me moments of joy that I cannot think will ever come my way. I know I will be able to talk to you all day about how wonderful you are and how much I love you. And maybe someday I will learn to love myself again.

Because I haven't been able to since that horrible night.

There were three of them. Their faces never leave my mind and I can still smell their sweat, the beer of their breath and the way they jeered and laughed and applauded each other. I can hear the zips on their trousers, the way they mocked my name and I can still feel the needle pierce my arm, and the heat pumping through my veins into unconsciousness. I can hear the theme tune of the late-night television quiz show that played in the background while those monsters played their very own game. I can still see the stream of daylight come through the window when I woke up, and the pain I felt when I tried to move from that shabby, broken sofa. I still feel dizzy and lost when I think of that long walk home in the morning. I knew I had to escape before I was stuck there forever. I plunged my sore body into a scalding hot bath and scrubbed my skin till it bled. Then I locked myself in my room and, when it came time to go to my parents' house, I had already decided on my vow of silence. I had learned a lesson about humanity and I had made a mistake in trusting someone with everything I had.

I never did find Singh after that. I never looked for her again. And I don't think she ever looked for me. I still think about her though and, funnily, I don't picture her as that vacant, pale drugged-up loser that she so quickly became. No, I prefer to remember her as the girl who made me laugh, who wore flowers in her hair and who read poems to me and sang songs when I was feeling low.

Maybe some day this will all end. Maybe some day, with you, my future will not be dark and grey. I hope to find my rainbow. I hope that you are my rainbow. You will always be my rainbow.

Your loving mother

Estelle xxx

I can barely breathe. The diary rattles in my hands, and I reach to the floor for a drink and then I gulp back lukewarm water until I can drink no more. My hands tremble and I feel sweat build on my forehead, dribble down my face and I shiver in the cold. I lift the photo which has fallen onto the sofa and I scan across the faces, looking for some sort of recognition. Singh is there, staring off camera in what appeared to be a drunken daze. The picture was taken in a hazy 1980s' nightclub with smoke-machines and green laser lights in the background. I cannot spot my mum in the picture but there are two young men to the side of the photograph who are looking at Singh. Neither of them seems particularly big or skinny like the guys she described in the diary. Each of them holds a beer bottle in his hand, and they seem happy and in a party mood but they aren't the focus of the picture. Maybe they weren't even supposed to be in it? Maybe it was just another photo of Singh? But it wasn't focused on her either or even a clear photo of her, so why had Estelle left it in this diary? Perhaps it was the only other picture of her she owned. I flip the photo to the blank side to see if it is captioned but there is nothing. I push it violently back into the diary.

I try to take it all in – the attack, the disappearance of

Singh, the horrible secrets my mother had been harbouring all these years, the fact that the man who fathered me could have been any one of three junkies and I feel my skin crawl once again.

I am now transformed. I am a totally different person. I have now gained a whole new identity and immediately I hate it. I look at my hands, at my arms, at my bare legs from beneath my crisp white shorts and I want to tear my skin off. I stand up and examine my face in the mirror, tracing my nose and mouth with my fingers, and then I grab my hair at each side of my temple and push it back from my face, staring into my own eyes which I no longer recognise. My skin is a pale grey colour and my brown eyes look full of fear, yet I can see *his* menace.

But what scares me the most is that I can't see myself or any resemblance to my late mother any more. All I can see is him. A mixture of three faces flash through my mind and the room begins to spin. I reach out for my phone. I need Caroline. I need someone. I want Ben. I am so hot, so dizzy, so thirsty. Do I look like him? Did I remind my mum of him? I feel faint. I feel like there is a monster living inside me and I need to get it out. I need to get it out now! Now!

8

"We are here to help you," said Father Bernard and Max pursed his lips, turning the leaflet over in his hands as he glanced down the list of Mass times, Holy Services, meditation, counselling, spiritual healing, personal development. The list went on . . .

Max looked up at the older man. His fine-lined face and tiny brown eyes were kind and thoughtful and he looked like he'd listened to a lot of problems in his day. He seemed like a good man and Max felt even more of a sinner in his presence.

The library where they sat was a magnificent room with old-style leather armchairs and floor-to-ceiling rows and rows of books in green and leather covers and cases. There were small round tables scattered around the room, which was oblong and dark, and each was dressed with a green-fringed reading lamp. Max wondered if anyone actually read the books, or if there were really books behind the leather spines at all.

"Our leaflet tells you what we can do for you if you need us during your stay here," continued the monk. "First and foremost, we are a retreat centre. We have a team of people who welcome anyone who needs to switch off from everyday life and find themselves again. At their own pace of course."

"Thanks," Max said, feeling inadequate. "I'll just have look through this in my own time and then I'll let you know. I don't really know where to start or if any of this is even for me. Sorry."

"Not the praying type?" asked Father Bernard. "Don't worry – we're not here to judge you or your beliefs. Take from us what you need."

"That's a relief," said Max. "Not the praying type is one way of putting it, I suppose, but I'm praying now in my own way, believe me. I'm praying for peace of mind and a new way of life."

Max barely recognised his own words as they trickled out to this stranger. He wasn't even sure if what he was saying made sense but the monk seemed to be concentrating on his every word.

"You don't need to tell any of us what is on your mind unless you want to, Max. You seem lost and confused and maybe you just need time to think. That's absolutely fine. There are no pressures here to tell any of us why you have come to stay at Blessington but, if you feel it would help, then we are here to listen."

Max pondered his statement. Why *was* he here? He couldn't put it into words and he certainly couldn't tell the truth.

"Em, I'm not sure," he said. "I just know that I need

to clear my head. I need to move on from the past. I need to forgive myself and I need to become a better husband, a better father . . ."

"So you'll be here for a while, then?" joked the monk.

Max gave a nervous laugh. "You think?"

"No, I don't think so. You know, sometimes reflection is the best way of finding our way forward. Even if you don't want to attend any counselling, just having some time to yourself might be enough to give you some guidance while you're here. Just take your time."

Max crossed his legs at his ankles, relaxing somewhat in these unfamiliar surroundings. Father Bernard's little voice with its Cork accent was obviously well trained in making people feel at ease.

"I think it's time I talked to someone who is impartial to me as a person," Max said. "I was going to just take a vacation, you know, somewhere by the sea where I could switch off and let the salt air clear my mind but I realised that being in my own company would probably tip me over the edge. Then my business partner suggested I come here. He said his brother-in-law had problems and he sought solace here and when he came home he was a different person. And that's exactly what I want to be. A different person. A better person."

He looked out through the long window opposite them and watched a stream of light come through, carrying dust in a beam that finished on a rug that covered most of the floor. He wanted to be a different person, but was he in the right place at all? He still questioned it and felt like he was imposing on these good people of God who took only voluntary donations for their time.

"Well, I cannot promise any miraculous cure, my friend," said Father Bernard. "Only you can turn your life around. If you ask for God's forgiveness he will grant it but it is up to you to accept it and move on. You cannot be punished forever if you are truly sorry for what you have become."

"I am sorry, Father. I am so sorry. But where do I start? What do I physically do now that I'm here? I don't think I'd get any solace from Mass just yet if you don't mind me saying and I'm not sure I need counselling as such."

Max stood up, paced towards the window and looked out onto the majestic grounds of the abbey. It was a beautiful scene, but Blessington was by no means a hotel where he could lie on a cosy bed out of sight and flick through numerous channels on satellite television until he drifted off to sleep, or order room service so he could drink and eat as he wallowed in self-pity.

This was more of a hostel than a luxurious counselling clinic, more of a self-help centre where you took from it what you could and helped out with chores. With its religious elements, the place promised to be more a soul-cleanser and perhaps therefore just what Max needed if he only knew where to start.

"Why don't you take a walk in the grounds?" said Father Bernard. "It's a beautiful day and much too nice to be cooped up in a dark room like this. Or indeed, we have afternoon Mass in the chapel just down the corridor if by then you want to come and sit in the back and just listen? Or there are therapeutic chores like cookery and gardening which you may soon pick up on."

Max smiled at the man. "As a chef, please forgive me if I stay away from the kitchen in this instance."

"Of course, Mr Kelly. Of course," said Father Bernard with a little chuckle. "I'll have your case brought to your room. Have a think and we'll help you along the way. I always start a new task or journey with a breath of fresh air. It helps me get my head around things."

Max gazed out the window as the monk spoke to him and he noticed how many people were walking through the gardens, some with their families, young and old, others couples hand in hand and some individuals who, just like himself, looked like they were lost in thought as they strolled along the gardens in the afternoon sunshine.

"You're absolutely right. I think I'll start with a walk," he said and he shook the older man's hand. "Thank you in advance for helping me and my family. I'm so grateful for your time."

He followed Father Bernard back out into the huge hallway with its mosaic tiles, mahogany furniture and cream-painted curved walls with their rows of plastic-held pamphlets. He selected a few random leaflets and made his way outside where the sound of summer made Blessington seem like a tiny slice of heaven and when he breathed in the fresh air and felt the sun on his weary face, he honestly began to feel better already.

9

"Hollie! Jesus, Hollie, you scared the life out of me. Hollie!"

"Ow! My head. My head hurts."

I open my eyes and I think I might be dreaming when I see a face I have been longing to see for weeks now. A face I know that soon I will never see again.

"Ben! How . . . where did you come from?" I mumble. "Oh Ben! Ben, I'm so scared!"

I am on the living-room floor. I have been lucky in my fall, he tells me, but the blow to the back of my head throbs nonetheless.

"I've been calling you since yesterday," says Ben. "When you didn't answer I thought I'd better come up to see if you were all right. Good job I did."

He cradles me in his strong arms and eases me up from the floor and I want to stay in his arms forever.

"I must have fallen. I must have fainted," I tell him. I still feel delirious and my mind is a blur. "Oh God, Ben I have so much to tell you. I . . . I am so glad you are here."

He carries me across the room. "What on earth have you been doing? What happened?"

I hold onto his neck and stare at him, so glad to see him that I can barely speak. He lays me down on the sofa and pulls a throw over me, then crouches by my side so that our faces almost touch.

"I'm so glad you're here," I whisper. "It's awful, Ben. It's so bad and it's getting worse and worse and . . ."

"Ssh, don't be upsetting yourself more," he says, rubbing my hair back from my face. "Have a rest while I tidy this place up a bit and get us something to eat. Rest for a while and then you can tell me all about it."

He lifts a collection of glasses from the floor, some crisp packets, empty Lucozade bottles, unfinished coffee cups and I watch him as he stoops and bends, searching round the living room with worry written all over his face.

He really is so handsome. No, really. Everyone says so. Ben Campbell is a real catch but everyone also knows that he is hard to hold on to. I had managed to do so for over a year but Ben had itchy feet and wanted to move on, much to my heartbreak and distress. But he is here now and I will savour his attention and the knowledge that he still cares, somewhere down deep in that dark moody soul of his. Although I'm probably mildly concussed, I manage to notice that he is wearing the Armani jeans I bought him for his last birthday. They cost me at least a week's pay. And together we chose the Converse trainers he is wearing. Even the cologne that I can still smell from my hands, from being round his neck, brings me back to better days when we would run away for wild weekends and do nothing more than eat and drink and spend long lazy days in bed. God, how I miss him and those happy times.

"Oh, don't touch that. Just leave it – no, give it to me," I say, attempting to sit up straight but the pain in my head makes me lie back down straight away. I hold out my hand for him to pass the diary to me and he does what he is told, but pretends he is going to have a flick through it first.

"Is this yours? I didn't know you kept a diary?" he says playfully.

Doesn't he realise I am in no mood for jokes?

"Please, Ben. It's . . . it's very important. Give it here. Give it to me now."

He does as I ask and leaves me while he takes the rubbish he has gathered to the kitchen. I listen to him whistle an indie tune as he opens and closes cupboard doors and stacks the dishes into the dishwasher.

"Do you mind if I make some coffee?" he calls. "Shit, this milk is off! It's way out of date. Christ, Hollie!"

"'Christ, Hollie!'" I mimic. He used to say that to me all the time. I hold the diary in my hands, staring at it, flicking through it once more. I speed-read through the last entry again and try to find more clues. I look at the photo. Who are the boys? Were they random passers-by or were they *the ones*? Will I ever be able to get some sort of justice or at least closure on my nightmare history or is this something I will just have to live with?

Ben appears by my side and looks at me sorrowfully.

"You really have gone off the radar, haven't you?" he says.

I nod, full of self-pity. "Suppose I have."

"So, are you going to talk to me about all of this, or will we eat first? It's up to you."

"Eat? Gosh, sorry, Ben, but I can't even think of food right now. And I can't believe you have found anything edible in my fridge. I don't know the last time I even looked in there. It was two days ago at least."

"I didn't," says Ben. "I'm going to pop out and buy some food, so how about you stay exactly where you are, then we'll have lunch and you can tell me as much as you want to? What do you think?"

"I think . . . I think I still love you," I say, reaching out to touch his T-shirt and I can see his face change from concern to pity and he bites the side of his mouth, squeezing my hand and looking away. "I'm sorry. I . . . I just ruin things every time, don't I?"

Shit! I don't intend to sound so desperate but once again the words just spill out when I see the tenderness in his face and hear the concern in his voice. He leans over and kisses my forehead. It is a brotherly kiss, like the way you'd kiss an old friend.

"We'll talk when I get back. Now, please relax. Just relax."

He helps me up from the sofa and holds me close and I feel a tear escape from my eye. I really don't want to cry.

"I *am* getting better, Ben," I say. "I even got dressed today. I put some perfume on too. See, I'm getting there."

Ben laughs and kisses my forehead again. More of the same.

"You're lucky you didn't do yourself serious injury when you fell. I'll be as quick as I can. Don't move until I get back. Promise?"

"Promise."

And I wait.

10

"Hey, mate, anyone sitting here?"

It was six o'clock now and dinner time. Max was sitting on his own at a table in the modest canteen. He shook his head and gestured to the young red-haired man to join him at the table.

"Cheers, man. I'm Jasper."

"Yeah, I remember you from before," said Max, recalling a brief introduction at one of the numerous park benches on the grounds of Blessington. He guessed the lad was no more than twenty-one but he spoke like a man of the world who had its weight on his young shoulders.

"Food's a bit shit but beggars can't be choosers, that's what my ma says anyway," said Jasper as he tucked into his cabbage and potatoes.

Max grinned. For one who thought the food was below standard, Jasper wasn't going to leave a bite of it on his plate.

"I still can't believe a young kid like you is staying in a

retreat centre," said Max. He was doing his best to take off his chef's hat and relax and eat what he could of the school-dinner type platter that sat before him. "I thought it was only old crazy guys like me who came here to hang out on holiday with the monks."

"Can't get off the white stuff, sir," said Jasper, tapping his nostril, his eye giving an involuntary twitch when he spoke. "It's either here now or jail later and it would break my ma's heart if I ended up in the clink. I'm doing all this for her. I wouldn't be here if it wasn't for fear of letting her down like the rest of the family already have."

Max smiled. "You're a mummy's boy, then? I think we all are at heart."

Jasper dropped his fork on the floor and Max saw how the young boy's hand shook when he bent to reach it. He didn't respond to Max's statement, just picked up his fork, wiped it with a paper napkin, and continued to shovel down his food, stopping occasionally as if to speak but then changing his mind.

"What about you?" he asked eventually. "You fond of the sauce? The old booze, eh? You don't look like it, mind. You look in pretty good shape for an oldie."

"For an oldie!" said Max. "Ah come on, I'm not that old, really. Old enough to be your father but not that old. Mind you, I have felt it of late."

His thoughts were disturbed by Jasper who dropped his fork again and swore as he stooped to lift it, then wiped it again and continued to eat and talk at the same time.

"My da is *way* younger than you," he said, talking with his mouth full. "My da's only, like, forty or something so I'd guess he's nearly ten years younger than you, I'd bet. But you look *far* younger than him. You look like you're loaded. My ma looks older than she is too but then she's the one who has to put up with all his shite, *and* mine, plus we're not loaded at all. We're skint. I feel real sorry for my ma, you know."

Max fidgeted in his chair and glanced around the hall. It was a cosy enough setting but it was quiet, with only about seven people scattered at the tables. He and Jasper were the only people who were keeping each other company and making conversation. One man sat on his own – he had been praying over his food for as long as Max had been in the canteen. Surely it would be stone cold by the time he got round to eating it?

"Have you been here before, Jasper?" Max asked, picking through his own rations of boiled potatoes, cabbage and bacon. If Will could see him now . . .

"Nah, but me brother has been here. He was going a bit off the rails too and my ma says God can help much quicker than any doctor when it comes to things like this. So, I'm on retreat, that's all. It's not like it's a loony bin nor nothing in here. You just clear your head and think about what a dickhead you've been and then hopefully you go home and make amends."

"Sounds simple," said Max, playing with his food. "If only it was that simple."

"Depends how big a dickhead you've been, I suppose," said Jasper. "The bigger the dickhead you were, the longer it'll take you to wise up, that's what –"

"Don't tell me! That's what your ma says?" laughed Max.

"Exactly," said Jasper, pointing his fork with a smile. "Now you've got it. Always listen to your ma. That's my motto."

They continued to eat in a more comfortable silence, each glancing at the other on occasion, with Max wondering what brings certain people to realise that they need help and direction.

"So, what about your dad?" asked Max, when he had finished his meal. He pushed away his plate and wiped the corners of his mouth with his own paper napkin. His dinner had tasted somewhat better than it had looked. "Where does he fit in? Does *he* offer any words of wisdom when you need advice?"

Jasper took a drink of milk from a small carton and wiped the remnants from above his lip with his sleeve.

"That asshole? Fuck! He couldn't even *spell* the word advice let alone give it!"

"Oh, that's –"

"No! Actually, hang on!" said Jasper, looking up at the ceiling as if he had been struck with divine inspiration. "He *has* taught me one thing I am truly grateful for – sorry, Da. He made me realise that if God ever blesses me with a child in future I know exactly what I *don't* want to do. That's the best lesson my da ever taught me. How *not* to be a father. How to be a pure one-hundred-per-cent shite-talking ass-wipe, that's what he has taught me. Great lesson in life, you know. Wonderful man he is."

Max sat up straight and breathed in. Jasper's words were stinging him but the boy was now on a rant.

"He's hardly ever at home and when he *is* home he's stuck on front of the TV like a silent stuffed toy, he never

74

talks to Ma about nothing, he goes on the odd bender on the old booze cruise for a day or three . . . Jeez, I could go on and on. He has her climbing the feckin' walls with worry. Kick him out, that's what I say but she never will. She loves him, you see. Love is deaf, dumb and blind, I tell her, but she never listens. It'll always be the same. And that's why I'm the way I am. That's why I'm an asshole and that's why I'm stuck in here eating cabbage and fuckin' spuds. Fuck!"

Jasper slammed his fist on the melamine table and then pushed his hands into his red face. His breathing was heavy and he sniffled hard. Max handed him a spare napkin and he buried his face in that instead. Max was startled. He looked around but no one stirred – they just continued to eat or pray or think or whatever the hell they were doing.

"Your da does sound like a right asshole," said Max quietly. He waited until Jasper lifted the napkin down from his face and the tears in the boy's eyes almost melted him. "He sounds like a prize asshole, in fact."

"You think?" asked Jasper. "Sometimes I think I might just use his antics as an excuse to cover up my own bad behaviour. Maybe it's my fault and I just use him as an excuse."

"No, no. Believe me, you're not the asshole. He is."

"And what about you, sir? Are you an asshole, or why the hell are you here?"

Max breathed in and then out and looked the boy in the eye. "'Cos, I'm just like your old man," he said. "I'm an asshole too but hopefully I'm going to do something about it."

"You're not as bad as he is," said Jasper. "There's no way you've done half the shit that he has. He has done some bad shit in his day. Really bad shit."

"Wanna bet?" said Max. "If only you knew. If only you knew."

Jasper raised an eyebrow. "I'd doubt it. You know, I didn't even ask you your name. My ma would kill me if she thought I'd forgotten my manners. Maybe we can start again. I'm Jasper. Just Jasper, no surname, like Madonna or Beyoncé or –"

"I get it. I'm Max and I'm married with two sons who are a few years younger than you. And just like your da, I've done some bad shit too. But hopefully that will all end today. Hopefully, all my shit will end today."

11

I stare at Ben and drink in his every movement as he uses up every space in the tiny kitchen, unpacking groceries from brown-paper bags like an eagle swooping in and out of each one, lecturing me on how I need to look after myself.

He pulls up the blinds and opens up the windows to let some fresh air in and I hear the sea in the distance and its sounds makes me feel calmer and at home. Naturally, I feel safer and more stable with Ben around me and when he speaks to me and looks at me with that caring look in his eye, it feels like a hug from my mother or like having a warm cosy blanket wrapped around me that I never want to let go of. With Ben I feel totally secure again. I feel safe, almost untouchable, invincible even. But I remind myself to be careful. I know I must not take his concern for my wellbeing as anything other than basic humanity.

"I'm so glad you called when you did," I tell him, watching as he chops salad leaves on a wooden board with ease. "You always seem to know when I need you most. You always did."

Ben glances over at me with a smile. I look at his arms, so strong, and I watch his hands that work with the food, almost bringing it to life. I have always loved to watch people cook and Mum would often join me for TV catch-ups of celebrity chefs and reality cook-in programmes when I came here to stay. Sometimes we'd even try them out for ourselves, jotting down recipes as we watched the telly or looking them up online with our mouths watering. I haven't felt like that about food for a long time now.

"Are you sure you don't want me to do anything to help?" I ask him. "I feel so useless sitting here watching."

"No, you just stay where you are," he says. "I think you've had enough action for one day. Just let me do this for you. Then all you have to do is eat it."

"I'll try, Ben. I'll try but nothing seems important any more. Now that I know what I know, I can't think of anything I want to do or who I want to see. It's all such a nightmare. And even though you're here right now, I know I have to face this nightmare without you by my side and I think that's what's scaring me the most."

Ben leaves his cooking station and reaches for my hand, but when I stand up from my chair to meet his height he gently pushes me back down again.

"Hollie, listen to me," he says. "I can see how vulnerable you are at the moment. I don't want to –"

"I know, I know but –"

"Sshh. I don't want to make things worse for you. I can see how much you need me right now and that's why I'm here, but we broke up a few months ago and I don't think it's a good time to jump right back to the way we were before. Do you?"

I can feel hot tears prick my eyes. How could I answer that? I never wanted it to end in the first place. I still wasn't over our break-up when Mum died and it's all been a tsunami of grief washing over me.

But when he's here with me it reminds me of better times when we would spend long lazy Sundays on the coast with Mum, and he would treat us to a home-cooked lunch while she and I relaxed with the afternoon papers in the garden, listening to the sea in the background and inhaling the healthy salt air.

"I'm sorry," I say. "It's not easy to switch off from how things were . . . but you know that already, anyway. It's all been said before . . . and I really am grateful for you being here. I don't mean to . . ."

I trail off and he squeezes my hand again and I can see that this is painful for him too.

"Let's just take it one step at a time, eh?" he says. "Let's just see how it goes."

I nod. "Yeah. I can live with that, of course I can. One step at a time is fine by me. It's how I'm living at the moment anyway."

I raise an eyebrow at him and smile just to show I'm not angry with him and he goes back to preparing the salad, then he checks the chicken fillets in the oven and gives the home-made salad dressing a stir.

In my heart I know he is right. This is hardly the time

to plunge back into something he decided had run its course. And we *had* parted on good terms, even though my heart was well and truly smashed into smithereens.

Yet, somehow, somewhere amongst those broken pieces, I could see how we had indeed branched off in different directions in the last few months of our relationship. Ben was becoming more and more busy with his rock band, playing gigs at nightclubs and bars across Belfast city and beyond almost every night and I found myself complaining to him about taking time out for me. We had become like ships in the night – I would work at my university classes during the day and he would work into the wee hours of the night. Soon it was like we didn't know each other any more. There just weren't enough hours in the day and, every moment we grabbed together, I clung on to as a last hope that everything was still okay while he saw it as another step towards the end.

And when he decided it was time to break up it was like I had been shot through the heart. I was in disbelief for weeks. So much so that I didn't tell a soul – not even Caroline, not even my own mother. Now it seems that only months ago my life was going somewhere, and now my whole world has collapsed around me, just like God has decided I have had enough happiness, enough time in my little sheltered bubble and now it is time for me to face up to reality – the reality of a life without my mother, a whole new past of mysteries to swallow and to top it all off, no Ben either.

Well, not in the way I want him anyhow.

"Good?"

"It's delicious," I tell him, pushing the lettuce leaves around the plate and then slicing some chicken to go with it. I know he is watching my every move so I take another forkful and I'm surprised that this time it tastes so nice.

"You don't have to pretend," he says with a smile. "I can tell you're forcing every morsel into you for fear of offending me. But you have to eat something."

"I *swear*, it's delicious," I tell him. "I've missed your cooking so much and I *have* been eating. Just not so much recently, I suppose. What? What are you staring at?"

Ben was watching me, his fork poised mid-air. "You," he said. "I'm staring at you. You really can look so convincing when you want to."

My stomach gives a nervous leap. I want him to stare at me but not like this.

"I'm not telling lies, Ben," I say, concentrating on what is on my plate and not on the man I adore who is just across the table from me.

"I just want you to be happy," he says and I glance his way. "For a split second you looked . . . well, you looked like . . . you again."

"Like me?" My guard is up but this takes me by surprise as there's no way I look like me. "I don't even know who I am any more! It's like I'm on this really scary rollercoaster ride and I can't get off and just when I feel it slowing down it goes whooshing off again and I'm totally out of control."

"I know, baby. I know it's hard . . ."

I hold my knife and fork in mid-air and eyeball him. "No, you don't know, Ben! No one knows! And don't call me 'baby' when you don't mean it!"

"Okay then, I won't. Jesus! I'm just trying to understand."

"Well, don't bother." I get up from the table and walk to the fridge. I take out some chilled sparkling water and pour two glasses. "You forgot the drinks."

"Hollie, please believe me. I have no intention of assuming I know what you're going through."

His voice is shaky now and he sounds so sincere and I wish I hadn't been so stroppy with him.

"I just want to see you content and relaxed and healthy," he continues, "and I'm worried about you. Just because we aren't a couple any more doesn't mean I don't care. I'll never stop caring for you. When I saw you lying on the floor like that earlier, it scared the shit out of me. You'll never know how frightened I was. I *do* understand and I *do* care."

I sit down again and move my food around the plate, already having forgotten the delicious taste from earlier. I concentrate on the pattern on the oilcloth and try to snap out of my feelings for Ben. He is a good man. He is an honest man. I will just have to ride this storm and see what happens.

"I know you do care, Ben. You wouldn't be here if you didn't and that means the world to me. But no matter how much you care or you say you understand, I cannot be happy. How can I be happy? I don't have you, I don't have my mother and I have absolutely no idea who I am any more."

I continue to focus on the tablecloth. It is a blue design with small squares and a white swirl on every third square. I had never noticed the white swirl before.

"So, is it the diary?" asks Ben. "Are you going to tell me? You don't have to tell me anything if you don't want to, but if you do –"

"Yes, it's the diary," I say and I drop my knife and fork onto my plate. "It's terrible, Ben. It's so horrific what she went through. And now I'm left with all these unanswered questions and I know I'm not who I thought I was. I mean, I didn't come from . . . oh God, I don't know."

Ben moves closer to me and I can feel his body heat and I want him to hold me and tell me all this isn't real.

"What did it say? Is this about who your father is?"

I lean on my hands and close my eyes. "I don't have a father. I've never had one and now I know I never will. My mother was brutally attacked by a pack of animals and I'm so ashamed that she was left with me as a reminder! I mean, how could she even look at me? No wonder she –"

"Hollie, Hollie, take it easy! Don't say things like that."

"But it's true. How would you feel if you found out you were conceived through rape? Even saying that word makes me want to tear my own skin off."

I know Ben is horrified. Of course he is. He probably sees me differently now too and is trying his best to hide it but, if he is, his face doesn't show it.

"Are you sure?"

"It's what she says in the diary. And Caroline knew about it too. And my parents . . . they all did . . . and hid it from me."

"And did she go to the police? Were they ever caught?"

"No," I say, then stop and sniffle and he hands me a tissue. "That's a whole other chapter. Whoever they are, they are out there and she said that their faces never left her mind. Can you imagine how frightened she must have been? No wonder she brought me up here in the middle of nowhere. It makes me sick. Really sick."

Ben grimaces and he glances around the kitchen in shock. I know he is picturing the brutality of the scene, just as I did, just as Caroline will when I tell her, just as I will always picture it now when I think of my mother.

"Do you think she wants them to be caught?" he asks me. "Is that why she left you the diary?"

"She didn't leave me the diary," I whisper. "I found it. She didn't want me to find it but then she killed herself and didn't think to destroy it. Or didn't care any more. I want to find out for myself anyhow. And for her."

Ben doesn't look convinced. He rubs his chin as he thinks and then runs his hand through his hair.

"Your mother wouldn't want this, Hollie. I can't see why she would want you to go back in time like this. What if you get into trouble? You don't know what or who you're dealing with. It could be very dangerous."

Of course I know it could be dangerous. Of course the very thought of coming face to face with any of these ghosts from the past – from a life I never knew – terrifies me. Of course I realise I haven't even thought this through but I'm afraid that if I do I might change my mind and let her down.

"I promise I won't do anything stupid, Ben. I will know where to draw the line and call it quits. But there's an old friend of my mother's who will make a perfect starting point. She's a Japanese lady called Singh Moshiro and she should be able to tell me more."

Ben knows I have always been content with what I have in life but now this diary has released an inner monster that I might never control until I have closure. I give him the diary and let him flick through it. He doesn't read it, but he studies the two photos and then sets them down on the table in front of us.

"This is her?"

I nod.

"But what can you gain from digging up the past like this," he goes on, "unless you want to catch the perpetrators and see them brought to justice? Will you push it that far? You're going to need a lot of evidence."

He gives a light nervous laugh and his reaction makes me stubborn in a way that reminds me of when I was younger and I would start an argument only to realise that I was wrong halfway through but that it was too late for me to back down so I'd continue manning my point.

"I think it's what my mother would have wanted," I say, and I feel a new jolt of adrenaline rushing through my veins, pumping up into my heart. My chin rises and I feel like the champion of a cause. "I think it's why she killed herself, Ben. She was raped and she never saw justice. She never had the strength. But I do and right now I want to hunt them down and I want to let them know just how much they ruined her life and how much they have now ruined mine. I want justice for my mother and I believe that finding Singh Moshiro is the place to start. I will find her and I will find those men. All three of them. Believe me, I will."

12

"Do you believe that some people are born evil?" Jasper asked Max as they walked through the gardens.

It had turned into a mild, pleasant evening and Max had planned on taking a quiet walk but his plans had been scuppered by Jasper's insistence on joining him.

Max clicked out of his daze when he heard Jasper's latest question. "Where the hell did that come from?"

The boy had a knack for talking non-stop and already Max knew of his every neighbour on every street, how many children they had and who was a "good skin" and who was trouble, if or when he might ever happen to be in or around the outskirts of Glengormley.

So far, there was Robbie the Boxer who was destined to be the next Barry McGuigan until he shattered his arm when he fell down the stairs of the local pub. Then there was Jim the Bouncer who knew everything and everyone and if Jim didn't know, then he knew someone who would. Jim sounded very useful, from what Max was told, and Jasper assured him he was. Or the shop assistant on the corner, Stacey the "local bike" as Jasper so eloquently put it and Bernie the hairdresser who had people calling at her door day and night because she had a charm that could cure the shingles.

But evil? Well, this was a different type of conversation altogether for Jasper.

"You know the way they say nature or nurture? What do you think, Max? Born evil or bred evil? I'm in a philosophical mood. Is that even the right word for it?"

"philosophical? Yes, it is. I believe, Jasper, that if you surround yourself by good people, you will see good and you will do good things. If you surround yourself with bad people, bad things happen and you are more likely to be a bad person. But sometimes good people do bad things and they can only blame themselves."

Jasper shoved his hands in his pockets and chewed his gum louder than normal.

"Is that what happened to you?" he asked. "'Cos you seem like a cool enough guy. You seem, like, dead on. I think if you were my da it'd be dead cool."

"Maybe that *is* what happened to me," said Max. "But it doesn't excuse or change what I've done, does it? And no, I'm not a very cool dad at all."

Jasper wasn't so sure. "Nah," he mumbled. "I can't see it. Do you know what I want from my da, Maxo?"

"What's that?" asked Max, laughing at Jasper's latest twist on his name.

"I just wish he'd listen to me. Just listen. You know, talkin's one thing and he does plenty of talking and shoutin' believe me, but he never listens to a word I say. You're a good listener, Maxo. You shouldn't give yourself such a hard time."

Max yawned for the third time since their walk began and he put up his hands in apology.

"I'm sorry," he said, "sorry for all this yawning, Jasper. And thanks for the compliment but I think it's time I got a bit of shut-eye. Old guys like me need their beauty sleep."

Jasper looked disappointed and Max patted him on the back as they parted ways.

"Maxo?" he called and Max stopped in his tracks. "Do you think I talk too much, Maxo? Maybe that's why nobody listens to me. Maybe I talk far too much?"

Max smiled at the young redhead who, for all his faults and admissions, was a likeable sort who just needed to be given a chance in life.

"You just keep talking, Jasper. Talking helps. I only wish I had talked a lot more when I was your age. A whole lot more."

Max climbed the stairs that led to the dormitories and changed out of his day clothes. Then he walked out onto the corridor where a communal pay phone stood. He lifted it and dialled home with a heavy heart.

"Dad? Dad, is that you?"

Josh's voice soothed his fears and he closed his eyes.

"Is that you, Dad?"

"It's me, son," said Max and he lay back against the wall, letting the voice of his younger son soothe away his troubles.

"Are you okay, Dad? Are you feeling better?"

"I am actually feeling better," he said. "A little bit better. Now tell me what you got up today. Did you have a game? Did you score?"

"Don't you want to talk to Mum first?"

Max could sense that Sandra was by their son's side, eager to talk to him or perhaps assuming that he wouldn't have time to talk to the children – in a hurry like he always seemed to be.

"I can't wait to hear Mum's voice," said Max, "but you go first this time. I want to hear all about how my little man got on at school. Tell me all about it. I'm listening. I'm listening now."

13

I wake up with this new-found energy still pulsating through me and the direct mission for the day ahead swimming around in my mind. Instead of the nightmares I had earlier predicted, I had slept more soundly than expected. I realise that for the first time since my mother's death I have focus. I have reason.

I may even have blame.

I never expected to have this reaction, but the urge to find these people and to get answers from between the lines of my mother's diary burns me now and I can't wait to get up and start my investigations, like a detective on a new case.

Ben stayed till late last night and I let him read the last entry of the diary, knowing that when he did he would understand how important it is for me to find out more. We had avoided any conversation about our relationship and how it might turn out but I smile now as I recall how he kissed my cheek at the front door and caressed the bump on my head with such attention. Just having him in my life, no matter what way, is enough for me right now.

I step into the shower and think of Singh Moshiro and the answers she might have. I don't know how I should feel about this strange Japanese woman who had become the object of my mother's obsession in her early days at university. As I wash my hair I try to picture what Singh might look like now. Was she now a mother too? Had she found her way out of the dark, seedy past she had lost her way in? Was she living near? Was she living here in Ireland at all?

I rinse my hair and the dreaded thought that Singh might be back in Japan or, worse, that she might have met a sorry ending like my mother flashes in my head. Was Singh even aware of what happened that night? From what I can gather, she may even have been as much a victim of those monsters as my mother was, maybe worse if that was possible. If she had failed to find a proper escape route.

I hear the phone ring when I step out from the shower. I grab my towel from the radiator and make my way into the bedroom to answer it, hoping it will be Ben.

"So, how did last night go?"

It's Caroline. I check my watch. Of course it's Caroline. She never misses her early morning calls.

"What do you mean by that?" I ask, knowing fine well what Caroline is hinting at. "Were you spying on me?"

Caroline laughs. "As if I would do such a thing! Let's just say, I was in the area and I saw a very familiar car in the driveway. Are things back on again? Please say yes!"

I hold the towel at my chest and sit down on the wicker

chair that sits beside my bed in a room that faces the front of the cottage.

"No, it's not back on again, but of course I'm working on it," I tell her. "Look, a lot has happened in the last twelve hours or so and I really need to talk to you. Had Ben not arrived when he did, I would have been calling for you last night to come and rescue me. I read the diary."

"What? Oh God, Hollie, I'll be right there. Is it bad?"

"It's bad," I say, as the words from the final diary entry chant in my head. I have read them so many times now that I could almost have been there in that seedy flat with my mother all those years ago. I can smell the stale alcohol, the sweat, I can hear the game-show jingle in the background, I can see the lights of the television flicker in the dark and I can almost imagine every feature on the faces of the men that raped my mother. I know now that I have to find Singh Moshiro and ask her to tell me the full story. If it means going to Japan and hunting her down, I will find her. By God, I will find her.

Caroline sits in silence, her tear-stained eyes worn out and empty when she closes the diary. She leans her cheek into her hand and shakes her head when I offer her a second cup of coffee.

"Hollie, I can't believe she went through all of this! It's like she has just died all over again. I should have helped her more. Oh God, what sort of useless bitch was I? How could I not have known what she was going through?"

"Don't say that, Caroline," I say, knowing exactly how regretful she feels right now. "You know Mum wouldn't want you to feel guilty for any of this. She chose not to tell us before. That was very brave of her but look where it has ended. How could any of us have helped her when she bottled it up inside and died without telling us?" Caroline blows her nose into a tissue and stares at the diary on the kitchen table.

"I knew it was bad," she says, "but I didn't think . . . I didn't think it still haunted her so badly. I tried, Hollie! God knows I tried to get it out of her. I asked her so many times but she wouldn't give in. She said I was too young to understand."

I rub Caroline's shoulders and then pull out a chair so we sit face to face and I look at her face which is like a younger version of my mother's and an older version of mine.

"I feel guilty too," I say. "Can you imagine how disgusting this makes *me* feel inside? I was her constant reminder of that horrible night. I was the end result, the living proof that it happened. Imagine how that must have felt. Imagine how that makes me feel right now? How did she look at me? How did she even love me at all?"

"Don't you dare say that!" says Caroline, her change of tone making me start. "Don't you dare suggest, not even for a second, that your mother didn't love you! Don't you ever say that again!"

She stands up in anger and I move away. I don't think I've ever seen Caroline so upset towards me. Sure, we disagree from time to time but now there is anger in her eyes and tears of resentment and disappointment fall down her face.

"I never once said that she didn't love me, Caroline!" I shout back in my defence. "I'm asking myself how she could have! I'm telling you that if it was me, I don't think I could have gone ahead with a pregnancy like she did and I don't think I could have been as brave as she was. Don't punish me for feeling sorry for her!"

"She was my sister!" sobs Caroline. "She was my sister and I know that she never, ever let any of that cloud how she felt about you. I just don't want you to have the slightest doubt about that. Don't ever, ever question that again!"

I remind myself of how shocked I was when I first read what Caroline was now trying to understand. I really don't want to rise to any arguments with her, but allowing for her shock doesn't change my gut feeling. To be a child of rape was something that no one – not Caroline, not Ben – could ever understand. How could anyone understand? I feel poisonous right now! I feel like an alien inside a human body. I feel that I, like my mother, have been wearing a mask all my life and that now the mask is beginning to shed its skin and I want to know exactly what is inside and it scares the hell out of me.

Caroline reaches for a face wipe from her handbag and sits her make-up bag on the table. I see her chest heave up and down as she tries to control her breathing, tries to compose herself.

"So you now want to find this Japanese woman, is that right?" she asks, a new-matter-of-fact tone in her voice and I know what is coming. "Is that what you are now going to tell me?"

"Yes, it is. I think it's important that I do find her."

"Well, I think you're mad," says Caroline. "I think you have no idea where this might lead to."

"I do – I know –"

"No, you don't, Hollie!" she snapped. "She sounds like a nasty piece of work to me. Imagine what she might be like now? Imagine where she may have ended up in life? You don't want to get involved in this, Hollie!"

"But she might have answers for me, Caroline. I need closure on this. Tell me you understand. Please at least understand that I need answers. Don't *you*?"

Caroline rubs her face aggressively and looks in her pocket-size mirror as she reapplies her make-up. She needs to get to work and I don't envy her the hour-long journey ahead into the city where she will probably wallow in all of this and be in tears again by the time she gets to work.

"I don't think I want any answers from her," she says. "Estelle ran after her and look how that ended up. Look at where it left her!"

"I know. But I don't plan on going on my own. I'm hardly going to turn up on her doorstep and expect a hero's welcome. I'll need someone with me of course, that's if I ever even find her."

"Huh. Well, don't plan on asking me. I think I'd murder the bitch with my own bare hands if I ever came across her. Look at the mess she has left here. Look at us!" She slams the make-up down on the table and dabs new tears from the corners of her eyes.

"I want to find out what she knows," I say quietly. "I want answers from her and then I'll walk away if that's what my gut instinct tells me to do. I'm not stupid, you know. I will know when to walk away!"

Caroline shakes her head and looks at me, her head tilted, and I know she is being protective but again that stubborn streak simmers in my gut.

"I don't think I can let you do this, Hollie. I think you're treading on very dangerous territory if you dare to even ask questions about Singh Moshiro."

"It's not up to you to 'let me'. I can make my own decisions."

"I mean it! I don't like the sound of this at all. In fact, I don't want to hear you mention her name ever again. Believe me, you are inviting trouble if you go looking for her."

My mobile phone bleeps and I read a text message from Ben.

"Too late," I say and I think my heart is going to explode with both excitement and fear at what I have just read.

"Why? Who is that?"

"It's Ben. About Singh."

I sit down and clasp my hand over my mouth and hand Caroline the phone to read it for herself.

"Oh . . . oh God, he thinks he has found her already? Hollie, no! Please, Hollie. No!"

14

"I think that's all for today," said Father Bernard and he gestured for Max to leave the library where they had finished their morning chat.

Max didn't like to think of it as a counselling session or a confessional but in a way that's what it almost was. He had been at Blessington for two nights now and already he felt the huge weight he carried in his soul being chipped away, little by little.

Will had paid him a visit earlier that morning and though it was nice to see a familiar face, Max knew he still had a long way to go before he could face the big bad world again.

"Have you called with Sandra?" he asked Will as they sat on the bench in the grounds that, next to Jasper of course, had almost become his best friend. He had whiled away hours on that bench, letting his thoughts float away into the afternoon sunshine and, the night before when he couldn't sleep, he found himself out here in his place of peace. Father Bernard had said he would find such a place in the physical world, and soon his place of peace would make its way into his mind.

"The kids are holding up well," said Will. "I took Josh to the cinema with my girls last night to see that latest Owen Wilson comedy so we had great fun. Charlie wouldn't hear of it but that's his age, I guess. It's amazing how a few years can make a difference, isn't it?"

"Charlie's not a kid any more, that's the difference," said Max sullenly. "He won't be as easily convinced as his little brother by Daddy's tale of woe."

"You've been teetering on the edge of a breakdown," said Will. "At his age he will understand that. I know it's rough as hell for him but you're all going through shit at the minute. Charlie will surprise us all, you'll see."

"And Sandra?"

"Sandra loves you, Max. She is stronger than we give her credit for and she's up for riding this storm. I can see it in her eyes. She's willing you through this. I know she is."

Max tried to recall a time in his life when he had talked so much and so openly about his life and he couldn't place it. His life was an open book here at Blessington. There were no secrets, no judges, just willing ears that would listen and sometimes say nothing. Sometimes Father Bernard would nod and ask the odd question but most of the time he would let Max do all the talking. He told Bernard of his early childhood, of his marriage to Sandra, of his affair, of his pride in Blue Heaven, of his failures as a husband and father . . . but never yet had he mentioned Estelle.

He remembered the last time he saw Estelle. She was Christmas-shopping in Belfast and she looked weary and lonely, wandering up and down the aisles of the department store, checking her list, trying not to bump into her fellow shoppers, standing in line at the tills waiting to be served.

She didn't know he was there of course, watching her every move. She didn't know how he longed to step out of the shadows and talk to her. She didn't know he dreamed of knowing her again and making everything better. He had watched her perform in orchestral concerts too. Once, he even brought Sandra with him to an Easter recital and he felt like a stalker as he watched her play the violin, easing the bow against the strings and, even though she played so beautifully, her face looked so sad.

He had stopped looking for her after that, knowing that his behaviour could become too intense and how dangerous it would be if she was to find out, if she was to spot him in a crowd. He deliberately stopped looking her up when he went to the north, and once managed a trip to the Carrick-a-Rede Rope Bridge with Sandra and the kids without letting her memory and the fact that he was physically close to her hometown ruin his trip. But she was never totally out of his mind.

Perhaps he *would* have to talk to Father Bernard about Estelle after all. Perhaps he would have to confess his guilt and take it from there. God would forgive him. He would take Bernard's word on that, but could he ever forgive himself? That was a different ball game altogether.

There were some things in life that just didn't deserve forgiveness.

15

I meet Ben outside my apartment in Belfast on a miserable afternoon later that week and the city smog repulses me now, having spent so much time on the secluded coastline at my mother's cottage. Even the noise of the city traffic and the mix of faces on the streets seem so alien and business-like compared to the easy-going surroundings of the beach and the laid-back holiday feel at White Rock.

Ben won't tell me exactly how he has tracked Singh down so quickly. A friend of a friend is as much as I can dig out of him but from his scant information I have learned that Singh's later life isn't rosy at all. She has a fine reputation with the men of East Belfast, his source told him, and is a kept woman of many well-known playboys of the city's underground. Nice.

Ben is there before me, like a nervous estate agent waiting on his first client. He gets out of his car and gets into mine, and then we change our minds and decide to travel in his because he tells me I'm useless in city traffic when I come back from the coast. He's right of course. Plus, he *is* the one with directions.

I take Jinx from the back seat of my car and lead him into my apartment which seems empty and cold so I turn the heating on ever so low and give him a bowl of water, praying he won't be too nervous in his new surroundings.

"So, you've already sussed this place out then?" I ask as Ben zooms us out of my street and onto the busy Ormeau Road.

"Yeah, I have," he says, squinting under the visor and I push it up out of his way. "Dean from the band knows this area well and he took me for a spin across to it last night. Not exactly *Location, Location* or your average 'des-res' but I've seen worse when travelling through the city on my way to gigs. Mind you, I bet when you see it you'll change your mind about your unexpected visit and get cold feet on this mission."

I ignore him and turn up the radio, then decide to choose a CD from his collection which sits so neatly in a case between the passenger and driver's seats. It's like being back in time, travelling in Ben's car, and I remind myself this is not the time for nostalgia. I choose a James Morrison album and slide it into the player, then try to relax as we pass the usual city-outskirts sights of KFC and several BP garages before we come out into the smaller mini-towns that line Belfast's boundaries.

About four songs later, we stop at a garage and I try to ignore the butterflies in my tummy. Of course I have a speech prepared in my head and I feel as if I am carrying my mother's spirit around with me when I hold my handbag close on my knee and feel the diary inside. Ben continues to scaremonger me with facts and figures on the clientele who live in the area.

He gets back into the car, hands me a fizzy drink and takes off again, asking me continuously if I am absolutely sure I want to go through with this "escapade" as he calls it. I ignore him and change the CD to James Blunt's "Undiscovered."

"So, here you go," he says and I sense an air of smugness in his tone as he parks the car across the street from a high-rise block of flats. The building is very seventies in style with its grey cement façade and brown wooden front-doors to each apartment, brightened only by white PVC window frames and the odd washing line that hangs from the balconies.

"This is definitely it?"

"This is it," he says with a nod.

"Wish me luck." I grasp the door handle in my fingers, totally unsure of what is ahead of me but with sense of wild abandonment that I can no longer control. "What number did you say it is?"

"You're not seriously going to go through with this?"

"What number? Sixty-three?"

"Please, Hollie. Please think about what you're about to do. Shouldn't we talk about this for just a little bit longer? I thought that once you'd seen the place it would put you off. You can't go up there. You don't know what you're doing!"

"It's sixty-three, right? Well, if you're too chicken to join me, I'll have to go it alone."

I get out of the car and head across the street and in

through a set of moss-green steel gates that have more rust than paint on them. I plod past them as though it is an everyday journey for me. Across the car park I see a group of youths loitering under a sheltered area away from the light rain and I look back, hoping that Ben isn't too far away from me.

He scurries behind and eventually catches up and we walk in stride, both equally nervous but only one showing it, and it isn't me.

"I think this is mental," he says but I don't answer.

I see the cement puddle-filled steps that lead to the floors above and I focus on them, blanking out the entire world around me, concentrating totally on my mission ahead.

We clamber up the steps and I continue to ignore Ben and dig my hands deeper into my pockets, grasping the square, yellowing photographs that had led me to look for this rundown apartment block in the first place. It had all been so easy. I can't believe how easy it is to track someone down these days. A quick phone call to a friend who had made a few enquiries and here we are, at an apartment block outside Belfast only a few miles from where I live myself and just over an hour's drive from my childhood home in the cottage by the coast.

Ben stops when we reach the sixth floor but I march on in defiance.

"Please, Hollie!" he calls. "This is insane. You can't just turn up unannounced like this. She won't even have a clue who you are."

But I stride onwards and this time I don't care if he follows or not. I dodge puddles of litter and cigarette-ends, my veins pulsing with determination. It is the first lead I've had so far and it feels like karma, like this is all meant to be. I feel my mother's breath on the back of my neck, her voice whispering into my ear, urging me on, willing me to have the strength that she didn't have to follow this through.

"You're heading for a fall, Hollie," says Ben but his words are muffled now even though he is still behind me. "I don't want you to do this. I really don't want you to do this. I'm sorry I ever gave you this damn address in the first place. If I'd known you were going to insist on visiting her so quickly . . ."

His voice trails into the distance. I am blind with fortitude now and Ben's words sound foggy in my head. I can barely hear him over the shower of summer rain that dances on the makeshift veranda-like roof of the corridor, making a rhythm with my solid footsteps and my heart beating in my chest.

Of course this is insane. I know it is. The whole bloody situation is insane but I can't stop now. Not when I am this close to the whole truth of my mother's past. Of *my* past. The can of worms is already wide open. There is no going back.

I hear Ben's footsteps gather pace from behind me, his feet splashing through pools of water on the broken tiles that line the sullen apartments.

"Let me do this, Ben. Just let me do this," I say, still marching, still not looking back. "I need you with me. Please don't stop me now."

I am reaching the end of the row fast. Am I definitely on the right floor? Am I definitely at the right part of town? One doorway runs into another as I glance at the numbers: 55, 56, 57, 58. Every door looks the same. Mid-brown, glossed with a golden diamond of stained glass at eye level and an oversized number emblazoned in black below it. I slow down, knowing that I am almost there and I force my fears to subside. 59. 60.

I stop, allowing myself one brief second to change my mind. Horns blow from the city below and I can hear the group of youths kick a ball against a fence, trailing tin cans along the ground and calling each other names. I could turn back. Perhaps I should. But I find myself walking again, my steps gathering pace once more. 61. 62. I look back at Ben. 63. And I'm here.

"You do realise this may not tell you anything, Hollie," says Ben and I listen to him now. "Chances are this woman doesn't even live here any more. From what I've heard she has moved around a lot. Just don't get your hopes up, please, babe."

I turn towards Ben and swallow hard. This is dodgy territory and I know it, but it is a risk I am prepared to take.

"I have to do this for myself, Ben. If I fail, I fail but I have to do this for her. You know I do."

Ben reaches for my hand and gives it a light squeeze. "I know, I know. I'm just scared for you, Hollie. I'm terrified of where this will lead. I'm terrified that you won't be able to cope with what you might find out . . . but hopefully it won't come to that."

I shrug my shoulders and then lean against him, wrapping my arms around his waist and snuggling my head into his chest.

"Tell me you understand. If it was you, what would you do? Would you want to know more? You would, wouldn't you?"

Ben's mouth twists the way it always does when he is unsure. He gently pushes me away from him and takes hold of both my hands, my fingertips like mini-icebergs peeping from my fingerless gloves, and he glances up and down from my eyes to my hands, my hands to my eyes.

"I'd probably do the same, I suppose," he says. "Yeah, I suppose I would do the same."

"Exactly. Now let's get this over and done with. If it's no good, then I start looking again, okay? I have to find her. You have to understand."

"I understand."

"Alrighty. Here goes," I whisper in a long breath.

I knock on the glossy door, resisting the temptation to squint through the golden stained glass and I wait. There is no reply.

"See, there's no one here," says Ben. "Now let's go. We can come back later if you want to."

"Ssh! Here they come. I hear someone."

The sounds of a baby crying spill out onto the corridor and I feel perspiration rise on my skin when I see movement in the hallway on the other side of the door. This is it. Oh sweet Jesus!

I bite my lip, look at Ben who stares at me with such pity and hope, and then I brace myself to deliver my explanation for turning up to a stranger's house unannounced, and with such a list of questions to hand.

The door opens and the woman who answers looks expectedly puzzled. She is more a girl than woman, really.

An interesting face and her mixed race makes her look so Eastern and exotic, just like the lady in the photograph in my pocket. She looks about sixteen, seventeen at the most and her unique appearance makes my heart leap. The woman I am searching for is here. I just know it.

"Yes?" says the girl, glancing around the doorframe to where Ben looks out over the city, afraid to witness the happenings unfold should it be the dead end he predicts it to be. Hopes it might be, really.

The girl's eyes are dark brown against pale skin and her hair falls around her face like black waves with golden tips mixed with blues and pinks. Her ears are pierced all the way round and she has a Japanese symbol tattooed on the side of her neck. I try to find the words . . .

"Em, I'm . . . I'm looking for a lady called Singh." My voice is hoarse with nerves and I swallow hard, finding it hard to wet my mouth as my throat feels gritty and dry. "Singh, er . . . Singh Moshiro? Does she live here?"

The teenager rolls her eyes and giggles and I note her heavy eye make-up that somehow heightens her beauty. She wears far too much and like her hair it is mismatched and colourful but it suits her so well.

"Singh *Moshiro*?" says the girl, mocking my pronunciation. "What do you want from her? Does she owe you money?"

I shake my head. "No, no. Not money. I just want –"

"Don't tell me then. It must be revenge, right?" The girl's tone drips with sarcasm. She seems wise beyond her years. "Did she steal your boyfriend? Or your father? Or your dreams? Believe me, I've heard it all before. Nothing will shock me."

"Hell, no!"

"Look, I think we've heard enough, Hollie," says Ben. "Come on, let's get out of here."

He puts his hand on my shoulder but I shrug it off. I am fearless now and more determined than I have ever been. There is no turning back. Not without giving this a fair chance. I have to find Singh. I have to talk to her and some jumped-up tattooed teenager is not going to stand in my way.

"Just tell me. Do you know her? Does she live here? Do you *know* Singh Moshiro?"

"Why should I tell you?" asks the girl, folding her arms and leaning against the doorframe.

"Because I need to talk to her. I need to find her."

The girl raises an eyebrow. "You and half this city! Trouble, trouble, trouble!"

"No, it's not trouble," I plead. "I swear. It's something that happened a long time ago. It's something she may be able to help me with. It's about my mother. I only want to talk to her."

The baby's cries grow louder in the background and the girl glances back over her shoulder into the apartment, and then she sighs.

"Look, I'm kinda busy here," she says. "I get people calling all the time. If I was to let everyone in who says they have dealings with Singh or Vinny, I could be standing at this door all day. *All* day. I gotta go. *Adios.*"

"No!" I reach out my hand and hold the door back from closing. "Please. I swear to you. Singh owes me nothing. She doesn't even know me. I need her help. I beg you."

"Who are you?"

"My name is Hollie. Just . . . just tell her I know Estelle. Just say Estelle. She'll understand. She'll tell you to let me in. Then you can see to your baby. I won't stay long."

"It's not *my* baby." She is adamant, defiant almost. "Look, Singh is sick. She is really, really sick so if she doesn't want to –"

"Please. Please. Just say Estelle."

"*Estelle?*"

"Yes. Just Estelle," I gulp, then quickly root in my handbag and lift out the photo-booth strip of Singh and my mother. I don't look at it at all and I hand it to the girl. "Here, give her this and I'll wait. If she still doesn't want to see me, then I'll go."

"Wow!" says the girl, her eyes glancing from the photo to me and then back again, eyes darting in disbelief. Then she laughs. "*This* is Singh?"

I nod. "I believe so."

"Shit! Wow! She looked so different then. Look, let me close the door and see to the baby. I'll give this to her and see what she says. But she is very tired today. No promises, okay?"

"Okay," I say and I feel an inch further towards victory. "No promises."

The girl closes the door and I put my hands back into my pockets, shuffling from one foot to the other and avoiding Ben's inevitable reaction. I have a gut feeling that even by seeing this mysterious lady in the flesh I am a step closer to my mother and to my past.

Yes, this sordid history will haunt my every move and

affect everything I do and the person I become if I don't at least try to follow on from the clues I have.

The door clicks open again, more suddenly than I expect it to, which startles me. I look back at Ben who is still close by and who is watching my every move.

"Singh will see you now," says the girl. "She smiled when she saw the photo. Now she's crying. I tell you, she is not up to much. And you leave when I say you leave. Do not upset her or you will see trouble like you have never known before. We do not have very long, I'm afraid, so don't be getting too cosy."

She leans out through the door and looks right then left, and then she pushes the door open and hurries us inside.

I look at Ben and he rolls his eyes in warning but I nudge him to play along and mouth "Thanks" to him when the girl turns her back.

The apartment is much cleaner and more spacious than I had expected on first impressions. Though grubby and grey on the outside, indoors it smells of lemon and its fresh décor gives it an airy feel. There are no photos on the walls, but there are tasteful Japanese paintings that match the walls and the only sound now is the faint hum of the television. The baby who was making all the noise from before lies snuggled in a Moses basket by the television and an older child, a boy of about six or seven sits on the floor, still in his pyjamas and super-glued to a kids' satellite TV channel.

"I'm Maria, Singh's daughter," says the girl who, having vetted us, seems a bit more relaxed now. "She said to introduce you to us all. Don't know why. Anyway, this is Reece, her son, and Little Miss Noisy in the corner is Niamh. He's Scottish, she's Irish and I have no idea what I am, apart from being me. One, two, three. Oh and Japanese mixed through, obviously. We may not be the most conventional family but hey, shit happens."

"Shit happens," says the boy and Maria swipes the back of his head playfully.

"Come with me," she says to me and I signal for Ben to follow but Maria gives a frightened look which says that Ben's involvement wasn't part of the agreement.

"Er, maybe I'll just hang out with Reece here and his superheroes," he says and he makes for a chair that sits by the living-room doorway. He looks uncomfortable and sits down slowly. "If Reece doesn't mind, that is. Hey, big guy, I'm Ben."

"It's *Ben Ten*," says the boy. "On the telly, that is. He has the same name as you. But you're not ten, are you?"

I give Ben a reassuring smile and he winks back at me, then Maria interrupts our interaction.

"I mean it, we better hurry," she says so I fold my arms to stop my hands from shaking and I follow Maria down a narrow hallway.

We stop and wait as Maria knocks on a bedroom door.

"Mama? The lady is here. Is it okay to come in?"

Sound from a second television broadcasting a familiar morning chat show trickles through the door and then the volume is muted.

"Yes," says a faint, nervous voice from inside the bedroom and Maria opens the door wide, allowing her mother full view of me, the wayward stranger who has interrupted their morning routine.

"Her name is Hollie," says Maria. "Like I said, it's about Estelle. Like I told you. And then it made you cry."

I step inside the room and look across to where a very youthful, yet very frail and petite Japanese lady lies propped up on pillows of pink satin, her long black hair in stark contrast to her very pale skin and the deep pink of the sheet as it hangs around her tiny shoulders. She is gaunt and sick, yet her beauty lingers on her face and her smile is captivating. How could a woman of such beauty fall into such ill repute, if that is truly the case?

"I'm Estelle's daughter," I say, but Singh's expression tells me I really don't have to explain. "I need you to tell me about my mother."

Singh Moshiro brings her tiny hands to her face and gives a theatrical gasp.

"Poor Estelle . . . I am so sorry for Estelle." She grips the bedclothes, muttering quietly to herself in her native language. "I have forgotten her. All these years I have forgotten her. It is my fault. Poor Estelle."

"She seemed very fond of you at one time, Ms Moshiro. I just want to know more about your friendship. I know what happened but I hope you can tell me more."

"Oh, her screams! I can still hear her screams . . . she had no idea. I didn't know what was going on! How did you find me?"

Fear prickles over my skin and I feel perspiration under my jacket collar. What the hell am I doing standing in an absolute stranger's bedroom, following a diary entry from my late mother and a photo from nearly thirty years ago? She says she remembers her screams. I don't want to know. I know enough already! I have changed my mind. I need to get out. I need to get out of this place. Ben was right. As always, he was right. This is insane.

"I'm so sorry to call on you like this," I say and I feel the room spin slightly. "I shouldn't have come here. I will go . . . yes, I'll go."

I take some steps back, and then turn and brush past Maria who wears a bemused smirk as if she has seen it all before. People from her mother's past with unresolved issues were obviously two a penny.

"No, don't go! Wait!" cries Singh. "I didn't mean to frighten you like that. It's just the shock from seeing you. You are like a ghost from my past, Hollie. Please don't go so soon."

"Mama, just let her go," says Maria. "This is not good for you. You are not fit to cope with any stress in your condition."

I pause at the doorway and turn towards Singh again, my body feeling like I should walk away but my mind steering it back in her direction. I need to find out what I can now that I am here. The fear in Singh's face has turned to remorse and pity, and tears fall from her sunken eyes.

"My poor Estelle," she whispers. "My poor, poor, sweet, innocent Estelle."

"I need to know who did it to her," I say, walking towards the bed once again. My voice has turned bitter and shaky and I can feel Maria's protective eyes bore through my skin.

"Mama?" said Maria. "Mama, are you okay? What's going on?"

Singh wipes a tear from the side of her eye and nods at

her teenage daughter then waves her out of the room with her frail hand.

"It is okay, Maria," she says. "Just let me talk to Hollie for a while. You go and see to your baby sister."

Maria is not happy to go and I sense that she will linger at the door for a while and listen. She seems like a smart girl and even though she is much younger than I am, she seems much more knowledgeable, much more worldly-wise and she has a look in her eye that could cut like a knife.

"Come here, Hollie. Come and sit down," says Singh. She lets go of my hand and pats the bedside and I half-heartedly move onto the edge of the bed, my clammy hands feeling cool on the satin bed sheets. I am unable to take my eyes off the woman who I hope holds the key to my mother's past and my own secret beginnings yet I cannot shake off the fear that I am on unsafe territory.

"I'm afraid of what I am about to hear," I say, cursing my vulnerability, and I get a flashback of Caroline saying she would hate Singh Moshiro.

She looks at me like she is reading my mind.

"Please don't be afraid of me. Please don't think ill of me. I am a dying woman," she whispers. "I will not do you any harm. You do not know how long I tried to find Estelle but they wouldn't let me. They wouldn't let me find her and I wanted to find her so bad."

"Who wouldn't let you look for her?"

Singh looked frightened. "I don't know. I don't know what I'm saying. I'm confused."

"I read her diary," I tell her, then I hear Maria's footsteps walk along the hallway and away from the bedroom. Despite what Singh says, I am afraid and I don't want to waste any time. I want answers from Singh Moshiro, not friendship or confessions. Just answers.

"Her diary?" asks Singh. "Oh, she did love to keep a diary. She was always jotting down notes and stories. I told her she should be a writer but her heart lay in her music. I always remember her as a fine musician. She could make that violin dance in her hands."

"I know what happened," I say, and I realise I sound like Caroline as I cut to the chase.

Though I try not to be, I am angry, and I know I have to make this quick or my temper will burst at this pathetic waste of a life in front of me. How dare she try and fluff this over! As if she doesn't know what I have just read! She heard her screams after all!

"It was all in the diary and it was vague at the end but it told enough to lead me to you. It told me a lot of things I didn't know about my mother. It told me she was raped. In your apartment. And I want you to tell me who did it to her."

Singh looks surprised at the frank way I have spoken to her. She obviously wasn't expecting such bluntness. She obviously wasn't expecting to be asked such questions straight out. Then she looks at me, as if dawning realisation has just came through the window and she puts her hand up to my face.

"Oh no, Hollie. No, no, no! Why on earth would you want to dig up the past like this?" she asks me with grave concern and her voice drops so low I can barely hear her. "Why? You have got to be so careful, dear. You are dealing with danger. Real danger. I think you should stop now. Go home and never come back here. Never."

"I have no intention of stopping, Singh! None! I want to know the truth, Singh! I have to know the truth!"

"But you shouldn't go behind your mother's back like this," she whispers. "She wouldn't want it. It is not up to me to tell you. It's up to her. If she wanted you to know, she would tell you herself. Why are you coming to me after all these years?"

I sense her shortness of breath and I know my time really is running short.

"She can't tell me. I mean, she won't. This photo?" I say, and I pull the nightclub picture from my pocket like an ace from up my sleeve. "I found two photos in her diary. This is the second. Look, look at this photo. Do you know who these people are?"

She reaches for a sip of water from the bedside table and nurses the glass in her hands, then squints at the photograph. Though her eyes look tired and glazed, I can see horrible flashbacks pierce through them and she shakes her head.

"God, no. Where did you get this? Put it away! Where did you get this?"

"From my mother. Now, tell me who they are! Please!"

"But where did she get it? She must have . . ."

"She must have what? Singh, this is so important to me."

"Estelle was my best friend. She needed me so badly," she says and she begins to sob, getting louder and louder as if years and years of guilt are pouring from her soul. "And I let her down. Oh God, I let her down so badly. I'm so, so sorry, Estelle. I'm so sorry!"

116

I stand up from the bed and stare down at her, not knowing whether to embrace her or shake her. The woman is obviously deranged with guilt and I am more intrigued, more confused and even more terrified than ever.

"Estelle, Estelle, I need you to know I'm sorry," she shouts at me, rocking like a baby so that the glass of water tips over and spills all across the bedclothes.

"I'm not Estelle," I say. "Tell me who is in the photo! That's all I want to know! Just tell me who these people are and if I'm on the right track! Tell me, please!"

Maria bursts into the room and hushes her mother, then looks up at me in disgust.

"Just who do you think you are?" she snarls. "How dare you treat a sick woman like this? You are all the same, calling here, wanting her to go back in time to settle what's on your selfish minds! Leave her alone!"

"But – but I just need to know who this is in the picture," I say, pointing to the men in the nightclub. "Did he do it, Singh? Or did *he*? Who is he? Who is the other?"

Singh buries her face in her daughter's shoulder and her wailing continues. I can hear Ben's voice from the hallway but I don't want to go. I need a name. My journey here is pointless without a name. Just one name will help me.

Ben appears at the doorway. "Hollie, let's go. I don't think this is doing either of you any good. Hollie! Come now!"

The little boy runs into the bedroom and cries out for his mother, then from the living room the baby wails.

I make my way to the door and Ben ushers me out of the bedroom, like I am a pitiful drunk in a bar and I hear him apologising as he guides me away.

117

"Oh, so *now* you decide to leave, you coward?" yells Maria. "My mother is sick and you make her feel like this and leave me with all this mess! I knew you were trouble. I knew you were. Get out! Get out of our home!"

"Please tell Estelle I'm sorry!" calls Singh. "That's all I ask. Tell her I'm so sorry. I never meant for that to happen to her. I was in a bad place. It was a bad time. It wasn't my fault. I'm so sorry."

I pull free of Ben and stride back into the bedroom.

"I can't tell her anything," I spit at Singh and I swallow back tears of self-pity. "I can't tell my mother anything any more because she is dead! My mother is dead!"

"What?" Singh chokes.

"Get out! Now!" yells Maria.

"You heard me. She is dead. She killed herself. My mother killed herself and I think you may know exactly why."

Ben turns the ignition in the car and the sound of James Blunt's "Undiscovered" blasts out from the CD deck, at the same point in the track where we left it when we pulled into the street-side parking spot, what seems like only minutes ago.

Part of me wishes I could go back in time to that very moment when I could have listened to Ben when he pleaded with me not to talk to Singh – but part of me feels hungrier than ever for information and my head spins with lack of direction and possibilities.

"Where do I go now?" I ask Ben, afraid that he won't answer me.

His strong arms steer the car out of the parking space and into the traffic. "Where the hell do I go now?" I cry.

Ben turns down the music and puts his hand on my knee.

"Home," he says. "Right now I am taking you home to your own apartment, away from your mother's cottage on the coast and away from the crazy life of Singh Moshiro. I think that you have had enough excitement for one day. I think you really need to consider if all of this is worth your while."

16

It is strange to be lying here without the sounds of the sea to help me sleep and so I toss and turn for hours, begging for my brain to switch off. Ben has left me to go to a gig across town and I sense it may be a few days before I see him again after today's episode.

Seeing Singh Moshiro was surreal at the time but now it has made this living nightmare seem so real and closer to home. Before I saw Singh face to face it felt almost like she was a movie character or a pop star or someone out of reach, but all this time she had been living just a few miles across the city from me. From what I can tell from her weak appearance, she hasn't much longer left to live and in a selfish way I can only think of how little time I have to find out what I need to know from her.

I am restless all night and at half past six I cannot lie in bed any longer. I hear Jinx whimper and so I give in to my racing mind and the dog's early-morning demands to be walked, thankful of his company and for giving me a reason to be.

I splash my face with cold water and dress in a comfy pair of track bottoms, trainers and a sports vest. I shove an apple and some water into an old canvas shoulder bag with my purse and phone and set off with Jinx, feeling just a bit better already.

The dew glistens under my feet as I walk across the Ormeau Embankment and, before I know it, we have made our way into the city centre. I stop for a takeaway coffee from an on-street vendor and sip it as we stroll along, the caffeine kicking my brain into gear another notch.

I haven't been up this early in Belfast since I was working at the stage school and the very scent in the morning air and the sounds of the morning traffic give me a reassuring sense of normality.

My mind is lost in thought as Jinx pants along ahead of me, dragging me on auto-pilot across the city. We pass through street after street – past City Hall and then back down along the waterfront of the River Lagan as the world wakes up and the morning commute kicks off. When we eventually stop to catch a breath, I can't believe we have been walking for over an hour and a half.

I lean against a wall to get my bearings, patting Jinx's head, breathing in and out and wiping my brow with my wrist. Where has my mind been all this time? I really hadn't intended walking so long, or so fast or so far. When my eyes lift from the ground, my stomach lifts too as I recognise my surroundings from the day before.

In the near distance, just about half a mile away I see

the same block of flats that Ben and I visited yesterday. I slowly begin to walk towards them, the urge to have a closer look almost uncontrollable, and I wonder if my subconscious has led me here in my dreamlike state. Jinx barks at a passerby and I hush him, still walking along the main street and then off the beaten track through a children's play park and up towards the flats.

A row of trees separates the park from the car park of the block of flats where Singh and her family live. A gap in the trees has been made to form a foot-worn short-cut towards the city centre. I move away from the path and watch through the trees and count the rows up the concrete mountain and then count the doors across until the entrance to Singh's home comes into my vision. I feel like a spy as I watch people coming and going from the neighbouring doorways, some down the steps and into cars and some in and out of each other's flats, perhaps borrowing milk or sugar or checking in on friends. I wonder what Singh is doing now. I wonder if she is thinking of me or have I gone out of her head as quickly as I appeared on her doorstep?

I wait there a long time, trying to keep Jinx quiet, but there doesn't seem to be a lot of life around the Moshiro family home at this early hour of the morning. A few older kids emerge from the sleepy hollow and begin their early-morning game of football in the car park and I'm surprised how the noise they make doesn't waken the dead. I listen to their banter and how they playfully slag each other's soccer skills and their favourite teams and I am lost in their carefree world of cheering and jeering and how they plan another happy-go-lucky day ahead.

Then, in my peripheral vision I see her. It is Maria! She is walking towards the gap in the trees and I want to run and hide. I feel like I have been caught on an early-morning stakeout. How did I miss her come from the doorway? I want to turn in the other direction but now she is too close and I will have to be swift in case she sees me.

She is wheeling a pram and talking non-stop to her young brother who is holding on to the side bar of the pram, his little legs bobbing along as he tries to keep up with Maria's longer strides.

I pull Jinx's lead and veer further up along the trees, praying they will disguise me. I can't walk away across the park or she will spot me in the distance so I huddle into the trees and hope we are out of sight. I can't let her see me. There is something about the younger girl that unnerves me. Well, a lot of things actually. I teach girls who are older than Maria at the stage school and at university but none of them have the accusing, world-weary look of Singh's daughter. Her beauty is unnerving too, and despite what I imagine her more than colourful upbringing to have been, she oozes confidence and is overloaded with loyalty to her mother.

"Just two shops, I promise, Reece," I hear her say over the hum of the pram and the weight of their footsteps on the other side of the trees.

Jinx barks and I tug his lead, nestling closer into the trees as Maria and the children pass through the gap and into the park. Jinx barks again and I close my eyes tight.

"Look at the doggy," says Reece to the baby and I dip my head and then march away from them along the line of trees that divides the park from the residential area. To my relief, it seems that the teenager is too focused on her daily chores to notice me.

"Come on, doggy!" calls Reece.

I grip the lead tighter and walk on, my spine tingling with fear that Maria might be looking my way. But then, when I relax my shoulders Jinx takes flight and the lead slips from my grasp. I watch in defeat as he bounds away from me, back in Maria's direction, almost knocking them down in excitement at his new friend's attention.

"Shit!" I mutter. "Shit, shit, shit!"

I see Maria stop the pram and allow Reece to pat Jinx who is lapping up the attention from the young boy. I try to busy myself and turn the other way, leaning down to tie the laces of my trainers, pretending afterwards to look in my bag for something. But it is too late. Maria has spotted me. I can feel her distinctive eyes glaring through me from the short distance between us and I know I have been caught.

"You just don't give up, do you?" she shouts through a mouthful of chewing gum. "I could have you done for loitering, you know. Or for stalking. Don't you have your own life to worry about?"

I have no choice but to try to explain so I walk towards her and hold my hands up in mock defeat. Her dark eyes are framed with midnight-blue shadow and huge false eyelashes, her black bomber jacket and skinny jeans suit her tiny frame. She really is like an exotic little bird and, though feisty and full of attitude, the way she looks after her little family endears her to me and I sense her bark is much worse than her bite.

124

"Stalking? I don't think so. I can assure you this is pure coincidence and, anyhow, isn't this a public place?" I remind myself that I am almost twice the girl's age. There is no way that I will ever be intimidated by her, no matter what she says or threatens me with. No way.

"What's the dog's name?" asks the little boy and my attitude softens. He has Singh's eyes as well and I see a resemblance to Maria in his dimples and cheeky smile which makes me forget any animosity.

"His name is Jinx," I say. "And I think he likes you."

"Yeah, I think he does. Oh, can I hold his lead all by myself and walk with him? Please? Just for a tiny second?"

I glance at Maria.

"We have to get to the shops," she says. "Come on."

"Please, Maria, please!" he says, looking up at her with a pleading smile. "I really will be only two *tiny* seconds. You can count if you like?"

"With you, Reece, everything is just for two tiny seconds," says Maria. "How do I count up to two tiny seconds? And besides, maybe Hollie doesn't have two tiny seconds. Maybe she has her own life to get back to?"

She gives me a cheeky look and stands with her hand on her hip, waiting for my reaction.

"I have time," I say and I hand the little boy the heavy lead and watch his face light up as Jinx walks alongside him. "And even if I didn't have time, I couldn't say no to such a handsome young fella."

Maria and I walk slowly in silence through the deserted play park, each of us in her own deep and awkward thoughts.

I marvel at how close to Singh I have lived during my working life in this city. Belfast has been my permanent home for only three years now but it isn't the biggest city in the world and chances of meeting someone you know are pretty high. I think of all the times my mother joined me on shopping trips, or out for lunch or to afternoon recitals and wonder if she ever saw Singh, or at least how much she was thinking of her when she saw the familiar landscapes of their friendship.

Belfast is such a different landscape to the little village on the north coast where I was reared and where my mother lived until now, and for a city girl like she was it was quite an unusual move to want to be away from it all.

She told me how, when she reached the final stages of her pregnancy with me, her father bought her the little cottage by the sea and she vowed she would never leave it. Then, when my job took me to Belfast, the thought of living alone almost made her pack her bags and follow but something stopped her and now I know what it was – a fear of the past, the opening of old wounds, the sight of old friends . . .

"He's always wanted a dog but since Mum got sick it's just not possible," says Maria, breaking the silence. "And anyhow, there is no way in the world we could fit a dog into our apartment."

"How sick is she?" I ask her in sympathy. "She told me she was dying. That must be so hard for you all."

"It is. The cancer is eating her insides and there's nothing they can do. So your mum died then?" She hands the baby a toy as we walk. She is quite the expert at parenting it seems and I wonder just how much responsibility this teenage girl has had in her young life. "That sucks, big time."

"That's one way of putting it, I suppose," I tell her and I kick a stone out of our path. "It sucks, big time. All the time."

"My mum will die soon too," says Maria, almost matter of fact. "She will die but it will take her slowly and painfully. It's a horrible disease."

"But you must have help? How do you manage?" I gasp, seeing the young family in a whole new light. "Who will look after all of you if . . . when Singh goes?"

Maria shrugs and laughs, just as she did the day before when Ben and I arrived at her front door. It is like she is hardened to the world, like she has seen it all and heard it all before.

"*I* will," she says. "I've always been the main one anyway, at least since these two came along. She was never supposed to have any more children, but I wouldn't change things for the world. They keep me sane, these two. They're all I really have, I suppose."

I long to reach out to Maria, to offer her help, but I don't get the impression that she is the type to be hugged or to show affection. Even with her siblings she seems business-like and to the point. I really do feel so sorry for her. I shudder when I imagine the upbringing the girl may have endured with different men calling at the house, different faces at the door, demanding time with her mother – and now I have added to her pressures.

"I'm so sorry about yesterday," I say, realising now more than ever that my unexpected questions could only have piled additional stress on Maria. "I have some issues

I need to clear up so that I can move on with my life, but I really shouldn't have burdened you with my problems. I didn't mean it to turn out so upsetting for any of you."

Again Maria just shrugs as if it is nothing new in her life.

"I think it took more out of my mother than it did me, if you want the truth. I had no idea who you were or what you wanted, but when you left we got talking. I suppose I understand now why seeing you made her react in the way she did. She feels very guilty, you know."

Maria's admission shakes me. She didn't need to know all of this torrid history at such a young age.

"Oh God, I feel awful now. I couldn't have realised how ill she is. I was just so determined to find her but if I had known she was ill I wouldn't have approached her in that way. Please pass on my apologies." I stop and extend my hand to take the dog's lead back from Reece.

Maria stops walking and takes the lead from her brother and then she hands it to me.

"She remembers one of the guys in the picture," she says.

My heart leaps and I can hardly breathe.

"She told me his name a while after you left but nothing else about him – or nothing I could make sense of."

"Which one? Who is he?" I ask, feeling a rush of nerves overcome me. "Did he know my mother? Was he there that night?"

"Settle down," says Maria, rocking the baby in the pram as she speaks. "You shouldn't get yourself into such a state, you know. You should be very careful, that's what she said."

"Tell me," I say, trying not to sound desperate. The little boy is staring at me now with saucer-like eyes and I feel like I have already upset the baby by the panic in my voice. "Please, Maria. Try to remember his name. This is so important to me."

"Oh, I remember his name all right," says Maria. "He is the one on the left. The other guy she says she has never seen before. I'll write it down for you. I don't know why I remember it so clearly but I do. In fact, how my mother remembers is anyone's guess. God knows she's had more men than hot dinners."

She takes a tiny notebook from her handbag and I notice a list of groceries scribbled on the open page. She writes down his name, tears along the perforation and hands the page to me. I put it into the purse in my shoulder-bag without as much as looking at it.

"Thank you," I say and I reach out and hug Maria so tight I fear she may break in two. "Thank you so, so much! You're sure this is the right name?"

"I'm sure. Look, it might be nothing," says Maria with a wise glint in her eye. "Don't build your hopes up. It's just a name of someone from my mother's past. There are many men from my mother's past so this might not mean shit."

"But it has to!" I am frantic almost. I fear she will stop talking and leave if I don't keep questioning her. "Tell me exactly what she said, Maria. You don't realise how much this could help me. Was he a friend of hers? Did my mother know him? Was he there that night?"

Maria rolls her eyes. "Oh, Singh seems to know him all right. She had no problem remembering his name and something tells me he wasn't flavour of the month, put it that way. She sort of spat out his name and then rambled as she does, but she certainly didn't seem to like him very much. But when I asked her if he was there that night she said she didn't know. That's about all I know. Sorry."

"No, don't be sorry. This is fantastic. Well, it's a start anyhow. Here, I want you to take my number and if you find out anything else you can call me any time."

"No!" she says. "Er, no, I don't think that's a good idea and anyhow I'm not sure I can get any more from Singh. She is very sick. I don't want to upset her and she says it's too dangerous for me to talk to you."

"Anything," I beg her, handing her a business card I find in my purse. I notice it is an old one with my coastal address as well as my Belfast one. I make her take it. "Please. If there is anything at all just . . . just call me. Goodbye, Maria. And thank you again."

I tug at Jinx and walk towards the swings in the play park where I sit on one, Jinx tethered to the frame. I swing higher and higher as Jinx barks and then slow down and reach into my bag where the slip of paper lies. I unfold it and read Maria's tiny handwriting. There is a name in capital letters and I read it over and over again until it is embedded so much in my brain I will never need this piece of paper again. Now I have a name. I can't believe I have a name.

My hands shake as I press Ben's number into my mobile phone. I have over an hour's walk ahead of me to get home and I can't wait to get to my apartment where I can Google his name and set about finding a match to the man in the photograph.

"You'll never believe it, but guess who I bumped into just now?" I pant down the phone.

"Hollie? Where are you?"

"I just ran into Singh's daughter, Ben! And she gave me a name. She gave me a name, Ben! A name of one of the men in the photo!"

"Hollie, Hollie, please remember to breathe. Where the hell are you? Tell me!"

"I'm on the far side of town. You see, Jinx and I went for a walk and before we knew it, we were near Singh's apartment block and then Maria was taking the kids to the shops and –"

"Hold on a minute! Are you trying to tell me you just happened to *find* yourself over on the other side of town? That you just *happened* to be there and you just *bumped* into Singh's family? This is insane, Hollie."

My mouth tightens in temper. I am so angry at Ben for reacting like this. Yes, I know it sounds strange but he is as bad as Caroline with her soapbox standards and her words of warning. They don't know how I feel. They never would.

"I *said* she gave me a *name*," I say, feeling tears prick my eyes. I close them tight and then open them again, willing myself not to cry. With one hand holding the phone and the other holding Jinx's lead, there would be no way of disguising it if I did burst into tears in public.

"Okay, okay. So she gave you a name?" says Ben with a sigh.

"Yes, she did. She says that Singh knew him and that he wasn't flavour of the month. Yes, that's what she said. That Singh didn't seem to like him very much. Maria seemed to know what I was talking about. She said she spoke to her mother about it after we left."

I feel defensive and am now more determined to continue my campaign on my own. It is my fight, anyhow, not Ben's or Caroline's. It would be nice to have Ben's support but if he is going to puff and pant and sigh every time I make a discovery, then I will gladly go it alone.

"And what's the name then?"

I give him the name and then sniff at his nonchalance. "Don't worry about it. I can look him up myself when I get home."

There is a moment of silence and then I hear Ben click on his keyboard on the other end of the phone.

"Hold on! I'm at a computer here and I already have him," says Ben. "I've done a Google search and the list is endless, but if I remember right from the photo, I can tell you that I've found your guy. If I'm right he lives in Dublin now. Rather well known he is too, is our Max Kelly."

17

Sandra Kelly watched the phone that hung on the kitchen wall and willed it to ring. The kitchen was shining clean now, unlived in almost. She had devoted her energies when the boys were at soccer camp in the morning to scrubbing cupboards, throwing out junk mail that had piled up on the dresser, dusting corners she never before knew existed, and rearranging notices on the fridge. She even had made some vegetable soup and its homely smell soothed her with its reminders of happier times when Max used to love to come home to a steaming bowl of soup, whatever the weather. It was her speciality, he always said.

They were married twenty years now. Two whole decades of ups and downs and roundabouts but still she couldn't imagine life without him. She remembered her wedding day like it was only yesterday. Her sister joked that Max was the playboy Sandra had always longed for with his spontaneity and moods and the way he could make her laugh and cry in equal measure. Theirs had always been a passionate and fiery relationship and it was the only way Sandra would have wanted it. But things had changed since his fling with that waitress girl in their early days of marriage.

Sandra remembered that day like it was yesterday too. The shock almost physically choked her when she overheard them in the kitchen of the restaurant and she still felt the physical pain in her gut when she thought of it.

She had called unexpectedly at Blue Heaven, just passing on her way from the school run. The boys were in the car and, as she would often do towards the end of the week, she thought she would offer a run to the cash and carry to take the burden off some of the staff.

Funnily, she had never noticed the girl before.

She wasn't a typical vixen-like husband thief at all. She was quite mousey and fragile and the only thing that made her stand out from anyone else was her foreign accent. She was French. Yes, she was definitely French.

"Is Max around?" Sandra had asked the sous-chef who pointed to the fire exit where Max spent most of his spare time, taking in the city views and listening to the sound of Dublin from his high perch on the second floor while puffing on a cigarette. She knew his routine so well, or so she thought. She admired how the staff worked so hard as she passed through the kitchen and, as always, she felt proud that Blue Heaven was a part of their family now. It was in their blood.

As Sandra made her way through the kitchen, no one stopped her in her tracks or delayed her or gave her a warning look or alerted Max to her arrival because no one else knew about it. No one at all.

She pushed open the door of the fire escape and stepped out onto the steel platform that led to the stairwell. She called his name but as she said it her face fell into a frown and, like a thud in her gut, she knew right then her husband was cheating on her. She didn't see them kiss, they weren't holding hands and they weren't even touching but it was from the comfort in their stance, the way their body language spelt it out that she knew. She just knew. And when Max looked up at her from his pew in the middle of the stairwell, she knew her reaction was one-hundred-per-cent right.

He didn't deny his relationship with the girl when she questioned him that night. They sat at the kitchen table, speaking in low voices as he confessed his stupidity and his fears of losing her and the boys for a moment of weakness. The girl disappeared from Blue Heaven as quickly as she had arrived and Sandra quietly got on with things, but she and Max had been different since then.

The seal had been broken on their marriage. There was a scar on their wedding vows, an open wound that wouldn't heal. He went through a lengthy period of self-hate after that, constantly beating himself up and declaring how pathetic and unfit he was, how he didn't deserve his family and he threw his entire life back into the restaurant, spending more and more time away from the family home.

Then gradually he came round again – softly, slowly he became the man she loved again. She remembered the very moment she knew he was back in their lives. It wasn't a big occasion nor was there any announcement, just subtle signs that her husband was content and relaxed again. It was a Saturday evening and she was on the sofa, waiting for her favourite programmes to begin. Charlie was at a friend's house and Josh lay across the armchair nearest the television. When Max came into the room, Sandra expected him to announce his plans for the evening and leave them to it, but instead he sat at the other end of the sofa and, almost like he had never changed at all, he moulded back into the way he used to be.

They had Sunday lunches out when he wasn't working, they went swimming and they even squeezed in a few days camping and life was back to normal for many years. But now he had gone off the rails again and she had no idea why.

She checked the time. It was twelve forty-five and soon it would be time to call her boys together for their lunchtime bowl of soup. She was trying to maintain a routine, if only for them.

Maybe he would call soon.

Her mobile was clenched in her hand at all times and she was on her fourth cup of coffee that morning. She hadn't heard from Max in over twenty-four hours and Josh was constantly asking questions as to when he was coming home and what he might be doing at the caravan and why they all couldn't have gone to have some family fun. Charlie had known from day one of course that his father wasn't at the caravan.

He had arrived in from soccer camp the day before and thrown his bag down with extra force in the utility room. Sandra had already sensed his anger from the way he'd

136

slammed the door of the car, the way he almost took the back door from its hinges.

He swore aloud when he noticed her sitting at the table as she did every day, waiting on Max's call.

"You're as pathetic as he is," he had told her when he'd come into the kitchen the day before. "Why do you sit here, day in, day out waiting for the phone to ring when you could be doing so much more with your time?"

"Like what?" Sandra had asked him, feeling bitter and sore that her son found her desperation for her husband to contact her so repulsive.

"I don't know. Go for a walk, go for a drive, or do whatever the hell it is you normally do! But don't just sit there like a puppet, waiting for him to tell you it's all okay when it so obviously isn't!"

Sandra had looked at her son in a different way since he spoke to her that way. He was seventeen years old and had always been her best friend, praising her on a daily basis, telling her how wonderful she was when she burnt the evening meal or how he loved her even though there was no milk in the fridge or if his football kit wasn't ready on time. He was so undemanding and mature and now he was telling her in his own way that she had let him down by her inability to get rid of the man she loved more than anyone in the world. She felt torn between the need to wait for Max's calls so she could reassure him that he was nearly there and the need to make out that everything was just fine as far as her boys were concerned.

Yet, here she was, another day later, doing the exact same thing. Waiting on the exact same chair in the kitchen and wishing and waiting for the same phone call.

18

I stare at the computer screen in Ben's apartment and feel my insides boil up like a churn of acid, bubbling under my skin and threatening to explode.

"The smug bastard," I whisper and take a sip from my wineglass.

Ben stands behind me, looking at the same computer screen and I know he is feeling exactly the same, but trying not to show it.

Max Kelly certainly looks like an arrogant prat in his profile picture on the website he uses to promote his Dublin-based restaurant.

"Like, who the hell does he think he is? Gordon fucking Ramsay?" I roar, gulping my wine this time until the glass runs dry. "I mean, look at him, all moody and sultry, looking up into the camera as if he's some movie star! And listen to this . . . 'Belfast-born Kelly is proud father to two teenage sons and is happily married to

Sandra.' Happily married to Sandra! Well, bully for him and Sandra, that's all I can say. I suppose he has the white picket fence to match. Why should he turn out so Goddamn perfect? Bastard!"

I slam my glass on the computer desk and hold my face in my hands.

"Oh, don't hold back, Hollie! Don't give any benefit of the doubt," says Ben, trying to lighten the mood. "Go for the jugular. Say it how it is and all that. I mean, the man could have nothing to do with this and may have rightfully earned all his successes but no, you have automatically written him off as a smug bastard and guilty as charged. Nice one. I never knew you to be so judgemental and knowledgeable of the law."

I hold out my glass and Ben fills it halfway but doesn't take any himself this time, and I remember that he has to drive Jinx and me home very soon. As always, he has a gig that night and I know he really would have needed some time to chill out beforehand, but he seems as hooked on finding out more on Max Kelly now as I am. Well, almost.

"Well, I think I have a right to feel this way for now anyway. Now, what else . . . he's a Michelin star chef who owns – and still cooks in – one of Dublin's top restaurants, he's happily married to 'Sandra' with his two-point-four children in case you didn't get that the first fucking time, and he lives in the city suburbs and life just seems all rosy in the garden, doesn't it?"

"Looks like it. Certainly looks quite idyllic from where I'm standing. He's a good-looking guy too," says Ben, and I raise an eyebrow as a warning that he is due a dig in the ribs for saying anything at all positive about the man.

"What?"

"Ah, come on, Hollie, you can at least give him that!"

"Suppose he is, for his age," I spit and Ben looks surprised at this admission.

I may already have the man packaged as the devil in disguise but I haven't gone completely blind to reality. The man certainly seems to have it all, that's for sure.

I turn silent and tilt my head at an angle, then zoom in on Max Kelly's face with his green eyes, his dark hair all floppy in a Hugh Grant way, his crooked but cheeky smile, his tanned complexion and his snow-white teeth. Hardly the sweaty, evil monster I had pictured at all. I try to imagine him in his earlier days, with his mob of animals, jeering as they attacked my mother when she was so young and innocent. Pouncing on her in the dark, drugging her, raping her . . . and my head begins to spin with anger again. I stare at his face so close on the screen until it becomes pixelated before my eyes, searching for physical resemblances to mine in case he might be . . . in case he might be my father.

"I'm going to find him," I mutter to myself, taking down the address of the restaurant and underlining his name at the top of the page. "I'm going to hunt him down and I'm going to make his life as miserable as he has made mine."

Ben shakes his head. "You don't know that, Hollie. You don't know if he had anything to do with it at all."

"You're right. I don't. But there's only one way of finding out."

"I thought you might say that," he says and he pats me

140

on the shoulder. "I was hoping you wouldn't, but I don't think hell or high water could stop you, could it?"

I look up at Ben and shake my head. "Nothing or no one will stop me until I find out the whole story, Ben. I want to know what this Max Kelly did to my mother and I want to know it now."

19

Young Charlie Kelly knew exactly where he could find what he was looking for. He knew the names, he knew the clubs, he knew what to ask for and he knew that at long last he finally might make his mother see that there was more to life than trying to mend his broken father. He just needed to distract her from his dad's petty, selfish behaviour and make her realise that there were other people in the family too.

The nightclub scene in Dublin was a haven for all sorts of students, tourists and regular socialites where a nod and a wink and the right money in your pocket could get you a cocktail of drugs within seconds.

At seventeen, he was a late starter on the drug scene but his attitude to life had changed of late since he watched his parents let their marriage dissolve. His dad really didn't give a shit about him *or* his brother. He was too busy finding himself at some religious hideaway Uncle

Will was financing and Charlie had no doubt that a woman was involved in some shape or form.

Women were the cause of all his father's downfalls. That dumb-ass waitress with her stupid accent and her short skirt was all it took for Max Kelly to lose all his senses. His father didn't know that Charlie knew about it but he wasn't thick. He heard the whispers, the tears, the hushed silences when he came downstairs at night to get a drink of water while his mum and dad were having one of their talks at the kitchen table.

He had lost all respect for his mother too. She was as bad as he was, the way she let him work twenty-four seven at the restaurant just so they didn't have to face up to their problems at home.

Like, the restaurant was where he met that silly French bitch – what's to say he didn't have a string of others since then to keep him occupied when he was never at home?

"Double vodka," he said to the barman and took out his wallet to pay for it. "No mixer. Just ice."

"Let me get that," said a girl to his left and she twirled her finger through her bleached blonde hair and suggestively sucked from a straw, staring him in the eye.

"No, thanks," said Charlie, turning the other direction but the stupid cow persisted, moving to his other side, heaving her breasts out as far as she could and rubbing against him to the beat of the music. "Look, I just want to get a drink," he said. "So can you please remove your tits from my face?"

"Don't you like me?" she asked him, putting her hand on his waist and thrusting her body closer. He could see right down her top which was, he guessed, the whole idea. "I only want to buy you a drink."

"Oh go for it, then, Barbie," said Charlie, rolling his eyes. He sank the vodka and then pushed the girl's leeching grasp out of his way, much to her shock. She fell up against the bar and he ignored the sideway glances a few of the punters gave him, pushed his way through the sweaty dance floor and swung open the bathroom doors where a familiar group of lads dominated a cubicle. The smell of danger was in the air and Charlie inhaled its poison, ready to take on a whole new edge to his clubbing experience. This would make them all sit up and notice, eventually.

"So you're finally ready to have some fun, young Charlie?" said a red-haired ringleader who had been pestering Charlie for months to join in on the weekend drug fest. "You won't regret it. I swear, kiddo, you won't forget it. First go is on me. Some Charlie for young Charlie!"

"I'm ready," said Charlie, feeling the heat of the vodka still in his throat. His stomach was on fire but already the alcohol had seeped into his bloodstream and the heavy beat of the club sounds in the background made a perfect combination. "I hope this is as good as you said it would be, man, 'cos you don't know how much I fuckin' need this right now."

He leaned forward and put his nose up against the finely ground white powder, covered one nostril with his finger, closed his eyes and sniffed the cocaine into his system. When he stood up straight, he was buzzing already. It was like nothing he had ever experienced before. Not through vodka, not through beer, not even through sex. This was it. This was just what he needed. Where had this pleasure been all his life?

"I'm ready to party!" he said and the other boys cheered as he danced his way back to the bar where the girl with the straw and the blonde curly hair was chatting up another man at the bar.

"I think I owe you a drink, pretty face," he said, leading her by the arm away from the competition and back into his territory. He waved to the barman for service and kissed the girl hard on the mouth.

At long, long last, Charlie Kelly was in control.

20

The journey back to the cottage at White Rock beach takes me much less time than normal and Jinx seems happy to be back on his own home turf. Every inch of the majestic scenery that surrounds me reminds me of happy times and I just can't let that go yet. I feel a release, a relaxation that I never, ever can experience in the city. The rugged coastline and iconic sights are breathtaking and more beautiful than any tourist brochure could ever describe. Castle ruins sit in the distance on lush green countryside that contrasts so vividly with a royal-blue ocean below, framed with curly white waves and steel-grey rocks pebbled with gold.

It is quiet here, silent almost, apart from the sounds of the sea and nature and I feel my head clear instantly as I drive along the winding roads. Jinx gets his bearings and his panting becomes heavier and his tail wags against the back seat, making a beating sound.

"Yes, Jinx," I call to him. "Settle down, baby. We're nearly there."

I haven't thought what I will do with him when I return to real life in Belfast. I do know it would break my heart to let him go to a new home, but how could I take him away from here? White Rock is the perfect place to while away the hours with a pet for company, but my life in Belfast is much too fast and my apartment is much too small to take him with me.

Perhaps I will stay in this cottage forever and commute the hour-long journey into work and stay here where the pain of losing my mother and losing Ben will eventually be easier to swallow. I know I will have to let both of them go soon but, while my mother's death is final, I have unfinished business before I can let her memory rest. With Ben, it is over and I know that but accepting it is more difficult than I ever thought. I now know the meaning of a broken heart, in more ways than one.

He told me to take it one day at a time but I realise that his love for me is now on a friendship level and I have to gradually wean myself off him if I am to deal with the future. But for now I will live between the two places until I can lay my mother properly to rest in my mind – not just in the cold soil of the cemetery in Belfast where we buried her in the family plot my grandparents bought some years ago, but in my head and in my heart. Then hopefully I will learn to live again.

I am in the shower when I hear the doorbell ring and I look out to see Caroline, clutching a bottle of wine under her arm, ring the bell for the second time, double-checking for any sign of life in the cottage. She will see the light on in the living room and the flashes of the television screen through the blinds, so I'd better hurry. She knows I'm here.

"Hollie, it's me! Can you let me in?" she calls through the letterbox. "It's your wicked aunt and I have a bottle of wine here to bribe back your affections. I hate it when we fight."

"Use your key," I shout but she doesn't hear me. "Use your key!"

I know that Caroline has a key for the house in her handbag as always and the fact she doesn't choose to use it signals the distance that has opened up between us recently.

I open the door and sense Caroline's surprise to be welcomed by a very different, more pleasant me than she obviously expected.

"Sorry I took so long. I was in the shower," I say with a smile. "Why didn't you just use your key, stupid?"

"Er, I forgot it," lies Caroline, and she follows me as I drip down the hallway. She sets the bottle of wine on the kitchen table while I bound back up the stairs, clasping the towel around me.

"I'll be with you in a sec," I call out to her. "Get that bottle of wine cracked open. I have so much to tell you. You'll never believe it all when I do."

Caroline did what she was told and reached for two wineglasses from the cupboard, hoping that tales of rekindled romance with Ben was on the menu for discussion. She closed the cupboard door and was met eye to eye with a smiling picture of her sister Estelle which was part of a tasteful collage of imagery that Hollie had placed in every room in the house.

There were photos from birthday parties and fancy dress with Estelle and Hollie wrapped around each other, sticking their tongues out for the camera. There were photos of toasts to the future, of nights out and nights in, of days on the beach, of Estelle with Jinx in the garden. Every room in the cottage was filled with her memories but it was in the kitchen that Caroline could feel Estelle's presence the most. The tiny kitchen was still so full of her personality that Caroline got mixed feelings every time she came in here. She could still see her sister making a pot of coffee, the radio humming in the background, the smell of lavender mixed through the scent of the freshly brewed coffee and the way she always appeared so happy to see you, just like you were the one person she wanted to see most at that very moment every single time you popped by.

She had a CD collection to die for and she would go to see a live band at the drop of a hat. They often used to joke that Estelle would have spent her last pennies on a concert ticket or a trip to the theatre or any excuse to see an orchestra play or even a jazz band down the local pub. Caroline picked up a selection of Estelle's CDs and examined them, putting Fleetwood Mac, Paul Brady and James Taylor back in their relevant cases, and feeling slightly pinched inside that Hollie had been listening to them, reminiscing probably, crying no doubt. She lifted Robbie Williams' latest collection and smiled, and then put him up on the shelf with the others. Estelle had an endearing crush on Robbie and she made no secret of it at all. Despite all her darkness and her worries, she had a lust for life that was bursting to get through. If only she had given life a chance to prove to her that it was still worth living. If only she had been as happy as she looked on the outside, or in her photographs.

Happiness was her mask, thought Caroline. It was a mask that she never, ever took off her face. Oh Estelle!

Caroline cursed herself for not asking more questions, for not pushing her sister to tell the truth but at the time all those years ago Estelle was determined that what had happened was brushed under the carpet never to be resurrected again.

In later years it was easier not to address why Estelle wanted to live so far away in a cottage on the coast on her own, and why she still slept with the light on, why she insisted on keeping a huge black Labrador in such a tiny house. Her fears were there. The signs were there the whole time, but Caroline had been afraid of addressing them as much as Estelle had been.

Caroline had been so afraid of knowing the truth. And she still was.

"Now, where do I start?" I say, combing my wet hair on my way into the kitchen. "I swear, Caroline, you will never believe how quickly this is all falling into place. It's all too easy. I can hardly wait to tell you."

"What is falling into place?" asks Caroline, smiling, hinting of course that my new-found enthusiasm couldn't be anything other than my blossoming relationship with my gorgeous ex-boyfriend. "You and Ben? Please tell me that's what you're talking about."

My face falls at her attempt to distract me from the inevitable.

"No. Not me and Ben, Caroline. You know fine well

what I'm talking about, but if you're not in this with me then I suggest you take your peace offering and –"

"And stop right there!" says Caroline holding her hands up. "I dread launching into another row before we even get started on the conversation, not to mention the wine. So, tell me then. You went to find the Japanese lady and then what happened?"

We sip our wine at peace and I tell Caroline about how upset Singh had been, how ill she had become, about her poor children and how eventually I had come across the name of Max Kelly. I lift my laptop from the sideboard and bring up the website of the Blue Heaven restaurant, my face bitter and twisted, yet I feel a rush of excitement when I point out the chef in his black and white photo that fills half of the screen.

"I'm going to have to confront him," I announce and see how Caroline is biting the inside of her mouth to try and hold back her outburst. "And I won't settle until I have every piece of information bled from this hot-shot chef with his happy family. Why should he have it all? Why?"

But Caroline is not on my wavelength at all. She doesn't share my determination or hatred for this man enough to want to see him suffer for his sins of the past. She thinks I've lost it, she thinks I'm crazy. She thinks I'm taking this too far but I don't really care what anyone says.

"I think you're mad, that's what I think."

I open my mouth to protest but Caroline continues.

"I'm sorry to burst your bubble but no, you can't do this, Hollie. You simply cannot do this. You cannot turn up at a restaurant and throw accusations around at someone you don't know!"

"I can!"

"No, you cannot! You have no idea who this man is! No idea at all! Just because he happens to be in a photograph from around that era does not make him a guilty party in what happened to my sister!"

"She was *my* mother!"

"I know that, but you do not know who Max Kelly is! For all you know he could be an old boyfriend. He could be a good guy. He could be just a random passerby, a fair-weather friend. Do you remember every single boy you met at university? Do you remember every house party, every face? I bet you have photos from your days at Queen's where you'd barely recognise yourself, let alone some young fella who just popped in for a few beers on his way through the Holylands? Why are you so sure that this Max Kelly is guilty without knowing the facts?"

I know I have no real case. I know this all seems mad to anyone living outside of my little bubble and my little one-girl mission to save the world.

"I just have a hunch!" I say and it sounds ridiculous. "Look, if it settles your mind at all, I'm not going to walk up to the man and perform a citizen's arrest for Christ's sake! I'm not going to burst into his fancy kitchen and demand an explanation and camp there until I get one. You could be right. Maybe he has absolutely nothing to do with all this. Maybe he won't even remember her. But what if he does? What if . . ."

Caroline stands up and pours the dregs of her wine down the sink.

"What if he's your father? Is that what you're thinking now, Hollie?"

I can't answer her. But the answer is yes. Oh my God, I feel so desperate but I need to know. I need to rule him out, don't I?

"Do you really want to find out?" asks Caroline and I nod. "But you hate the man already, Hollie. I can see it in your face that you can already picture him attacking Estelle and I mean it, love, this is not going to get you anywhere. This is dangerous. Please listen to me. Listen to me for once in your life. This is dangerous, Hollie. You could ruin an innocent man's life with your notions and conclusions. You could ruin your own life too."

Her words sting me to the core. I know she has a point, I know this could be dangerous but I also know that if I don't follow it through, I will never forgive myself. Yet if I do and if I am right, I don't know how I will react or cope. I just have to trust my instincts and investigate this man. I just have to.

"My life is already ruined," I say. "What the hell do I have to lose?"

"Don't say that, Hollie. You have so much to live for. You are young and beautiful and talented and you have your life ahead of you. Don't get bogged down in the past. It's not worth it."

"You can go now," I say to Caroline, setting my own wineglass by the sink to demonstrate that our conversation is well and truly closed. "I would rather do this with your support, but if that's not the case, well, I'll just have to do it alone. Either way, I'm going to see what I can find out about Max Kelly and there's nothing, and I mean *nothing*, in this world that will stop me."

21

"He didn't come home last night, Will. Charlie didn't come home and he hasn't phoned to say where he is. He has never done this before."

Sandra Kelly marched around the house as she spoke, her nerves frantic at her son's absence which was so out of character.

"Who was he with?" asked Will from his office desk at Blue Heaven. This was all he needed. So far, two staff had phoned in sick and the sous-chef was demanding more help in the kitchen. The place was falling apart without Max. It was a living nightmare and now young Charlie had decided to add fuel to the fire through his disappearing act.

"I have no idea who he was with. He left in a temper like he's done every evening since Max went on his retreat and he's acting like it's all my fault. It's like he's punishing me because he is so angry with his father."

Will opened a pack of painkillers and swallowed two of them.

"None of this is your fault, Sandra," he said. "It's no one's fault and Max will be home tomorrow like a new man. Gina! Can you get the other line? Please God it's the temp agency! Sorry, Sandra, but this place is like a minefield at the minute."

"I'm sorry. I'll let you go get back to work," said Sandra. "I shouldn't be bombarding you like this with more and more of our problems. You've been such a good help to all of us lately."

Will's finger hovered over the button for the other phone line which was flashing orange to indicate another call waiting.

"Look, he'll show up. They always do. Give it to midday and if he still isn't home, call me back. I'll make a few calls round the pubs and clubs but, in the meantime, keep trying his phone and seek out some of his mates. Chances are he's crashed on a sofa and will saunter in with a sore head to you any minute now."

Sandra hung up the phone and sat on the edge of the armchair. She could hear Josh rustle about upstairs and she knew how it would upset him if he found out Charlie had stayed out all night without telling anyone. He was a sensitive young boy and, at a time when most boys his age were enjoying their days of summer freedom, he stayed cooped up in his room or by his mother's side in a gesture of support, counting the days till his father came home.

The phone rang again and Sandra answered it immediately. She pushed the lank hair from her face and held her hand on her cheek as she spoke.

155

"Hello? Hello? Charlie, is that you?"

There was no answer. She could sense that someone was listening but they weren't speaking.

"Charlie, can you hear me? Where are you? Are you okay?"

The phone went dead and Sandra dialled the number back but it wouldn't register. She sat back on the chair and stared at the ceiling. Where was her son? Where was her husband? Her life was spinning out of control and she had no one and nowhere to turn to.

22

I hang up the phone and already I feel guilty for making the anonymous call to Sandra Kelly. I shouldn't have tracked down Max Kelly's home number like that. Like finding Singh, finding his number made me feel invincible, like making contact with them was all meant to be. Like I was in control from the shadows, just waiting to pounce on their lives and shove them into the ruination they deserved.

I had no expectation of being given his phone number but when I called Blue Heaven I couldn't believe my luck when the dumb-ass on the other end was more than willing to look up and give out his boss's mobile number because I said I was a journalist from a foodie magazine. Then, when his mobile went on to voicemail and diverted back to the restaurant, the same waiter gave me his home number as an alternative and even apologised for my inconvenience!

But I chickened out when I heard his wife's voice on the other end. I felt like an intruder but in a sick kind of way I got a slight power-kick from being in control, feeling like I was after him but that he didn't know. I instantly felt sorry – no, I felt pity – for his wife who was no doubt oblivious to her husband's sordid past. But she will know in time if I have my way.

She did sound a bit desperate, calling out for "Charlie" whoever the hell Charlie was. Maybe she was having an affair? Maybe she and her lover had had a row and I had called in the middle of it?

I can't wait around any longer. The cottage is making me feel claustrophobic and the energy that buzzes right through me like an electric current will not subside. I have to find out more.

I feed Jinx and put him outside into his pen and set off to see my mother's neighbour, Mrs Jenkins.

Mrs Jenkins lives alone just up the laneway and she promises every time she sees me that she will look after Jinx if I need to visit friends or go back to the city alone. She has taken care of him a few times in the past.

I knock on her dainty ivy-clad door and smile as her gentle face greets me with a crinkled charm.

"I have to go to Belfast, Mrs Jenkins, and –"

"You need me to look after my old pal?" she says in delight.

"Just for a little while – a couple of days," I tell her. "His food is in the usual place. He doesn't eat quite as much as he used to – I think his years are catching up on him."

"Just like mine," laughs Mrs Jenkins. "Are you okay,

my dear? You look pale and a bit out of sorts. It can't be easy."

"It isn't easy. It isn't easy at all," I mumble. "Look, I really can't thank you enough for looking after Jinx for me. I know he's a bit of a handful at times and if it ever gets too much for you don't be afraid to say no."

"As if I would!" says the old lady. "Now you go and do what you have to do. Me and my old pal will have a great time together. I love the company to tell you the truth and it's nice to have someone to talk to, even if he doesn't talk back."

"Thank you, Mrs Jenkins. Thank you so much."

I take one last look back at my mother's cottage as I drive up the lane that overlooks the seafront and I get that horrible empty, guilty feeling that fills me every time I drive away from here, as if I am leaving her behind. Somehow, I don't think of her lying in a cold Belfast cemetery or even in heaven as yet. To me, she is still in the cottage, still at home, waiting for me to sort out her troubles so that she can rest in peace.

Just over an hour later I reach my apartment in Belfast and make a check around, making sure that everything is safe before I leave on my journey. I pick up a few essentials from my wardrobe, pack my violin and take a few CDs from my bedroom to listen to en-route.

I have never driven to Dublin before, but I have no fear of getting lost or feeling alone. I have the address of Blue Heaven, my sat nav fully charged and ready to go, and that is all I need to know. Everything else will come later.

As I fix my make-up in the hallway mirror, I do a quick

last-minute check in my head that I have everything with me: euros, check; phone fully charged and charger in bag, check; sat nav programmed, check; phone numbers for both restaurant and Max's home, check; a photo of my mother, check; my mother's diary and the photos she left with it, check. I have everything organised. I am ready.

I go out, blessing myself at the holy-water font on the wall by the doorway, then turn the key in the door. It is a glorious morning in late August and the birds sing in the trees and the smell of fresh-cut grass gives me a spring in my step as I walk to my car which is parked a little further down the street. I have butterflies in my tummy but a fire in my gut and I know that I have a point to prove to Ben and to Caroline who have been so accusing and so judgemental. What would they know? It wasn't their mother this happened to. It wasn't their past.

I have just got into my car when I hear a familiar voice from behind.

"Hollie! Hold on, Hollie, wait up!"

"Oh, hiya, Ronan. Has Caroline sent you to check up on me?"

"No, not exactly," says Ronan and he leans on the side of the car, looking in at me through the driver's side window. I put on my sunglasses and put the window down slightly, trying not to give him any hint that I am up for conversation. How clever of Caroline to send him here! Caroline knows how much I admire Ronan and that I take his words of wisdom as gospel. Well, I won't tell them anything from now on. None of them. They don't need to know my business.

"It's just that, well, I'm in a bit of a hurry," I say,

knowing that the quicker I get away, the less guilty I will feel for lying to him about where I'm off to. "I'm meeting some old school friends for lunch in town and I'm late already. We might go for a few drinks so I might stay over even though I'm not so keen on that idea."

I'm trying to cover all my bases in case my trip to Dublin lasts into the night and Caroline suspects I have gone, against her better judgement.

"Okay then, have fun, Hollie," says Ronan. "But when you get a moment I need to talk to you about coming back to work. We really need to talk about it."

"Oh . . . I thought Caroline had sent you here to check up on me . . ."

"This has nothing to do with Caroline," says Ronan. "The Board are putting the pressure on and they want to talk about setting a date to have you back in action. It's been a long time now, Hollie, and they think it's time you rejoined the gang. I think it would be for the best for you too. Help you get back to what you do best."

For a second I remember the old times at work. I really do love my job and the summertime brings such a wealth of talent our way that every day is a new challenge and introduces us to so many different gifted musicians. I have been so focused on delving into my mother's past that my job and anything else to do with the real world, the right here and now, has seemed alien and unimportant. It's like I have been living in my own little bubble and I don't know if I want to face reality just yet.

"Look, I'll think about it and we'll talk tomorrow. I promise," I say, pushing my sunglasses back onto the top of my head. "Please just give me another little while to get my head around this, and then I'll be back to the old Hollie who gets on your nerves by messing up room bookings and who steals your biscuits in the staff room."

Ronan smiles and winks at me. "That's more like it. We're just worried about you, Hollie, that's all. We want you back."

I hold out my hand and Ronan squeezes it tight. I want to tell him the truth and for him to tell me he understands and that he is on my side and I want him to wish me luck and say that he hopes I find the answers I am looking for.

But I can't tell him because deep down I know that even Ronan wouldn't back me on this one.

"Have a nice lunch and go easy on the drinks," he says and I turn the ignition in the car knowing that on this journey I am totally alone.

"I will go easy on the drinks, don't worry. I always do. And I'll be back at work before you know it. Thanks, Ro."

"What for?"

"For not telling me I was off my head lately."

"Doesn't mean I don't think it," he says with a smirk. "Now, off you go and remember you can call me any time, day or night, if you need a shoulder to cry on."

"I will," I say and I put up the window of the car, put my sunglasses back on and drive off on my mission to find the mysterious Max Kelly.

23

"Inner peace, inner child, inner flippin' organs. I swear, Sandra, it's like being pulled through a wringer here. I've never been so mentally exhausted in all my life."

Yet Max sounded on top of the world and Sandra was relieved to hear his voice on the phone. She hadn't told him about Charlie, who was still sleeping off a disgusting hangover despite the fact that his lunch had been served over an hour ago. He had been a right mess when he got dropped off earlier and he didn't have enough money or any sense to pay the taxi driver. Sandra had been so embarrassed at needing to go outside in broad daylight to help her drunken son into the house and Josh had been horrified at the sight of his big brother, all limp and giddy and his face twisted in a drunken ball. He had blood on his shirt too, but Sandra would address that with him, as well as everything else, when he finally woke up.

In the meantime she would hide his behaviour from

Max who was on such a high and she really didn't want any arguments right now. As long as Charlie was home and safe, that was the main thing.

She had checked on him every twenty minutes to make sure he was breathing okay. She had opened the windows in his bedroom to let out the fumes of alcohol, taken off his shoes and jeans and put a spare blanket over him to make sure he was comfortable but, as the day went on, her relief was slowly turning to anger and she was well ready to have it out with him when he finally came downstairs.

Max was oblivious of course to her concerns and when he asked about the boys, she gave him a generic reply and put Josh on the phone to tell him about his day at football summer camp.

"So do you think you're ready to come home tomorrow?" she asked when Josh had finished going into every detail about a goal that shouldn't have been allowed because the player was blatantly offside.

"I feel more than ready," he said. "I feel refreshed and rested and, most of all, this time out has made me realise just who and what are the most important things in my life. I will never let you down again, Sandra. Never."

Sandra drew circles with her fingers on the kitchen table. She could feel her heart beating in her chest at the sound of her husband's remorseful voice and she wanted him back now more than ever.

"Shall we come and pick you up tomorrow? Me and the boys?"

"Yes," said Max and his voice broke into a deep sob. "You don't know how much that would mean to me. Thanks, Sandra. I love you. I love you all so, so much."

24

I drive across the bridge at Drogheda and pull in on the side of the motorway, switch on my hazard lights and wait till sense prevails, whatever that means. I can barely breathe. I put the window down in the car and listen as traffic zooms by, hoping that someone will stop and tell me if I'm wrong or right in what I'm doing. I need impartial advice. I need someone to come with me. I am scared.

Time passes, about twenty minutes I guess, and I see a Garda car in my rear-view mirror and they indicate and pull up behind me.

"Everything okay, Ma'am?" says the young officer. He has a row of beaded sweat on his upper lip and he looks like I am the last person he wants to help right now. All he wants is a long cool drink and to get rid of his uniform and put his feet up in his own back yard on this warm summer afternoon.

"I'm fine. I just felt a bit faint in the heat and needed to pull over, but I'm good, thanks."

"You sure?"

"I'm sure." I flash him a smile and shake a bottle of water to show I'm refreshed and ready to drive on and he leaves me to go about his daily business and clock up the rest of his hours before sinking that cool beer that waits for him at home.

I continue on my expedition along the motorway, reassuring myself that I need not make myself known to Max Kelly if I sense in any way that he may react badly to my presence in his restaurant. I will wait for him if I have to, and I will speak to him if I can, and then leave and draw any conclusions that I might come to.

I turn off the M1 to Dublin just before I come to the Tunnel and follow my sat nav's directions to the city centre. I feel hot and sticky and I long to freshen up. I need to stop somewhere to use the loo and touch up my make-up, hair and perfume to give me a much-needed boost of confidence. But I am stuck in traffic now and the best I can do is give my hands a clean with some travel wipes, run a brush through my hair and touch up the basics of my lipstick as I sit in line on Dublin's busy roads.

I wonder what he'll think when he sees me. Will he see me as a younger version of Estelle or will he recognise someone else in me? Himself? I shudder at the thought.

I have planned my meeting outfit carefully to suit the occasion. Smart casual was the look I opted for with black crop trousers, a plain black T-shirt with flat pumps and a multi-coloured neck scarf to brighten it up. My hair is in need of a cut and a few more highlights but, since this impromptu visit didn't allow for a trip to the hairdresser's, I have tied it loosely to the side of my neck, allowing large natural curls to fall at the front and frame my face, and this lets me get away with it and shows off my girly side. A smart yet innocent look.

A look, I hope, that will bring him back to the past.

"Nearly there," I whisper and turn down the volume on the radio so I can concentrate more on the sound of the directions from the sat nav. I have checked out the parking facilities at Blue Heaven online and it seems to be well catered for. Its website was most helpful, telling me how it is quite a large building and is on two floors, with the pub-grub-style menu on the bottom floor and the à la carte and more exclusive wine bar on the second floor, closest to the semi-open-plan kitchen. It appears to be a clever set-up and one that had earned Max Kelly and his business partner a lot of respect and a lot of money.

Of course I have practised what I am going to say to Max a hundred times over in my head. I needed a reason to see him, so I have planned to introduce myself as a classical violinist and ask for an appointment to see him to discuss the possibility of some live entertainment for private functions at his restaurant. My research tells me that Blue Heaven already hosts a jazz band bi-monthly and has a "piano-bar" theme night on occasion. I have brought my violin in case he asks to hear a live sample of my work. And then, when he is comfortable in my presence, I will casually mention where I am from and I will drop in the story of my mother's recent death. And then I will take it from there. I will watch his face very closely and I will take it from there . . .

It is much groggier in the city centre than it has been on

the journey down to Dublin and I feel perspiration on my upper back as I wrestle to park my car in a multi-storey car park not too far from Grafton Street where Blue Heaven is located.

I wind down the window and click off my seat-belt, then pull down the visor to check my appearance once more. I look exactly how I feel. My face has tiny beads of sweat above my lip, just like the young Garda, and my make-up looks greasy and shiny. Shit! I can't go searching for him like this! I reach into the back seat of the car and yank my tote bag in beside me, then rummage inside to see what I can find. Deodorant, face wipes, extra perfume and chewing gum. It would have to do.

I reapply my make-up and the cool spray of deodorant makes me feel slightly more refreshed. I am so, so nervous now but every time I feel this way I imagine the words from my mother's diary echoing in my head. I remind myself to be brave yet at the same time not to jump to any conclusions when I meet this man.

I step out of the car, place my overnight bag in the boot, flick my hair back from my face and straighten my T-shirt, then walk out onto the busy street. I catch my reflection in a shop window and, for all intents and purposes, I look pretty good. The sun kisses my cheeks and I look slim and stylish, despite having travelled for over three hours to get here.

Grafton Street is a hive of activity with the melodies of buskers mixing in the air and a jumble of nationalities bustling in and out of the upmarket shops. I know I can't be far away from the restaurant and then I see its sign, just a few feet away, and I am nervous again.

I feel like I am on a movie set. This doesn't seem real. A waiter serves a customer drinks from a tray on the outdoor terrace amid laughter and chat and when I see the Blue Heaven logo on his T-shirt I know that this is not fiction. This is all very real and this is where I am right now.

I look up at the sandstone restaurant and realise how Blue Heaven is much, much smaller on the outside than I had imagined. I walk past the wicker terrace and into the entrance porch, then turn right and push open the glass doors that lead to the bottom floor. Inside it is cooler yet much cosier, more intimate and not at all as highbrow as its website suggested. The interior is dreamy and night-like with midnight blues and soft lighting and a flurry of good-looking staff dressed in indigo jeans and plain white vests with the Blue Heaven logo. They buzz around the floor and in and out of a lift which is obviously a short-cut to the kitchen area upstairs. A spiral staircase indicates the more formal route and the entire place, with its low unobtrusive reggae beats, has a tangible atmosphere that I am automatically impressed by. This is a very slick and very stylish establishment.

"Table for one?" says a waitress, interrupting my intensive observations.

"Er, yes, I mean, no. Em . . ." Shit! "I'm here to . . . can I see Max Kelly, please?"

The girl looks at me like I've asked for a date with the Pope and swings her head to the side.

"Hold on a second. Gina!" She looks at me again. "Gina will look after you. She'll be right here. Now, is there anything else I can get you in the meantime? A glass of water? The interviews here can go on and on, believe me."

"Interviews? No, I'm fine, thanks," I say and I see an older lady, in her mid-forties perhaps and wearing a different uniform from the floor staff, coming my way.

"Thank God you're here," says the lady in a broad New York accent. "I was beginning to think they had forgotten about us. I'm Gina. You ever been here before?"

"No," I say, realising she has mistaken me for someone else. "I was just hoping to –"

"We are so under pressure today! Boy, am I glad to see you! Come this way." I don't seem to have a choice except to follow her up the stairs.

"You'll soon learn the ropes. Now, I'll give you a quick tour, get you signed up, find you a uniform that fits and then hand you over to Jackie. You start at six but I'm sure they told you all that."

"Sorry?"

"Yeah, six till eleven, that's right." She looks at a notepad. "Great! That's what I thought. It's only weekends for now but don't worry – if we like you, we'll keep you. That's the way we work around here."

I think of my violin in the boot of my car and of my original plan to bluff my way into meeting the elusive Max Kelly but maybe this is an even better idea? She obviously thinks I'm a new member of staff. Should I play along? I have waitressed before back at home and the set-up was surely the same here? Share the tips, don't spill anything and be sure to give out the right food to the right people and the right change at all times.

"You look the part, anyway," says Gina when we

reach the top of the spiral staircase. She is still making notes as she talks and glances at me with a relieved smile. "Tall, blonde, well-groomed and most of all, not local. You'll find all sorts here – French, Russian, Italian, our staff are from everywhere apart from Dublin. It's a cosmopolitan thing. We seem to attract a lot of students. So, like I say, I'm Gina. What's your name again? I don't think they were able to give us a name at the agency?"

"I'm . . . I'm Hollie. Listen, Gina, would you mind if I –"

Gina throws her head back and puts her hand up to stop me. "Sorry, excuse me, Hollie." Someone is calling her. "I'll be right there, Will! Give me a second. Look, I'll have to let Jackie take over. I'll be in the office if you have any questions. It's absolute bedlam in here today but you look like you're up for the challenge. See you at six and good luck."

I plonk down on a high stool against a wooden railing that overlooks the bottom floor and try to catch my breath. I remember seeing a picture on the website of the wine bar which stands in the far corner, the polished flooring, the circular tables and the low-level lighting, but most of all I recognise the open-plan kitchen that is straight ahead of me now on the first floor. I can hear the chefs talking, shouting almost, and Gina is right. It does look like bedlam! I wonder if he's in there? I wonder if he can see me and, if so, will he recognise me from Estelle?

"Now, let's get this all out of the way," says Jackie, who seems to appear out of nowhere.

I was expecting a girl, but Jackie is in fact a small Oriental man who carries a clipboard and a pen and looks very efficient. "It's Hollie, right?"

"Yes." I want to tell him this is a mistake. I want to come clean and revert to my initial plan but the words won't come out and as he speaks to me I am unable to take my eyes off the kitchen where I watch numerous chefs and kitchen staff spinning around, managing to avoid bumping into each other as they fry and sauté and take orders from the waiting staff.

"Can I get a glass of water please?" I ask. "It's very warm up here."

"Of course. Give me a second." Jackie is gone and back again in a flash. "Are you okay, Hollie? Sorry about all the rush but we always tell the agencies not to send us anyone during lunch hour and yet they always do. It sometimes scares potential staff away when they see how manic it can be in here on any given day. Blue Heaven is not for the faint-hearted."

He laughs knowingly, as if his last sentence is a line he has used many times and one which he is quite proud of. I sip my water, the ice cold hitting the roof of my mouth and the back of my throat and Jackie waits with his pen poised, his eyes darting around the room indicating that he needs to move on to his next chore.

"Here, let me," I say and I take the clipboard from him. I glance around the room and use the first name I see from one of the optics on the bar – Murphy. That will do. I write it and a false address on the file, deciding that I will keep up this façade for one night only so I can find out more about Max Kelly. I want to see him face to face. I want to see how he reacts when he hears my mother's name. I don't need the staff of Blue Heaven to suspect that I am anyone other than a temporary member of relief staff. What I do need though is to see Max Kelly or my mission here will be pointless.

I leave the madness of the restaurant and my phone rings as I step out onto the busy street, but I ignore it.

I can't believe what I am doing here. I can't believe what I have just agreed to. Part of it makes me feel nauseous, part of it fills me with dread and just a tiny part of it feels strangely exciting. There is a gentle breeze now on Grafton Street and I inhale the fresh air and welcome the chance to prepare for my shift at Blue Heaven and find somewhere to stay the night. Max Kelly's face from his website picture is all I can see in my head and I even scan the faces on Grafton Street for him as I walk past Brown Thomas and other familiar shops I have read about in magazines. On my tour around the building I couldn't match his face to any of the staff but the kitchen was so busy that Jackie only gave it a fleeting pass-by, explaining how they processed the orders from the floor. Contact with the chefs is to a minimum but, when I see him, I will make it my business that he notices me.

My phone rings again and I find it and see that it is Ben calling me. I don't answer but wait until he leaves a message and then I listen.

His voice is stilted and urgent. *"I have been trying to get you for the past hour. Jesus, Hollie, I've been climbing the walls with worry. Why don't you answer your phone? Where are you? I've tried to call Caroline but she's not answering either. Just let me know that you're okay. I have a gig tonight out of town so I'll be leaving early but please just let me know that you haven't done anything crazy. If you've gone in search of that man . . . look, just call me."*

I hang up the phone and stand still in the middle of the street as people rush past me, swearing under their breath that I have blocked their path. Am I crazy? Is this mad?

Maybe so, but I'm riding this one out. I think it's the least I can do.

I send Ben a text. "Don't worry! Good luck with the gig. I'm fine. Chat soon."

That should hopefully keep him off my back for a while.

The bed and breakfast is averagely kitted out but it feels quite homely with its old-fashioned décor and friendly family staff, which ranges from an elderly grandfather to a boy in his late teens. It is walking distance from the restaurant and I have booked in for one night only, promising myself that I will leave first thing in the morning once I find out what I need to from Max Kelly. I sit at the mirror in the poky bedroom with its floral walls and beige bedding but I don't see my own face in my reflection. I am a stranger now.

I eat a sandwich which I brought from home and make a coffee, then sit again at the mirror and eat slowly, wondering how or where I got the strength from to go on this venture alone.

I convince myself that I am doing no more than anyone else in my position would do. I feel like a part of me is missing, like a lost limb or a disability which can be healed if only I find this man. Never do I consider that I am on the wrong track. I have a raging gut instinct that cannot be tamed and I feel like there is an energy inside me that I have only just discovered.

There were three men, she said. And I truly believe that Max Kelly was one of them. I have to start somewhere, and Blue Heaven is the place to start.

Waitressing in the evening in Blue Heaven is a lot calmer than what I have witnessed during the day. The staff seem more chilled and the atmosphere has toned down to a much more sophisticated level, which I welcome as it gives me more time to absorb my surroundings. I must not get my hopes up but I will use every second of my time here to learn more about this man – his lifestyle, his reputation and most of all, his past.

Because it is my first shift, I am given responsibility for drinks orders only which means that I have no errand to the kitchen on the first floor, much to my annoyance. But it doesn't stop me from doing my homework.

It does mean that I work closely with the head barman, Emmett, who keeps me on my toes by insisting I smile more and look happy to be here. If only he knew.

"Come on, Hollie. This is a jolly place to work. The food is beautiful; the drinks are too, the people are shit hot. Think happy, happy, happy!"

I'll give him happy! I fake a smile and glide round the floor and every time I look in his direction he makes happy faces at me and soon I find that I can't help but smile when I catch his eye. In a normal life, I would enjoy Emmett's banter but in this case I can't. I don't want to get to know anyone here. This is business, not pleasure.

Soon I have a five-minute break and I am shown to a

small staffroom on the first floor where two of the other waiting team members gulp a quick coffee down their necks and try to make the most of their speedy breather from the floor.

"Hi, you must be Hollie," says the girl, stirring sugar into her coffee at lightning speed. "I'm Beth. Welcome to Heaven." Her accent is English.

"Or should we say 'Hell'!" says her colleague who seems to be French and is on his second cup of coffee already.

"Hell? It can't be that bad, eh? I'm loving it so far."

The girl rolls her eyes and taps her spoon on the side of her cup. "Well, of course you are because you're working with Emmett. We have noticed, you know. You're making a lot of the girls jealous already."

I frown in her direction and she hands me a cup to help myself. I don't care if I'm making them *all* jealous. I'm not here to flirt with Emmett. I'm here to find Max.

"I've heard a lot about this place," I say, casually. "I've heard the Head Chef, what's his name again . . .?"

"Max?" says Beth, rising to my bait. "Max Kelly. Everyone knows his name!"

"Yeah, that's the one. I've heard he's a bit of a character. What's he like?"

Beth looks at her colleague for help but he just shrugs so she gives her own opinion. "Okay, where do I start? Most of us fancy him loads, I suppose you could say. It's like this power thing, like he's untouchable, nearly in a Simon Cowell type of way."

"Yuk!" says the boy and he makes a camp gesture with his hands. "I see what you mean with the whole 'untouchable' thing though. It's like he's way up there and if he says hello to you it's like your day has just been made. Some of the boys fancy him too which is quite sick if you ask me. He's way too old!"

Beth playfully slaps her colleague's arm. "No, he's not, Christophe! He's in his forties and he looks much younger. Anyway, who cares about age? It's all about charisma and charm and . . . and power. Yes, power. I swear if he even as much as looks my way I nearly melt. Of course he has no idea that I even exist!"

I am already intrigued. I want to meet him and wipe his smug power right from his face. How dare he command such attention? If only they knew.

"So, when do I get to meet him?" I ask tartly. "I'd like to see for myself if he's as handsome and powerful as you all seem to think he is."

The boy and girl glance at each other and then they burst out laughing.

"Meet him?" says Christophe. "We don't *get* to meet him, that's the point."

"What? Why not?"

"We deal with Gina and that's as high up as we get round here. None of us have ever met Max Kelly. He's like God in this place. Anyway, he's been on holiday this week but he's due back in over the weekend, I heard, so you won't even see him tonight. Everything about him we hear only on the grapevine but, having said that, he's the reason why most of us want to work here in the first place."

"Holiday? He's on holiday?"

Shit! Could my timing be further off? I will never get this opportunity again. I can't afford for him to be on holiday!

"Yes, holiday," says Christophe, looking puzzled at my reaction. "Rumour has it that he treated his wife and kids to a last-minute week in the sun. You know, it *is* that time of year and all that. Why do you look so surprised?"

"No, it's just that I hoped he would be here. I just wanted to see what all the fuss is about. I want to –"

"Ahh, look how disappointed she looks, Beth. Like a number-one fan who turned up to the gig when it was over. Aw!"

"Did you hear the other version though?" asks the girl, interrupting me excitedly. She nudges Christophe and he shrugs her off. "No, what's that?"

"The rumour mill is crazy around here, so this might not be true," she says. "But I've heard that all is not well in Max's marriage. They say –"

"That's enough, Beth!" says Christophe, nipping in. "Give Hollie a chance to settle in before she's poisoned by rumour and gossip."

"I'd love to know," I say but Christophe is already guiding Beth out through the door.

"I'm serious!" he says as he leaves. "If you want to keep a job here, then don't listen to and don't believe everything you hear in this place. Best to keep your eyes and ears shut, your nose clean and do what you're paid to do. Wait tables. Now, let's get back to work before Gina has us out on the street."

My shift is over and I feel defeated, almost cheated by Max's absence. I wonder if this a sign that I should I pack it in and go home but I feel part of his life now. I knew it had been too easy so far.

No, I can't stop now. My defeat about seeing him makes me all the more hungry to finish what I've started and I decide to stick it out here at Blue Heaven. It's the weekend after all, so it is unlikely that the agency will check up on me, or that Gina will smell a rat. She seems far too busy and understaffed to worry anyhow.

I linger around upstairs and slowly brush around some of the tables even though I should have left ten minutes ago, all the time glancing over into the kitchen where I imagine Max issuing orders left, right and centre to his staff who believe he is some god-like creature. My obsession with him is growing and I know that as long as it takes, or as long as I can keep my true intentions to myself, I will stay here at Blue Heaven until he returns. Be it tomorrow or Sunday or even Monday, I will wait.

He isn't on holiday. I know he isn't on holiday. Well, not with his wife and kids anyhow. Sandra was at home and I know by the look on Christophe's face that he was covering for the "boss man" as he seems to be affectionately referred to. One thing is for sure around here – Max Kelly has all his staff eating out of his hands, or at least that's how they have been told to behave. He is the most respected man in the building and his absence has caused rumour overdrive which I need to find out more about as soon as I can.

"Ah, Molly!" says Gina, when she spots me as she comes to the top of the stairs. "So, you've survived your first shift? How did you get on? Jackie seems pleased."

"It's Hollie, actually. And it was fine." I don't want to talk to Gina. I think it's best I stay out of her way in case she catches me out. "Thanks for the start. It's nothing I haven't done before."

Gina purses her lips and looks me up and down. "So . . . what is it then?" she asks with a smirk. "Acting, music or modelling?"

"Sorry?" I lean on the shaft of the brush and eyeball her. What the hell is all this about?

"I've heard you were asking about Max so I assume you're the same as the rest of my casual staff?" she says. "Most of the kids here use this place as a stepping-stone to their big break and sometimes it works. We get a lot of famous actors, directors, pop stars, producers, you name it. They all call in for a slice of Blue Heaven when they're in town and, if Max thinks you're worth it, he might get you an introduction. But you knew that already, right?"

"Actually, no, I didn't. And the staff tell me they never see him anyway." I raise my chin. "I'm not angling for any introductions. I'm a musician. A classical violinist actually."

Gina looks a bit hurt by my snappiness and I suddenly realise I have read her character all wrong. She is not accusing at all. In fact, she seems motherly and caring and I know I can use this to my advantage so I quickly shift into a different gear.

I paint on my best bashful smile. "Okay. I confess. I was hoping to meet him. You've seen right through me."

"Thought as much. But don't worry, it's no secret that Max is the man with the contacts and I can tell you he has a real thing for classical music. In fact he is in love with the violin. I don't think we have any classically trained staff here at the moment so you've certainly got an edge."

She looks as if she has had a light-bulb moment and she goes to speak but then stops.

"What is it, Gina?" I ask sweetly. "Look, I'd really, really appreciate your help. If you could get me a one-to-one with Max Kelly really soon I'd be over the moon. You're right. He is the main reason I wanted to work here."

I can sense that Gina takes great pride in her position as Max's keeper. She could be my fast pass to seeing him without causing a stir or fuss. Yes, this is definitely my best approach.

"No promises, but I'll do my best," says Gina. "I'll see you tomorrow at six?"

"Tomorrow at six!" I say with an appreciative nod and when she leaves I drop the floor brush from my grasp. Now, I just need to check in at home to avoid suspicion about my whereabouts, knowing that my search for Max Kelly is finally coming to fruition.

25

Sandra drove up towards Blessington and savoured the beautiful summer morning. It really was set in the most beautiful part of the country and she could fully understand how this was the perfect setting to find peace within the soul.

The boys had been quiet on the way up to County Louth. Charlie was in a different world with his iPod and Josh had his nose permanently stuck in his Nintendo DS. Sandra hadn't minded though. It gave her time to reflect, to think about the future and how this new effort that Max had made would make things look so much brighter. At forty-one, she was six years younger than her husband but she also knew that in just a few years' time, their sons would have moved on and they needed to be as strong as they could be together if they were to make their marriage last in the long term.

She saw Max as soon as she turned the corner and

recognised the bench he was sitting on as the one which featured so heavily in his stories of Blessington. A red-haired boy, not much older than Charlie, sat by his side and they smiled and talked until Max looked up and recognised the family car.

"Dad!" said Josh and he unclipped his seat-belt before Sandra had time to properly bring the car to a halt. The moment it stopped, he bolted and ran across the lawns and into his father's arms.

Sandra's eyes filled up as she watched them embrace. Max swung Josh round like he used to when he was much smaller and Josh gripped onto his father's arms.

"Aren't you going to greet Dad?" Sandra asked Charlie who didn't reply. She turned around to face him and then nudged his leg. "Charlie, I'm speaking to you!" "What?" he snapped and pulled the iPod headset from his ears. "That was my favourite song!"

"I said, aren't you going to say hello to your father?"

"And I said no!"

"No, you didn't. You didn't answer me. Charlie, I mean it. He is trying his best so please give him a chance or I'll –"

"Or you'll do what, Mum?" Charlie spat back at her. "You won't do anything. You never do! That's the fucking problem!"

Charlie opened the car door and slammed it behind him, then marched off across the gardens in the opposite direction to where Max and Josh stood. Sandra saw Max direct Josh back to the car and signal at her to stay put while he went after his eldest boy.

"I'll go after him!" called Sandra.

"Leave him to me," he said, marching after his son. "I'll deal with it. I should have dealt with it ages ago."

"Talk to me, Charlie," said Max when he caught up with the boy. "I said talk to me for Christ's sake! I'm your father!"

Charlie stopped suddenly and pulled the earphones out, his mouth tight with anger and his face paler than Max had ever seen it before. He reached his hand forward and thrust Max out of his way, then walked ahead, Max marching after him.

"You're not a father to me at all," said Charlie. "You haven't been a father to me in years and years! All you care about is yourself and that goddamn restaurant you spend most of your life in. You missed my birthday! You even missed my birthday, Dad!"

The boy stopped again and heaved giant sobs, his shoulders shaking and his head down. The iPod he carried fell to the ground. Max bent to pick it up and offered it to his son.

"I promise you, Charlie. I promise that it's all over now. I've been chased by demons in here." He pointed to his temple. "I've been wasting so much time worrying about people from my past that I'd forgotten all about how the important people, the really important people, are right here, right now. They are you and Josh and Mum. Our family. Please give me a chance to make us a family again."

He put his hand on Charlie's shoulder and Charlie looked up at him. For a boy of only seventeen, he had witnessed far more of his parents' marriage troubles than he should have – far more than either them realised.

"Do you love us, Dad? I mean, do you *really* love Mum and me and Josh? Because if you don't, then maybe it's time to walk away. I can't bear this any more."

Max gulped, clenched his hand into a fist and punched his chest over his heart three times. "I'm telling you, Charlie. Man to man, father to son, that all of my mistakes are in my past. I have a future to concentrate on and I plan to fight to win back the love of my family because I love them more than they will ever know. It's just up to me to make sure I am man enough now to convince them."

Charlie sniffed and nodded, and wiped his eyes on his sleeve. Then he began to walk back in the direction of the car, focusing straight ahead without continuing the conversation or responding to what Max had said. His father was close behind him.

Back at the car, he put his earphones back in and turned the volume up as high as he could stand it, then climbed into the back seat beside his brother.

"How're you feeling?" asked Sandra when Max climbed into the passenger seat.

"Better," said Max. "Much better."

He clasped her hand where it rested on the gear stick and Sandra felt a warm glow of hope for her family and for her marriage for the first time in years.

"What do you say we order in some takeaway for dinner?" asked Max when they arrived home and pulled into the driveway. "I think we all deserve a treat and Mum certainly deserves a night off from cooking."

Sandra pulled the handbrake up on the car and turned

to the back seat to where her sons had sat in silence for the past hour and a half.

"What do you think, boys? You fancy some pizza or Chinese? What do you say?"

Josh lowered his game system down onto his lap and looked at Charlie for guidance.

"Whatever," said Charlie. "I'm not hungry."

"Come on, you two. It's Saturday night. What do you fancy?" said Max, rubbing his hands together to try and liven up the mood. He felt so refreshed inside that he could burst and he yearned to prove himself to his young family.

"Suppose pizza would be nice?" said Josh.

Sandra thought her heart was breaking in two. She could tell that Josh was dying to make out that everything was back to normal but that he didn't want to betray his brother's feelings by seeming too keen.

"Pizza okay with you, Charlie? We could rent out a movie too? What's the name of that comedy you said you wanted to see?"

Charlie shrugged. "I said *whatever*."

He got out of the car and walked indoors, using his own set of keys to enter the family home.

The others followed him.

"Oh my God, I can't tell you how good this feels," said Max to his wife as he inhaled the familiarity of his own kitchen. "I have missed out on so, so much lately but I plan to make it up to each and every one of you."

"Take it one step at a time," said Sandra, filling the kettle at the sink. "I know what it's like when you come out of one of those intensive retreats. It's like going to a conference or training workshop and you come out feeling all rejuvenated and full of ideas and positivity. Then in a few days' time, maybe less, you're back into the mundane old day-to-day stuff and all your gusto is gone."

Max was genuinely hurt. "I can't believe you're comparing a week at Blessington, with intense therapy and counselling, to a conference! That's hardly fair. I even prayed for goodness' sake. Like, really prayed. To God."

Sandra managed a giggle at the thought of Max in intense prayer. He barely remembered the Hail Mary at times and she couldn't remember the last time he attended Sunday Mass. Will had done quite a job in convincing him to spend time at Blessington but she wanted her husband to be himself, not some reformed preacher type who believed he had found a cure for all evil.

"I just think that sometimes therapy can be like fast food for the soul," she said. "Unless you keep it up, it can be very easy to fall into the dark side again. And I don't want you to do that."

She poured them a coffee each while Max flicked through the evening paper.

"It's funny how you can switch off though. I never thought I'd last a day with no emails, no mobile phone ringing constantly, no news to keep up with. It really puts everything into perspective. It's like being on a totally different planet."

Sandra sat down and watched him as he spoke. She had never seen his eyes so alive before. She had never seen him speak about the simple things in life with such passion, such belief. She had never, ever seen him so content in his own skin, in his own surroundings.

Whatever it was that was haunting him before had now been dissolved and she promised herself she would never bring it up with him again. If she was to save her marriage, save her family and guarantee the happiness of her boys, she could only look forward now. She could never look back again.

26

My second day in Dublin is spent mostly in bed as I sleep off the exhaustion of yesterday's drive and my unexpected waitressing shift at Blue Heaven. It took a bottle of wine to make me sleep last night and even with the anaesthetic affects of the alcohol I still tossed and turned with nightmares during the night. I could hear her screams and I could smell the dirt of the men who pounced on her, who raped her one by one, who drugged her and kept her in a drunken state as they partied and used and abused her young body.

In my nightmare, I could see Max Kelly as he looked now, grinning at me like he knew exactly what was going on, like he was in full control of my life. He was the puppeteer, pulling the strings and in this nightmare my mother and I were together and for him we would play the violin and do anything else he wanted us to do. He was our keeper, our mastermind, he controlled and steered every movement in our lives.

I had awoken with a start and outside I'd heard a cat scream and the curtain on the small bedroom window fluttered in the light night-time breeze. I felt alone and frightened and I pulled the bed covers around me, too scared to get up and close the window tight or use the bathroom. Instead I lay there in the dark and dressed for breakfast when the first light filled the room. When I returned from a half-eaten breakfast I lay down and I eventually fell asleep when the rest of the world was waking.

I have lain in bed thinking about my evening ahead for hours now, delighted with my new friendship with Gina. Using Gina was a much quicker route to seeing the elusive Max Kelly and I cannot afford to let such an opportunity pass me by.

I change into my Blue Heaven uniform, pull a light jacket over it and set off in the direction of Grafton Street which according to my previous journey the day before will take approximately fifteen minutes. With over an hour to spare, I snack on a sandwich on a summer bench and watch busy shoppers shuffle to and fro from the street's busy stores. I admire a street performer's statuesque stance and throw him a luck penny and watch a caricature artist capture a doting mother and her toddler. When I have seen enough and with still some time to spare, I take up a pew in the cosy pub a few doors down from Blue Heaven. I remove my jacket and order a 7Up and ice from the bar.

"You must be a new start up the road?" says the barman and I nod, taking in the bar's ambience, so different from its exclusive neighbour. The barman,

Damien, is handsome and Canadian I guess from his accent. I flash him a smile, realising that he could also be useful to my enquiries.

"It's just my second shift – I start in approximately twenty minutes," I tell him, checking my watch. "I just thought I'd catch the end of the match on the big screen while I wait."

"Ah, so you're a football fan too?" says Damien, clicking the lid off the lemonade bottle. "Well then, you'll settle into life over there quite nicely. Max and Will are Chelsea fanatics."

I spot my first opportunity for information.

"Chelsea? Really?" I say with a giggle. "So he's not all perfect then?"

The bar man pours my 7Up and the clink of the ice on the glass heightens my thirst.

"Depends which one you mean," he says with a grin. "Max or Will."

"I've no idea which is which," I say to him. "Like I say, I'm brand new. Totally green. I just heard that the Max guy was one to watch."

I guess he knows I am testing him but nonetheless he takes the bait. I take a long drink from the straw he has placed in my drink and watch him think.

"I suppose he has his moments," he says with a shrug. "I see him in here a lot. He and Will argue, then one of them leaves in a huff and then they are best buddies again the next day. It's a bit of a well-known comedy routine amongst us staff. Mind you, they run a damn fine restaurant in there so something must be right between them."

I nod and stifle a yawn, my messed-up body clock beginning to take its toll. How can I still be tired? I decide I have beaten around the bush for long enough. It's time to get down to the nitty-gritty and ask some real questions about Max.

"I heard he's got a bit of a way with the ladies," I say and flick my hair back from my face. "Should I keep a look-out for his roving eye?"

The barman looks puzzled and I kick myself for suggesting such a thing when I have no idea where it came from.

"Can't say I know," says Damien. "But then, there's only so much you can tell from a guy who orders a pint or two from you once or twice a week. He keeps himself to himself but, from what I know of him, I like him, womaniser or not."

Once again, I wonder where I have found the strength to go through with what I am doing right now. Here I am, in the middle of Dublin on my own, in a bar asking accusing questions about a man I don't know. It is like I have adopted a new character since I began this mission to find Max Kelly. I am fearless, ruthless almost, like I have nothing to lose by seeking answers on my mother's and on my own messy past.

"Mind you, I know Max has had his troubles lately," says the barman eventually, bringing me back to reality.

"Don't we all?" I say, trying not to sound too eager for information.

"Yeah, but I think this is really rough. Poor guy," says Damien. He is polishing glasses as he speaks and seems genuinely concerned. "I mean we all have troubles but it must be pretty bad when he keeps disappearing like that."

Disappearing? I try my best to keep it cool. Ah, his holiday . . .

"Yeah, I heard. Yeah."

"This latest thing sounds nasty, eh? I mean, things must be bad when you have to do that. Hardly a holiday being stuck in there! It must be so tough on the family, not to mention the business and . . . you have no idea what I'm talking about, do you? Shit, I've said far too much."

I try to look like I'm only casually interested but fireworks are going off in my brain. Has Max Kelly been in trouble? Has he been in hospital or in prison or where has he been?

"Sorry, I have to go," I say then. "Didn't realise the time."

I jump from my stool and make my way into Blue Heaven with more nerves and more determination than ever before. So it isn't all paradise in the life of Max Kelly after all? What goes around, comes around – isn't that what they say?

27

"Hey, Gina," I chirp, pulling the strap of my bag over my head and taking off my jacket like I've worked at this restaurant forever. I have already won over Max's first lady and I need to keep it up. So far, so good.

"Can we have a word?" asks Gina, her fine, dark eyebrows arched so high that her forehead's wrinkled. She looks like she has been waiting for me and seems much more assertive, much more prepared than at our previous encounter. "I think it's important that you and I have a quick chat before your shift starts."

I nod and give her a bright smile which I know unnerves her and I follow her up the spiral staircase and into a small office where there are three desks. Mummy Bear, Daddy Bear and Baby Bear . . .

Gina gestures to me to take a seat at the tidiest desk of the three and I notice from a photo that sits beside the computer station that she has a very handsome son, or else a very good-looking and much younger boyfriend.

"He looks nice," I say, and Gina shoots me a look without explaining her relationship with the boy in the photo.

"Why don't we cut the crap, Hollie," she says, her New York accent sounding clipped and much stronger with her sharp tone.

I sit up in my chair, feeling my defences rise. Oh God! "Excuse me?"

"Now, I don't take no shit round here," says Gina. "I run a very tight ship and yesterday there was a blip that I ain't proud of. You're not from the agency, are you, Hollie?"

My stomach gives a leap. Do I play this hard or do I take the softly softly approach?

"Well, to be fair, Gina, it was a pretty stupid mistake. I mean, this is supposed to one of the most exclusive restaurants in the city and yet I was hired without even an interview or a question. It was more than I expected and I didn't know what to do. Imagine if you were in my –"

"We had asked the agency to send someone over!" she says. "We are incredibly busy at the moment and I don't appreciate that you lied your way into this job."

Lied? I didn't tell any lies. Apart from my surname but she wasn't to know that . . .

"I didn't lie. It was your mistake and I took advantage of it. It's not my problem, is it, that you didn't do your job efficiently?"

"I don't want it to be a problem for either of us, Hollie!" says Gina, a little louder and more pinched than before. "But if you want to play hard ball, I'll match you every step of the way – that I will promise you now. If, however, it's a private audience with Max Kelly you're after, then I can help you because that is my job. It's your choice. You can go against me, or you can make all this very easy. It depends just how much you want him to notice you. He is a very, very busy man. Everyone knows around here that to get to Max, you have to go through me first."

My initial reaction is to argue with her but what am I to gain? I already have overstepped the mark. I should have apologised. I should have given her a sob story about my musical dreams.

"Okay, okay, maybe . . ." I whisper, wringing my hands. "Maybe I *did* come across a bit too . . . well, a bit too strong just now."

Gina leans on her hand and raises her eyebrow again. "That's one way of putting it, I suppose."

"I didn't mean that you were in any way inefficient and I know you have been under pressure," I say in a total U-turn. Then I rack my brains for a quick explanation. "You see, I've been trying so hard to break into the music scene for the last few months now and to be honest . . ." I blink a few times and bite my lip. "To be honest I've been through a really rough time of late. It's been terrible . . ."

I glance up at Gina, hoping my tale of woe will spark some empathy but she is stoic, waiting on a full explanation. I swallow and wipe my eyes.

"My mum . . . she's . . . well, you see it was her dream for me to be a professional musician, ever since I was little. It was my dream too but I got in with the wrong crowd earlier this year – you know, clubbing till late, missing rehearsals and when I got kicked out of the orchestra I knew I had let her down so badly. It was like I'd thrown it all back in her face."

To my surprise, real tears stream down my face and I take a tissue from my sleeve and dab under my eyes. I can't believe I am using my mother's name to keep on side with this woman.

"I had to get away," I continue. "I couldn't look at her face when she found out I'd thrown away such a golden opportunity. She had put in so many years of commitment, not to mention all the financial pressure, to put me through music college and I failed her. So I came to Dublin, and someone told me about Max Kelly and how if you got a corporate gig in here, you might at least be heard by the right people."

Gina hands me a fresh tissue, her face softening. "So you came in here and I handed you a uniform and you thought it was your lucky day?"

Both of us laugh, me rather shakily, each accepting her own responsibility in this hiccup.

"Something like that," I say, relieved now to see some compassion in the woman's eyes.

"Well, I suppose we've both got off to the wrong start and we can take our fair portion of the blame," says Gina. "Ambition is a wonderful thing, Hollie – but sometimes it blinds us."

I breathe out. Thank you, God, thank you, I chant inwardly.

"I'm happy to hold my hands up," I say. "I should have explained myself from the start but I'd waitressed before and I thought this might be like a back door in, if you know what I'm saying."

Gina nodded. "I admire your drive, Hollie. I too had to knock on quite a few doors before I was made General

197

Manager of this place. I trod on a lot of toes and lost some friends along the way, but I would like you and me to start again. Let's put this behind us, eh?"

"I think that's for the best," I say and then a flush of panic rushes through me. "And Max? Have I burned my bridges about meeting him?"

Gina looks me in the eye. "I'll cut you a deal. If you can keep this little faux pas to yourself, I'll make sure you get the full attention from Max that you deserve. How does that sound?"

"It's a deal! I won't tell a soul, I promise."

She takes out a diary from her top drawer and flicks through it, stopping when she comes to the date she is looking for.

"Now, how does this sound for a start?" she asks. "I had this idea initially last night but I decided to sleep on it and then the other little matter arose. But since we are talking second chances . . . tomorrow night we're having a bit of a comeback party for Max. It's a private gathering and it is after hours. Just a few drinks and nibbles for some of us oldies here to show him how good it is to have him back from his . . . from his break."

Oh my God. I feel prickles on my skin and my blood runs cold.

"What . . . what do you need from me then?"

"Well, what would you say if I asked you to provide some background music for Max and some of his closest friends, only for an hour or so?"

She looks at me like she has handed me a golden ticket to my future fortune. I feel dizzy at the thought. Could I do it? Could I play for him?

"I . . . oh my God, this is . . . yes. Yes, I would say yes."

Gina is beaming at me but then her tone steps down a gear.

"Excellent! Now, you don't need to be nervous at all, Hollie. The important thing is to be yourself. I know this is probably more than what you had expected but he isn't a monster. He's just the boss. A very influential man indeed, but don't be scared. Embrace the opportunity. You are a very lucky girl."

Her words swim in my head. I cannot speak. I don't know if I really can do this. She is still talking.

"Just hang around after your shift and I'll give you the nod when we're ready to start. It will probably be towards midnight so just bring your stuff, have a few tunes in mind – a few popular classics – and we'll take it from there. It will all be very relaxed."

She stands up and extends her hand to me.

I stand and take it. "Thank you so much, Gina. Thank you. I'm so sorry if I came across so brash earlier. I was too eager and maybe a bit tired into the bargain. It's been a rough time lately."

Gina walks out from behind her desk and opens her office door.

"I'm just glad we can start again. As a rule I want my staff to both like and respect me and to know I'll always give them a chance. Now, wait till your mum hears that you're playing a private gig at Blue Heaven in Dublin. That would make her very proud, wouldn't it?"

"Yes," I mumble and I follow her out onto the busy restaurant floor. "Wouldn't it just."

28

Max swirled the brandy in his glass and savoured its rich aroma. The evening had been quite pleasant, considering its rocky start, and once the pizza had been cleared away and the family shared a few games on a console that Josh had hooked up into the main television set, there was laughter and a relaxed mode that Max hadn't experienced in a very long time.

The boys had gone their separate ways now, with Josh taking a DVD to his room and Charlie heading out with the lads.

With the house so peacefully quiet, Max and Sandra sat side by side on the sofa, their arms skimming each other and he smiled when he saw the contentment and relief on her face. He was the luckiest man alive to have such a strong woman by his side and he was determined now, more than ever, to make her as happy as she deserved to be.

He noticed how she had cleared out the spare room without mentioning it and he took this as a very positive sign indeed. They had so much catching up to do, so much to look forward to and they had both agreed that there was no looking back. It would never work out if they did.

"Knock, knock! Oh, I'm sorry. I should have called."

Will popped his head around the living-room door and Max and Sandra both jumped, never expecting any visitors at this time of the evening.

"No, no, come on in," said Max. "Good to see you, buddy. Can I get you a drink?"

Will looked sheepish, as if he had walked in on a courting couple, but he couldn't help but smile at how the atmosphere in the Kelly household had changed for the better.

"No, I won't stay. I just wanted to let you know that tomorrow evening, well, Gina and I have a table reserved and we thought that you, Sandra and my Patsy could have a bit of a bite to eat with us, followed by a few drinks to settle you back into the place. What do you say?"

Sandra glanced at Max and then at Will. "Oh, I don't know, Will. Isn't it a bit soon? I'd hoped Max could spend a few days around the house, you know, just relaxing before he was thrust back into reality again."

Will looked slightly hurt but he held his hands up and nodded. "Whatever you say, I'm happy. It's entirely up to you. We just thought that if Max showed his face on a social basis, it would give the right impression to staff and some of the regulars who have been asking for him."

Max felt defensive now. "But I thought Gina had given

a message out loud and clear that I was on holiday? My God, a man is allowed a holiday in the middle of August!"

Will sat down on the arm of a chair and took a deep breath. This wasn't being received as he'd planned it at all.

"Look, guys. The staff can only be shielded from so much. They're fiercely loyal, you know they are, but the rumour-mill is rife in any place of work and the last thing we want is fuel thrown on the fire by any one of them speaking out of school. I thought it would be reassuring for them to see you back on the premises, and in the best of form. And it would be good to have a nice relaxing drink together. Like friends do, you know? It would help to put the past few months behind us. But if you'd prefer not, that's okay too."

Max took a swig from his brandy glass and nodded at Sandra. "It's entirely up to you, Sandra. If you aren't happy to go, then we'll give it a miss. What do you think?"

Sandra looked from one to the other and sighed. "I don't know. I really don't. Look, why don't you two have a chat about it and I'll go clear away the dishes and get my head around it. I can see where you're coming from, Will, but I'm not sure if Max and I are ready to make any big public statements. I'll leave you to it."

Max sat back down on the sofa but Will seemed uncomfortable.

"I think I'll make tracks," he said. "Max, walk me out to the car – we can talk on the way."

"I don't see what harm having dinner at Blue Heaven would do," said Max as they approached Will's vehicle in the driveway. "It's just I feel as if I've come so far over the

202

past five days and I'm still digesting it all. Making me go to Blessington and take time out is the best thing you have ever done for me, Will. You have saved my marriage. You may even have saved me."

Will clasped his hands and leaned forward. "I'm delighted for you, Max. Really thrilled. But I don't want to rush you into anything. What you told me in the office that night –"

"Is in the past," said Max. "The best thing I've learned this week is that we cannot change the past. Man, I have been chasing it for years now, wondering about her, even following her when I got it really bad, to see if she was still alive, to make sure she had not crashed and burned over what happened. Then she did crash and burn and I am responsible for her death. But all that has gone now. Estelle is gone and I have to move on and make up for any past mistakes by doing the best I can in this life. I have to let my old life go."

"Whoa!" said Will. "I think I'll need a quick brandy after this conversation! That's deep stuff, kid, but it's the only way forward I suppose. But, Max, don't beat yourself up too much – you didn't actually *kill* anyone, after all."

"No, I didn't actually kill anyone but I do feel like I played a big part in what became of her. She took her own life, Will. That I know for sure, but her ghost had been haunting me for years and years before she passed away. I have to let her rest now, for my own bloody sanity, whether I deserve it or whether I don't."

29

Caroline opened the cemetery gates and felt a shiver run down her neck. She had yet to find any comfort from visiting her sister's grave and, since Hollie had told her what was in Estelle's diary, she had avoided the place completely. Today, however, she had found herself going there on a whim and she felt bad that she had no flowers or ornaments that she could leave at the graveside.

She shoved her hands in her pockets and looked at the ground as she walked, still finding it hard to believe that this was the only way to visit her sister now. The graves were neatly lined and the Parish had given the cemetery a lot of care and attention with its neat lawns and rules on size of headstones and other practical conditions. Estelle's grave was one of the most recent.

Caroline dropped to her knees at its side, automatically blessing herself and saying a silent prayer.

They hadn't erected a headstone as yet. It was almost time to do so but she hated the thought of putting Estelle's name and age on a slab of marble, making it all seem so final, so real.

"Why did you have to run away like this?" she said aloud, staring at the rich mound of soil in front of her. "We could have helped. Why didn't you tell us what happened back then?"

The sound of cars passing the cemetery was the only other thing Caroline could hear apart from her own voice which echoed in her head.

"You could have got over this, I know you could. No one would have ever let them come for you again, or hurt you again. Now, Hollie has taken on the role of Miss bloody Marple and is obsessed with finding a man she believes is guilty of ruining you, all because she found a photo of him in your diary. There's just no stopping her, Estelle. What on earth have you started?"

A rustle behind her startled Caroline and she looked around to see a young girl who was ferociously chewing gum staring down at her, holding a bunch of garage flowers limply in her right hand. She had her other hand on a pram and a young boy stood by her side.

Caroline squinted in the sunshine back at her.

"Er, hello?"

"Is this Estelle's grave?" asked the girl. "Estelle Lynch, right?"

Caroline stood up and brushed some soil from her jeans. She pulled a stray hair from off her face.

"Yes. How long have you been standing there? You shouldn't just creep up on people like that!"

"I'm sorry. We were just out for a walk and I thought I might leave off some flowers. Sorry if I'm intruding. I really didn't mean to."

The girl laid the flowers carefully on top of the soil and Caroline felt guilty for her harsh reaction.

"I'm sorry, it's just I didn't realise anyone else came here. Estelle was my sister. Did you know her through her music?"

The girl scrunched her face and shook her head. "No. I didn't know her at all, but I sort of feel like I should have. She was a friend of my mother's. She's dying too, you see."

Caroline's brain kicked into gear. Singh. The Japanese lady. She should have known by the girl's appearance.

"Oh, well, then it's my turn to apologise. I'm Caroline. Hollie's aunt."

"Maria. Look, it's no big deal. It's not like we should be best friends or anything. I just know that when Hollie called the other day, it sent my mother right back in time and she seems to believe she has making up to do with Estelle. A bunch of flowers isn't much, but it's about all I could think of."

Caroline looked at the young girl with a new sense of pity. She was an intriguing sort with her extreme beauty and heavy make-up and the little boy had the patience of a kid twice his age. He just waited for Maria to finish without complaining like most other boys his age would do, or so Caroline imagined.

"That's very kind of you," she said. "Look, I'm at a bit of a loose end at the minute. Do you fancy joining me for a quick coffee? My shout? It is Sunday after all so

206

maybe I can treat the kids to some ice cream to make up for being so rude?"

"Nah, no worries," said Maria. "We're not a charity case just yet."

"I'd love some ice cream," said the little boy and Caroline leaned down to his level.

"Same here," she said. "Strawberry flavour with chocolate sprinklings is my favourite."

The boy's eyes were like saucers and he licked his lips. "I like an extra large vanilla with a huge, big flake the size of a house!"

He used his hands to demonstrate and both Maria and Caroline laughed.

"You know what they say about taking sweets from strangers?" said Maria, ruffling the boy's hair. "Have I taught you nothing?"

"Let's go," said Caroline.

She walked on and the girl and her little family followed.

"I don't think we are strangers at all," said Caroline. "I think we share a lot of history and I would like to know more. I certainly feel like I know you."

Maria shrugged her shoulders and giggled. "Okay then, a coffee it is."

"Or . . . they do a mean Sunday lunch around the corner? I get the impression we have a lot to talk about."

Maria rolled her eyes. "I suppose it *would* save me cooking and I can take home a doggy bag for my mother, not that she's up to eating much. It will keep these two out of her way for another while, I suppose."

"Great," said Caroline. "The place on the corner does

the best Sunday lunch and it has the biggest portions of vanilla ice cream ever! I've tried almost everything on the menu. Come on, let's go."

"Do you look like her?"

Maria was wolfing down her roast beef and mash but managed to talk ten to the dozen as she did so.

"Yes, quite a bit," said Caroline. "We were like chalk and cheese as children but as the years went by we grew more and more alike – but she was blonde like Hollie whereas I am darker. Some people thought we were twins, much to Estelle's delight because she was quite a few years older than me. Well, six years to be exact."

"Wow! She was still very young when she died. Don't you think it's a pity she and my mother grew apart like they did? Singh has told me so many funny stories over the past few days. They were two peas in a pod, she says, and she laughs so hard I can't even make out what she is saying. But then she cries and I don't understand. If they were so good for each other, why did it all go wrong?"

Caroline realised for the first time since she met Maria that afternoon that the young girl was not as worldly wise as she first took her for. She seemed oblivious to her mother's early years and had moulded into her current way of life, unaware that her upbringing was in any way out of the norm.

"You enjoying your ice cream, Reese?" Caroline asked the boy and he nodded.

The baby gurgled in the pram and Maria fed her another spoonful of dinner from the mixed-up bowl of potatoes, meat and veg that she had so expertly ordered for her.

"I suppose you feel sorry for us," said Maria, pushing her hair behind her ears. "Most people do but we're doing okay, you know."

"That's good," said Caroline. "It must be tough for you playing 'mum' twenty-four seven. Don't you have any time to yourself?"

Maria shook her head and fed the baby some more dinner. "Not really, but I'm not missing out on much. In a way, looking after these two sort of keeps me out of trouble. Vinny says if it wasn't for my mum getting pregnant with my brother and sister, I'd probably be out on the game by now. This way, I was needed more at home to help her look after them."

Caroline almost choked on her food. The way Maria referred to prostitution in such a casual way was frightening to say the least.

"And he's probably right," Maria continued. "Even my mum's sickness has made all of our lives a bit easier. Things are a hell of a lot quieter now. You have no idea what it used to be like. There are so many skeletons in that woman's closet they could have filled that cemetery we just visited. It was hard to keep up with. You have no idea."

Caroline pushed her plate to the side and noticed how Maria eyed up the leftover meat and the odd potato.

"Who . . . who is Vinny?" Caroline asked. She couldn't help watch the innocent little boy lick his plate, oblivious to any of the conversation taking place around him.

"Vinny is just Vinny. He sort of lives with us, some of the time," said Maria. "It's weird but I feel safer when Vinny is there. No one would ever mess with him, that's for sure. But sometimes he has to go away for weeks and weeks and we're on our own. We still have Mum, of course, but it's always like we're on our own when Vinny isn't around."

"Vinny bought me *Ben Ten* shoes," said Reece and Caroline was then aware that despite his concentration on his food, the boy was in fact very tuned into what was going on around him.

"So, tell me more about Singh and Estelle, then," said Caroline. "You said she had some funny stories. I'd love to hear them."

Maria set down her knife and fork and rolled her eyes. "I've had to listen to stories of Estelle for days now. Okay, here is one. The day they went to their first lecture together and they got lost on campus. This is really funny."

Caroline settled her elbow on the table and leaned her head on her hand as she listened to Maria's recollection of some of her mother's most precious memories and she felt like she had known this young girl forever.

Ronan was reading the newspaper when Caroline got back to his city apartment. He looked over the top of it and then took off his glasses and twirled them in the air.

"That was a long trip," he said. "Where the hell did you get to? I've been so worried I could hardly concentrate on the Sunday sports news."

"Ha ha," said Caroline, leaning across and kissing his cheek on her way past. "How was your recital?"

"Quite good actually," he replied, folding the newspaper and setting it on the coffee table. "We are really missing

Hollie though. I'll have to have some more convincing words with her when she gets back from her friend's place tonight. Her compassionate leave ran out ages ago and unless she can convince her doctor to extend her sick leave, she's really going to have to make a decision."

Caroline flopped down on the settee and swung her legs up to the side.

"It can't be easy for her," she said. "All of these questions, all of these maybes and mysteries just suck. Plus she's still immersed in grief and guilt and a host of whys and what ifs. I know I am too but somehow being in work gets me through it. And I haven't had to cope with any horrific revelation about my conception."

Ronan nodded. "So what did you get up to while I was gone? Lunching with Brad Pitt again, no doubt?"

Caroline threw her head back and talked to the ceiling. "Of course he has been pestering me since the moment you struck up your first note on the viola, but no, I turned him down. I actually had a very impromptu lunch with Singh Moshiro's daughter. I learned a lot about my sister today. A lot."

Ronan was intrigued. "You had lunch with *who*?"

"She's only sixteen, Ronan, and I swear it's pitiful how she has to rear her little brother and her baby sister while her mother lies dying of cancer. Singh Moshiro has come to a very sad ending and I find it uncanny, considering that she and Estelle were best friends. There is definitely a rich history between them and even though their friendship only lasted a number of months it has certainly paved the rest of their life out for them."

Ronan stood up from the armchair and, on the

suggestion of coffee, Caroline followed him to the kitchen.

"So, what you're saying is that whatever happened around the time Estelle was referring to, shaped not only her life but also that of Singh Moshiro?"

"So it seems," said Caroline. "The gang who Singh had fallen in with led her into a life of drugs and prostitution which unfortunately she stayed in for the rest of her life until now. Estelle had a lucky escape of sorts, but the memories of what she went through haunted her so much that even now she couldn't cope with it."

Ronan joined her at the table and set down two steaming mugs of coffee, paying attention not to spill any.

"Do you think those same guys are still in Singh's life then?" he asked.

"Maria didn't say that as such," said Caroline, "but there is one man called Vinny who she seems to hold in very high regard. He seems to be their protector since as far back as Maria can remember and she feels safe around him. She has a lot of time for him, but I'd like to know more."

Caroline shivered and she knew by the look of Ronan's face that he felt the same. She wanted to know more but she was afraid of getting in too deep. People like Vinny had trouble written all over them. Surely Estelle wouldn't have wanted Hollie to put her life in danger by getting in the path of such dangerous people?

30

It's Sunday and today is my big day.

I comb my hair and apply an extra coat of lipstick. Tonight is the big meeting with Max Kelly and I hope it will be as fruitful as I imagine.

I clip my hair into a loose "up do" with a few light grips, planning that when I finish my waitressing shift, I will take it down and let it fall around my shoulders for my debut performance at Blue Heaven in front of my exclusive audience.

I wonder what his wife looks like? Is she pretty? Is she smart? Does she know his secrets and can she see through his lies?

I spent this afternoon shopping and treated myself to a neat, black strappy dress and silver heels, topped off with a chunky silver bracelet and matching necklace and earrings. I know my preparations are a step too far, but I have checked my mother's diary and noted that her favourite scent back in her university days was Georgio – a popular, mysterious fragrance by Georgio Beverly Hills, which is certainly not suitable for everyday wear. Its sharp, flowery scent is musky and feminine and it smells of power and intrigue. I searched until I found it in one of the larger department stores in Dublin city and now that I have applied it to my pulse points and its scent has filled the room, I'm pleased with my effort and attention to detail. The fragrance is distinctive all right, and I am certain that if Max Kelly is as guilty as I think he is, this might subliminally help spark a reaction.

Amidst my preparations, I think about Jinx who is so many miles away. I call Mrs Jenkins to ask if she can extend her doggy-sitting duties for just one more night and, with that sorted, I send Ben and Caroline a quick message to let them know that I am fine and that I am having some well-earned time out with my imaginary friends.

Caroline calls me straight away but I need to stay focused so I ignore the call, deciding that I will have plenty to talk to Caroline about once tonight is over.

The anticipation of meeting him is immense, now that I have spent two evenings in his restaurant, getting to know the people he knows, picking up titbits of information along the way so I have analysed his character as much as I can before we come face to face. Like an undercover detective, I feel like I am living in the darkness of his shadow and, as I'm now within touching distance, the rush I feel is very hard to control.

Gina had opened up quite a bit when I called her earlier to check the final arrangements for tonight. We chatted like old friends and I had managed to casually glean from Gina that Max had lived in Belfast until the age of nineteen when he had dropped out of his university course and made a new life in America where he trained to be a chef. It was on his return from the States that he met Will Langdon, a risk-taking entrepreneur who proposed to him that they form a business partnership – and the rest was history.

I wonder if Gina is in love with Max. She is so protective of him, and she gushes about his every characteristic when her barriers are down. She has taken a shine to me and I must use it to my advantage and ignore any liking I have towards this lady. I must not let emotions get in my way so I avoid any personal questions from her and kept our conversation centred round tonight and the man of the moment.

My heart skipped a beat when Gina told me that Max had left Belfast in 1981. He "had fled" were the words she had used but, when I probed her further, she gave an impression that it was Northern Ireland's troubled political situation that made Max want to escape. I didn't buy it for a second of course, but I played along with her and threw in some comments about my own relatives who did the same during The Troubles.

I'm almost ready now. I have my dress, my heels and jewellery packed in a bag and I am dressed for my evening shift at the restaurant. Max's dinner party is known to only a few in Blue Heaven as yet. Tomorrow of course all the staff will know. But my plans are known only to me.

31

Sandra was trying to select an appropriate outfit for their late dinner with Will and guests. The idea had unnerved her at first but, when both Max and Will had agreed that the "happy Blue Heaven families" element of the occasion would be toned down, she decided it was something to look forward to.

Max had suggested that they bring the boys along, too. Of course Charlie was having none of it and offered to baby-sit, with a response along the lines that he would rather "slam his balls in the door than listen to Will Langdon talk shite".

Sandra and Max had no answer to that and so decided to make use of the offer to spend some time as a couple amongst friends and make the most of dining at Blue Heaven before Max returned to work there.

She had narrowed her options down to three dresses when Max came into her dressing room, a towel round his waist and smelling of cologne and soap and manly freshness.

"The red one," he said. "You know I've always loved you in red."

"You are so predictable," said Sandra and she turned to face him, feeling romantic at the sound of his voice as well as excited that he was helping her choose a special outfit. It had been so long.

Max slipped his hands under her robe and caressed the small of her back and she gasped under his touch. He pushed the dressing-room door closed and turned the key, then pulled her closer to his semi-naked body. She took the towel from his waist and let it drop to the floor, just as he slipped her robe from her shoulders.

"It's so good to have you back," she whispered, "I –"

His mouth cut her words short, kissing her hard and so passionately she wanted him more than she ever had in her life.

"I love you, Sandra," he said. "I love you so much."

32

I begin my shift at six as planned and I leave my violin and change of clothes in a locker in the staff room before taking my place on the restaurant floor. There are rumours that Bono has reserved a table for later in the evening and I am certain that I recognised a well-known Irish television presenter and his family pass me by on my way in tonight.

I am still on drinks duty only but it keeps me busy and in a strange way I never notice the hours going by like I did in previous waiting jobs. Emmett, the barman, is glad to see me and he has a twinkle in his eye that tells me he is up for some *craic* – but I mustn't take my eye off the ball. He really is cute though and underneath my armour I am very flattered that he has noticed me. The rest of the staff are friendly too and we share the odd joke. When I forget for the odd brief moment why I am really here, I actually enjoy Blue Heaven and all that comes with it.

"All set?" asks Gina as she breezes through the bar where I am waiting with a tray of cocktails and exclusive wines for Table Eight. She looks different with her hair done and her red lipstick heavily sitting on her lips.

"I can't wait," I tell her and my stomach twists. "Does he have any idea you have all of this planned?"

"Not a clue. I can't wait to see his face when he sees the effort we've made to show him how much we care. Max is irreplaceable around here and we've missed him terribly. A bit of music and some after-hours banter is the least we can do for him."

I can hardly believe it, but I feel a pang of guilt run through me right now for all my planning and deception. What if I am wrong about Max? What if I make a sorry fool of myself and he really is a nice guy who has no connection with me whatsoever? I haven't heard a bad word about him all weekend. Stay focused . . . I must stay focused.

"I really hope he enjoys it," I say to Gina. "You've gone to a great effort. You really have."

On my break I go to the Ladies' and run my wrists under the cold tap. I have managed to spill red wine over my white vest already and had to find a spare in the staff room, plus I have delivered the wrong order to at least three tables within the space of fifteen minutes. I spill my make-up onto the counter and begin a quick fix-up.

"What am I doing here?" I ask the stranger in the mirror and I lift my hands behind my head to tighten the clips in my hair, holding a spare clip between my lips. I glance into the mirror again where I now see my mother looking back at me. The excitement I felt earlier is swiftly turning to dread and I get the awful feeling that I am about to make a very sorry mistake.

Beth and another waitress burst into the bathroom seconds later, full of gossip and surplus energy.

"You'll never guess what!" says Beth and I look at her, not knowing what to expect.

"What?"

"You'll never guess who is coming in here tonight!"

"Er, Bono?" I suggest, checking my appearance one last time as the other two girls nudge each other like schoolgirls.

"No! Max Kelly! He's back," says Beth.

"Isn't that supposed to be a secret, Beth, for the moment?" I ask, feeling defensive of Gina's hard work. God, but I am softening so fast! I have been here too long already!

"Oh, so you know?" She looks startled at this. "Well, one of the head girls took sick and now *I* have to cover. I have to serve him his food! I swear I'll probably spill something over him. Oh my God, I am so nervous! Apparently he only eats in here once a year and all the staff are terrified of making a mistake when he does. I am *so* shitting myself!"

I gather my make-up into my bag. "You'll be fine."

"No, I will not," says Beth. "I mean, after where he has been, he might be like, really grumpy or sensitive."

"Shut up," says the other girl. "You know we're not supposed to know any of that."

"Any of what?" I ask.

"Nothing!" sing both girls in unison and I fold my arms and wait. I have already gauged that Beth is a loose cannon. Gina must be desperate, to let her work at the dinner party tonight.

"Well, it might not be true," whispers Beth, "but apparently he has been in therapy. Therapy! The word on the street is that he has major issues from his past, like this huge ball of guilt about something really bad he did before, and apparently he went a bit loopy in here one night and then Will signed him into some centre in the country! *Apparently*, one of the junior staff was on duty that night and he overheard them talking. I can't believe it. He is always so strong and . . ."

Beth's voice sounds foggy now and I feel like I am going to be sick. I grasp the sink unit behind me but my hands slip and I almost fall backwards.

"Je-sus!" says Beth, grabbing me. "Are you okay, Hollie? I swear, sometimes I think there are places in this restaurant where you take your life in your hands. Honestly!"

"Please! Just stop talking," I tell her, rubbing my head. My uniform is grubby again from a rub against the sink and what Beth has just told me has knocked the wind from my sails. I have mixed emotions – guilt, denial, fear, dread.

I mutter an apology and leave her. I go back to the staff room and change my top once more, then straighten my back and walk out onto the restaurant floor again, hoping and praying that what I am doing is right. Yet I also pray, for Max Kelly's sake and for Gina and for all who look up to him, that I am terribly wrong.

33

The car arrived at ten on the dot and Max straightened his tie on his way past the hallway mirror. "Charlie, look after your brother and don't let him play video games all night!" called Sandra, making sure she had her purse, keys and phone and not to mention lipstick and perfume in her handbag.

Max kept his hand lightly on her waist as they walked to the car and he opened the door for her, watching her with a knowing twinkle in his eye.

The early part of the evening had been wonderful and both Sandra and Max had agreed that they would finish what they had started when they got home that night. They both had developed a healthy hunger for supper at Blue Heaven and Sandra had already enjoyed a glass of sparkling wine as they waited for their chauffeur – a treat from Will – to take them into the city centre.

Sandra loved to drive into Dublin at night. The M50

was quiet and the road from Malahide was smooth with no disruptions. The radio played low in the car and the leather seats felt cool on the back of her bare legs. She was looking good and she felt equally good in her red dress and low kitten heels that allowed just a few inches of height difference between her and her husband. Friends often joked that in stilettos she would tower above Max and despite his 5'11" frame it was true. Sandra's long legs were the envy of many women and the topic of conversation of many men. Tonight, at just forty-one years old, she felt fresh and youthful and born again.

Soon the bright city lights surrounded the car and she snuggled under her husband's arm as their driver weaved in and out of traffic to find the fastest route.

He pulled up alongside the restaurant and left the engine running, then ran around the far side of the car to let his customers out.

Max tipped the driver generously and agreed on a pick-up time, then extended his arm for his wife to link him.

"Do you fancy a drink next door or should we go straight in and take our seats?" he asked.

"I need food as soon as possible after that drink I had," Sandra said. "I don't want to be talking nonsense to Patsy and Gina or, worse, to Will. I'd never hear the end of it."

They pushed open the doors of the restaurant and Max's heart soared as the noise of knives and forks clattering and stimulating conversation filled his ears and the smell of barbecued steak and fresh fried onions warmed his insides.

He was back. Max Kelly was back at last.

34

Gina ushers me with the rest of the head staff into the staff room shortly before Max and Sandra arrive.

"Give us half an hour to order our drinks and get settled," she says, "and then we'll eat as the rest of the clientele leave. I've set Table Ten upstairs as it's the furthest and most secluded. Jason is in charge and will start proceedings when I give him the nod, Beth and Anton will follow and take our orders. Hollie, you can stay here and relax and Jason will give you your entrance cue around dessert time. Thanks everyone for all your discretion and professionalism. I do appreciate it, as does Will. This means a lot to me. Good luck."

She winks across to where I sit in the corner of the staff room, feeling like a nervous wreck. Could this man, who they were treating as some kind of hero, really be a reformed monster? Could it really be that he didn't deserve this princely treatment from anyone?

"Are you really terrified? 'Cos I am," said Beth and I nod, chewing the inside of my jaw.

"I'll be fine," I say. "Don't know what all the fuss is about, really. If you all weren't acting like it was the Second Coming it might help us calm down, you know."

My nerves make me snappy. I don't mean to be.

"But it is quite an honour, isn't it?" says Beth. "I mean, when I first moved here and started my university course, all my friends told me that this was the place to earn a few quid and meet all the best contacts if you want to be an actress. They said that if you impress Max Kelly, and very few do, then you are sure to get up at least one rung on the ladder. The man knows everyone in the business and they all adore him."

"So it seems," I say. "Look, I think I'll go practise. Take my mind off things."

I fetch my violin and walk into an adjoining room that Gina had shown me earlier. It is a meeting room of sorts but it doesn't look like it has been used much. A small table and four chairs sit to one side and apart from a water font, a few trade magazines and a plant, there isn't much else to see. What I do notice, though, is a window with wooden Venetian blinds that looks straight across the restaurant floor with a bird's-eye view of Table Ten.

I peer out through it, terrified of being caught, and I draw a sharp breath because right at this very moment, Max Kelly and his gorgeous wife are taking their seats. It's him at last. It's really him.

"Wow, this is splendid," said Patsy Langdon, taking her seat between Will and Max. "Sandra, darling, you look amazing! We should do this more often. We really should."

"I know! Isn't Gina just the best?" said Sandra. "You've gone to such an effort arranging all this at such short notice, Gina."

"It's what I do," said Gina, taking her seat. "I've had plenty of practice, believe me."

"But you're still the best," said Max and Gina blushed. She was more than pleased with her efforts though. Her timing was impeccable and the table looked delightful with its tasteful candle arrangements and gleaming silverware. She really had pulled out all the stops.

"I thought it would be best if we ate late so we can have at least this area to ourselves in a little while," she said. "I think it will do us all good to spend some relaxed, social time together. Things have been quite tense around here of late so it will be nice to let our hair down together for a change."

"I'll drink to that," said Will, raising a glass. "To the future!"

"To the future!" said the dinner party and they put their glasses together then relaxed into friendly conversation.

I watch through the window from the meeting room and my face falls into a frown.

"To the future!" I mime. My mother has no future because of that man and his repulsive past. Now that I have seen him in the flesh, my determination returns and my insides once again turn sour. Singh didn't have a good word to say about him. Just because he has transformed into a smarmy Mr Popular doesn't change his early days.

I check the door is locked and I slip off my jeans and uniform vest top, then let my new black dress fall over my head, across my shoulders and over my body till it skims my hips and settles into a tapered edge below my knees. I spray some extra perfume on my wrists and put on another sweep of rich red lipstick which I know looks striking in contrast to my lightly bleached blonde hair. Then I slip out of the meeting room, down the spiral staircase and order a double vodka and a tiny dash of lemonade from Emmett at the bar.

"Steady on, Hollie," says Emmett when I sink the drink in one. "It's not that bad. He won't bite. Well, maybe he would bite you. I would."

"I'll take that as a compliment?" I hold out my glass for a refill. "Now hurry up and get me another. My nerves are frazzled and Gina will murder me if I'm seen downing some Dutch courage."

"Your secret is safe with me, honey," says Emmett and I pay him for the drink and take it back upstairs with me.

I sneak back into the meeting room and sink most of the contents of my glass, letting the alcohol warm my insides and settle my knotting stomach. I have never been good at controlling my nerves. Even though I have performed as a soloist and as part of a recital group in front of hundreds, I always suffer pre-stage jitters. This is only an informal background performance for an audience of six, most of whom probably won't even know if I hit a bum note or not, yet it is probably the most nerve-racking audience I will ever play in front of.

"Oh my word, he is so sexy!" says Beth, fanning her face with a napkin.

She catches me unawares and I scramble to hide the dregs of my drink.

"You think?" I say.

"Oh, I don't think it. I know it. They've just started their main course and he said I was doing a great job. Imagine! He spoke directly to me. I swear I heard Gina telling him my name and that I was an actress and he said he'd remember it. You should see the way he looks at you. It's like you're the only person in the room!"

"You really have it bad," I say, hoping that I haven't overdone it on the alcohol stakes as the room gives a light spin. I hear my phone ring from my handbag but, without checking who the caller is, I switch it off and put it away again.

"So are you all ready?" asks Beth. "I really wish I could play a musical instrument. I always wanted to play the piano and it's one of my all-time regrets. Can you play the piano?"

I open my mouth to answer but I'm interrupted by Jason, the head waiter, who looks flustered when he comes into the room.

"Five minutes," he says. "Are you okay?"

"Yes," I say and try to look cool. "I don't know what all the fuss is about. You two are acting like it's an audience with the Pope. He's not all *that* important."

My insides are doing somersaults and the excitement of my colleagues isn't helping. Beth and Jason glance at each other and then laugh.

"Oh yes, he is," says Jason and he fixes his white towel

over his forearm. "Be assured that around here he is. I'll call you when they're ready."

"So far, so good," whispered Gina to Will who sat to her left. Max was in fine form and the subject of his time in Blessington had been politely avoided.

"You are a genius, Gina," said Will under his breath. "Gina the Genius! This was the best idea you have come up with in a long time. Look at him. He's the old Max we loved and adored back in the day. And Sandra looks serene too. I'm so glad we did this."

"Me too," said Gina, dabbing the sides of her mouth with her napkin.

Max was commanding the table with stories of days gone by and the rough and tumble start to Blue Heaven. Gina was dying to hear when he planned to take up his position in the kitchen again but one step at a time was as much as she could expect from him. He really had made good use of his week away and he looked refreshed and content and the way he looked at Sandra showed a new spark of life in their marriage. She made a mental note to congratulate her staff on their excellent but unobtrusive manner, then thought of Hollie waiting in the wings with her violin. This would truly be the icing on the cake.

"Compliments to the chef," said Max, and the whole party laughed aloud. "The duck was truly delicious and if the crème brûlée is of the same standard, then I needn't worry about rushing back to work. And of course the service was excellent as always. Great job, Jason."

Jason beamed and Gina's heart swelled with pride. The

waiter then met Gina's eye and she gave him the nod to show Hollie out to her position.

"I hope you don't mind, but I have arranged some background music during our dessert," she said.

The top floor of the restaurant had cleared and they now had the place to themselves. Gina knew how Max loved to digest his food in comfort and she hoped that she hadn't overdone it with the live musician.

"Wow, you really are spoiling me," said Max. "I'm not sure if I deserve all of this after what I've put you through lately."

Gina watched as Patsy and Sandra's heads dropped at the mere hint of Max's recent state of mind but Will came to the rescue.

"We all have our crosses to bear," he said. "We all have our skeletons, our ghosts that come and haunt us and we are adult enough to know that sometimes life can be a tough old bitch. The most important thing, though, is our determination to kick back on the bad times and stay in touch with what is really good for us. You are good for us, Max. You are good for this place, you are good for us as people. Welcome back, old buddy. We've missed you."

At that, the first notes of Beethoven's "Für Elise" sounded and Gina smiled from ear to ear as she watched Hollie. The table party applauded and Max looked thoroughly impressed. He had his back to Hollie, who stood under a soft light in the opposite corner of the room and he turned around in his chair to get a better view.

Hollie looked amazing. Her blonde hair tumbled across her shoulders and her silhouette cut a dash as the violin hummed out its velvet tune. From where she stood, it was hard to make out her features but Gina noticed for the first time how beautiful she was and she knew that Max would be smitten. Hollie the waitress would have absolutely no problem getting a glowing review from Max Kelly.

My heart. Oh my God, my heart is thumping and my hands shake as I move the bow across the strings. I have my eyes closed and I wonder has he noticed me yet. I sense them staring at me and my legs feel weak as the first tune comes to an end.

I open my eyes and step into a stronger light as they applaud and then I see him and our eyes lock. He blinks once or twice and then glances around the company, watching them watch his every reaction. He doesn't speak.

And so I play on . . .

Max clutched his napkin into a ball and shifted in his seat. His mouth was dry and his skin ran cold at the sight before him. He knew they were waiting for his approval but he couldn't move. He wondered was his heart still beating as his vision blurred and everything around him went silent. He couldn't hear the music or the applause or the whispers at the table. He wasn't in the restaurant any more. He was back in time and Estelle was in front of him, full of life and energy and beauty and when she moved closer to the table he could only hear himself breathe in short pants and he held his hand to his chest.

"Max?" Gina's voice was like a fog in the distance. "Max, you don't look well. What's the matter?"

231

"Max, are you okay?" whispered Sandra and pulled him round to face her but he shook his head and turned his back on her again, staring at the vision across the room.

She was beautiful. More beautiful than he could ever have imagined and he knew right then that Estelle had no intention of letting him lay her ghost to rest.

He didn't realise that he was crying. He was so sorry.

I cannot close my eyes as I play now. My fingers have taken on a life of their own as if on autopilot and I can no longer hear a note I am playing. He is staring at me and I am locked in his gaze, a mixture of emotions racing through my veins.

He looks terrified, meek and not like the powerful heart-throb that everyone has made him out to be. My presence is having the effect I had wished for. He can see Estelle in me. I know it.

Yet I can't take my eyes off him, nor he from me and as I play "Ave Maria" I am sure that he is as deaf to the sounds of the violin as I am. I play faster and faster and my breathing becomes shorter and quicker and then I hear Gina calling my name and I drop my bow to the floor.

"Thank you!" says Gina, standing up from the table and I now realise that she has been asking me to stop for some time. "That will be all, Hollie. You can go now."

The group gives a light applause as I bend down to lift my bow from the floor. I breathe in, trying to think of something to say but I cannot find the words. My mind is blank and I search and search for the conversation I had rehearsed for days now. My anger has turned to a numb emptiness and I know I have been crying as I played and to my surprise so has Max Kelly. I have never experienced a moment so intense, so surreal, yet I have to escape.

I turn away from Max Kelly and make my way back into the meeting room where I find the remainder of my vodka which I down with trembling hands. I have to get out of here now.

"We will have dessert now, Jason," said Gina quietly and Max turned back to face his company, his face waxy and sullen.

Will excused himself from the table and Gina looked across at Sandra who was glancing from Max to the others and back to Max, unsure of how to react to the bizarre scene which had unfolded.

"Who was the girl?" said Sandra eventually, staring now at the flickering candle in the centre of the table. "Who the hell is she, Gina? Or should I ask my husband?"

"I have never seen her before in my life," said Max. "So I will ask the same question. Who is she?"

"Her . . . her name is Hollie," said Gina.

"Hollie who?"

"I don't know."

"What do you mean, you don't know? You hired a violinist without knowing her name? Don't you have her card or her details anywhere?"

Max's tone sounded edgy and aggressive and Gina had never heard him speak to her in such a tone before.

"I . . . she works here. I hired her on Friday but –"

"You hired her but you don't know her name?"

"Not her full name, but I'm sure it's on file –"

"Well, go and get it then. Go and get her name and tell me who she is."

Sandra put her hand on Max's forearm and hushed him, realising that Jason was behind them with the dessert tray.

"I'm sure Gina has all the appropriate information in the office," she said. "There really is no need for your overreaction, darling."

Max was in a different world, unable to let the subject go. He didn't care about dessert; he didn't care about his overreaction. He wanted to know all about this girl and he wanted to know it now.

"I'll go and ask her myself then, shall I?" he said and got up from the table, marched across the room and burst open the door to the room labelled "Staff Only".

"Hollie!" he shouted. "Hollie, where are you?"

"She's gone," said Will from behind him. "I went after her, got as far as the car park but it seems like she just fled. What the hell is going on now, Max?"

Max turned around to face his partner and held his face in his hands.

"It was . . . it was just like her. She won't go away, Will," he said, shaking his head. "No matter how hard I try to forget, Estelle just won't go away."

35

I push open the door of the bed and breakfast and run up the stairs, my legs weak under the weight of my violin and my bag of belongings. I am still in my dress and heels but I have no time to change. I grab my clothes from the floor and stuff them with the rest of what I own into my bag. Is that everything? I really have to go! I remember my phone charger which is still plugged into the wall, so I pull it out and stuff it into my handbag. I have to get home. I have to get home. I pull the door closed behind me and race down the stairs of the place that had become my secret home for the past two nights. I ring the bell at the desk for assistance, then I ring it again and again. Please hurry!

"I need to check out now," I say to the elderly man who shuffles into the hallway, looking like I've disturbed him from his sleep.

"Now?" he grumbles, moving behind the counter. "It's almost midnight. I'll have to charge you for tonight."

"That's fine. Here."

I throw him my key and he slowly adds up what I owe and I long to just give him what I have in my purse and call it quits, but he gives me a total and I pay in cash then run out through the door.

My hands are shaking so much I can hardly get the key into the ignition. Please, come on! I need to call Ben. I need to call Caroline. I reach into my bag to find my phone and I switch it on, and then turn my attention back to starting the car.

A knock on the window makes me scream. It's him! Oh my God, he has followed me!

"No!" I scream. "Please don't hurt me!"

"What the hell do you want from me?" he yells through the window.

I check that the doors are locked and my hands are shaking so hard.

"Who are you and what do you want from me?" he yells.

He glares at me through the passenger-side window as another man tries to calm him down on the pavement. It's his business partner, I think. Jesus, they have followed me!

I can't breathe. I put the car into gear and put my foot to the floor, steering out onto the street without checking it is safe. The tyres screech and I race along the busy street, afraid to look in my rear-view mirror in case he is behind me.

What the hell have I been thinking? The man is a lunatic. He raped my mother for Christ's sake. Or did he? Yes, he did! Jesus, I am so confused right now. All of my bravado is left behind me and I just want to be home with

Ben and Caroline and Ronan and forget all about Max Kelly.

I reach across to the passenger seat where my phone lies. I need Ben. I need normality. Ben answers within seconds, which is more than I deserve considering the string of missed calls I have from him in my call log.

"Ben!" I sob. "I'm driving out of Dublin. Everything has backfired – I just want to get home!"

"Hollie, what have you done? What the hell are you playing at?"

At the sound of his voice, I burst into tears and I can barely see out through the windscreen but I am too afraid to stop. "I just want to come home, Ben. I've been so stupid."

"Tell me exactly where you are. Ronan and I are just outside Dublin. We've been trying to reach you all day! We had this terrible feeling you had gone to confront Max Kelly and when we couldn't get you we just had to come and see if you were okay."

"I'm sorry. I don't know what I was thinking. I can't stop. He might be following me."

"Who? Hollie, you're freaking me out right now! Who might be following you? Max Kelly?"

"Yes! Max Kelly!"

"Hollie – pull into the next service station and find out its address and we'll be with you as quickly as we can. Okay?"

"Okay."

I pass two service stations before I have the courage to stop. My hands are still trembling as I park as near to the shop door as I can get, then I run inside and ask for its address, all the time checking out through its window in case they have kept up with me this far.

"Everything all right, Miss?" asks the shop assistant but I don't answer. I run back outside, get into the car, lock the doors and I wait.

Max sat in the car outside Blue Heaven with Will, wishing his partner would give it a rest. He knew he shouldn't have followed her. He knew he could have lost his licence for driving under the influence and he knew he should have listened to Will who'd felt he had no choice but to accompany him, in case his actions with the strange girl got out of hand. But most of all, he knew that he would have a hell of a lot of explaining to do when he went back inside.

"Just tell me I'm not going insane," he said to Will who was now urging him to come into the restaurant and try to mend things before it was too late. "Tell me I'm not imagining things. Jesus!"

He punched the dashboard and put his head down on the steering wheel, questioning his sanity and hoping he had just overreacted to what had happened.

"You're freaking me out, that's for sure," said Will. "I can't make sense of it all when you won't tell me exactly what's going on."

"I *told* you what's going on!" yelled Max. "I told you why I reacted like that!"

A fresh wave of panic engulfed him and he jumped from the car and ran back inside with Will following close behind.

"This is such a mess," he said, taking the stairs two at

a time. "Such a fucking mess. How the hell do I explain this to Sandra?"

"Sandra's gone," said Gina who was standing at the top of the stairs. "She left in a taxi a few minutes ago. She's in pieces, Max. In pieces. What the hell . . . ?"

Max put his hand on his forehead. "I'll tell you what the hell!" he roared. "Your violinist nearly gave me a fucking heart attack, that's what the hell! So much for moving on, huh! So much for forgetting the fucking past and for inner peace and so much for fucking happy families! What the hell do I have to do to move on from this? Tell me!"

He pushed past her and swept a centrepiece from a nearby table onto the floor as the two waiting staff watched all agog. Gina noticed them and shooed them into the staff room while Patsy Langdon began to clear up the mess.

Max was seated now, but his breathing was unsteady and it seemed his outburst had only started. But instead of shouting and raising his temper again, he put his head into his hands and sobbed like a baby.

"What do I have to do?" he cried. "Tell me and I'll do it. She follows me. Everywhere I go, everything I do she is there. On the street, on a bus, in Church, at home . . . even when I look at Sandra I sometimes think it's her. She's dead but she's still here."

Will and Gina shared a glance and Gina pulled out a chair beside Max and put a hand gently on his arm. "It was just a girl playing a violin, Max," she said. "How can you get so upset by it? Do you know her?"

"It wasn't just a girl playing a violin. It wasn't just any girl . . ."

"Then who was it?" said Gina. "Who is this Hollie Murphy?"

Max shook his head. "I don't know."

"Look, buddy, maybe you need more help," said Will. "We can get you the best therapists out there if that's what you need. I know a guy who –"

"I don't need a fucking therapist," Max said, blowing his nose into a tissue. "I saw her with my own two eyes! I need to lay her ghost to rest once and for all. I need to find that girl. I need to know why she came here, why she –"

"Max, stop it now! This is ridiculous! It's bloody ridiculous!" said Will. "Pull yourself together, man. Stop with all this crazy shit about laying ghosts to rest and go home to your wife and family who need you! I've had enough. I've tried to help you but you won't help yourself. Come on, Patsy. We have a baby-sitter to drop home."

Patsy and Will left the restaurant and Gina fetched Max a large brandy to try and settle his nerves. She sent the remaining waiting staff home and poured a drink for herself – a long cool white-wine spritzer which she hoped would take the edge off the tension headache. Max looked pitiful and her heart bled for him, whatever his issue with Hollie was. He had been good to her down the years. When her husband left her and she had no one to turn to he had been a friend. When her son got into trouble with the cops he had given him a man-to-man talk that probably saved his life. When she lost the baby she was having with her last boyfriend, he sent her flowers and gave her extra time off to grieve. Now, as extreme as his reaction to the girl with the violin had been, he desperately needed a friend and Gina was more than happy to return the favour.

"I have a confession to make," said Gina. She had poured them an extra drink each and was just taking her seat again.

"Go on," Max said.

"The girl, Hollie . . . she didn't come here for a job. She came here to see you."

Max gripped the glass in his left hand and his face crumpled again. "What? What did she say?"

"I . . . I had asked the temping agency to send over some relief staff and when she arrived the place was so busy I just assumed that's who she was. She asked one of the staff for you but when I came down to her and talked her through the procedures etcetera, she just played along. To cover up my mistake, I said I'd let her play tonight for you. She said she was a musician just trying to get a break and she heard you could help. Maybe that was a lie too."

The look on Max's face changed from disbelief to relief and back to surprise and shock again.

"Oh my God," he said, and then he repeated in a whisper. "Oh, my good God. What does she know? Please tell me she doesn't know what I've done!"

Ronan and Ben arrive at the service station and pull up alongside my car. I am huddled in the front seat, my jacket pulled up under my chin and I have never been so frightened in all of my life.

"Take me home," I whisper when they open my car door. "Please, Ben. Take me home."

I reach out and Ben holds me close, allowing my limp body to sink into his and he rubs my head as Ronan looks on.

"Never, ever take off like that again, you maniac!" says Ben.

"I'm so sorry to have worried you all. I'm in a daze at the moment and I don't think I could have driven much further. I'm scared. I'm so scared."

They ushered me into the passenger seat of my car and Ben slips into the driver's side, having agreed to meet Ronan back in Belfast.

Our journey up north is spent mostly in silence apart from the low hum of Classic FM and the noise of the motorway. I sleep for a while and reach out for Ben's hand when I wake up, wanting to feel his touch and to know that he is beside me.

I don't tell him about my temporary job at the restaurant or how I befriended Gina to get a meeting with Max or how I ran out when the intensity of being in the same room as him was too much to bear.

Ben doesn't question me and I don't offer the information and the warmth of the car and the relaxing journey settle me, but every now and again I look behind us and Ben hushes me and tells me that he is here now and that I am safe.

I see lights on in my apartment in Belfast and Caroline's car is parked outside. Ronan has beaten us to it and is there too and I am weary at the thought of explaining it all to them. I am exhausted, physically and emotionally. I am drained.

"He definitely did it," I whisper.

Ben looks straight ahead and then when he finds a parking space he turns to me, his voice gentle but firm.

"Let it go," he says. "You have got to let this go or it's

going to eat at you for the rest of your life. It will ruin you. It's already ruining you."

"I don't think I can," I tell him and I take my keys from him and open my front door, feeling far away enough from Blue Heaven and Max Kelly to feel safe, but a tiny step closer to the truth.

By the time Max came home Sandra had fallen asleep on the settee. It was almost four in the morning and she mustn't have heard the taxi leave him off. He watched her sleep, her blonde hair tucked behind her ear and her make-up that had been so carefully applied now streaked from her tears. She was grasping the phone in her right hand and an empty glass of wine stood by her side. At that moment he wanted to lean over and kiss her and wipe away the memories of what had turned out to be possibly the most horrible evening in the history of their marriage.

"I'm so sorry," he whispered and he fetched a blanket from the hot press and laid it over her. She was still in her evening dress and still wearing her earrings but he knew if he woke her up, there would be an unmerciful row and he didn't want his boys to hear them argue.

He switched off the lights and tiptoed up the stairs, a sick empty feeling flurrying in his stomach. Gina had been so kind to sit with him and he was glad she had come clean about how Hollie came to be in the restaurant, plus it reassured him that his mind wasn't playing tricks on him. In fact, it made him realise that what he had feared for years and years was true after all.

He stopped at Charlie's bedroom and peeked in to

where his eldest boy slept soundly, the low hum of a radio in the corner still playing late-night tunes. Max crept across the room and switched it off, then pulled the covers up around his son and closed the door tight.

Josh's bedroom was further down and he checked in on him too, realising that if he told Sandra the truth he wouldn't have the luxury of seeing his sons sleep very often.

Josh had left a night-light on and Max sat on the edge of his bed watching his face, the picture of innocence lost in dreams so far from reality. He felt like his heart was going to break in pieces when he thought of what was ahead. Sandra would never forgive him for tonight. She was humiliated in front of Will and Patsy and Gina and was probably convinced by his desperate reaction that Max was having an affair with the young violinist.

He really felt like ending it all. Estelle couldn't live with the memory and neither could he. Perhaps that was a way out, but that would be worse on his family than having them live through it – or would it? He pushed such thoughts out of his mind and watched Josh's eyelashes flutter as he slept. How could he even contemplate inflicting such pain on his children? He would be a man and face up to his mistakes if it came to the crunch.

"Daddy?" said Josh, still half asleep as he turned on his other side. "Did you have a nice night?"

Max felt like he was choking. He couldn't find words for a reply.

"Did Mummy look pretty?" asked Josh, a little more awake now.

"Yes, Mummy looked very pretty. She always looks

pretty," said Max. "Now you go back to sleep, little man. You just go back to sleep."

I can't sleep. I have tossed and turned in bed for hours now and Ben's wise words, not to mention Caroline's disgust at my behaviour are ringing in my ears.

"You have no idea how worried we have been," she said. "You can't just take off like that, Hollie. I thought . . . I really thought . . . you had . . ."

"I wouldn't do that," I told her defiantly. "My God, I know too well the mess it leaves behind. I know I was stupid and selfish but there is something about him. He followed me to my car. He followed me!"

Caroline did not want to know. I think her anger at my lies and how I had ignored all her advice has blinded her to anything else I have to say. She is staying with me tonight but I don't want to be here in Belfast. I want to go back to the cottage on the coast where my memories are and I want to close the door and leave them all to get on with their own lives and let me continue what I need to do to live mine.

I can't think of my next steps. I can't really see past the next stage.

In a perverted way, I want to see him again already. He scared me, he really did, but I want more. Am I wrong?

36

Ronan wakes me before eight with breakfast on a tray. I have eaten nothing more than a few sandwiches for days and his kindness brings me back to when I was little and my mum would surprise me on days off school with a similar scene.

I can still see her, popping her head round the door, the tray wobbling in her hands, and she would sit with me, cherishing every moment of watching me eat what she had prepared. It made her heart sing, she would say and then she would cry again.

Funny I am only remembering her tears now. She must have been so alone, so frightened. I would ask her what was wrong and she always said it was because she was so happy but she wasn't. Of course she wasn't. I know that now.

"I can't believe I've caused such a fuss," I say to Ronan when I accept his offerings. "And I don't really deserve any special treatment, do I?"

Ronan sits on the edge of my bed and shakes his head.

"Probably not," he says, "but you know I'm a soft touch where you are concerned."

I want to hug him. He really is one in a million and Caroline is so lucky to have him.

"Oh, I get it now . . . this is a bribe to get me back to work?" I say playfully as I take a sip of tea. "You know me too well. Feed me and I'm yours."

He laughs but it is a distant laugh. His eyes are sad as if he is remembering the past.

"Suppose you could say it is," he says. "Well, I'll leave you to it. Some of us have work to do. Catch you later."

"Thanks, Ro," I call but he is already gone and I hear him bid Caroline goodbye and the apartment door close behind him.

It is silent now.

I wonder if Caroline has gone too? She must be due at work in the boutique soon. I imagine I am alone in the apartment but then I hear the hum of a vacuum cleaner and the faint sound of the radio from the sitting room and realise that she hasn't left me yet.

She is so like my mother it hurts sometimes and I know she is trying her best to be firm with me but still be a friend. I know also in my heart that everything she does for me and everything she says to me is for the very best. But, apart from Ben, she is the only one I can scream and cry to. She is a gentle soul with strong beliefs and I cannot deny her loyalty and how she has adjusted her own lifestyle lately to make sure mine gets back on track, yet she is suffering this loss on an equal level. I owe her more than I will ever be able to give back and as much as she irritates me with her words of wisdom, I hope she knows how much I appreciate her right now.

I savour the warmth of the tea and toast, in dread of Caroline's inevitable demands for me to get out of bed. She made no bones about it last night as to what her plans are for me to get my life back on track, with a to-do list which included getting my butt back to work, locking the diary away and either make it or break it with Ben (as if I have the choice on that one). She even went so far as to quote the Bible to me and after the journey from Dublin and all the demons in my head I wanted to scream at her to get out of my face.

"There is a time to mourn," she'd said piously, "but there is also a time to cast away stones. Now is your time to cast away stones and learn to dance again, Hollie. I just want to see you dance again."

She cried of course as she said it, even though her anger was bursting from beneath her very skin and when Ronan comforted her I felt betrayed by him. He was supposed to be on my side. He was always on my side. Christ, but I feel like a child in a playground right now with all these immature thoughts amongst such heightened emotions.

The knock comes to the door as I had predicted and Caroline comes into my bedroom. It is a very different scene to my room back at White Rock. Where the cottage is floral and cosy with heavy duvets and curtains, my bedroom here in the apartment is cool cream with plain coffee-coloured walls, plain beige carpets, white wooden doors, clean lines and matching blinds – a much more modern setting. A photo of Ben and me on holiday and a simple vase of fake red dahlias sit on my bedside locker and my wardrobes are neat and tidy. I love this apartment but right now I love the cottage more and the longing in my heart to go there is overwhelming.

"I've given the place a general tidy round so you needn't worry about cleaning," says Caroline.

"Thanks. You didn't have to."

I want to go to the cottage. I want to go back to the sea air and Jinx and my memories and I want to hide away from everyone and think about what I need to do next.

"Now, what are your plans for today?" she asks.

I don't answer. I am planning my escape. I need to get out of here. I can't go back to work yet. I have still so many questions.

"Hollie?"

When she leaves for work I can go. Even just for a few hours. I can think better there. Everything will be clearer in my mind when I am back in the cottage.

"Hollie, will you answer me?"

"What? Sorry. My plans . . . em, not too sure."

"Ronan and I have been talking. Hollie, we think you need some counselling to help you get through this."

"Counselling?"

"Yes. We feel you need some bereavement counselling to help you deal with things a bit better. You have had such a shock finding Estelle and now all this. I think you need –"

I can't believe I'm hearing this. Counselling? What the hell do I need counselling for? I'm perfectly fine. I know exactly what I'm doing.

"No way."

"Hollie, please listen to me. You're not coping at all. Look at you. Hollie, you ran away to Dublin to seek out a man you know virtually nothing about. You can't seem to think of anything else apart from this Max Kelly character and it's ruining you. You've even given up on Ben."

"What? What are you talking about? Ben gave up on *me*!" I want to scream at her! "He gave up on *me*! My mother gave up on me! I haven't given up on anyone!"

"But *I* won't give up on you, Hollie. I promise I will never give up on you. That's why I'm here. It's why I'll always be here and I'll help you get through this, every step of the way. Tell me you'll think about it at least. Tell me you'll think about talking to someone who can help you more than I can right now."

I sniffle and look away from her and wipe my eyes. "If I could just . . . if I could . . ."

But I don't know. I don't know which way to turn and I don't know what to do. I don't know who I am any more.

37

"I don't want any breakfast!"

"You have to eat something."

"I don't have to do anything."

"I'm just saying . . ."

"Well, don't say anything. What you did last night said it all."

Charlie listened at the kitchen door as his parents argued and he clenched his fists so tight his nails drew blood on the palms of his hands. Things were never going to change. No matter how many times his dad made promises, they would always be broken. It would never get better. Never.

"What's all the shouting about?" asked Josh, still groggy and wearing mismatched pyjamas when he came down the stairs.

"Nothing," said his older brother. "Nothing at all. Why don't you go watch some telly and I'll fix you breakfast."

"Really? Thanks."

Josh made his way to the living room and then stopped to have a listen but Charlie ushered him on through.

The back door slammed and the sound of their father's car started up but neither of the boys mentioned it to each other. But they watched from the window as their father drove away.

"So what do you fancy? Cereal?" asked Charlie.

"Nah, it doesn't matter. I'm not that hungry any more. Thanks anyway, Charlie." Josh flicked on the television and stared at the screen, trying to block out the sounds of his mother crying in the kitchen.

Max drove towards Malahide Marina, pulled in, yanked the handbrake and leaned his head on the steering wheel. He had left the house without his wallet, his mobile and his keys to the restaurant and he had a sick feeling in his stomach which didn't sit well with the pounding headache he had woken up with. This morning's conversation with Sandra doubled with a hangover from too many medicinal brandies the night before was not a healthy recipe.

She said it was over. She said she was humiliated by his behaviour. She said she could never trust him. She said it would never work. She didn't want to know the story. She had heard enough.

"My God!" he said, gripping the steering wheel with both hands. "My God, help me sort this out! What do you want me to do? Tell me and I'll do it!"

It was a glorious day in Malahide and the Marina was busy with yachtsmen preparing to make the most of the sunshine. What had become of him? Where was the confident, fiery chef now? Where was the man who was fully in control? The man people looked up to, admired and envied even? Did he really exist? Or was it all just a smokescreen for the sad, pathetic person he had become?

He had even considered a full confession, was on the verge of telling Sandra the whole thing, every dirty detail but she said she couldn't take any more.

The façade was over and the truth wasn't even out yet. One night of his life. One sorry, stupid, drunken night from years ago had shaped him into the person he had become and he didn't feel sorry for himself at all. It was his problem. It was his fault. And he would have to fix it.

38

I promise Caroline I'll be okay on my own while she is at work. I promise her I'll be right here when she comes back later. I promise her that I'll consider counselling to help me get through this. I promise her everything she wants me to promise and she leaves a little more content than she was earlier.

"We'll get through this," she says. "Just stay calm and focused and we'll get you through this."

But as soon as she leaves the panic sets in again. I feel like the walls are moving in and I can hardly breathe. The minimalist style of the apartment doesn't suit me any more. It is just an empty shell and its clinical feel does nothing for me. I grab a jacket and my phone and I go outside and begin to walk, knowing exactly where I have to go.

It doesn't take as long as I thought it would to reach the park beside Singh's apartments. On a day like today with the sun shining and the clear air, it is a pleasant place to be so I sit on a swing and watch the apartment block as its residents come and go.

It's after eleven now yet some blinds are still closed. The same group of boys kick the same football against the same wall, saying the same chants and calling each other the same names. It is like looking into a different world or watching a reality television show on repeat from where I sit and I am hooked on the basic everyday existence that these people live.

I wonder about the man who comes out to tell the kids to keep the noise down. Is he happy? Does he live alone? Is he in good health? I see a young mum struggle with a toddler and a baby and I worry that she has no one to share her burden with. Where does she find enough money to buy her children clothes and feed them? I wonder when she last treated herself to an evening out or a new outfit or if any of that even matters to her. I wonder about the young couple who walk hand in hand to their car. I hope they are good to each other, and that they appreciate their togetherness and I pray that no one comes between them and ruins their hopes and dreams.

But most of all I wonder what Singh and Maria are doing now. I wonder if Singh is suffering from her illness and if she is thinking of me at all.

I see a man leave their apartment and make his way down the steps and get into a car. He is smartly dressed and I wonder is it her doctor? Or worse, is he an undertaker? Is Singh dead? Oh God, I hope that Maria is coping with the children and my blood runs cold when I think that sooner or later she will have to do it all on her own. She is only sixteen. Perhaps I should go and see her? Maybe I can help?

I untangle myself from the chain of the swing and march towards the apartment block as the man's car zooms off into the distance. The lift is broken so I take the steps, which are much easier to climb on a dry day. I walk along the row of brown wooden doors until I come to the Moshiro home and my hand freezes in mid-air, just before I knock the door.

What am I doing? Oh God, maybe this is all wrong.

I start to pace along the walkway again, back towards the steps, telling myself this is crazy. I don't even know these people, for goodness' sake. Why would they need me? They probably don't want to know me or have anything to do with me.

And then I stop. What if she needs help? What if she feels lonely or tired or if she needs a friend? And then the questions in my head begin again. I want to tell Singh that I found Max Kelly. I want to ask her more about him and tell her that he recognised me and that he followed me to my car and that I worked in his restaurant and that I saw his wife.

I walk back to the door and I knock on it with force, unable to control the urgency to see these people again. I do not have long to wait as I hear footsteps come across the hallway and then the door opens.

"Jesus, do you have to knock so hard! Oh! Oh, it's you . . ."

Maria doesn't look happy to see me. Her hair is untidy and one of her eyes which are always so beautiful is coloured this time by a bruise.

"Maria, what happened? Are you okay?"

"You have to go away, Hollie," she whispers and I hear her little brother call in the background. "It's just a salesperson!" she says to him. "Go and watch TV."

"Really, Maria, are you in trouble? Can I help?"

Maria rolls her eyes and then gives an ironic laugh. "No, Hollie. You most certainly cannot help. Now go. Please go away from here and never come back, I'm begging you."

"But –"

It's too late. She closes the door and when I knock again she doesn't answer. I wait around and look out over Belfast city from the heightened view of the apartment block and I feel more alone than I have ever felt in my whole life. I am like a lost soul, floating around in mid-air, not knowing where I belong or who I belong to. I will go home now, but I don't even know where that is either. Nowhere feels like home to me any more.

39

It drew down dark and Max made his way back to the car having walked around Malahide Castle in a daze, wondering where he should be and what he should be doing to fix the mess that was his life. He felt drunk and dizzy and he was no further on with his plans than when he started out earlier that morning.

Everything seemed hopeless. He was lost and alone.

He started up the engine in his silver Audi Q7 and reversed from his parking space, then drove out of the castle grounds and towards his home with a heavy feeling in his gut.

He pulled up in the drive and walked in through the back door where he found a note on the kitchen table.

He lifted it and his heart wept as he read his son's handwriting.

"Dad. Mum doesn't know I'm writing this, but I wanted to let you know we're just staying in Gran's for

tonight. Just in case you are worried or wondering. See you tomorrow. Josh."

He threw his car keys on the table and walked into the living room where he lay on the sofa and stared at the ceiling until he fell into an unsettled sleep.

At 1 a.m. Max's phone rang and startled him awake. He scrambled to find it and squinted to see who was calling him at this hour, hoping it was Sandra but knowing she would never back down so easily.

It was Will's number.

"Hey, Will, what the –"

He had been dreaming about the girl with the violin as he had done the night before. She was calling him, following him, torturing his mind with her haunting tunes and ghostly features. In the dream she was Estelle. She was not at rest and she didn't want him to be either.

"Max! Max are you there?"

"Yes, sorry, I was asleep. What is it?"

"You have to get down here now! Quickly!"

"What? Where are you?" Max sat up on the sofa, shivering. The temperature had substantially dropped in the night.

"Come right now! The restaurant is on fire! It's blazing here right in front of my eyes. Jesus Christ, Max, I think we're ruined. Blue Heaven is no more. It's burning down here right in front of my eyes."

Max and Will sat in the Garda Station and listened in shock as the Fire Chief – a Mr Brian Doherty – listed possibilities of how the fire at Blue Heaven might have been started. A Garda flanked his side but let the fire expert do the talking. It was why he had been called in after all and the small meeting room of the cop shop seemed somewhat overcrowded with the presence of four grown men who were used to throwing their weight about in their own working environment. It was a dull grey room with nothing in it but a plastic potted plant and a table which had seen better days.

Will and Max sat at one side, with the Garda and the Fire Chief on the other.

"Arson? Jesus, I just don't believe this is happening," said Will.

Max was yet to speak. Instead he sat still, his face pale, with the look of a truly broken man.

"I'm just saying we cannot rule arson out at this stage," said Doherty, a tall, lean man who spoke gently but straight to the point. "It is, after all, the single most common cause of fire in business premises. Corrupt insurance claims, mostly."

Will stood up in anger. "I can assure you, Mr Doherty, that this is most certainly not the case with our restaurant. We run a thriving high-end business, a *respected* business, and in today's economic climate we are proud to say that we have managed to continue to see our profits rise. We have taken great pride in building Blue Heaven to be the fine establishment that it is and we have no reason to scupper its potential and future growth. None whatsoever!"

"If you'd let me finish, Mr Langdon," said Doherty, not changing his cool, calming approach. "I understand your frustration right now and I am merely outlining possibilities as we await the investigator's report. The list is endless aside from the more obvious causes such as an electrical defect or an appliance fault. I have checked and your fire certificates are all up to date."

"Totally up to date," said Will, jutting his chin forward. This waiting around for answers was torturing him, as was Max's unbreakable silence. "We run a clean, efficient operation, Mr Doherty, and this morning I had to contact twelve members of staff to tell them they could stay at home today. This is devastating for us all. We need answers and we need them now."

"And I thank you for your patience, sir," said Mr Doherty. "But I've told you all I can for now. The report should be back by early afternoon and you've done all you can at the minute. Your insurance providers have been made aware of the situation, your staff have been informed and you've given an official statement to the Press for the benefit of your customers' so I'm afraid we'll have to wait until the report comes through before we can do any more. I have contact details for both of you and I assure you that as soon as I know any further detail, I will be in touch immediately."

The Fire Chief stood up and shook both Max and Will's hands, then the Garda walked him to the door, thanking him for his contribution to the investigation.

"Er, Mr Doherty?" Max said and Will did a double take at Max's long overdue input.

Doherty swung around. "Yes?"

"Can I ask you one more thing?"

"Yes. Yes, of course." The silent one speaks, thought Brian Doherty, and he leaned against the doorframe of the grey room.

"You mentioned the possibility of arson . . . but why do you think someone would want to burn down our premises? Is there some sort of psychological profile on people who carry out such attacks? Do they always have a reason?"

Brian Doherty shrugged and rubbed his tired eyes. It had been a long night and he had a feeling there was more to this fire than at least one of the Blue Heaven partners suspected. Max Kelly looked drawn and grey and full of worry. His silence until now spoke volumes.

Doherty stood away from the doorframe and used his arms in an animated way as if it was a well-rehearsed routine.

"Em, well, where do I start? Revenge? Excitement? Thrills? Jealousy? Many arson attacks are not targeted at all – the vast majority are down to opportunistic vandalism."

"You make it sound as if it's impossible to track such people down!" said Will. He could feel his blood pressure rise and he physically tried to keep calm by controlling his breathing patterns. If vandals had deliberately ruined his livelihood and his every dream then he would personally hunt them down and make sure they paid for their actions. "Can't you give us something more precise than that?"

"What do you want?" said Doherty somewhat sharply, at last shifting from his monotone. "Picture profiles?"

"I want to know the kind of person who might have carried out this attack!"

Doherty folded his arms. "I've told you: teenagers for kicks, pyromaniacs for pleasure, thieves to cover their tracks, someone with a grudge – the list goes on."

"Someone with a grudge?" said Will. "You mean we might know the perpetrator?"

"Yes. In that type of case, arson is often committed by

262

someone who is angry but who doesn't know how else to release it. It's this combination that is a catalyst: anger and having no means to express it." He sighed. "But there is no evidence to say it *is* arson as yet. Mr Langdon, Mr Kelly, I think we all need to seriously calm down right now. We must avoid jumping to conclusions. You asked me for possibilities, I'm giving you possibilities."

"Calm down?" said Will, feeling anything but calm. "With all due respect, Mr Doherty, I know that you deal with this on a daily basis and I realise that you see hundreds of people going through this – families, businesses, community buildings burnt to the ground for a million and one reasons and in a million and one ways – but this is our life, the very core of our existence. It's our livelihood, it's how we build a life for our families and now our life is gone and we need to know . . ." Will felt his chest tighten and he swallowed hard, and then continued. "We need to . . . we need . . ."

"Will?"

"Just give me a minute . . . I'm fine. I'm . . ."

Will clutched his chest and leaned on a nearby table and breathed in, out, in, out. The pain seared in his chest now and he felt weak and dizzy. He tried to speak but the words wouldn't come. He tried to signal for help and though he could hear Max talking to him, shouting at him, he had no idea what he was saying. Pain shot down his arm and he tumbled on to the floor.

"Jesus! Will!"

Brian Doherty dropped to his knees where he felt Will's pulse and checked for breathing. "Call an ambulance and tell them it's cardiac arrest," he said to Max. "Quick!"

The Garda made the call while Brian Doherty moved Will into a recovery position and raised his feet off the ground.

Then Max rushed to Will's side. "They're on their way," he said. "Come on, Will, hang in there, buddy! They're on their way."

Max sat in the hospital waiting room. A thousand thoughts ran through his mind about his marriage, a future without Sandra and the children, without Will, without Blue Heaven.

His whole world was in tatters and he could see no hope of finding a way to get back in the driving seat and take control.

He thought of the Fire Chief's words – revenge, jealousy, anger – and the burden of responsibility lay like a heavy stone on his shoulders as he prayed for an accidental reason for the fire at Blue Heaven, but he had a sinking feeling it might have something to do with him.

He remembered how different his life was a year ago. He and Sandra had spent two glorious weeks in the Maldives, chilling out from everyday pressures and switching off from real life back in rainy Dublin. It was their first holiday as a family in over ten years and they had vowed to do it more often and live the lifestyle they deserved to make up for Max's long unsociable hours at the restaurant.

The boys had glowed from the time away from home and he had never seen Charlie, who was then sixteen, as content as he was back then as he entertained his younger brother and eyed up girls his age on the beach.

That's how life should be, he thought now. That was a
time when he had it all figured out – to work damn hard
but remember to take time out and prioritise so that the
important things, the really important things, take first
place. Their happy family mode lasted until Christmas
that year and then Max fell into his old habits of working
all hours, of feeling stressed and tired when he got home,
of losing touch with his family's wants and needs and of
their everyday existence. He and Sandra gradually grew
apart as he neglected to make time for her and the boys
and he became nestled in his old cocoon of working and
sleeping all week round.

And then he heard of Estelle Lynch's death and after
that his life had become a living hell.

He would never forget the day he got the phone call
from an old acquaintance back home up North. He
refused to call the man a friend. He was never his friend.
He had spent time with him, yes, back then but they had
been young and stupid and always drunk. Yes, very, very
drunk and always high as kites on drugs too but even that
didn't excuse their sordid actions.

He had been at work when the call came through on
the restaurant's office line. Gina had taken the message to
him in the kitchen but she had no more information apart
from the caller's name and that it was of a personal
nature.

Max had been stunned by the mention of the man's
name. He had never heard from him since those early days
at college and, when he left for America, he tried not to
think of him again and was glad to escape from his filthy
circle.

"Well, isn't this a blast from the past?" the caller had said with a cackle. "Checked you out and can't believe the big-time hot-shot you turned out to be! How the hell did you turn away from the dark side, Kelly?"

Max had glanced around the office helplessly and Gina, realising that this was indeed of a personal nature, had left him in privacy to hear what the man had to say. Max felt like a young boy who was pinned against the fence by the most notorious school bully.

"It's none of your business what I get up to. Now why the call? What the hell makes you look me up after all this time?"

The man snorted and cleared his throat and Max remembered this as an old habit and it disgusted him as much now as it did back then.

"Well, all this time I've been thinking you were still in the States and that you'd left this homeland forever. But then, like a blast from the past, I happened to come across some posh magazine with your name plastered all over it. Couldn't believe my fuckin' eyes! 'Max Kelly is now the dog's balls! He is the man!' I said to the missus. We had a right laugh!"

"So, is this a congratulatory call?" asked Max. "Or are you just curious? Maybe you're looking for some business advice?"

Max didn't have time for this shit. He had a restaurant to run and he didn't want to hear from ghosts of the past after spending almost thirty years avoiding them.

"Stuff your business advice, young Kelly!" said the man and Max heard him clear his throat again, then spit on the other end of the line. "I'm calling with news on an old *mutual* friend of ours, if that's what you'd like to call her. Yes, I think this lady was fairly mutual."

Max hoped he didn't say her name. He could feel his heart-rate build and his skin went cold. He didn't want to hear her name. He hadn't heard her name mentioned by anyone in years and he wanted to keep it that way.

"What's that sound, Max?" said the man on the phone. "What's that sound? Is that you shaking or are the bones from the skeletons in the closet threatening to come out? They're coming to get you! *Boo!*"

He gave a raucous dirty laugh and Max wanted to hang up but he didn't want this bully to get the better of him. He didn't want to hear Estelle's name again from such circles but he needed to know what had happened to her.

"Just cut the crap and tell me! Tell me what has happened to her."

"It's not crap, Max. She wasn't the crap at the time, was she? I remember you, Max. Dripping with guilt, threatening to tell all to the police, to come clean! You stupid bastard. You could have ruined us all! You could have had us all locked up, you fucking asshole!"

"But we were in the wrong! You know we were! I've never forgiven myself for what happened that night. Maybe you don't give a shit but do you know how much I've thought about it since? Do you? Every fucking night, that's how much! Every night and every day! She has never left my mind!"

The man guffawed. "Well, worry no more, Mr Michelin Star Chef with your glossy magazine photos and your fancy house and fancy wife and fancy lifestyle! What would they all say if they knew your dirty secrets? Your dirty, rotten past!"

"Don't you dare threaten me, you bastard! Don't you fucking dare!"

"That's the thing, Max, old chum. I'm calling to save you. I'm calling to ease your poor, guilt-ridden conscience. Your secret has gone to the grave. It's finally gone!"

"What? What are you talking about?"

Gina came back into the office and, on seeing Max's face and his pose and how he gripped the phone so hard his knuckles were white, she left again.

"Well, you know young Pete kicked the bucket a long time ago and he was the only other one who knew, but he was never going to squeal anyway. But now . . . now the main concern is now gone too. The bird herself has flown the nest."

"Estelle? Estelle is dead?" Max sat down on the office chair and his face went pale.

"She sure is. She's dead as a doornail! Kicked the bucket! So our fears are over at long last, Max. Our secret is safe. The wolf in chef's clothing can cook at peace and the world of celebrity can breathe out and eat happily at their favourite fancy restaurant."

Max loosened his Le Chef white jacket and dropped the phone to his side. She was dead. Oh my God, she was dead. His head spun and he put the phone to his ear again.

"How?" he asked. "How did she die?"

He pictured her face on the occasions he had followed her. She was always forlorn, so sad and troubled, and he hoped that her death had not been too painful after all she had suffered in her younger years.

"A DIY job," said his informant. "She did it all by herself."

"Suicide?"

"Suicide. You got it in one. So, on that note, I'll let you get back to the heat of the kitchen with your new cleaner conscience and who knows, maybe someday I'll visit this wonderful Blue Heaven of yours to see what all the fuss is about? Isn't it funny, how you ended up in 'heaven' and Estelle must have still lived in hell?"

Max stuttered but he couldn't find an answer and the man rambled on.

"Good name for the joint, though. I like a good steak and so does the missus. It's a long time since I gave her a treat so it might earn me some brownie points? Or maybe riff-raff like me would be refused entry? Would we? Would we be allowed a slice of your heaven, Max?"

Max still didn't answer him.

"Ah come on, say something! Are old friends welcome in your big posh place in Dublin or is it only for reformed offenders?"

"Stay away!" said Max. "Don't you or any of your kind dare come near me or my restaurant! Just stay away from me and never call here again! Never!"

He hung up the phone and leaned back in the chair, perspiration bubbling on his forehead and trickling down the back of his neck. He didn't feel relieved at all at the news of Estelle's death. How could he? How could his conscience be cleared just because she was gone from this life? She had taken her own life. And by doing so she had taken his life too.

40

I am going back to work on Monday, or so I'm told. I'm now under strict orders from Caroline and she has even drawn out a timetable of milestones for me to adhere to and, I have to say, having something to aim for is comforting and makes me feel a lot more secure.

The apartment seems cosier too and I've made a real effort today, rearranging furniture, watering plants and I even hung a few pictures with Ronan's help when he called in for coffee earlier this afternoon.

His delight at my return to work is so obvious and I can sense he is as happy for Caroline as he is for me that there seems to be a focus and a way forward that doesn't involve my mother's turbulent past.

He brought me some paperwork home today and I am delighted to say that I genuinely can't wait to get stuck in and get lost in the world of my music the way I used to.

I haven't told Ronan or Caroline about my latest visit

to Singh Moshiro's house because I don't want to burst their bubble. They both think they are doing a great job on boosting my progress over the last two days, and they are.

And though I haven't turned my back on any of my investigations into finding my mother's attackers, I have found solace now in planning a routine for the next few days: reading the morning papers over breakfast, watching some chat shows on television and then working on my papers after lunch.

I am tempted to get Ronan to bring Jinx here from the cottage. Of course my apartment is in no way suitable for an animal but he brings life to the place and makes me feel less alone so we'll see how it goes.

I heard from Ben today too and the best news is that he is taking me out for dinner tonight. I turned his offer down at first but he insisted and, when Caroline heard, she brought me a new dress from the boutique in case I might use a lack of fashion as an excuse to refuse to go.

My feelings for Ben have changed over the past few days. Maybe it was my Max Kelly distraction or obsession, if you like, that has made me less needy of his time and attention. I know I have not yet reached any solutions or gained any justice for what happened to my mother, but I now realise that going to Dublin – crazy as it may have been – has given me a tiny bit of closure.

I saw him and he saw me and now he knows that a piece of Estelle Lynch still exists and that what he did to her will never be forgotten.

I know by his reaction that he was one of the three, and the look on his face when he banged on the window of my car with such desperation will not leave my mind. It has even made me wonder: does he know he is my father? Could she have told him? Or, if not him, does he know who is?

I know he is suffering now. I can feel it inside that he is suffering for his actions and it has settled me. But is he suffering enough?

I may never know.

41

It had been a long day at the hospital and with Will hooked up to every type of monitor known to the medical world, Max left the hospital with a heavy heart. For the second day in a row he had no idea where he was going.

He sauntered across the hospital car park and got into the car and waited, trying to decide if he should go home and battle it out once more with Sandra or if he should bite the bullet and look about for another place to live.

The investigator's report had been delayed but at least Will had survived the worst of his heart attack and was now on a long road to recovery. Max didn't know where to turn as far as the future of Blue Heaven was concerned. Will had looked after all the business side of things and without him he would have no idea how to clear up legal and insurance matters, not to mention having Blue Heaven rebuilt.

Perhaps he should consider a temporary relocation? He knew of a few empty premises which were victims of the recession that he could have a look at. Yes, that made sense. He would ask his solicitor to look into that and deal with all insurance matters in order to get Blue Heaven back up and running again. He would show Sandra that he had commitment and loyalty to her and their family's future by doing so. He would do it for his family, for his wife, for Will. He would do for his own sanity.

He started the car with a sense of purpose at last and when his mobile phone rang, he prayed it was the Fire Chief with the investigator's report. With that out of the way, he could at least attempt to get his life back on track.

"Hello, Max Kelly speaking," he said, steering the car into a reverse out of the parking space.

"Max."

It was a woman.

"Hello? Yes, this is Max."

"I'm calling you about . . . about something that happened a very long time ago."

"What?"

"I'm calling you about a lady you once knew . . . a young girl. Do you remember, Max?"

Max put his foot on the brake and knocked the car out of gear in the middle of the car park.

"Who is this?"

Her accent was northern and she sounded quite young and Max felt his blood run cold.

"A girl called Estelle Lynch. What did you do to her? She is dead now because of you."

"Jesus Christ! Who are you? What's going on?"

"She is dead now, Max. And it's all because of you. I hope you are suffering because I am too. I'm suffering and you should be living in hell right now for what you did. I hope you suffer more."

The girl aborted the call and Max tried to get her number to return it or trace it but it had been withheld. She was definitely northern, Belfast probably, but how the hell did she get his number? It had to be the girl at the restaurant.

She was out to torture him. She was determined he would never forget his past.

Then he thought of the call to the restaurant after Estelle's death. Yes! It was *him* behind it. It had to be him, and Max knew exactly where to find him.

He rang directory enquiries and got the number for a bar in Belfast he knew his old "friend" frequented back in the day. His instincts were right and when he asked for him by name he was given his number straight away.

"What the fuck are you doing now?" he said when he heard the man's gravelly greeting. "Are you trying to send me over the edge?"

"It's the Super Chef! I have no idea what you're talking about. What's the problem? Bad dreams again? Nightmares like the old days?"

"Who is she? Who is calling me? What are you trying to do? Invent ghosts to make my life even worse than it already is?"

"Ah, ghosts," said the man. "Funny you should say that 'cos I've heard that one exists all right. Out to scare the bejaysus out of you, I'd imagine. And me too if she's brave enough to find me."

Max hated the bastard even more now than he did thirty years ago. He wouldn't let him mess with his mind like this any longer. He'd had enough of his silly games.

"Don't fill me full of shit about your ghosts! I want to know what you're up to sending lookalikes to my restaurant, making nuisance calls and now my business has been burned to the ground! Just how much of this are you behind? All of it?"

"Whoa, boy! Steady on! I have no idea what you're talking about but I have had reports about a girl sniffing around lately. Do you have a name?"

"What?"

"The girl who visited your restaurant? Do you have a name?"

"Don't play ignorant with me, you dirty bastard. You sent her. You know her name. She gave me a false name, she even got a job here. Clever stuff, buddy. Very clever."

"Max, you have to believe me. I sent no one to you, I made no calls. Now tell me the girl's name, even if it is made up. I think it's in our best interests to know. Both of us."

Max wasn't convinced. "Look, I've told you before to stay away. I have had enough of Estelle Lynch over the past while. I've suffered enough. My penance is done. I've lost my family, I've lost my business, my partner is lying hooked up to a heart machine and most of all I've come close to losing my fucking mind! So you can tell your little Hollie Murphy chick or whatever the fuck her real name is to call it quits now or I'll do something about it!"

Max heard a loud, raspy laugh on the other end of the line.

"That's more like it, old boy. That's the Max I used to love. Now, hold that thought. Get fired up and hold on to your temper and use it so that this bitch, whoever she is, doesn't ruin you any further than she already has. I hope she doesn't come my way. Good luck, Max."

He ended the call and his phone rang again with another withheld number, Max was at the end of his tether. Was it her again?

"What the fuck is it now? What do you want to throw at me now?"

"Mr Kelly?" said a male voice.

"Yes, that's me. Sorry – I thought –"

"Obviously. Mr Brian Doherty asked me to call you directly but I sense this a bad time?"

"Go on."

"It's the Fire Investigation Unit and I'm calling to let you know that the Incident Report from the blaze at your business premises has now been received."

Max didn't want to hear. He couldn't take much more in one day.

But the man talked on. "I can confirm that the attack was malicious and that the fire was rapid and accelerant with multiple origins, and all sites of origin at ground level. It looks like the fire was caused by a flammable liquid such as diesel or petrol and the full report is here for your information. I'm sure you will be in touch."

Max chewed his bottom lip and closed his eyes. "Yes, I'll be in touch," he said, throwing his head back on the headrest of the car. "I'll be in touch."

I instantly regret making the call to Max Kelly. I know I've broken every rule I set out for myself with Caroline when she was trying her best to help me move on from all of this but I can't help myself. I cannot control my obsession with knowing that he is aware of my existence and that I am out to get him.

I feel sickened at hearing his voice and I know I've taken this too far but I can't get him out of my head. It's like a drug, wanting to know more and more about him and the hunger for him to know that I exist and that I know what he did to her and how it made her so sad and angry and how it drove her to take her own life.

When I picture her . . . when I picture her lying in bed that morning so cold and lifeless on what was going to be such a joyous weekend for us with great celebrations and all we had planned . . .

We were to have lunch in our favourite seafood restaurant, while away the hours with a long walk on the beach and then share a bottle of wine on the patio before retiring inside with a few movie classics.

I remember now that I never got round to cancelling our booking at the restaurant and the DVDs I brought with me are still lying in their wrappers on the hall table at the cottage. I never got round to moving them into the sitting room or taking them back to the shop where I bought them. I know I'll never watch them.

Ben is picking me up at eight and I have laid out my dress and my earrings and shoes and I know that when I get to the restaurant I will loosen up at bit. I need to relax. I need to switch off.

I run a long hot bubble bath and turn up my favourite CD, *Classic Collections,* and then I soak for an hour, easing myself into a more relaxed mode. I think of Ben, of how he has always made me feel so special, so unique and how this evening could be the start of a new day in our relationship. We need to try again. I need to concentrate on building my future and forget about the past. I think about all the wonderful times we shared, the holidays we spent together, the way we laughed together and the way he laughed at me when I cried at soppy movies. I think about us dancing and how he had two left feet but the confidence to carry it off. I think about how when he looks at me that way I feel like we are the only two people in the world who exist and when he holds me . . . when he holds me I feel like I am floating on air.

I feel refreshed and pampered after my bath and even my mind is rejuvenated once again and I look forward to my preparations. I style my hair carefully into a straight, sleek bob the way Ben has always liked it. I apply a shimmer of instant tan and paint my nails a deep burgundy, then begin on my make-up. I've always loved make-up – the different colours and textures and how it can instantly lift my mood when I wear it.

When Ben calls me on the phone I smile at the sound of his voice but my instant elation soon turns to disappointment at his news. He has to cancel.

"I am so, so sorry, babe. You know I hate to do this to you. It's just too good an opportunity to miss and I can't afford to turn it down. We've been waiting to gig there for ages and this cancellation is a golden opportunity. Hey, I know! Why don't you come with me? It could be like old times. You could sit with the rest of the girls and Dean has a new girlfriend you haven't met yet. What do you think?"

Disappointment clogs my throat and I look down at my new dress, think of my make-up, my hair, my earrings . . . all my efforts to look forward in life and not look back seem pointless once more. Everything is pointless.

"Don't worry about it, Ben. It's no big deal … I don't want to go to the gig with girls I don't have anything in common with any more."

"Are you sure? They're nice girls. They'll make you feel really welcome."

"Sure, I'm sure. Good luck with the gig. Goodbye."

I sit down on the edge of the bed and realise once and for all that where Ben is concerned, I will always come second best to his band. I always thought that because we were both musical we would have an understanding of how each other's schedule works but I know exactly how his works and ours will never combine.

I love Ben. I will always love him for the time we spent together and for how he has been there for me, but now I realise that like Max Kelly, like my mother, like my whole beginnings in life, and what I have learned of late, Ben will only ever be part of my past and never part of my future.

42

Max pulled his car into Gina's driveway and knocked forcefully on the door. She answered with a concerned look on her face and he charged past her into the hallway, and she closed the door behind him.

"Max, you look terrible! How's Will?"

"Terrible? Is that all? How about fucking off my head? Is that how I look because it sure is how I feel?"

"Here, sit down." Gina led him into her sitting room and sat across from him on an armchair. "Can I get you anything? A coffee? Something stronger?"

Max was in such a foul temper he couldn't settle. He stood up and paced the floor, rubbing his forehead and swearing repeatedly.

"Everything is *shit*, Gina. It's shit! Will is seriously ill in hospital and now I learn that someone burned Blue Heaven to the ground deliberately! It was arson! Who the hell would do that? Who?"

Gina was startled, frightened even. She had never seen Max like this before. His eyes were bloodshot and bulbous and his skin was sallow and grey. He seemed to have aged overnight and was barely recognisable from the dashing, handsome and confident chef she knew and adored.

"I . . . I don't get it. I don't get it at all. Arson? Jesus!"

"And then that girl who you conveniently let into my restaurant decides to call me up today just to let me know she hasn't gone away. She's got my number now and I imagine this is only the start of it. My God, Gina, I have tried so hard! I even went into a fucking religious centre to try and get release from all this but my life is in ruins. Will could have died today on top of everything!"

Gina felt sorry for Max but she didn't want to carry blame for any of this.

"Max, if I had suspected for one second that she was playing some silly mind games with you, you know I would never have let her in through our doors at Blue Heaven! She tricked me and she used me to get to you. I'm so sorry. I really am. Please don't blame me for any of this!"

"Well, someone has to be blamed! Someone started all this. My God, *I* started this. I started it and now I don't know how to finish it." Max looked demonic. He rubbed his jaw line as he paced the floor, put his hands in his pockets, took them out again, physically wrestling with his emotions. "Tell me her name again. Tell me her name."

"Hollie Murphy. I've told you before."

"That's not her real name, though, is it? I need her real name!"

"It's what she told me but, no, I can't imagine she

would give her real name if she was trying to fool us. Then again, who knows? It's just an assumption that she would use an alias."

Max sat down on the edge of the settee and with shaking hands he scrolled through numbers on his mobile until he found the one he needed. The phone rang and rang and then it was answered.

"Maxo! How goes it? Delighted to hear from you again, old friend."

Jasper was as chirpy as ever but Max had no time for small talk.

"Jasper? Jasper, I need your help and I need it fast."

"At your service, Maxo. At your service."

"There was a conversation you and I had and I need you to remember it. You told me there was a bouncer guy in your part of the world who seems to know everyone in and around Belfast?"

"Ah, Jim the Bouncer! Yes, I remember. Why, what's up?"

"I need to find someone. I need you to give Jim the Bouncer a name and see if he can help me track her down. Jasper, this is really important. The name is Hollie Murphy, she's in her late twenties, blonde, shoulder-length hair. She plays the violin. And if he gets no matches to that name, then try the surname Lynch. Hollie Lynch."

Jasper sounded excited. "You got a mission with this woman? Oh, Maxo, you old fox! She sounds like a right looker!"

"Yes, I *do* have a mission with her but I have to find her first. I need an address and I need it fast. Thanks, Jasper! Now, get working on it!"

43

Social Services would be arriving in half an hour and Maria Moshiro was like a nervous kitten. She knew the end was near and she dreaded what the future held for her young family when the authorities became involved but she knew she had no choice in the matter. Her mother had grown weaker by the day until even the doctor's regular calls and the Marie Curie nurses couldn't help her enough any more. They had moved her to the Hospice on the Knock Road which was much more suitable with its round-the-clock care and home-from-home atmosphere. But this made it difficult to see her now because it was out of town and it was no fun dragging a baby and a young boy around on public transport.

She missed her mum terribly and she hated the thought of officials landing at the door and threatening to change the way she looked after her brother and baby sister.

It was an evening call and Maria was well prepared.

The apartment was gleaming and she had lit a scented candle and dressed in her best clothes for their arrival. She had settled the baby into an early evening nap so that she wouldn't be tired or cranky when they called and she had laid out a cerise pink dress and matching socks and a bow for little Niamh's fine, wispy dark hair.

Vinny would be here soon. She hadn't wanted him to come but he had insisted on helping her fight her case and showing that she had support from family friends. She didn't need that – she had compiled a list of people she could call upon – neighbours, acquaintances of her mother's, even the local Co-op owner who she had befriended when she became a regular buying groceries on a day-to-day basis.

She had even put down Caroline Lynch's name – the kind lady who had taken her and the children out to lunch that day and who had secretly kept in touch with her by the odd text message. She had warmed to Caroline and she felt that some day she could warm to Hollie too, given the chance. She felt a true connection with them and when Caroline left her a contact number, she honestly believed that she would actually call her sometime. Secretly, of course.

"Brush your teeth when you get out, Reece!" she called to her brother who was having a bath. She had laid out his Sunday best to make sure he looked as handsome as ever and he had been on his best behaviour all day, helping her tidy the house. She was doing a good job as a young mum and she took great pride in how she kept her household and was delighted at the fruits of her labour.

"I already did brush them," said Reece and when Maria popped her head into the bathroom, he breathed out to let her smell his fresh minty breath, then gave a toothy grin.

"Good boy," said Maria. "We're all set then. I'll get you a towel."

Maria had managed to keep social services off her case for months now – insisting that she and her brother and sister could not be split up but now that the inevitable visit was almost here, she felt panic rise from her gut again at the thought of Reece and Niamh being taken into care.

She could look after herself, of course. She was almost seventeen after all and lots of people her age lived independently but looking after two children was going to be a huge challenge. She could do it, though. She could do it and no one in this world could tell her any different.

She heard the key in the door and then her ears tuned into Vinny's trademark whistling sound as he made his way into the tiny sitting room of the apartment. The sound of him coming made the hair on the back of her neck stand as it always did.

She was adjusting family photos on the mantelpiece, determined to give the impression of a stable, happy home life. The apartment was fresh and clean but his very presence automatically made her feel like she had to start all over again.

"Hi, babe," he said. His voice was gravelly and it sent shivers down her spine. "How are you bearing up? All ready? Place looks great."

She gulped and didn't turn around to face him. She could feel her mouth curl in repulsion as she felt him come too close to her and goosebumps stood on her skin. The smell of cigarette smoke from his clothes and his hot breath made her want to scream as it filled the air. He stank of body odour too and its stale stench overwhelmed the scented candle she had bought at the Co-Op. The kind lady behind the counter had recommended the vanilla fragrance and it had just begun to take effect until he came in and ruined it. She was scared but she wouldn't give him the satisfaction of knowing. Where Vinny was concerned, she always, always put on a brave face.

"I'm okay," she said, clenching her nails into the palms of her hands. She turned to face him now, her chin tilted with pride. "I'm nervous about them splitting us up, but I'll be fine. I've been through worse shit than this. Much worse."

He reached out to touch her face, his hands large and clumsy and stinking.

"What about your eye? Does it still hurt? It looks nasty, babe. Here, give us a look . . ."

She stepped back and swung her head away so that he couldn't reach.

"No," she said, and then she saw his face twitch. "Don't touch it. It stings. Just a little, but it stings. It's getting better. It really is."

"Good," he said and he snorted bile to the back of his throat.

The sound of it made Maria want to gag.

"Look, I can't always be here to protect you, Maria. Trouble comes, trouble goes, and that's just the way of the world. I'm just glad I stopped it before it went too far."

She ignored him and fixed the photos once more. She didn't want a thing to be out of place and she had laid out the best tray with cups and saucers in preparation for the occasion. She had borrowed them from the Co-Op lady. She had borrowed a lot from her lately.

She checked the clock and realised she'd better get a move on.

"Well, I'm just glad you're here now so we can get this over and done with," she said to Vinny. "I think I have everything ready now. I just need to dress the baby in her new clothes and get Reece sorted. I'll go hurry him up now. You know what he's like when he gets into the bath. A little fish, that's what he is . . ."

She would be glad to be out of Vinny's way for even a few minutes. She knew he despised the ground she walked on. She made him feel guilty. She made him realise that he had fucked up so many times with Singh. He allowed standards to slip three times to be precise, but no more. The cancer had made sure of that.

"Hurry up," said Vinny as he flicked on the television and made himself at home.

"I'll be as long as it takes," she said as she left the room. Who the hell did he think he was?

"Well, make us a cup of tea when you're done, for fuck's sake!" he shouted and Maria rolled her eyes. "I'm parched. Do you realise how hot it was out there today? I'm bloody sweating like a pig, running here, there and everywhere. The least you could do is make me a fucking cup of tea. Can't believe I even have to ask."

Maria breathed out through her nose and her heavy eyes blinked under the pain of her injury. Her eye felt like it was on fire but she would never admit to anyone how much pain she was in. Vinny hated to see her in pain. Again, it made all his actions seem more real to him.

"Lucky you!" she called back to him from the bathroom and her voice echoed off the walls. "How the

288

hell would I know what the weather is like? I haven't seen daylight in days except to go to the local shop. I've been stuck in here, haven't I?"

She heard him clear his throat again and her insides churned.

"True, true," he said. "You're a good one, Maria. You know I think the world of you. You know I do. Your mother did too."

"My mother *does* too, you mean. She's not dead, you know."

She heard Vinny grunt as she held out a warm bath towel to coax Reece from the bath. The little one looked worried and he shivered when he stood up from the warm water.

"Yet," he said, his little teeth chattering.

"What, my lovely?"

"You said your mother isn't dead. You forgot to say 'yet'. She isn't dead *yet*. I know she is going to heaven soon. Everyone knows that."

"Come on, Reece!" said Maria. "Our visitor will be here any minute and I don't want her to think I leave you sitting in water all day. Look at your hands, wrinkled like a prune."

Reece groaned and held his arms across his waist as she struggled to lift him out over the side of the bath.

"What's a prune? Can we go and see Mum tomorrow? I really, really miss her. This much!"

He held out his arms to their full span, giving Maria the opportunity to lift him from the bath and set him on the bath mat to dry him off.

"A prune is a very wrinkly fruit. Well, let's just see how

it goes today. I need you to be on your best behaviour when the lady calls to talk to us. You're doing really well so far."

Reece stood in silence as his sister dried behind his ears and scuffed his hair with the towel. She sprinkled baby powder all over his little body and smiled as he rubbed it in.

"Are they going to take me away from you?" he asked from underneath the towel when she gave his hair a final rub. "I don't want to go away. I want to stay here with you and the baby."

Maria held him close and breathed in his fresh smell. She swallowed back tears and all the fears that she was desperately trying to hide from her precious little brother.

"No way, baby," she whispered and rocked him gently from side to side. "Don't you dare even think about that. There's no way anyone will separate us. I'll make sure of it."

She wiped a tear from her eye and it stung when she touched the bruise that still lingered. She had covered it up as best she could with make-up but the bruise was still shining through and it throbbed so badly that it had kept her up most of the night. If the social worker saw that . . . well, she had a "walked into a door" story all prepared. She just hoped they would be convinced.

"I want to see Mummy, Maria. I really do," said Reece, and at that the baby's cries filled the air from the nearby bedroom, urging Maria to hurry along.

"I said we'll see!" she said. "I promise you I will do my very best to take you very, very soon. Now, come into your bedroom and I'll bring Niamh in while I get you dressed. Then we'll make Vinny a nice, hot cup of tea, okay?"

"Okay," said Reece. "But only if you carry me."

He let out an exaggerated shiver and Maria playfully scooped him up.

"I'll carry you, you little rascal," she said. "Now, best behaviour, you hear? Let's show these people that we are perfectly fine the way we are. Just you, me and Niamh. We don't need anyone else. No one at all."

44

Evenings are the worst.

I sit alone in the apartment and flick through the channels on the television, wondering how I can put the hours in till bedtime. I tried to work on the papers that Ronan left me but my brain won't operate at that level no matter how hard I try. I call Caroline, but thinking I am out for the night she has obviously made plans for her own social life so I accept there is no point in calling Ronan either.

I think of all the friends I had before my life turned out like this. I think of all the times they tried to contact me and I refused their calls, unable to face up to explaining the horrors surrounding my mother's death. I built a barrier of pride and independence, for fear that anyone would judge her and I only let my nearest and dearest into my circle of grief.

They tried their best to wean me away from my

morbid state of mind but I blanked them and eventually their efforts trailed off. At the time it was exactly how I wanted it. I wanted to be left alone to wallow in my own self-pity and to channel my thoughts on how I was going to cope with this upheaval in my life. I had no idea just how much I had still to find out about my mother's state of mind and how she lived a false life for all these years, masking her own feelings and her own fears and hurt just so that I – the fruit of all her pain and suffering – could live a somewhat normal life.

The rose-tinted glasses have long been shed as far as my memories are concerned. I know now that I blanked out times of despair and remembered what I chose to recall about my childhood – sporadic bursts of celebration, moments of laughter and spontaneous gifts and every practicality I ever needed plus all the love in the world. I chose to forget the days I would come home from school and she wouldn't be there. I would make some tea and toast and watch out the window and then she would breeze in with a painted smile, saying she fancied a walk on the beach and didn't realise the time even though it had got dark. I ignored the memories of her drinking during the day and how, when I'd try to help her cook dinner, she'd snap at me and then leave the pots on the stove until they burned.

I'd chosen to forget the nights when I'd find her sleeping in the bath tub, a bottle of gin by her side and the water running cold and I'd have to lift her out and get her to bed.

But I was a child back then. How could I remember? And why would I want to unless I really thought about it?

As I grew into my teens she must have learned to hide her true feelings from me. I don't recall any such scenes or dramatic cries for help in my later years and when I left for university she made me feel that it was all she had been waiting for.

And perhaps it was.

Perhaps she had been waiting until I was old enough or independent or settled enough to do what she had been trying to do for years. I wonder now how long she had been planning for it, how many times she had considered it or unsuccessfully tried it and then hated herself after for being so weak as to let those monsters from the past eat into her soul?

I picture her sitting in that cottage by the sea, all alone with her thoughts and her fears and her demons from the past and it kills me to think of how I left her to do so. What was I doing when she was having such devastating thoughts? Where was I? At work? Out for dinner? Partying at a gig with Ben?

How could any of that be as important as nursing my mother back to health? How could I have been so selfish as not to notice her pain, her heartache, the fear she felt inside? How could I have been blind to her needs and yet so tuned in to my own?

I turn off the television. I scurry into my bedroom and stuff the first items of clothing that come to hand into an overnight bag. I switch off every electrical point and I fetch my car keys and my handbag. Then I race out the door.

I want to go home now. I've had enough of sitting here in this alien city with my futile existence and replaceable friends. I want to go where I can be near her, where she can feel me near her. I want to be where I can tell her I'm sorry for not noticing her despair. I want to say thank you to Mrs Jenkins for looking after Jinx but explain that I won't be needing her kindness in future. I will be looking after him myself all the time from now on.

And then I want to draw a line under all of this heartache and I want this all to stop so I can start all over again.

I will go to the cottage and then I will try – I will try my best to start all over again.

45

Jasper rang Max as he was having dinner at Gina's house and her teenage son was eyeballing him as he ate, as if he suspected Max should have no place in his home. So, when his phone rang, Max was more than glad to excuse himself from the table.

He felt like a down-and-out, like a dirty stop-out who had to scrounge a meal or bunk down on the nearest couch he could lay his head on. Jasper was in full spirits and Max went outside into the still evening air to take the call.

"I've got your girl," said Jasper. "I've got the very one, Maxo. It took a bit longer than I thought but Jim is known for his extensive knowledge and –"

"Jasper, cut the crap. Where is she? Who is she?"

Max knew Jasper well enough to sense a build-up and a build-up was something he neither had the time nor the patience for. He wanted to put an end to this saga and he wanted to do it now. The rage he felt within him was uncontrollable and he needed to find this girl and make sure he put a stop to her efforts to ruin his life.

"Her name is Hollie Lynch, not Hollie Murphy. She's a music teacher at the university and she lives in the city."

"And? Where the hell in the city can I find her?" asked Max. He could feel a rush of adrenaline race through his veins and he feared he might explode with the sudden urge to go and find her and put everything to rest at last, no matter how he had to.

"Well . . ." said Jasper. He sounded out of breath, like he had just found out the information and was calling Max en route from Jim the Bouncer who knew it all. "She lives on the Ormeau Road during term time, helps out at a summer school normally at this time of year but her mother died recently and she has been spending a lot of time at her home place on the coast."

"The coast? Where on the coast?"

"It's a cottage overlooking White Rock beach. I have the address. It's on her business card for her music teaching so it was easy enough to find. Do you want it?"

Max could feel his temperature rising and the food he had eaten churned in his stomach. "Yes, yes, I want her address. But tell me, you said her mother died recently. Did you get her mother's name?"

Max already knew the answer. He knew it from the moment he set eyes on Hollie. He knew it from the very moment he heard the sound of the violin in his restaurant that night. But he needed to hear it for real. He needed reassurance that he wasn't going mad.

"Hold on," said Jasper and Max felt irritated as he

waited for the boy to answer. "Yes, yes, I have it now. I told you Jim the Bouncer knew everything. Her mother's name was Estelle. Estelle Lynch. Does that sound right?"

Max stared out across Gina's landscaped garden, out across the brick housing development which was full of anonymous people who were oblivious to his fate and his eyes widened and his head throbbed.

"Estelle . . . yes, just as I thought. Estelle."

So Estelle had a daughter. Hollie was her daughter. All his greatest fears rushed from the pit of his stomach and boomed in his head while his heart screamed for mercy.

"Max? Max, are you there?" asked Jasper. "Max? Are you all right, mate?"

Max couldn't answer. It was all clear now. Estelle had a daughter who knew exactly what had happened, or at least she knew enough to open this great big can of worms. She had found out his name and his family details and now Hollie Lynch was out to ruin him and so far she was doing an excellent job. It all made sense now. She was out to ruin him but he couldn't let her. He had to stop this. He had to put an end to her games and her plots to take him down. He'd had enough of her power trip. He had a wife and family and a business to think of and he was going to match this girl at her wicked games.

"Yes, I'm here, Jasper. Now give me her address. Give me both addresses."

Jasper coughed and rustled for the business card that Jim had given him.

"Okay . . . you aren't going to do anything stupid, are you, Max?"

Max could feel his jaw tighten and he didn't answer.

Getting the message, Jasper called out the addresses. Max jotted them down and hung up the phone with a curt "Thanks".

He didn't exactly know what he was going to do. He couldn't think straight. He couldn't see sense.

All he could see and hear was Gina pleading with him to wait as he stormed out through her house, onto her garden path and into the car where he spun off in search of Hollie Lynch.

He thought of his marriage, of his sons, of his restaurant, of Will. He thought of all the years he had given to punishing himself over Estelle. But the game was over. It was time up for Estelle, and it was time up for Hollie Lynch. And in a way, it was time up for Max Kelly and he knew it.

46

Maria pursed her lips and listened as Sylvia Armstrong, the pristine and to-the-point social worker, tried to reason with her. She was a tall, lean woman who was kindly and who seemed to genuinely care about her clients, but Maria couldn't bring herself to agree with her.

"At sixteen –"

"Nearly seventeen. I'll be seventeen in September."

"Well, even at seventeen, you still have your education to consider. You shouldn't *have* to leave school and your mother has stated clearly that she wants you to go on with your studies. You will have to repeat your GCSE year, Maria, and I can assure you that we will do our very best to find foster care for all of you with the same family so that none of you are split up. It's just too much responsibility and the law doesn't allow for a seventeen-year-old to run a household on her own."

Maria sat with her back straight and her hands resting

on her knees. Vinny hadn't spoken a lot but was keeping the baby entertained while Maria tried her best to convince the social worker that she was capable of being the sole carer for her brother and sister. It was a long shot, she knew it was, but she was giving it her all – blood, sweat and tears if it took that – to try and convince Sylvia that she could look after her family.

"It's just until my mum comes home. Everything was fine until she had to go to the Hospice but when she comes back, you'll see. We'll manage until then. You can check on me every day. Every single day. I don't mind."

The social worker glanced across at Vinny for support but he had one eye on the television screen and another on the baby. At least that was something. He seemed like a useless, arrogant piece of shit and Sylvia saw his type all the time unfortunately. She didn't see Maria's type very often, which was making her job painfully difficult right now.

"Maria," she said and she took the young girl's hand. "Maria, your mother is very, very sick. She is terminally ill and I understand that the chances of her coming home are . . . well, there is virtually no chance of her coming home, Maria. Do you understand?"

Maria wiped her nose with the back of her hand and then scrabbled in her pocket for a tissue, her head down so as not to let this do-gooder see that she was fighting back tears. But when the tissue met her face, the tears flowed and she couldn't fight it any longer.

"But I've been running things here for months now," she said through heaving sobs. "And Vinny is only a phonecall away, aren't you, Vinny? *Vinny?*"

Vinny paused from his entertainment routine. "Of course. I'm here a lot and like Maria says, only just a phone-call away when I'm out of town. Leave the kid be. She runs this house anyway. Always did."

The social worker made a few notes and Maria looked at her with damp, pleading eyes.

"Maria, you are a very, very brave girl and I don't know of many seventeen-year-olds who would want to take on the responsibility that you have already on your very young shoulders. But I have to consider all options. If Vinny is supportive, I will make a note of that." She darted her eyes across to where Vinny sat and was more unconvinced than ever when he began flicking through television channels again. "Is there anyone else you can rely on for help? Any family? Close friends? Any other adults that you trust to lend a hand when you need one?"

Maria brightened up, pleased that she had done her homework for this question. She handed the lady a sheet of A4 paper on which she had written the names of as many neighbours and friends as she could come up with. She hadn't had time to check with them all if they minded that she put their names forward, and some of them she barely knew but she was desperate to show that she had a lot of people she could call on.

The social worker nodded. "And these people have come forward to say they that they can help with what exactly? You have a lot of people on this list."

Maria's eyes darted around the room and she wrung her hands as she spoke. She hated telling lies but she would have to stretch the truth on this occasion.

302

"Well . . . er, well, general things I suppose, like baby-sitting and shopping and . . . em . . ."

"You *suppose*? Maria, you have got to see the bigger picture here. Listing people you *suppose* will help does not guarantee you any assistance at all. You have got to think this through. Think of your own life, of your social life, of your education –"

"Maria has a lot of close friends who are more than willing to do their bit," said Vinny and Maria gasped at his sharp tone. "She has her head screwed on, has our Maria."

"So you can verify all of these people as close acquaintances, can you?" asked Sylvia in an equally nippy tone.

"Let's see," said Vinny and he stretched across to take the sheet of paper from the lady, the baby bouncing on his knee. He snapped it from her hand.

"It doesn't matter, Vinny," said Maria and her voice began to shake. "Some of the names are people you may not know. But I know them all. You probably have no idea of who half of them are. Really, it doesn't matter . . ."

She winced. She knew what was coming next. And she knew what would happen when Sylvia left the apartment. Oh no. How stupid had she been?

"Interesting," he said as he scanned down the names. "Very interesting. Yes, like I say, Maria has her head screwed on, *most* of the time."

He glared at her, his eyes bulbous and bloodshot, and her skin prickled like it had done so many times before.

"I . . . I was just trying to show that I have support and I do have great support. There are some of them who I'll never have to ask for help."

Vinny handed the paper back and eyeballed Maria, much to the discomfort of the social worker. She made a mental note on the sudden strange and quite disturbing interaction between this man and the young girl.

"Is everything okay?" asked Sylvia. She slowly gathered her files from the coffee table, sensing now that she had heard and seen enough to fill out all the relevant paperwork on the Moshiro case.

"Fine," said Vinny. "Everything is fine. Now are we nearly there because it's getting late and we'll have to get these kids ready for bed? They don't like to be knocked out of their routine."

"Yes, I'm finished," said Sylvia. "I'm finished for now. Maria, I'll be in touch with you first thing in the morning to formalise and activate your care plan based on the information you've given me this evening. Thank you for your time. And you too, Vinny."

She fixed her handbag on her shoulder and walked out of the room and down the narrow hallway that led to the front door, with Maria following her close behind.

"I can manage. I swear I can," said Maria as she opened the door for the social worker. "Please believe me, Miss. I don't care about education any more and we'll manage on whatever finances I'm entitled to. Please, Miss Armstrong. Reece and Niamh are much more important to me than any qualification will ever be. Please don't take them away from me. They're all I have."

Sylvia nodded, a slow sympathetic nod that told Maria she was on her side but her hands were tied.

"Do you feel safe, Maria? Do you feel confident and safe in this environment?"

Maria didn't answer. She scrambled with words in her head but everything seemed to be an obvious lie. She had to think of something fast. She had to lie. She had to save her family.

"And your eye, Maria?" asked Sylvia. "What happened to it? It looks like a nasty knock."

Oh, this was an easy one . . .

"I bashed it against the corner of a cupboard door in the kitchen. You know, one of the cupboards high up. Reece wanted a biscuit and I didn't close the door properly. It looks worse than it feels, honestly."

"And Vinny?" said the social worker. "Tell me, Maria. Is he supportive? I need you to tell me the truth."

"Yes, yes, he is. I swear to you. He is fantastic support," said Maria. "We have great support in Vinny. We couldn't be without him. Thank you, Miss Armstrong. Chat tomorrow?"

"Yes," said Sylvia. "I'll be in touch first thing. Now, take care of yourself, Maria, and we'll make decisions in the morning that will best suit you and your family. Goodbye."

Maria closed the door and leaned up against it with a sigh.

That was close, but worse than that, she could almost feel Vinny's rage through the walls, in the air, on her skin. She knew what was coming and she closed her eyes and counted to ten to try and calm down as she mentally prepared for the beating she was about to receive for being in touch with the Lynch girls. She prayed to St Jude, her favourite saint, the Patron of Hopeless Cases. Not that he was ever able to help her. She was more hopeless than the most hopeless case in the world so this time she didn't beg him not to let it happen . . . it *was* going to happen. She prayed to him and begged him that it would not happen in front of Reece.

"Please wait till he is sleeping," she prayed. "Please."

Reece walked out of the living room and into the hallway where his sister stood, physically shaking as she awaited her penance.

"Night night, Maria," he whispered, his fresh clean face pale with worry. "Vinny says it's bedtime but it can't be. The news is on and I always go to bed way after that. Is it bedtime already? I haven't had my supper yet."

Maria nodded and a huge tear dripped down her cheek. Reece knew what was happening. He always did and it broke her heart to think of what was going through his young innocent mind which was poisoned by times like this.

"You go to bed, Reece, and I'll be in really soon to tuck you in. Just put on the telly for a while and close the door tight. How about a big treat?" She sobbed out loud and then tried to swallow her fears as her breathing rode into a pant. "How about . . . how about I bring your supper to your room in a few minutes? I'll just be a few minutes, baby."

"Okay," said the boy and he tiptoed down the hallway to his bedroom. "I'll close the door tight? And turn up the volume?"

"Yes," said Maria, closing her eyes. "You do that. Good boy."

She left the doorway and made her way to the living room to bring the baby to her cot but the firm grasp of his clumsy hands met her arm and he pulled her to his side and slammed the door. Maria braced herself for what she had ahead of her but when it came, the shock and pain cut through her like a knife and took her breath away.

"How many times?" he yelled, his spit showering her beautiful face. "How many fucking times have I told you never to speak to those people again? How many fucking times do I have to pull you into line like this?"

Maria tried to answer but she couldn't get her breath back. She could still feel his fist when it left her stomach and she leaned on the sofa, gasping for air when he struck her again across the back, then pulled her towards him by the hair. It stung so badly and her mouth dropped open in reaction but she refused to make any noise.

"Please, Vinny!" she gasped. "Not in front of her. Not in front of the baby!"

The baby screamed from where she sat on the floor and she could hear the sound of cartoons coming from Reece's television down the hallway and the volume growing louder. Good boy, thought Maria despite the searing, gut-wrenching pain she was feeling. Keep the volume up nice and high. Turn it up so you can't hear anything else.

"Answer me!" shouted Vinny. "How many times do I have to tell you never, ever to even say their names? I have warned you, bitch! I have warned you so many fucking times! You're as bad as your pathetic mother!"

"I . . . I can't . . . Vinny, no!"

"You can't what? You can't keep your mouth shut, is that it? Yes, you're just like your mother, you little slag!" He threw her onto the coffee table and she fell on the floor, beside where the baby sat crying on the carpet. "You never fucking listen! No matter how many times I tell you, you still do what you want. Was that Lynch bitch back here again?"

"No . . . no, Vinny. I swear she hasn't come back here since."

Maria had found her breathing pattern again but the pain was still as sharp as ever. Every time this happened was like the first time. Every punch, every blow, every kick he gave her felt worse than the time before. She couldn't get used to feeling the wrath of Vinny's temper, not like her mother seemed to, but Maria would much rather take the beatings than ever watch her mother go through the physical and emotional torture he inflicted on her like this again.

Her head ached from where he had yanked her hair from behind and she had twisted her wrist with the fall, but she reached out to where the baby sat and lifted her across to comfort both of them on the floor. She snuggled the baby closer and rubbed her downy head and urged herself not to let him see her cry.

"You're on your own from now on, you lying tart!" spat Vinny and he looked at her with venom where she sat on the floor, cuddling the infant to her shoulder. "I've had enough of you milling about behind my back and letting that bitch and her family into our lives, snooping around and asking questions. If she comes about here again, tell her fuck away off and I mean it! I mean it, Maria! This is your last warning! In fact, if I find her, I will do more than tell her my fucking self! I will fucking kill the two of them whores! And I'm not finished with you yet!"

He slammed the door shut on his way out and Maria could hear him swearing as he marched past the window of the apartment and she didn't move until minutes had passed and she heard his car zoom off into the distance. Then she lifted the baby up into her arms, wincing at the ache in her wrist as she moved.

"There, there, baby," she whispered, holding little Niamh tightly. "It's all over now. It's all over. Let's get some supper for you and Reece, shall we? Will we make some supper? Yes, that would be nice. Yes, it would. Let's get Reece his Cheerios."

The road to White Rock is quiet for this time of the evening and I barely notice the time go by. I feel the frost that has chilled my heart melt when I see the cottage in the distance and, when I drive closer, I see Jinx in his pen and his ears prick up at the sound of the car engine pulling into the drive. Even in the dark he recognises me and I release him to let him express his delight at my return.

"Hello, old boy," I say, fluffing his fur just the way he likes it. "Yes, I've missed you too. I really have. I really, really have!"

I turn the key in the door and walk inside the cottage, feeling the warmth of home immediately and I can't stop smiling. This is where all my memories are, good and bad. This is where I feel the safest and where I can lock myself up with my thoughts in peace. Everything is exactly how I left it. A magazine lies on the sofa, a cushion is scattered and out of place and I remember noticing it when I was last here but was too determined to get to Dublin to fix it.

It seems so long ago now and I feel a change inside me, like a metamorphosis which is guiding me to redirect things in my life and to focus on what is best for me as a person.

My mother's death left me with questions that I cannot find answers for and maybe it's for the best. I'll try and hold that thought for as long as I can. It feels much better this way.

I am wearing my new dress but I don't want to take it off. It signals a new me and a new attitude and the strength to look forward in my life.

I don't want to go backwards again. I can't look back in time any more. My future is much more precious than that.

When Caroline calls I don't answer, but she calls again and again and again and eventually I pick up. She is so highly strung I can barely make out what she is saying.

"Lock the doors," she says to me. Her breathing is shallow and I can hear a baby cry in the background. Its wailing drowns out her voice and I have no idea what she is trying to tell me.

"Caroline, slow down! I'm at the cottage –"

"I know you are. I'm on my way. Please just lock the doors and don't answer to anyone. I have Maria and the children with me. You're in danger, Hollie. We all are. Just sit tight and we'll be there within the hour."

"Don't cry, Maria. He will never find us at Estelle's cottage. He doesn't even know it exists, how could he?"

Caroline's hands gripped the steering wheel and she leaned forward in her seat, concentrating on the road ahead. It was growing dark and the baby was unsettled in the back seat. Maria leaned in between the seats and found her soother, then fixed a blanket around Reece's knees and under his chin as his eyes drooped closed, despite the baby's screeching.

"Try and get some sleep, Reece," she said. "Don't fight it. We'll be there very soon."

"Can I build sandcastles on the beach?" he asked, his voice deep and full of sleep. "I have never built a sandcastle before."

"Oh, we are going to have such fun!" said Caroline, wondering if she should chance overtaking a slow-moving vehicle in front of her. A light evening drizzle warned her against it. "We can get some ice cream tomorrow and take Jinx for a run on the beach. He has missed you so much."

Reece gave a throaty laugh and Maria sat back into her seat in the front of the car.

"I can't thank you enough," she said to Caroline and the sharp pain returned in her waist where she had knocked it earlier as she fell against the coffee table. Her stomach and back felt like one big painful bruise where he had beaten her. "He is probably at our place now, tearing it apart and going mental trying to find out where we have gone."

"If it's me he's after, and indeed Hollie," said Caroline, "he will search for us in Belfast first. I have told Ronan not to call at my house and Hollie's ex, Ben, is working tonight so there is no chance that he will bump into anyone at either of our places. We're safe enough." She was quite unsure about how safe they were but there was nowhere else she could take them.

Maria had something to tell Caroline but she didn't know how. She was afraid that Caroline would blame her for it, plus the throbbing pain she felt from head to toe was making it very hard to concentrate on anything more than breathing right now. Her mobile phone rang and a blanket of fear prickled over her whole body. It was him.

"Answer it," said Caroline. "The baby is quiet now and he will have no idea where you are. I'll pull up here so he won't hear the noise of the car. Just answer it and see what he knows. It will help us gauge if he has any clue who you're with."

"No, Caroline. I don't know what to say! I can't! He will know!"

"He won't," she said. "We need to test him. We need to know if he's on our track."

Maria closed her eyes and pressed the answer button on her phone.

"H–hello," she whispered.

"Where the fuck are you, you little bitch?" she heard him rasp.

She held the phone out from her ear as tears stung the bruise on her eye.

"You think you're smart with your little Houdini act? You can't hide from me, Maria. Your mother never could and neither can you!"

Maria didn't speak for fear of choking. She couldn't find any words to say. Caroline held her finger over her lips and nodded, telling her she didn't have to speak, just listen and find out what he knew.

"You think you can pull the wool over my eyes, do you? I told you I wasn't finished. You always said you weren't afraid of me, but you're running away from me now. You're afraid, aren't you, Maria? You're afraid of me?"

Maria shook her head and pressed her lips tightly closed.

"I – I'm not afraid of you, Vinny. I'm not afraid of you."

"Well, you fucking should be! Who are you with? Who is it? Maria, I will find you! I will fucking find you and when I do –"

Maria hung up the phone and threw it on her lap, then hugged her waist as she shook uncontrollably.

"No, no, no," she said, shaking her head from side to side. "You don't know what he's like, Caroline. He will find us. He will find us in minutes if he has to. He knows people. Vinny can find anything or anyone anywhere. I've seen it all before."

Caroline turned the key in the ignition, put her foot down on the accelerator and zoomed along the open stretch of road. There really wasn't far to go before she would have to nip in off the main road onto the coastal route that led to White Rock and its peaceful, secluded surroundings.

"How bad?" she asked, not sure if she wanted to know. "Just how bad is he? What would he stop at? How far would he go? He wouldn't . . . he wouldn't kill you, would he?"

Maria glanced into the back seat where Reece and baby Niamh now lay fast asleep. She brought her voice down into a whisper just in case.

"I saw him kill before," she said, her voice in a tremble. "He killed a man one night. Shot him dead while me and my mum waited in the car. Caroline, Vinny will stop at nothing. He killed that man because he opened his mouth once too often about Vinny's business. Nobody talks about Vinny and gets away with it. Not even family."

"Jesus!" said Caroline, wiping a line of sweat from her forehead. "Jesus! Is that how you look at him, then? As your family?"

Maria didn't answer straight away. She stared ahead as the white lines on the road bled into each other and then she shrugged.

"I look at Reece and Niamh as my family," she said with a forced sense of pride. "But Vinny . . . Vinny could be my father. I don't think he is and I hope to God it was some random client that planted a seed in my poor mother because if I knew for sure I was of the same bloodline as that monster, I would kill myself. He is evil, Caroline. He is more evil than you could ever imagine."

Caroline felt her blood run cold through her veins. Maria was almost seventeen years old and yet she had seen so much more in her young life than Caroline had in her forty years. How could life be so cruel to one young girl? She had witnessed a murder, her mother's life as a dead-end prostitute and suffered at the hands of this monster who beat her and . . . oh God, no. No.

"Did he ever . . . Maria, did he ever . . . abuse you in any other way?" she asked, praying for a negative answer. Perhaps if he thought she could be his daughter he wouldn't touch her in that way?

Maria let herself go now and she cried great heaving

sobs that stung like crazy on her broken skin. She dabbed her face as salty tears diluted her rich red blood on the white tissue. She had never, ever spoken about this before. She had blanked it out down the years as if it had never happened. No one ever needed to know.

"Do you know what, Caroline?" she said through her bitter tears. "Of all the cuts and bruises and bloodstained clothes that Vinny left me with, nothing ever hurt as much as what he did to me in my bedroom."

Caroline slowed the car down, unable now to concentrate on her driving any longer. She couldn't stop in case there was no time, yet what she was hearing now was blurring all her senses as her deepest fears about Maria came true.

"I don't remember it starting," Maria continued. "I could guess I was about seven years old but it has been going on since."

"Oh, Maria!" gasped Caroline and she pulled the car to a halt on the side of the road. She just couldn't drive any further. Not right now.

"Niamh is my baby," said Maria, looking down at her hands and the twisted bloody tissue that sat between them. "I have never told anyone. But she is mine. And Vinny is her father."

48

Max knew he was well over the speed limit as he approached the country roads on his way to White Rock. It was a scenic route and he knew it quite well, but it was dark now and the winding road that led to the picturesque coastal hamlet was tricky when driving so fast.

He tried to calm his nerves and slow down but the thought of finding Estelle's daughter was like a major adrenaline rush that he couldn't control. It was like Estelle was alive again in his mind and he had to see her. He wanted to see her again in the flesh to make sure she truly existed and after that . . . well, he had no idea what it would come to. He passed a restaurant and a small petrol station and he pulled the car in to catch his breath and to try and settle down.

"She is dead!" he chanted. "Estelle is dead. This is her daughter. It is not Estelle. It is her daughter."

He put the window down and gasped in the fresh air and

then he opened the car door and stretched his legs with a walk across the forecourt. He could see the counter assistant crane her neck from inside to see what he was up to and, realising he was causing suspicion, he walked back to the car and drove out of the station and onto the quiet lonely road that led to Estelle's cottage. The sat nav had led him across a more scenic route than usual but he was grateful to have an address at all, thanks to Jasper's prime investigations. He thought of Sandra and Josh and Charlie at home in Dublin and all the pain he had put them through because of his guilty conscience and obsession with Estelle Lynch. He thought of Will lying in hospital awaiting life-changing surgery. He thought of his precious business burnt to the ground and his mouth tightened at the thought of how his life was in ruins.

With the cottage only a few miles away at most, Max put his foot to the floor. It was time for him to face her, once and for all. It was time to lay Estelle's ghost to rest so he could get on with the rest of his life.

I let Jinx out into the back garden for some space and I breathe in the cool sea air. Apart from the crashing of the waves in the distance, this is the quietest, most peaceful place on earth. I close my eyes and listen to the sounds of the sea and I feel more at home than I have felt for a long time. This is where I belong. I need to stay here, I decide. It's the most beautiful place in my world and it's where I want to stay forever.

I think of Caroline's warning but it seems unreal in the context of this tranquillity. Something terrible has happened but it can't touch me here.

I go back inside and decide to celebrate my new strength with a toast to the future, so I take a bottle of white wine from the fridge and I pour some into a champagne flute. The television is on and I plan to settle onto the sofa and watch my favourite game show while I wait for Caroline and Maria.

I raise my glass and just as I am about to make my speech, I hear something outside.

I pause, my glass still in the air. Jinx is barking loudly and I hear a car pull up in the driveway. Is it Caroline? Surely not – the dog's barks sound ferocious and I hear him growl. Remembering Caroline's warning I suddenly feel afraid but perhaps it's a lost stranger or a tourist wanting directions to their accommodation? We get that sometimes at this time of year. The nearest town is just a few miles away but some travellers prefer to take the coastal route and find they've lost their way.

I put my glass down on the sideboard and go to the door.

Lock the doors. You're in danger, Hollie. I can hear Caroline's frantic voice in my head.

When I open the door he marches towards me and I know immediately that this is not a social call. He has come to find me and he means business.

49

"Max Kelly," I say calmly and I fold my arms. My coolness throws him off course and to be honest it has thrown me too. I don't know why but I am not afraid of him any more. He doesn't look like he's going to put me in danger. He holds his hands up to say so.

"Can we get this cleared up, once and for all?" he asks.

"I want closure, Max. That's all I want. And answers."

"You'll have them. But I need to ask one question: did you play a part in burning down my business?"

"I did not. I am not a criminal."

He nods as if he accepts that. "Hollie, my life is ruined," he says, "and I think yours is heading that way too. I just want to explain my side to you and then you can do what you want. Call the police, have me arrested, anything to put all this to an end. Anything."

I look behind to his car and he reads my mind.

"I am alone," he says, holding his hands up again.

"Pardon the cliché but I do come in peace. Please let's try and end this nightmare, once and for all."

I open the door and let him inside. Into my mother's world, into my own little world that I have created like a cocoon of protection. I feel like I am on auto-pilot and I probably am. He is very handsome and I am puzzled how I can even think along those lines right now. But he looks different to how he looked that night in the restaurant when he seemed weak and vulnerable and I felt completely in control.

I don't feel out of control right now, nor do I feel like he has the upper hand. We are even on this. We have both had enough and I am ready to hear him out.

"Drink?" I ask and nod at him to have a seat. He cagily sits down on the Laura Ashley floral settee and I see his eyes dart around the room, taking in all our photos, our memories and I want to fucking kill him.

"I – I'll have a drink, yes." His eyes seek mine. "Really, Hollie, I don't know where to start. I just don't know what to say . . ."

My anger turns to a frown as he crumbles right before me. His hands, his strong, clean, manly hands reach up to his face and he buries his head in them, pushing his fingers against his skin like he is clawing at the pain to go away. I feel a shiver run along my spine. I've always done exactly the same thing.

"I'll fetch you a brandy," I tell him tartly. I have no sympathy for his tears or his pain. I need to know more before I will soften to him in the slightest.

My hands tremble as I pour two glasses of cognac from my mother's living-room drinks cabinet. The bottle was sealed and I feel a connection with her when I realise that she must have bought this with an occasion in mind. She wasn't the type to stock alcohol for the sake of it. She used to joke that it would never last if she did.

I walk towards him, my hands shaking, and I hand him the drink. He doesn't make eye contact, but sips the warm, brown liquid and I see the colour slowly come back to his face.

He looks at me now with huge brown puppy-dog eyes and they glisten with tears.

"I do not want your sad stories," I tell him. "I do not give two flying fucks if you have spent most of your life with regrets and what-ifs and if the guilt has ruined you. I don't care! I just want to know what you did to her and I want to know why!"

I clutch the glass and I back away until I find a seat. I don't have the energy to stand up and argue with this man.

He doesn't have the energy to shout back.

"I don't expect anything from you but hatred and anger," he said and he gulps back his brandy and drains his glass.

I go and fetch him another, wondering where on earth I have found the inclination to be any way hospitable to the man who has consumed my every thought for weeks now.

"Do you know something?" I ask, my voice more settled now as the warmth of the alcohol rushes through my veins. "She was the most amazing woman you ever could meet."

He bites the inside of his jaw and looks at the floor.

"Look at me!" I shout at him and he does. "She was

kind, she was generous, she loved to listen to music, she lived to play music. She was beautiful and fun and –"

"I know," he said. "Hollie, I know she was. My God, I know she was."

I am flummoxed by his admission. "How do you know?"

He gripped the glass tighter, so tight I fear it might smash in his hands.

"Jesus, I followed her so many times." He lifts his head now to speak to me directly. "I wanted to tell her how sorry I was. I wanted to tell her I was not like the others. I knew she would believe me, Hollie. I knew she would if I could only have gathered the courage to tell her to her face. You see, she knew me. She knew I was not a bad person. I did a very bad thing, Hollie, and I am riddled with regret but I know that if I had just . . ."

I lick my lips slowly. They feel dry and chapped from the heat that lies in the air of the cottage. So my mother knew this man. She knew him yet she didn't say she did in her diary. Why was she protecting him? Why didn't she say his name?

"She was in love with me, Hollie. And through one stupid, drunken, drug-filled horrible night I let her down more than I have ever let anyone down in my whole life. I just wanted to tell her I was sorry."

My head is spinning. This could be a crock of shit. This could be a carefully contrived plan to divert me from his monstrous actions.

Then I remember the boy in the library. The one she thought that she might be in love with. The one who raped her and broke her heart and her soul. And I know he is sitting before me, himself now a broken man.

"Did you rape her?" I ask him and the words feel sour on my tongue.

He nods and does that thing with his hands on his face again, the way I do. He heaves giant sobs now.

"You bastard!" I take a deep breath. "Do you think you could be my father, Max? Do you?"

He doesn't answer, nor does he take his hands from his face.

A frantic knock on the door tells me Caroline has arrived and I go to answer.

"He knows!" says Maria and she huddles the baby to her chest. On her shoulder are two tiny backpacks with cartoon characters – one pink and one blue – and a larger one which tells me she and the children are planning to stay.

"Just let's get inside and then we can explain everything," says Caroline.

I am confused so I step back to let them into the cottage, unable to tell them that I have company and that they have interrupted a crucial moment. Caroline is holding Reece who begins to stir in her arms and she stops dead when she gets into the living room.

"What the – ? Hollie, what is going on here?"

I take a deep breath, in through my nose and out through my mouth. Caroline knows who he is. She knows because she looked him up just like I did when I told her about him. I always knew she had, even though she never brought herself to admit it.

"Max Kelly," I say in the calmest tone of voice I can find. "This is my aunt, Caroline. She is Estelle's only sister."

The fear in Max's eyes has heightened now and he sits

upright on the armchair, with one hand on each of the armrests as if he is about to take flight. He is surrounded by us. Estelle's daughter, her sister and the children of Singh Moshiro who stare at him and I know that it is as if all his nightmares have come true at the same time.

Caroline cannot find the words. I know what she wants to ask him. I too have lists of questions in my head that just won't register to come through but I know they will in time. But first of all I need to know why Caroline has brought Singh's children to White Rock at such a strange hour and why Maria looks like she has been thrashed around, much worse than I have seen before.

"Maria? Who the hell did this to you? Come and let me clean you up. You're bleeding."

I look at her stunning face and all the worries that are etched between the lines of her cuts and bruises. Her face has paled and even her tattoos that once made her hard and weathered-looking now look pathetic and lifeless. She is only sixteen, yet she has witnessed more than most people twice her age would ever dream of.

"I don't have time," she whispers, unsure of Max Kelly and his presence. "Just hide us, Hollie. Hide us all before he comes to find us. He is on his way, I just know it."

I glance at Caroline and she gently pushes Reece's head back down on to her shoulder and hushes the little boy as she takes a seat. She kisses his forehead and gives me a look that tells me to do what Maria says. Caroline looks terrified, more terrified than I ever thought she could be.

"It's Vinny, isn't it?" says Max Kelly and he stands up from his seat. "Does he know you're here? If he comes here, there will be big trouble. You don't know what you are dealing with, believe me!"

"Don't we?" says Caroline, the bitterness dripping from her tongue. "Look at that girl! Look at that young girl and tell me I don't know what I am dealing with! A monster, that's what, and I don't need you to come here from your fancy life with your fancy restaurant and fancy wife to tell me that!"

She raises her voice and the baby cries. I see that even carrying little Niamh is hurting Maria so I take her and make a hushing sound, as much to Caroline as to the baby. Reece stirs again and lifts his head.

"Why are you shouting, Caroline? When are we going to the beach?"

"Soon, baby. We'll go to the beach as soon as morning comes."

She hushes the boy and I marvel at her maternal instinct.

"Take them to the spare bedroom," I say with a note of urgency now. If Vinny did this to Maria, I hate to think what he has planned to finish the job. "Maria, come with me and let me check your face, it will only take a minute. Then you can go to the room and stay there too."

"I'm hungry," says Reece and I lay the baby down on the sofa beside Caroline who is holding Reece on her knee. She puts a protective arm out to the baby and my heart stops when Max Kelly approaches Caroline to help her. She turns away and lets Reece slide down her body onto the floor.

"Let me help you," he says. "I can take the boy. At least let me help you."

Caroline looks at him and lifts her chin. "I can manage these children myself, thank you," she says, her mouth tight with disgust and anger. "Come on, Reece. Let's get you all tucked in nice and tight and I'll bring you some supper to your new room. It will be a nice treat. We can take Niamh upstairs with us."

The boy stops and looks at Maria like he has heard those words many times before. He doesn't like having supper in his room. His body language tells me so.

"Do as Caroline says," Maria tells him gently. "She won't leave you and Hollie won't leave me. We are safe now. We will be okay, wait and see. Go to bed and dream of sandcastles, baby boy. I will be right there."

I take Hollie to the kitchen and leave Max alone on my mother's favourite armchair. He doesn't try to make any conversation even though the door that leads from one room to another in the cottage is wide open. I make sure I seat Maria in the kitchen in a spot where I have full view of his movements. I watch him as I pat the cuts on Maria's face dry and try my best not to hurt her any more than she is already feeling.

"Sorry, babe," I tell her when I feel her gasp beneath my touch. "Vinny cannot get away with this any more, Maria. This has gone on for far too long. Why should you have suffered like this? Why should you have suffered at his beastly hands for all your precious life?"

I speak a little louder so that Max can definitely hear me but Maria doesn't respond to any of my questions.

Max does eventually. "He is scum," he mumbles, his hands clasped in front of him as he leans forward on the chair. "He is a dangerous, dangerous man and I rue the day I ever was introduced to him. People like Vinny manipulate and destroy lives with their gutter ways. He destroyed yours and he destroyed mine. And he will keep destroying and destroying and . . ."

He gets up from his chair like he had been suddenly possessed and makes his way towards Maria and me.

"Does he know where you are?" he asks Maria. His eyes are bullet-like and his face has gone pale again. "Is there any way he might know you have come here?"

Maria nods and I step back from her.

"Maria! How could he possibly know? How could he know to come here? No, he can't. There is no way. Is there?"

She looks up at us both and I see her eyes fill up again. She nods again. She tries to speak but her words don't come out.

"Tell us, love," says Max and the gentle way he speaks to her throws me. "I know you are scared and I don't blame you for that. I know Vinny and I know what he is capable of. If he can leave you in a state like this, and if you believe that he might be on his way here, even if it is only a fleeting fear, you have to tell Hollie because you could be in grave danger. All of you could be in grave danger. But then you already know that, don't you?"

Again, Maria nods and then she gulps back her fears.

"You gave me your card one day," she says to me, her breath catching at every word. "It had your address on it both in Belfast . . . and here. He saw it, Hollie. He took it from me. I don't know if he will come here, but if he thinks for one second that I could be with you, he will make it his business to find me. And you. Hollie, I'm afraid what he might do to you and Caroline. I really am."

Max paces the floor and I watch him, his brain kicking into overdrive, and I realise that I have temporarily forgotten his role in all this and now he is slowly changing from villain to hero. I can't let that happen.

"Max, why don't you let us get on with things?" I say to him. "You came here to explain what you did to my mother, not become our hero in the 'let's save these girls from Vinny' episode. I think I've heard all I need to hear from you. Please go."

I am terrified inside. I do not want him to leave but foolish pride makes me think I have to get him away from here. He stops and he looks at me, a mixture of anger and hurt etched on his face.

"You have no idea, Hollie!" he says and his voice rises into a crescendo. "You have no fucking idea what you are dealing with here. This man could kill you! He wouldn't even think twice of how he would cover his tracks until after he had caused his trail of destruction. Just who do you think you are? I am not trying to be a hero! I am trying to protect you!"

"I don't need your protection. I don't want it."

"Well, how about the others around you? That young boy and girl and the baby? Don't they need protection?"

"Not from you! And not from Vinny either. You are all the same!"

"No!" he shouts. "No! Don't you dare categorise me with that monster! I am *nothing* like him! I never was. And that is why I choose to stay and protect you."

I stare at Max Kelly – the man who has consumed me,

who has been the subject of my obsession, the man who has stopped me from laying my mother's ghost to rest for months now. The man who I believe might be – just might be – my father.

"We need to call the police, Hollie, because if we don't have back-up I dread to think what may happen here tonight!"

"You can go now," I say to him even though I am shaking inside. "Just go, Max."

He bites the inside of his jaw again and glances from me to Maria. "No, Hollie. I will not go until I know for sure you are safe. If there is any chance that Vinny is on his way here, then I can assure you, hell and high water will not make me leave. I will circle this place if I have to, but I will not leave you."

"Do what you have to," I spit back at him, even though the thought of him leaving sends a chill through my bones. "But get out of my mother's house!"

"I won't be far away," he says and he leaves.

50

Maria and I both jump when the front door closes, even though Max has taken great care not to make any noise to frighten the children. We look at each other in silence and Maria's broken face breaks my heart just that little bit more.

We listen as Max's car starts and drives up the lane, its sound fading into the distance. And I feel desolate.

"So, are you going to tell me who Max is and why you wouldn't let him stay?" she asks me. Her lip quivers as she speaks and for the first time I see a vulnerable sixteen-year-old girl and not a brave young woman who has had to grow up too fast. I wonder just how much I can tell her.

"He . . . he is the man from the picture. The one I showed to your mother on the day I came to see her."

Maria rolls her eyes and she nibbles the back of her hand. She breathes out slowly. "Why did my mother have to end up like this?" she asks me and her tears flow freely now. "How on earth did she get messed up with such bad people? She is a good person, you know. She is not just what you think she is . . . what everyone thinks she is."

"Of course not, Maria. Singh is your mother and you love her very much. It shows. It really does."

I take her hand and we go into the living room again and when she sits down on the soft armchair, she opens up to me again. This time I am careful not to interrupt her.

"She didn't have much to give," she says. "But she was always there, always at home and her eyes would light up when I came home from school, like she had been watching the clock for me all day. She used to call me her little angel, and she would envelop me with hugs and kisses when it was just the two of us there in the evenings. And then Vinny would call and he would have a man with him – different men with all sorts of faces, different accents, different colours. Rich men, poor men, druggies, salesmen, you name it. And Vinny would send me to my room and tell me to turn on the television nice and loud. He bought me the television for my room and when Reece came along he bought him one too."

I swallow back my horror. What a horrible way for a child to live! I feel like taking Maria in my arms and erasing all her memories but I know that will never happen. She has scars so deep that I could never find them all.

"In the summertime, he would send me to the shop because the evenings were bright and he would tell me to take Reece and not come back for an hour. I would sit on the swings in the park and watch every minute go by on my wristwatch, and sometimes Reece would want to go home and I couldn't take him and he would try to count up to sixty as many times as he could, knowing that each minute he counted was closer to home time. One evening it rained heavily and we just sat on the swings until the hour passed by and when we got back we were soaked right through and came down with terrible coughs and colds. My mother cried for four days after that. She said she would never forgive herself. But it was Vinny I blamed, not Singh. He created her and he broke her and now he wants to break me too. Please don't let him, Hollie."

I look up to see Caroline in the doorway. She has been listening and her face says it all. She comes inside and sits beside Maria, stroking her shoulder and unable to find the words she needs to comfort and reassure her. I'm not sure I have the words either.

"Has Max gone?" she asks.

"Yes, I told him to go. I told him we didn't need his help. He . . . he . . ."

I don't know what I want to say. I can't think of what I want to say about Max Kelly and then I look at Caroline and at Maria and I think of the two children asleep and of where we are in the middle of nowhere . . .

"You were right to send him away," says Caroline. "You don't know enough about the man. Oh God, what if he tells Vinny? Jesus, he might tell him we're here!"

"No, he won't," I say. "He wouldn't do that. There is no way he would do that."

Maria looks at me, then Caroline, then me again like a spectator at a game of tennis. I am so aware of her fears and her vulnerability and I don't want to frighten her any more than she already has been.

"Caroline, I think Max Kelly made a horrible mistake when he was just a few years older than what Maria is now. He wanted to stay here and protect us from Vinny, but I told him to go."

Caroline looks frightened now. She turns to Maria. "But Vinny would never come here. He has no –"

"He does," Maria and I say at the same time and Caroline's face falls all the more.

"Jesus!" she whispers. "Jesus!"

Her words echo in the room and I take my mobile phone from my handbag. I can feel the fear in the room and my skin prickles cold.

"Maria, go to the bedroom and stay with the children. There is a lock on the inside of the door. Lock it and do not come out until I say."

She eases herself off the chair and goes to leave, then stops when she reaches the doorway that leads to the hall.

"Thank you," she says, her beautiful face crumpled into a frown. "Thank you both so much for rescuing me." She leaves before we can reply.

"Well, are you going to call the police then or are we going to just sit and wait for him?" asks Caroline. "He will come here, you know. I can feel it."

She is peeping out through the blinds and wringing her hands as she does so. I have never seen her so nervous. My stomach is sick yet numbness has washed over my mind so that I just sit and stare as if time has stood still. The cottage is eerily silent and outside it is pitch dark with not a sound for miles apart from the crashing of the waves in the distance and the faint hum of traffic from the nearest roadway that runs a couple of miles from where we are.

"I should have asked Max more questions," I mumble,

staring at the floor now. "There is so much more I need to know from him. He said she loved him, Caroline. She mentioned someone in her diary – but could it be him? I wonder if he is telling the truth?"

"Hollie! Will you bloody snap out of it! Do you realise what we have got ourselves into here? We are in such danger from an evil animal who thinks we have been snooping into his business and you are caught up in some 'what if' love mystery from years ago? We have to make sure he doesn't know we are here! We have to protect those poor children that are lying asleep and who are depending on us to help them get out of this disgusting lifestyle they were born into!"

I nod slowly as the realisation washes over me. Yes, we need to do something. We need to call the police, just like Max said. Yes, I will do that. I will do that now.

I lift my phone again and am shocked to see how my hands are shaking. I begin to dial the number and then I stop.

I hear a car in the distance.

"Hollie, call them! Give me the bloody phone!"

The car comes closer again and we freeze and stare at each other, like proverbial rabbits in headlights as the car's beam shines through the blinds. It is him. I know it and Caroline knows it and we both know we have left this too late. I have left it too late.

"Oh, sweet Jesus," mumbles Caroline as she dials. "Oh, please help us."

"Hollie Lynch," says Vinny, striding across our garden. I remember in all the commotion that I have left Jinx outside when I hear him mark his territory but Vinny ignores the barking dog as if he doesn't exist. He lifts his foot and kicks Jinx hard in the stomach and the animal's howls go right through me as I crouch under the window with Caroline by my side. We cling to each other as he roars from the other side of the wall.

"Hollie fucking Lynch! You stupid, nosey little bitch! I know you are in there and you have my children. Open the fucking door!"

I think about Maria and all the times she has suffered the wrath of this monster. I think about my mother and how he ruined her life too. How his dirty actions led to her suicide and all the guilt and horrific memories he left her with. I think about Max . . .

"Fuck! Play it this way then!" he shouts and the sounds of smashing glass makes us both yelp a little, like two cornered animals who know there is no way out. I hear him rummage at the door as he searches for the lock and then the thud of the door opening. He is in. Oh my God, he is in the house!

"Hide, Caroline," I whisper to her and I push her away from me. "Go into the kitchen and hide."

"No!"

"Go!" I tell her. "If he sees both of us he will know the kids are here. Give me time to bluff him, or at least try. Quickly!"

"But he'll see my car!"

"Go, Caroline!"

I shove her through the door that leads to the tiny pantry-style kitchen and I lock her in, knowing that he is only feet from me. I can sense his presence in every corner.

I can smell his sweat before I even see him, but when he comes into the room and looks me in the eye, the smirk on his ugly face makes me squirm inside more than I could have prepared for.

"How cosy!" he says and he clears his throat, then spits onto the floor and I feel my stomach heave. "What a nice little nest she had here, eh?"

"You bastard," I mutter but my voice sounds weak and feeble in comparison to his gruff arrogance. "You heartless, evil bastard!"

"You look just like her, you know. Has anyone ever told you that? A dirty, rotten whore who needs to know her place in this world. A silly little do-gooder who should know when to keep her fucking nose out of other people's business! Out of my business!"

He moves closer to me and I step back until I reach the wall and can go no further and the cold on the wall tells me my time is up. His hands are in his pockets and he breathes in and out through his nose, the temper rising and pulsing from the veins in his red neck and a straight line of sweat sitting above his thin lips. He is a big man, an ox of a man and I can't imagine how Singh and Maria have suffered at his filthy, dirty hands for so long, as he ruled their lives and their everyday existence. There is so much I want to say to him right now. So, so much but I know I daren't.

"Where are they?" he snorts. "Where are my children?"

"They are not *your* children, Vinny. You have no say over their wellbeing. Not any more."

He grabs my throat and pushes me into the wall so that my head bounces off the cold brick and I can't breathe.

His breath stinks of alcohol and he smells of stale sweat, his coarse hand gripping my neck.

"Don't fucking talk to me like that, bitch! I told you to mind your own business! Where are they? Where is Maria?"

His nails press into me and he squeezes harder and harder.

My eyes are watering now and I close them. I don't want to look at him. He repulses me. I try to raise my knee to defend myself but he finds it and pushes my leg to the side, then shoves his hand up under my dress and pulls at my underwear, tearing it in his hands.

I pretend this isn't happening. I try to blank my mind and bring it to another place. The beach. Yes, I am on the beach and it is sunny and there are lots of people and . . .

"You want this, is that what you want, you filthy little bitch? You want what your mother got, don't you? Well, you will fucking get it! You will get it!"

"Please! Please stop!" I find my voice but it doesn't sound like me. This is not happening. I turn my head to the side as he paws at me, mauls me in his huge hands. He pulls my face back towards him and squeezes my jaw.

"Look at me, you slut. Look my fucking way when I'm talking to you! Not so clever now, are you?"

He lifts his arm and slaps me with the back of his hand, so that his rings scrape my skin and I taste blood as it trickles into my mouth. He shakes me when I don't answer and his thumbs dig into my shoulders so hard that I can feel my bones move.

He pushes me further into the wall again, so hard I hear my back crack and I can see my mother watching me, her eyes filled with sorrow and she is reaching out to me trying to help, calling me, but I can't get free from his grasp.

"What was it you wanted from me? What were you trying to find out with all your snooping around, playing stupid detective games? You didn't know what you're messing with, did you? Don't you ever, ever dare dig into my past!"

"I . . . I just . . ."

"You just thought you'd try and make your poor old dead mother proud, is that it? Oh, you really are quite the chip of the old block, aren't you? She didn't have much to say for herself either. She just lay there and took it like a good girl and you are going to do the same."

He lets go of my neck and I hear a scream and it is me.

I scream at the top of my voice and I feel my lungs empty as the piercing sound of my voice drowns out the jingle from the game show on the television.

I hear Caroline rattle the kitchen door handle and call my name. He must hear her too but he doesn't react. He is focused on me now and me alone.

He is a monster. He is much more brutal than I thought. My poor mother. Even now I think of her and I sense how terrified she must have been. There were three of them, I hear her say. And now one of them wants me to suffer just as they made her suffer all those years ago.

"You bastard!" I yell and when he comes closer to me again I spit in his face and regret it instantly. His face distorts with rage and his fist comes crashing into my ribs.

"You should have known better! You should have known that I would come after you when you were sneaking around like that."

339

I try to ride the pain, hearing Caroline's voice as if it were in the far distance.

"Your mother was a snoop just like you. She didn't know how to stay out of other peoples' business either and look where that got her!"

"She got *me*!" I scream. I want to punch him. I want to hurt him but I am powerless. "You might think you ruined her but she still had me. You couldn't take that away from her!"

His breath is repulsing me as he pulls me towards him, then throws me onto the sofa. He pins me down, leaning all his body weight on top of me, crushing me, working his knee so that it pushes up between my legs and it hurts so, so much.

"I'm just about to take you now," he snarls and his hand moves down to his zip.

I hear the back door slam and another voice. Oh please God, let it be help. Please don't do this to me.

I open my eyes and look up to see Max towering over me. Oh God, thank you. Oh thank you, Max!

"You bastard!" he says, pulling the heaving weight off my body and knocking him to the ground. "Is this your idea of closure? What the fuck are you trying to prove?"

Max stands in front of me as Vinny wipes his bloodied nose with the back of his hand.

"Ah, Max, are you looking some of the action too, old friend? Looks like you've come to the right place. It's just like old times."

"Don't ever compare me to you, Vinny. You and I are two very different people. I never was in your league, no matter how you care to remember it."

340

"You never wanted to finish the job, did you, Max? We had to make you do it! You had the same opportunity as me and Pete but you just stood there, looking on, watching us get our piece of pie until you knew you had to give in and take yours too. You wimp! You're still a fucking public schoolboy wimp!"

Vinny gets to his feet with a slight wobble and Max walks up to him and grabs him by the neck. He throws him against the wall and yells into his face as I cower in a corner.

"You can call me what you like, Vinny! I don't care about you. You ruined my life that night and I have tried to forget the horrors you put that girl through and now you're back to do the same to her daughter? I have had your filth on my conscience every day and every night since. A few beatings from you were never going to make me forget what I saw. You can't beat me now and you can't beat those kids any more!"

Oh no. Oh Max. Why did you have to mention the kids?

Vinny finds a new lease of life and he wrestles Max away from him, then locks his arm into a twist so that Max cannot break free.

"You know nothing about those fucking kids! You know nothing about me either. You always did want to play the hero," croaks Vinny and I can see Max's arm shake under the strain of being held in place. "How does it feel to finally rescue your girl? Does it feel good? I bet what I was trying to get from her would have felt much better."

Max shoots me a look with horror in his eyes. "Did he touch you? In that way?"

I nod and huddle back into the corner, cover my face and pray for this to be over.

"You dirty bastard!"

I hear a click and when I look up Max is pointing a gun in Vinny's face. He has wrestled free and he has a gun. My skin goes cold.

"No! No, Max, don't do it! Please don't!"

Vinny smirks at Max as his hands shake holding the weapon and Max takes a few steps back.

"You're like a little boy scout," laughs Vinny. "You wouldn't even know how to use a fucking gun, would you? Not since you played Cowboys and Indians with your poncy friends at your posh school all those years ago. Go on, pull the trigger. I fucking dare you! But you can't. You're just not cut out for this, are you, Max?"

"Do it! Do it now! Kill him!"

Maria is standing in the doorway, clinging to the doorframe as she stares at Vinny with a hatred that a girl of her age should not even know of. Her face is stern and desperate and she stares at Vinny, nodding her head.

"Maria, baby," says Vinny and his hands go up into surrender when he sees her. His voice softens so much it makes me want to gag. "I thought you were in trouble. I came to get you. Where are your brother and sister?"

Max keeps the gun steady. I know it is killing him to even hold such a deadly weapon but Maria looks like she could easily use it. Not even a problem.

"But I don't have a sister, do I, Vinny?" she says to him, her eyes glazed and focused on her prey. "She's not my sister, is she? You know it and I know it! Pull the trigger, Max. Kill him!"

Max looks at me, then at Vinny and then at Maria. His feet shuffle and the gun quivers in his hands and like a flash-forward I see what is about to happen before it does.

"No!" I shout but it's too late. Vinny pounces forward and grabs the gun, then raps it under Max's chin and sends him to the floor as blood oozes from his nose and mouth. He kneels on Max's chest and points the gun into his face then waves it around the room, pointing it at me and then at Maria and back again at Max.

"No, no, Vinny!" says Maria and she covers her ears with her hands. "No, don't kill him! Don't do it! I can't watch this again. Don't do it!"

Max is eyeballing Vinny as the gun points in his face.

I close my eyes in horror but am compelled to open them again.

From behind, Maria – little brave Maria – lifts a picture from the wall and slices it across Vinny's face and he yelps like a wounded animal. The gun slips from his grip onto the floor. I hide my head in my hands. No! I cannot look to see where it has landed. There is a slight pause. And then the trigger clicks . . .

The sound of gunfire rattles through the house and the baby screams from down the hallway and I know that this moment will never, ever leave me. The click of the trigger and the muffled gunfire shot . . . I can't look up from my place on the floor and I shiver and shake as a trickle of blood skirts along the wooden floor and stops in a pool just before it reaches my foot, like a river that has nowhere else to go . . .

51

After she fires the gun, Maria drops it like a hot potato onto the floor and screams so loudly I believe she has been injured herself. She is almost dancing with fear of what she has just done and she claws at her clothes, terrified beyond belief of what fate might await her now.

"It's okay, baby," says Vinny, his eyes glassy and cold. "Daddy knows you didn't mean it. Don't worry."

He clutches his leg, plugging his gun wound with his stubby fingers in a way that makes me think he has done this many times before. Then he leans back onto the floor, stubborn and wounded but far from defeated. Max sits up, gasping for breath. The gun lies between Maria and the men on the floor but nobody moves.

"You're a rapist, Max Kelly," Vinny spits. "A dirty, rapist bastard and I was there to see you do it, just like *you* watched me. You are no better than I am, with your celebrity lifestyle and glossed-over history that you thought you could shove into the background of your past. You thought you had got away with it, didn't you? No, no, no. Long runs the fox, isn't that what they say? But you have my blood on your hands now too. Pity you missed your aim though, isn't it?"

Max has almost as much blood trickling from his face as what oozes from Vinny's light bullet-wound on his thigh.

"I didn't fucking do it. I didn't shoot you," says Max, holding his jaw.

"Oh, but you did. You did shoot me. Your prints are all over the gun. He shot me, didn't he, Maria?" Maria doesn't answer and Vinny roars at her. "Didn't he, Maria? Didn't he?"

She nods like an obedient puppy and turns into the wall, her wrists unable to wipe away the flow of tears that pour down her face. A police siren, all too late, sounds very faintly in the far distance. The baby cries louder so I signal to Maria to make herself scarce. She looks at me, her eyes pleading with fear, but I urge her to leave right now.

"It was always your way, Vinny," says Max, lifting his bruised body from the floor. "No one could keep up with you back then. It was always your way or no way, wasn't it?"

"And it still is, Max," said Vinny. "It still is that way and maybe now you and your little team of Charlie's Angels will finally realise that. The cops have nothing on me. They never have. I'm clean, Max. I always keep my nose very, very clean in this game so they know nothing. Not a thing . . . but look at you, lying there with your prints all over that gun and my leg bust open."

"You broke into my mother's house!" I tell him. "You have no reason to be here!"

"My children are down the hall!" he roars back at me. "I came to get them and you wouldn't answer the door. I'd be careful if I were you! *Really* fucking careful!"

"They are not your children!" I shout. "Maria despises you. She always has despised you! You raped her too, didn't you, Vinny? Didn't you rape your own daughter? You raped Maria! That's why she wanted you dead just now!"

"Maria will stand by me in the end, you'll see," he says with smugness written all over his face. "We've been round too many corners together, young Maria and me. But as for Max here? What the hell is he doing here anyhow? Come on, Max. Let's play cops and robbers while we wait. Why did you come here? What did you have in mind? Go on, Mr Celebrity, tell us!"

Max's breath is rasping and shallow and I worry that he is more seriously wounded than had first appeared. His nose is definitely broken and perhaps his jaw is too and he finds it very hard to speak.

"I . . . I wanted to find Hollie," he whispers. "I needed to tell her the truth."

"The truth?" says Vinny and he throws his head back laughing so that I see his mouth, his huge pink tongue and his yellowing teeth. "There *is* no truth in all of this, is there? There is yo*ur* version, my version and Pete's fucking version and he don't count for much, does he? He's dead, the bitch is dead and her darling daughter here is playing with fire with her detective work and she knows it. So it's just you and me, Maxie boy, and I've nothing to lose. *You're* the criminal now, Max. At least it looks that way from where I'm sitting. Illegal handgun, anyone? Fingerprints?" He sniggers. "Hard to watch your whole life go up in a puff of smoke, isn't it, Chef? Pardon the pun, but that's what you get for playing with fire."

Max jolts, as if Vinny has hit another nerve and it stings.

"So it *was* you," he whispers. "Why, Vinny? Why are you out to ruin me? Even my business? My livelihood. You burned it all down. Why? You couldn't stop until it was all away. Everything! Why?"

Vinny's snarling laugh curdles my insides as the sirens come closer.

"Because I could, Max. Because I could. *And* I wanted to wipe that smug grin off your face once and for all. Why should you have the good life, Max? Why should you live in luxury while the rest of us struggle?"

I pray that Max keeps his cool.

"My life is no luxury and you know it!" he shouts at Vinny, his voice raw and full of emotion. "You saw to that all those years ago! You ruined me years ago!"

Vinny surveys him coolly. "Oh, Max, Max, come on! Stop blaming me for all your wrongdoings. I can ruin you even more and the beautiful thing is, no one will ever know I exist in your world. No one will suspect a thing!"

The police are outside now. I hear their tyres on the gravel and the twirling lights from the siren swirl around the room like a scene from a nightclub.

"And what about me?" I shout from across the room. "What about what I know? What Maria knows? You can't get away with his, Vinny! You won't get away with it! I will make sure you don't!"

"I've been getting away with this for years," says Vinny and he spits again onto my mother's floor. "Don't ever think you'll stop me. This is not your field of expertise. Stick to playing your little violin, or I'll come and get you and next time, Hollie, I will finish you off. Now we'll get rid of the gun and we'll get rid of the cops. There was no gun, do you hear?"

I look at Max and he is as confused as I am as Vinny scoops the gun up and shoves it down the back of the sofa.

"We will all go down if they find the gun. It was a row that got out of hand. Let's call it a domestic since we're all related, aren't we?"

He sniggers and the police knock at the door.

I unlock the kitchen door and a weeping Caroline throws her arms around me. Then she gasps when she sees the destruction in the living room.

The cottage is unrecognisable with the furniture askew and the bloody stains on the floor and the stench of stale sweat and cigarette smoke lingers in the air.

A police officer takes blood samples from the floor and another hovers around asking questions but none of us are in any fit state to answer.

"An ambulance is on its way, sir," says a policewoman to Vinny who is still lying on the floor, wearing a very brave face.

I can't tell the police about him or it will get Maria and Max into trouble. I want to grass on him so much but my hands are tied.

"None of us need an ambulance!" says Vinny.

"Somebody get my Maria. Where is Maria? I just want to take my family home."

Maria comes into the living room, holding the baby on her shoulder, Reece by her side. She drops the little backpacks they brought with them at her feet – the larger one is on her back. A rush of fear and dread runs through me. The boy huddles into her leg and she winces, but she doesn't push him off. Instead she pulls him closer to her, like a mini-shield or a blanket of security that she needs close by her at all times.

"Yes?" she says to Vinny.

"We're going home once I get this bleeding stopped. You all ready?"

She nods and pulls Reece closer.

"Maria? No!" I say but she just stares at the floor and ignores me. "Maria, you can stay here. You can all stay here. You know that. Officer, you cannot let him take them home. He is dangerous. He –"

"He what?" says the police officer.

I can feel Vinny watching me and Maria's eyes warn me not to say anything. They plead with me. She shakes her head.

"He is not who they need right now," is all I can manage to say. "Please don't let them go home with him. Maria?"

"I'm ready, Vinny," she says and my insides flip over. "I'm just going to fetch the baby a drink while we wait – is that okay, Hollie?"

"Fine," I say and I watch helplessly as she makes her way past me and into the kitchen. I am shocked and afraid, but I know this is out of my hands.

The police officer leaves the room.

"Maria's coming home with me," says Vinny to me from under his breath. "And if you open your fucking mouth again I will gag you with my own bare hands. Shut the fuck up and take this as your final warning. If I don't get you, I know about half a dozen people who will gladly finish you off on my behalf."

"You can't even *take* her home," I say to him and his eyes pump fear through my body. I have no doubt that he could order a hit crew for me within minutes so I try a different approach. "Look at you. Look at the state of you. You can't drive with your leg injury. It wouldn't be safe for the children."

He laughs. "I'm sorry to disappoint you but this is just a flesh wound – my little princess here didn't aim very well – she didn't really want to hurt her old man. The bullet just skimmed me. A bit of bandaging and we'll be on our way home."

Every time he refers to Maria and the children as his family I flinch inside but I know I cannot help her any more. Something inside her has been switched off and I know she is giving up her fight, just as her mother once had all those years ago. Vinny is in control once more. Vinny is set to win again and even I don't know which way to turn now to make it better. Telling the truth in this case is putting my own life on the line and I guess that Maria knows that it would put her in the same position.

"Max? Are you okay?" I mutter but of course he is not okay. How could any of us be okay?

He sits on the edge of the settee, his head in his hands as the commotion continues around us. A million thoughts race through my head but words escape me. Where did Max get the gun? Why did he feel the need to pull it out on Vinny? Was this supposed to be an act of revenge? Was it a power trip he thought he could see through? Or was it merely to protect us?

"I'm sorry, Hollie," he says and he meets my eyes.

A shiver runs down my spine and I can't place why but I suddenly know with no shadow of a doubt that the familiarity I see in him is for the reasons I have suspected all along. He knows it and so do I.

"I'm sorry," he repeats. "I shouldn't have left you. I didn't go far. Just as far as the petrol station on the main road – I pulled in there to call the police on my mobile – I was afraid you wouldn't do it. He must have passed by while I was doing that. Then I came back. Thank God I was in time."

I say nothing. I cannot bring myself to thank him though I am full of gratitude for my deliverance.

When the ambulance arrives, Vinny is led outside to have his leg strapped up and I get the opportunity to talk to Maria, with Caroline by my side. We prop Reece up at the table in the kitchen with milk and cookies and the baby chugs a bottle in Maria's lap.

"Why are you doing this?" I whisper but she is stunned and she cannot answer me. "Maria? You cannot go back to that life. You know you can't. Where is your fight? This is your opportunity to get rid of Vinny and all that comes with him. If you don't tell the police now, you never will."

"My mother is dying," says Maria, staring across the kitchen and not even sounding like she did earlier. My heart sinks when I picture how feisty and strong she once was, then the vulnerable and emotional teenager that I saw earlier that evening and now she is a shadow of both of those people.

It is like she is dead inside.

"Maria, Singh is dying but she wouldn't want you to die too, would she? Come on! Where is her little angel? Where is the one she used to envelop in kisses and hugs before Vinny would come in and shatter your dreams? You don't want that for Reece or your baby, do you? You don't want to live under his command for ever like she did? You are better than that. You deserve better. You know you do."

A police officer comes into the kitchen and asks for a glass of water.

"I will need full statements from each of you," she says. "Obviously no one here is prepared to talk much right now and neither of the wounded parties want to press charges, so for now, unless you are willing to talk, I don't see what else we can do for you."

"And that's it?" asks Caroline. "He broke into this house – we didn't invite him!"

"He says you were holding his children captive. Anyhow, this is not the place for arguments, ma'am. I will need a statement in full."

"But these children are running scared," says Caroline. "Maria, tell this lady what he has done to you. Tell her!"

Maria watches Caroline plead with her but doesn't react in any shape or form. There is no way she's going to sink Vinny. No way.

"If Vinny is not going to press charges, then I guess I should get him home," she says and she gets up from the

352

seat with the baby in her arms. "Reece, you can carry the backpacks, okay?"

Caroline helps him to put his on his back and he picks up the baby's.

"Well, if you ever change your mind," says the police officer, "you can talk to me anytime. Ask for Officer Clements. I'm on duty for the next twelve hours. When you're ready to talk . . ."

"I don't need to talk to you, Officer Clements," says Maria and I want to shake her. "I have no reason to talk to you. I am fine."

"Maria, you are not fine!" I cry. "Please, Officer, she has so much to tell. She is in danger with this man. Please believe me!"

"Maria?" asks Officer Clements. "Tell me now before we leave."

"When I'm ready," she whispers and she brushes past the police officer and bundles her family together for the terrifying journey ahead.

Max sits in the back of the ambulance having his own injuries cleaned up. I walk out to him, my arms folded against the evening breeze.

"So, what do we do now?" I ask him and he looks back at me, his bloodied nose and blackening eyes a pathetic sight.

"I would perfectly understand if you never want to see me again," he says, biting his lip. "I've even managed to mess this up. I should have shot him. I should have just finished the bastard off."

I kick a stone and watch as it bounces across the yard and disappears under my car. Jinx has given up barking and is crouched in the garden, his head on his paws.

"I think we still have a lot of unfinished business," I whisper to him. "I think we have only scraped the surface and I don't think we have heard the last of Vinny either. But on a personal note, I still don't feel like I have closure on what you and Vinny did to my mother. Part of me wants you to suffer more. I want Vinny to suffer for what he did to her."

"An eye for an eye?" says Max and I nod slowly.

"Yes, an eye for an eye. Revenge," I say. "I want revenge, Max. I want him dead. I want you to finish him off."

When the ambulance and police leave us, I watch Maria, Reece and Niamh move out of the cottage and back to the only life they have ever known. The huge monstrous Vinny, his leg heavily bandaged, leads the way and Maria and her little family climb into the back of his car.

"I will look after them," says little Reece when I ruffle his hair as he shuffles past me. "When I'm a big boy I will look after Maria and Niamh. Don't worry, Hollie. We'll be okay. And Mummy will be home soon."

52

We don't speak much after that. Max's car outside is the only reminder that anything happened this evening and with him gone to hospital for treatment, a shocking silence lingers in the air between Caroline and me. Both of us drift into sleep as we sit and I am woken eventually by the smell of coffee and the sounds of Caroline moving about the kitchen. I think it is morning until I open my eyes and find it is still dark. I force myself to get up and shuffle into the kitchen.

Wordlessly I sit and wordlessly she puts a mug of coffee before me. Then she sits too and we sip our coffee, both of us lost in thought.

"She had her chance," says Caroline at last. "I just can't believe that she sided with him like that. Oh God, Hollie, what have we done?"

I have a dead, empty feeling in my stomach. I want Ben here to hold me and tell me we did all we could for Maria but I know in my heart that Ben has had enough of my obsessions with my past. And I have more on my conscience now than ever before and I could never expect him to carry that burden.

"I want to call her to see if she is okay but I'm afraid that he will be manning her phone," I say. "He'll have people watching us too, you do know that?"

Caroline nods and I feel so sorry for her. She warned me about this so many times and now I have dragged her into it and put her life in danger as much as I have mine.

"As long as Vinny is around, our lives will never be the same," says Caroline. "I think you should go home, Hollie. Home to Belfast where you have people around and jobs to go to and try and gradually get your life back on track. There are too many memories here and I think it's about time we closed the door on this as much as possible."

"No," I tell her. "I can't do that, Caroline. I can't rest until he is dealt with in the proper way. I have told Max."

"Hollie, I beg you to stop this. I beg you to know when it's time to draw the line. We have crossed the line, way further than we ever should have and if tonight has not taught you that, then I don't know what will!"

"But the police can't touch Vinny, can they? Why should someone like him be able to roam our streets when my mum is lying six feet under and Singh and Maria's lives have been ruined? And what about little Reece and the baby? What will become of them if I give up now?"

"Give up!" says Caroline. "I am not asking you any more, Hollie. I am telling you. Leave it be!"

I drum my fingers on the table. Every syllable of Caroline's speech sounds like thunder in my ears. I imagine Vinny driving like a maniac around the windy coastal roads. I imagine Maria's face, terrified and sore, and her mind racing towards what she will have to suffer when she gets home. I picture Reece, shivering in the back seat of the car, covering his little ears as Vinny thumps the steering wheel with his huge iron fist and I feel my heart pound and scream at me to do something to stop him.

"You don't understand," I mutter, my monotone almost unrecognisable. "He will kill her tonight. I know he will."

"Hollie, no! Don't say that. Don't even go there. It would be too risky in the circumstances – he has the wits to see that."

I stand up, my heart beating like a drum now. My head is spinning. My mouth is dry and the nausea is so bad that I feel like I could be sick. The energy I feel though is uncontrollable like a sugar rush gone overboard and I can feel every pulse in my body, every vein pumping now as the fear rushes through me, taunting me, calling me. I know she is in danger. I can sense it. I think of the gun. It is in the sitting room, thrust down the back of the sofa. I think of Max and what I asked him to do. Why did I ask him to do something that I know I can do myself?

"I have to go after them," I tell Caroline.

"No!" She stumbles as she gets to her feet.

"I will not have this on my conscience. I just cannot sit here and let this happen. He has killed before and he will kill again. You can stay here. I am going after them."

I walk to the living room in a robotic state and like a magnet to a piece of metal, my hand finds the gun and I lift it like an expert and feel its cool, hard exterior. It is heavier than I thought it would be and the cold metallic sensation on my skin sends a thrill of power through me that I have never experienced before. I want to use this weapon. I want to go after Vinny and finish him off myself and no one will stop me.

"Thanks, mate," said Max as he paid the taxi driver at the end of the lane that led to Estelle's cottage.

"Are you sure you're okay from here?" asked the driver.

He hadn't stopped talking throughout the entire journey from the hospital and Max now had a thumping headache to add to his other injuries. Still, a broken nose and a few bumps and grazes were easier to live with than having a murder on his hands. He had been so close to pulling the trigger, inches from it. He would never forget the weight of the gun in his hands and the look on Vinny's face as he pointed it his way. He looked cocky and fearless as the weapon was aimed at him, but Max knew it was a mask. Flashes from the past circled in Max's head – the bullying, the pressures, the drugs, the dirty rotten lifestyle that Vinny had lured so many into and the lives he had taken and ruined. Now that beautiful young girl and her siblings were set for a lifetime of misery and pain and God knows what else. He should have finished the job. He felt cowardly in one way, but the bigger man in another.

"I'll live," he said to the chatterbox taxi driver and he threw him an extra few pounds just to get rid of him quickly. "Thanks for the company. Have a nice night."

He walked away from the beam of the car's headlamps and into the darkness of the winding lane. He could see there were lights on and as he approached the house his heart-rate increased and the fear of what was still to come throbbed more than his bloodied nose.

He would take his car and leave this tiny place and drive straight to Dublin where he had so much still to fix with Sandra and the boys. Perhaps he could convince Hollie to let Vinny and his poison simmer into the background of all of their lives. He had done more than enough damage already and Max feared that if they pushed him any further, there would be so much worse to come. Max was not a killer, but Vinny was.

His pace quickened down the bumpy lane, past a scattering of similar cottages and he took a short-cut through a mossy field that brought him out the back of Estelle's place. He stopped and drew a breath, his head pumping with exhaustion, worry and the rant of that damn taxi driver's voice not to mention the haunting look on Vinny's face as he watched him leave with those children. But one image stayed with him even stronger than that. One image would never leave his head for the rest of his life and that was the way Hollie looked at him when she said she wanted to see Vinny dead. Her eyes, her mouth, the way she stood, the way she pursed her lips tight in anger.

It was like looking at his mirror image.

Yes, she resembled Estelle too in almost a ghostly way. When he had first seen her play the violin that night at his restaurant, he was convinced he was being haunted by the past he had never properly shut the door on. She was Estelle, in flesh and bone, staring at him, reminding him of his deadly sin as she played the strings on that instrument. The way she stood, the way she played – everything was a carbon copy of her mother but now, in almost every move she made, the way she spoke, the way she looked at him, he could see a definite trail of characteristics that came directly from him. And he couldn't decide which of the images frightened him more.

He reached the front door of the house and stalled as his hand lifted the knocker on the green door. He could hear raised voices, panic even, and his skin prickled cold.

"Hollie? Hollie are you okay?" he shouted as he banged the door as hard as he could. "Hollie!"

The other woman, Caroline, swung the door open and pulled him by the arm inside.

"You stupid bastard!" she said. "You brought a gun into this house and now she has it. Please, you have to talk to her! She's lost her mind. She says she's going after him. Please, Max. Maybe she'll listen to you."

Max pushed his way through the tiny hallway and into the sitting room where Hollie sat nursing the gun, caressing it like a baby one second, then examining it in the tiniest detail the next.

"Hollie, listen to me," said Max softly. He tried to meet her eye but she just stared at the gun, mumbling to herself. "Give me the gun, Hollie. Come on. Give it to me."

He was terrified and felt vulnerable and an easy target. Hollie's eyes were vacant and he wasn't totally sure that she wouldn't decide to turn the gun on him instead.

"I have to go now," she said, her voice flat and without rhythm. "I have to go and finish this. I started it so I will finish it. I will never contact you again, Max. Go home to your wife and family."

She gripped the gun now, so tight that her knuckles turned white, and Max's heartbeat raised a notch. He could feel Caroline behind him, equally terrified as Hollie's eyes squinted and stared at the deadly weapon in front of her.

"Give Max the gun, Hollie," whispered Caroline. "He needs to return it. We don't want to get into any more trouble and with a gun in the house we are asking for it. Come on, Hollie. Give it to him. Give it to him now!"

But Hollie looked as if she was in a different world right now.

"He deserves to die. He killed my mother, he is killing Singh and he is killing me now. I have to kill him before he kills me. Before he kills Maria. This is nothing to do with either of you. Just let me get on with it. This is my problem, not yours."

Max glanced at Caroline's pale and shocked face.

"Maybe I should call Ben?" suggested Caroline. "If Ben was here, she might listen."

"I haven't gone anywhere, Caroline!" said Hollie sharply. "Don't talk about me like I'm not here. And there's no point phoning Ben. He doesn't care any more. He gave up on me a long time ago."

"Ronan then? Do you want Ronan here?"

"I don't want anyone here! Why won't you listen to me? I just want to go to Singh's house and talk some sense into Maria and pull this fucking trigger so that Vinny is out of all of our lives forever. That's what I want to do and neither you, nor Ben, nor Ronan will stop me!"

She got up, pushed past Max, and charged towards the doorway with both Caroline and Max on her tail. She was fast and strong but she held the gun loosely at her side as she approached the front door and Max saw his opportunity. He scooped his arm around her waist and wrenched the gun from her hand, then fell to the floor when it dropped. He had it. He had it nestled under his stomach and when he reached his hand under his belly and grasped it tight the relief he felt was momentous, as if he had saved her life.

"No!" she cried. "I have to do this! Please let me do this, Max!"

Max slowly pulled his body up from the floor. He tucked the gun inside the waistband of his jeans, pulled his bloodied shirt over it and stood against the wall. He could see her watching it under his clothes, wondering if she could wrestle it back into her possession, but her eyes had softened somewhat, as if she was realising how close she had been to doing something incredibly dangerous.

Her expression slowly changed from that of a wild-eyed crazed revenge-seeking young girl to a frightened, vulnerable woman who had no idea what to do next.

"Hollie," he said softly, "you are angry and confused. Let's just take a deep breath and think this through. We both hate Vinny and my God we both have good reason to want him gone, but this is not the way to do it. We cannot take his life into our hands, as much as we wish we could. Come inside, Hollie. Come on."

He held out his hand to touch her shoulder but she flinched and walked ahead of him, back into the warmth of the sitting room.

"Thank you," Caroline mouthed to Max and then she slid down onto the sofa.

The sense of relief was tangible in the room and it was like they had been given a new beginning, a fresh start. Hollie's colour slowly returned to her face as they sat in silence, each aware of nothing other than their own heart beat and how close they had come to making their very messy situation a whole lot worse.

"Can I get anyone a drink? Tea? Something stronger?" asked Caroline at last, sensing she should make herself scarce. The atmosphere may have simmered down but there was a building tension in the air that spelt unfinished business.

"I'll have a brandy," said Hollie. "Make that two. Max will join me, I'm sure."

"Not for me. No," said Max. "I have quite a journey ahead of me tonight. I really, really should be making tracks."

He looked at the clock and calculated that he would be back in Dublin by two in the morning. But where would he go? He had no home, no family to welcome him back and listen to what he had been through. Gina had been more than generous so far and Will was in no fit state for visitors to his house.

"Call your wife," said Hollie and she looked into his eyes which were filled with regret and sadness. "Call your wife and sons and tell them you are coming home."

He shook his head and looked at the floor. "They . . . they don't want me home, Hollie. It's too late for that. I have let them all down by my behaviour. I've been a lousy husband and a worse father. For years I have carried the guilt of that one horrible night around with me, using it as a crutch of blame when things in my life went wrong.

A few years back I even had a brief fling and almost wrecked my marriage and I justified it by telling myself I didn't deserve normal happiness. I drank too much, I worked too hard and all the time I have been running away from my actions, instead of facing up to a few home truths. You have made me realise those truths, Hollie. You have awakened the ghosts from my past and, my God, I tell you it is frightening."

He reluctantly took the glass of brandy from Caroline, his hands shaking ever so slightly and when he put the glass to his lips, he shocked even himself when he gulped back the dark liquid, its heat instantly rushing through his cold veins.

"Looks like you won't be driving too far tonight," said Caroline. "But don't think you're staying here."

Max handed the glass back and wiped his mouth with the back of his hand.

"I will drive to Dublin now and leave you two girls to get on with your lives if that's what you want. But, Hollie, I think I should stay a while – we have more to talk about, don't you agree?"

Hollie was sipping her drink, embracing the soothing qualities even though it burned the back of her throat.

"You're right, Max. You're not going anywhere yet. I want to know where you got that gun, why you brought it into our house and when you are going to face up to the fact that the night you raped my mother you happened to plant the seed that made me. You are my father and I want to know more."

53

Daylight has crept in through the blinds on the small window that looks out onto the sea and my eyes sting with its presence and lack of sleep. My throat feels like it has been scratched by a bed of nails and my head is screaming at me to switch off and give it a rest.

Caroline lies fast asleep on the sofa with an old checked blanket over her.

Max looks even wearier than I do. He has aged since I saw him in the restaurant when I surprised him with my visit to Dublin. He is a different person to the man on his website who boasts about his celebrity-filled lifestyle and award-winning restaurant with his toothy handsome grin and swarthy complexion.

Now, he is no more than a criminal who pulled a gun on a smarter man just a few hours ago. Oh, how the mighty have fallen. On the other hand, he is my father. I know I shouldn't want to – I know I should push him

back out of my life and close the door on his existence –
but I want to know him more and more.

"Did you know about me?" I ask.

"No, I didn't. I swear to you, Hollie. If I had known
about you before now I would have made damn sure I
found you. I am not a bad man. Yes, I did a very stupid,
cruel and horrible thing when I was younger but I am not
a bad person deep down. People like Vinny . . ."

"Don't pin all the blame on your company, Max. You
were so weak you joined the mob that night and took
advantage of my mother. You said she was in love with
you. How could you do that to her?"

He held his hand to his chest and let out a long deep
breath. "I was very, very wrong," was all he could muster.
"I was in a bad way with drugs and alcohol but that doesn't
excuse me. And that one horrendous night has stayed with
me forever. I promise you, Hollie, I will do whatever I can
for you. If you want me to disappear, I will disappear. If you
want me to answer your questions, I will. If you want to
beat me, shoot me, whatever, you can. Whatever you want
me to be, I will be that for you. It's the least I can do."

"Why did you bring a gun here, Max?"

"I brought it to kill Vinny."

"Where did you get it?"

"A friend. Someone I met recently. He's a local lad, has
contacts. He had it for me within the hour."

"And why didn't you use it?"

"Because I'm not a killer, Hollie. And neither are you."

"You know nothing about me."

"I want to, though."

"I don't believe you."

"I do. If that's what you want."

"What about your sons? How are you going to explain this to them? And your wife? This will be the last blow for her. It has to be."

"I have a lot of bridges to cross. I just hope that in time they will understand. I made some terrible mistakes and –"

"I am a mistake. I am your mistake. Just another one of your mistakes."

"No, Hollie! No. You are not a mistake. You are you. Please believe me when I say I am not like Vinny with his brutal ways and sadistic lifestyle where he abuses people to make his mark on the world. If you only knew how many times I travelled up here looking for Estelle, wanting to make amends for what I put her through. I followed her to her work, I followed her around the supermarket, I even watched her perform a recital one summer's evening and I cried as she played. I could see it in her face that what we had done had never left her. I hurt her in so many ways, Hollie, but I never ever knew about you. If I had known about you, I would have made myself go over to her, be a better man and face up to what I had done instead of watching from afar in the shadows. I would have begged her forgiveness. I should have begged her forgiveness."

I watch him crumble before me. A broken man, a man who has watched every part of his life crash to the ground because of what he has done. One night of his life has ruined him, just as it did my mother. Yet others – people like Singh and Vinny and maybe even Maria – have made a choice to go down the other path in life. They chose a life of destruction or perhaps they were brainwashed into thinking that life had no other options for them.

I look at this man, crying into his hands before me. His marriage is in ruins, his business is destroyed, his conscience is in tatters and now he has found out that he has a daughter he didn't know existed.

"Do you believe in second chances, Max?" I ask him and he looks up at me, a tiny glimmer of hope in his eyes, laced with a doubt that tells me he thinks this may be too good to be true.

"Do *you*, Hollie?" he asks me. "I don't know that I deserve a second chance in life, but by God I would beg for one. I would beg you for one."

"I believe you deserve one, Max. Don't ask me why, but I do. I'm happy to give you a second chance."

I look at the clock my mother bought the day before she died. It is five fifteen in the morning and I am physically and mentally exhausted but somehow things seem clearer now. Much clearer. I say a silent prayer of thanks that I read her diary and that she left it for me, either accidentally or because she wanted to lead me to find Max Kelly – the man she once loved.

A huge fog has lifted from my mind and I can see everything clearer now. I feel . . . I feel just a tiny warmth of contentment at last. By God, I have waited on this moment for what feels like forever. Maybe this is my future. Maybe it's more than the closure I was expecting. It feels good.

54

Maria lay in bed, watching the clock tick by second by second, minute by minute, hour by hour. She hadn't slept yet for fear of Vinny's return. Instead she chose to lie here in her mother's double bed, with her arm around Reece on one side and the baby on the other. She had heard every move of the night time: people on the streets below, rowdy neighbours coming and going, doors slamming shut and sirens wailing through the darkness, but the one sound she dreaded to hear most was the sound of Vinny's arrival back at the flat.

It was cold in the room and she huddled the children closer to her. Her fingertips felt numb and her chest heaved up and down, up and down as she became more and more conscious of every single decibel that filled the space around her.

"Shhh, baby," she said to Reece when he stirred in his sleep, his favourite pyjamas crinkled around his little torso.

Maria wanted to fix them but she was too afraid to move, afraid that if she as much as made a noise that Vinny, wherever he was, would hear her and come after her.

The journey home had been the single most frightening experience of her life. Vinny didn't know whether he would scare her more by going faster than the speed of light around roads he didn't know so that Maria feared for her life and that of the children in the back, or crawling at a snail's pace so that the tension in the car built up around them like a smothering fog, threatening to suffocate them all.

Then when they got home to the apartment which was dark and cold and full of bad memories, he chilled her into thinking he was going to do his usual and beat her to a pulp once the children's backs were turned. But Vinny was playing a different type of game tonight. His silence was as deafening as his blows to her body and his piercing look of disgust sent a deeper fear inside her than she had ever known before. He walked them to the door of the apartment, his beady eyes skirting around in the dark and when Maria turned the key on the door, he was gone.

She had looked out through the window to see if she could see him in the distance but he was nowhere in sight and so the thought of him lingering outside or in the car park was like a time-bomb ticking in her head.

"Mummy," said Reece in a groggy, sleep-voice and Maria hushed him once more.

"Maria is here," she whispered, terrified still that Vinny might be within earshot. "I will always be here for you, Reece. Go to sleep."

She lay there and stared at the ceiling, wishing the hours to pass and praying for the first signs of daylight to creep through the window and take the darkness away. The night was deathly quiet now and the sound of her heartbeat and the sleepy slumber of her babies was all she could hear. Slowly, her eyelids felt heavier and heavier and she couldn't fight her tiredness any more. She concentrated on her breathing and allowed herself to drift off until what seemed like seconds later she was woken suddenly by the ring tone of her mobile phone.

She reached her arm out from under Reece's warm neck and pressed the answer button without checking her caller's identity.

"Maria," said the voice on her phone. "It's Susan from the Hospice. I'm calling about your mother, darling. I'm so very, very sorry . . ."

The rest of the nurse's words were a blur as practicalities swam through Maria's head like a never-ending 'to do' list. Her mother, her dear mother who had suffered so much for most of her life was at peace at last. She felt a tear trickle down her cheek and she wiped it swiftly away and tilted her chin, swallowing the threatening signs of grief that lurked in the back of her throat.

She hung up the phone and slowly she crept out of the bed and walked into the sitting room where she drew the curtains and let the morning sunshine fill the room. She looked around, deciding that a fresh lick of paint would make a world of difference. Reece's bedroom needed a facelift too and she knew if she asked Caroline she would let them stay with her while the place had a bit of an overhaul.

She opened the front door of the apartment and looked out over Belfast City, then took a deep breath and went back inside where she blessed herself at the Holy Water font her mother kept at the door. She lifted the phone that sat beside a framed photo of Reece as a baby, and dialled a number she should have dialled a long time ago.

As she waited on someone to answer, she looked at her reflection in the mirror. Her bloodied face, her bruised eye looked back at her and the feel of that gun she had aimed so wrong was still on her fingertips. She had to leave this lifestyle behind once and for all. She had to save her family.

"Can I speak to Officer Clements?" she said, her voice strong and confident and self-assured. "Good morning. It is Maria Moshiro. You can tell her I am ready to talk. I'm ready to talk to her now."

The End

If you enjoyed *The Truth Between* by
Emma Louise Jordan why not try
Playing the Field by Emma Heatherington also
published by Poolbeg?
Here's a sneak preview of Chapter One.

Emma Heatherington

Playing the Field

POOLBEG

PROLOGUE

Cara's rusting Fiat Uno grumbled along the country road, its wipers scraping the windscreen as the English summer rain finally subsided.

"Crap!" she said aloud. Was it right then left, or left then right? She couldn't remember.

She pulled the car in alongside a neatly trimmed hedgerow, turned off the engine and scrabbled in the depths of her handbag for the typed list of directions to Wimbledon that the recruitment agency had given her a few days before. Whoever her new boss was, she would not be impressed if her new "domestic assistant" was late.

List in hand, Cara turned the key in the ignition and the car spat back. Not a kick.

"Oh no, please don't do this to me now," she said, patting the dashboard and looking around her for help. She wanted this job. She needed this job if her career break was to work out as she had planned. Her glasses had steamed up and she took them off, gave them a quick wipe with her sleeve and said a silent prayer that she wouldn't be late.

She turned the key again and, as if the car had just been giving her a warning not to doubt its capabilities, it shot forward. Cara clung to the steering wheel, her eyes pinned to the road ahead. Then the car slowed down to its usual struggling pace.

Indicating right she took off again, chugging along the road and surveying her surroundings for another few miles, until she saw a huge set of gates that matched the recruitment agent's written description. Then she saw chimney-pots towering over trees far in the distance and she knew this had to be her new workplace. Yes, there was the name: Summer Manor. She slowed down further, glanced in her rear-view mirror and took a right turn through the gates.

"Oh holy shit!" she said as she made her way through sprawling lawns up a winding drive which led her to the front of the house, a modern home based on an old design. Its sandstone walls were a background for tall Georgian windows and a huge red door which was framed with ivy. Who lives in a house like this, she wondered, and she fought an involuntary urge to let her mouth drop open.

She wound down the window when she saw an older man who was watching her approach with a friendly smile.

"Ah, hello there," he said, leaning on a spade next to a mass of greenery. A black Labrador circled his feet. "You must be the new start."

The man's skin was a weather-beaten brown and his face was framed at either side with soft white curls that looked like candyfloss. If everyone at this "Summer Manor" was as friendly, Cara reckoned she would feel right at home. He looked so cute in an old-man sort of way that she could have put him in her pocket.

"I'm Cara," she said, extending her arm out through the car window. "Cara McCarthy."

"Cara McCarthy. Well, that's a pretty Irish name," said the man. "I'm Sam Potts, and this old scamp is Buster. He belongs to the man of the house but sometimes he thinks that's me."

"Lovely to meet you, Sam," said Cara. "And you too, Buster." The dog wagged his tail and panted up at her and Cara reached out to pat his shiny black head.

"He likes you," said Sam. "That's you off to a great start. Now, why don't you park up and I'll show you around?"

Cara surveyed the magnificent landscape once more and realised that whoever lived in this glorious home would hardly appreciate her hunk of junk standing out like a sore thumb.

"No doubt my trusty little motor will blot the landscape around here but it's the best I can do at the moment. I'll just park between these two beauties, then?"

"No, no, better not park there!" called Sam but Cara was already nosing her way between a nifty MG and a BMW jeep.

She locked the Uno into reverse and tried to straighten up the tiny lump of green metal, feeling dwarfed among such grandeur and wealth.

"Is that okay?" she panted, wishing for power steering, which evidently hadn't been invented in the land of Uno pre-1997.

"Sort of," said Sam, his blue eyes wrinkling into a smile. "Your new boss likes to have plenty of room to manoeuvre in and out of here when it suits her. Best to stay well out of her way in future and park down the side of the house.

But I don't think she'll dock your wages for parking in the wrong place on your first day."

Cara stepped out of the car and squinted in the morning sunshine. "Honestly, I'm normally an excellent driver but I guess I'm just a bit, well . . ."

"Nervous?" asked Sam.

"Yeah. Nervous." Cara shoved her hands in her pockets and then took them straight back out again, hearing her mother's "tomboy" remarks echo in her head.

"Don't be nervous," said Sam and he signalled at her to follow him towards the sprawling home. "There are a lot more rules to remember than parking your car in the correct position around here, but you'll soon get the hang of them, don't worry."

Cara closed the car door gently and followed Sam and Buster.

"I'm afraid I'm not very good at playing by the rules, Sam," she said as they made their way to the entrance of the magnificent home.

"Well, then that makes two of us," said Sam, opening the huge ornate red door. "Now, let's go inside and I'll introduce you to Sophia and Dylan."

"Sophia and Dylan?" said Cara. The names sounded somewhat familiar.

"They live here. Well, this is Dylan's home but his girlfriend Sophia moved in only a few weeks ago and already she's making her mark by making lots of changes around here. You, my dear, are one of them."

Cara followed Sam in through the front doors and into a wide, marble hallway which was the size of a small ballroom. Sophia and Dylan. Sophia and Dylan. She rhymed off the couple's names in her head. The house had a faint smell of summer fruits to it. Sophia and Dylan. Their names went together like tea and toast. They sounded all too familiar and then, like a slap on the face, the penny finally dropped.

She stopped in her tracks and stared at the gigantic framed photo at the top of the stairwell and gulped in realisation. A striking black-haired girl lay with her head on the lap of her Adonis boyfriend and her eyes glared confidently in Cara's direction. Her brand-new boss was none other than Sophia Brannigan, the all-new high-maintenance, highly strung girlfriend of Premiership footballer and babelicious hunk in a pair of trunks, Dylan Summers.

"Yes, that's our Sophia," said Sam and he threw his eyes up towards the portrait, laughing at Cara's reaction. "She wasn't here five minutes till she had that portrait commissioned."

Cara let out a nervous giggle and pushed her glasses back on her face. Dylan Summers and Sophia Brannigan. She was going to work for Dylan Summers and Sophia Brannigan!

Oh holy, holy, holy shit.

1

Don't You Step in my
Red Suede Shoes

"*Cara! Cara!*" The sound of Sophia's screeching tone pierced Cara's ears from the intercom that linked one room to the other at Summer Manor.

"Yes, Sophia?" Cara wriggled her way out from a pile of laundry in the utility room, wondering what the hell the demanding cow wanted now.

"Just an observation," called Sophia who was pinning her long, raven hair into a trendy twist in her dressing room, "that you have been here for weeks now and I am absolutely no further on in my career as a celebrity." She finished the look off with a pale pink neck-scarf and admired her own beauty, almost kissing the mirror. "To say I'm disappointed is an understatement." When Sophia was in a mood like this, her Liverpool accent became a little more posh.

Cara wondered how Sophia's celebrity career, or lack of it, could possibly be her fault, but then remembered that when Sophia went into a "poor me" rant, the world and his wife were to blame. Or the nearest person to hand: usually

Cara. Fly in her chardonnay? Blame Cara. Lost lipstick? Cara again. War in Iraq? Cara, how could you be so cruel?

"I have to say I don't really understand what that has to do with me," said Cara as she folded the laundry, rolling her eyes as the intercom light flashed before her. "As you keep reminding me, I'm just your cleaner."

She could sense Sophia's frustration a mile off. It was one of those days when her boss would argue a black crow was white and no one would convince her otherwise.

"Well, you wouldn't understand," said Sophia. "You see, I am using your arrival as a yardstick of my success and if I do not make some progress soon, it can only mean one thing."

"Which would be?"

"That you are simply not a good omen."

Cara nodded to herself. She was not a good omen. She could live with that. She'd been referred to as frumpy, clueless, hopeless, useless and any other word with "less" at the end of it as a daily punishment-beating for just, well, breathing since she took on her job at Summer Manor. Being a bad omen was merely a minor flaw.

"I had hoped that by hiring you to keep this house on its feet I would have more time for social networking and extending my contacts, but to date there has been no progress on my commercial success at all. Nowt. Nada. Nothing."

The intercom flashed off and within minutes Cara heard Sophia's stilettos march towards her. Then she appeared at the door, all dressed up to go out.

"I have some shopping to do for tonight," Sophia ranted. "So, don't expect me back too soon and if I were you I would start praying that some sort of miracle occurs in the near future that gains me the profile and publicity I deserve. Oh, and by the way, if my package from Belle's Boutique arrives, leave it upstairs outside my dressing-room. Goodbye."

Cara felt like the weight of a rhino had been lifted from her back when she heard Sophia's car vroom away from the house. "Don't expect me back." Those were her favourite words of all time from Sophia and they were normally only said once a week, whereas "do not go into my dressing room" had been drummed into her repeatedly since day one.

She looked at the clock. It was eleven o'clock. Sophia's shopping trips were usually all-day events so she would give herself an hour before she made her way up the stairs to see if she could get a peep at what all the fuss was about in the dressing room. Sophia always locked it when she went out, of course, but by now Cara knew where she kept the key.

Yes, curiosity about what lay at the other side of that door had haunted her during her brief employment as general dogsbody to Sophia Brannigan and now she was about to give in to temptation. Like a forbidden fruit hidden on the second floor of the luxurious residence, the room was calling to her, daring her to open its heavy, gilded doors, assuring her that no one was around to find out she had broken the rules in her brand-new job.

Come lunchtime, Cara tightened her pony-tail and glanced outside to make doubly sure the coast was clear, then took a deep breath and climbed the winding staircase. She retrieved the key from a drawer in the master bedroom and made her way to the dressing room. Her heart pounded and adrenaline pumped through her body as she turned the huge knob and pushed the doors open.

"Wow!"

She gave a ballerina twirl across the fluffy, cream-coloured shag-pile carpet, into the centre of a room which was even more lavish than she could have imagined.

It was huge. At least five times the size of the family sitting room she had been reared in back in Donegal and it was shelved from ceiling to floor with not an empty space in sight. The entire room smelt like new leather, with railings of clothes on hangers labelled by designer and boxes and boxes and boxes of shoes. The ceiling had so many lights that the room was almost floodlit, and a deep cream podium made a magnificent centrepiece in front of a floor-to-ceiling mirror.

Cara looked out through the window onto the extensive lawns of the house. She took a deep breath, longing to pinch herself back to reality but allowing herself just one more moment of fantasy where all of this was hers . . . A haven of luxury that was so out of her reach it was almost impossible to believe she was standing inside it right now. And she was getting paid for it. Not paid to stand around of course, but when the cat was away and all that . . .

She imagined the man of her dreams waving to her as he finished a game on the tennis court at the far end of the manicured walkway. She imagined her top-of-the-range sports car – no, actually, a Space Wagon – sitting on the golden stones of the gravel driveway, with baby seats for her adorable twin baby boys who were the spitting image of their father. Yes, in this dream she drove a top-of-the-range Space Wagon with tinted windows and a key code that would open the huge electronic gates of the big house especially for her.

She pictured herself chilling out in the heated, kidney-shaped swimming pool, after a hard day's shopping, or lounging in the extensive drawing room that was never used. She dreamed of choosing outfits for charity dinners and awards ceremonies, where she stood right now in the long rectangular dressing room.

For a few precious hours every day, Cara McCarthy truly loved her job. As she scrubbed and cleaned her way around its nooks and crannies with no one to disturb her, she would allow her imagination to run wild and pretend that she was the true lady of Summer Manor. Tucked away in the country-style suburb of Wimbledon Village, where rolling hills and country hideouts hid the fact that the bright lights of London were only a stone's throw away, its private grounds were a nest of tranquillity and the perfect space for a dreamer like Cara who could easily lose herself in a world of peace and luxury.

She allowed herself to run her hands along the Prada section, she tried on a Galliano scarf and put it back exactly where she found it. Then she felt brave enough to go a little bit further by trying on a pair of Sophia's high-heeled shoes which luckily were just her size.

"Where did you get those shoes?" she asked her reflection, then stumbled and fell into a clumsy bundle before pulling herself together again.

She stared in awe at how dainty her feet looked in the full-length mirror and how lean her calves when she didn't try to walk, or move or breathe. The shoes were blood-red pure silk, with a fine, real-platinum slinky heel and a pretty red bow which sat on the edge of dainty peep toes.

"I think I've discovered fashion," she laughed, realising she was actually enjoying herself more than she had in a long time. "Have I really been missing out on so, so much?"

Cara didn't normally talk to herself, but then again, she didn't normally try on shoes either unless she really had to. Unlike most women, Cara McCarthy had always viewed clothes as one of life's necessities rather than an adrenaline-inducing passion. In fact, if push came to the shove and her life was in danger, she would actually confess to preferring hiking boots to high heels.

But these shoes were different. These shoes had beckoned to her from beneath their bed of soft, cream tissue paper. She'd even taken a quick peek at the label which was still stuck on the box and had almost choked at the price tag. To own only one of them she'd have to live on Super Noodles for at least a month and hobble to work because she wouldn't be able to afford petrol for her clapped-out motor car, let alone afford the match of the shoe.

"Perfect, just perfect," she whispered, wishing she could keep the glorious beings in her possession forever and take them home to the poky apartment she shared with her friend Natalie. She would never, ever wear them outside of course, but would just stare at their beauty on a daily basis as they lay in their shiny box, and when she'd feel like it, maybe once a month or so, she would put them on and dance around in the safety of her own apartment.

Hell, she wouldn't even show them to Natalie and she always made sure she showed every item of clothing to Natalie. As her best friend and fellow "let's spread our wings and see the big smoke" buddy, Natalie was the one who had eventually told Cara that navy and black didn't go and that horizontal stripes made you look like a fat zebra, unless you had a frame like Kate Moss.

Feeling foolish, but brave, Cara maintained her

balance and opened the heavy doors that led back onto the landing of Summer Manor. She made her way towards the stairs where the sassy drumbeat of a Girls Aloud song called to her from the kitchen.

Pretending she was as tanned and gorgeous as Cheryl Cole, Cara shimmied down each step of the spiral staircase in Sophia's stilettos to the beat of the music and made her way in the direction of the succulent aroma of her roasting chicken which filled her senses and added to her good mood.

She made her way carefully across the reflective white tiles of the hallway, through the double doors that led to the dining room and through a huge open-plan area that brought her into the kitchen, allowing her mind to drift into a world of glamour, perks and parties where everybody knew your name and everybody wanted to be your best friend.

Into a world where the biggest daily dilemma was which shop to visit on which day of the week, where your diary was bursting at the seams with parties and where the man of your dreams played a poncy ball game for a living in return for a salary that would feed a small nation for the rest of their days. Into a world where jotting down a few remarks on other celebrities' fashion sense made you a "columnist" in a weekly magazine. She could be a "columnist." Not even a fecking problem.

But this wasn't Cara's world at all. This was Sophia's world. This was a WAG's world. But, right now, for a few stolen moments on a Thursday afternoon in August, Cara "Cleaner to the Stars" McCarthy was living it – and she was loving every flippin' minute of it.

Even her rubber gloves and checked apron didn't feel out of place when she slipped them on and continued with her chores in the kitchen. She turned the volume up to the max and allowed herself to feel the music as it took over her body. The shoes had become so comfy she would have forgotten she had them on only for her tendency to look down and admire how delightful they made her feet look, approximately once every ten seconds.

With a dramatic *whoosh* she wiped down the draining board, and then let out an "Ooh!" as she dusted the dresser. She felt her heart surge with excitement as the gentle clip-clop of the heels kept to a rhythm on the ceramic floor beneath her.

She lifted a photo from the solid oak dresser in an over-exaggerated sweep of her arm.

"I'll just give you a quick facial," she joked to it as she ran the duster over Sophia's glowing face. Sophia grinned back at her (it was an old photo – Sophia didn't smile any more in real life – she pouted) and she found herself giving the glass on the frame a little more elbow grease than she normally would with just a tiny pang of jealousy added in for good measure.

For Cara knew that the shoes she wore, the shoes that fitted her so well and introduced her to the dizzy heights of haute couture didn't belong to her and they never would.

They belonged to the real lady of the manor – the one person who could make Cara McCarthy feel like scum on her gorgeous shoes with just one sly comment or degrading cackle; the person who paid her a measly cleaning salary that was less than her own humungous weekly clothing allowance; the girl whose claws were so deep into her footballer boyfriend's existence that Cara could almost smell the gloss of the magazines she planned to sell her wedding to, if he ever proposed.

"Shallow cow," she said, vowing she would stop muttering as soon as she took off the shoes, which she would do in a few minutes of course, and she gave Sophia's rare grin another extra-hard polish. "Lucky, lucky, shallow cow."

The sudden crunch of tyres on the gravel from outside the house made Cara's heart skip a beat as she gave an extra fast dance spin on the kitchen floor. Who the hell was that at this time of day? Sophia didn't normally attract visitors. She didn't appear to have many friends.

"Jesus – shit," she stammered, glancing around and trying to decide on which direction to run. Sophia couldn't be back . . . could she? Cara clip-clopped over to the window and peeped out to see her worst fears come true. Sophia was back early.

Her pinched face framed by a long ebony mane and clad in oversized sunglasses was all Cara could see as she drove down the side of the house, yapping nineteen to a dozen into a tiny phone. Her personal number plate was emblazoned across the front of the car, just in case anyone would happen to forget just who she was.

She was early and Sophia was never early. Not from a shopping trip.

And she was coming in through the back door. And the back door led through a cloakroom that led into a hallway that led to the kitchen, where Cara stood in Sophia's red shoes that still had the price tag on them. A price tag that was the length of Cara's mobile phone number. Shit, shit shit!

Cara glanced down at her feet and dropped the duster into her apron pocket, then made a mad dash for the main hallway and towards the stairs, praying that Sophia's telephone conversation might hold her back and give her a few minutes' grace.

"Shit – bitch," she said, not knowing which word to use first. "Shit, shit, shit, shit, shit," as she took the stairs, two at a time. Sophia would sack her on the spot if she found out that she had as much as sniffed her brand-new shoes. Hell, she only let Cara use the cooker because she couldn't be arsed to use it herself and had a terrible fear of everything domesticated and electrical unless it could straighten her hair.

Cara opened a window at the top of the stairs and listened briefly to Sophia's conversation from below as she to-ed and fro-ed from the house to the car in a bad temper.

"But, honey, you promised!" she heard Sophia shriek into her cellphone as her heels clicked across the patio. Sophia didn't call her phone a "mobile". No way. That was too UK. "I have everything organised and we simply *have* to work on your profile, whether you like it or not."

Cara heard the car door open and then slam. That would be to fetch her shopping. A mountain of shopping. Cara hoped it would take her ages to unload it without her help, which Sophia was sure to scream for any second now.

"With the Beckhams gone Stateside everyone wants to park their pert little bottoms on their vacant thrones," said Sophia, "and this party is the ultimate opportunity to show the country that we have arrived." A pause, then an ear-splitting yell: "*Cara! Cara!* Come immediately and help me with all this!"

The intercom let out a shriek on the landing and Cara raced towards Sophia's lavish dressing room, silently complimenting herself on how she had learned to run so easily in such glorious footwear. To hell with cat-walks and premières, these shoes should be promoted as road-runners.

"Shit," she said again as she opened the dressing room doors. Then she reached down to take off the shoes. Her right foot felt naked without its new companion but she had no time to sympathise. She had to be cruel to be kind.

But, as she reached to slip off the left shoe, she lost her balance and bounced off the doorframe, then wobbled back into an upright position. She pushed the doors of the dressing room open further and hobbled quickly towards a chair. Faster than lightning she swooped down to remove the other shoe but suddenly her heart stopped.

It didn't skip a beat this time. It stopped.

For Jimmy Left Choo was now injured. Fatally injured. And Cara thought she was going to die too as the heel broke from its base and fell into her hand.

•◆•

If you enjoyed this chapter from
Playing the Field by Emma Heatherington
why not order the full book online
@ www.poolbeg.com
and enjoy a 10% discount on all
Poolbeg books

See next page for details.

•◆•

POOLBEG WISHES TO
THANK YOU

for buying a Poolbeg book.
As a loyal customer we will give you
10% OFF (and free postage*)
on any book bought on our website
www.poolbeg.com

Select the book(s) you wish to buy
and click to checkout.

Then click on the 'Add a Coupon' button
(located under 'Checkout') and enter
this coupon code

 USMWR15173

POOLBEG   (Not valid with any other offer!)   POOLBEG

WHY NOT JOIN OUR MAILING LIST
@ www.poolbeg.com and get some
fantastic offers on Poolbeg books

*See website for details